Paul Grover

Book One of The Vale Series

ARK OF SOULS

BOOK ONE OF THE VALE SERIES
ARK OF SOULS

First Published 2017

This Edition 2019 AoS Books.

ISBN 978-1-9161267-0-1

www.paulgrover.co.uk

With thanks to
Sue, Ryan and Luke
For support

Kevin, Kevin, Naomi and Mike
For encouragement and feedback

Carmilla
For working dark magic on my words

And you
For taking a chance

ARK OF SOULS

CHAPTER ONE

THE *FSS Berlin* exited hyperspace in a discharge of exotic energy. Her braking thrusters fired to stabilise her forward velocity as she broke free of her faster-than-light envelope.

Her sudden arrival scattered the pirate squadron, driving them away from a crippled long range freighter. The *Berlin's* forward turrets targeted and fired at the aggressors. Three of the fighters exploded in quick succession. One survivor was caught in the blast, its ion engines flamed out and the ship tumbled in the void. The remaining pair built hyperspatial envelopes and engaged their faster-than-light drives.

The warship's turrets retracted as she matched the relative velocity of the stricken cargo vessel.

Berlin was an old ship, one of the last three Europa class vessels in fleet service. Like her sisters, she was seeing out the twilight of her career patrolling the outer edges of human space.

Despite her immense size the *Berlin's* crew accommodation had been a secondary consideration to housing her propulsion and weapons systems. Officer's cabins were no exception. They were small enough to be uncomfortable yet large enough to allow for crucial equipment to be lost.

Mira had started to lose a lot of things. She hoped it was not a sign of further short-term memory degradation, preferring to blame the clutter of her cabin for her inability to keep track of her belongings. It was an easy, comfortable delusion.

She rummaged through the pile of discarded clothing on her bunk before dropping to the floor and peering into the dark, dusty space beneath. She located the beeping com-link. It lay between an illicit stash of pain killing medication and a pink rabbit.

She keyed the tiny in ear device to receive the call.

"Thorn."

"Commander, Central Ops." Suzanne Walton, the ship's Executive Officer omitted to mention the delay in Mira's response.

"We are conducting an anti-piracy operation and have intercepted a vessel in distress. We have dealt with the insurgents and the sector is secure. The Captain has assigned you to lead the inspection team."

Mira sighed; inspections were a tedious reality of deep space patrol. Most of the time they were fruitless searches through cargo holds on squalid ships while equally grubby crew looked on.

"Understood," Mira replied. She slipped an eye patch over her left eye socket with a fluid and practised motion. She checked it was in place by touch. Her fingers lingered on the scars that ran like a road map over one side of her face. She shook her head and her still damp raven hair fell forward. The non regulation style obscured the worst of the damaged tissue.

"What type of vessel is it, Sue?" she asked.

"Corporate, it's a Kobo, registered to Lightfoot Developments. We can't raise the pilot and the ship has sustained severe damage. Captain Adams will brief you before you leave. He is waiting in bay three."

Corporation vessels were always preferable to independents as they usually complied with government hygiene and safety standards.

"When do I go?"

"Captain wants to launch in 15."

"Roger, understood. Thorn out."

And I was hoping for an easy day.

Instead of the calm, predictable peace of the flight deck she would be spending the next eight hours rummaging through the hold of a freighter that could be loaded with anything from manufactured goods to bio waste.

This would be Mira's first inspection in three months and she had to admit it was probably overdue. She had been pulled from the last one due to a minor medical issue and Alex Kite had been sent in her stead. Kite had contracted a skin infection so severe he had been confined to medbay for three weeks. While the rest of the crew had enjoyed a week of leave at the Proxima Anchorage, he had spent his downtime in an iso-booth.

Kite was an academy golden boy with straight firsts in every discipline. He should and would have had her job had she not been assigned to the ship's crew two years ago. Mira knew Kite resented her yet she tolerated his passive aggressive snipes and his thinly disguised put downs. He was both the best and the worst the academy could produce.

Mira understood his ill feeling. Kite was a gifted officer with a bright future. She was a broken drop ship pilot who held onto her commission by virtue of her combat record. It did not take two eyes to see their careers were heading in different directions.

She unzipped her fatigues, kicked off her boots and tossed them to one side, further adding to the chaos of her cabin. She shivered in her underwear and danced from one bare foot to the other.

Mira opened the gear locker at the foot of her narrow bunk and removed the base layer of her battle suit. She pulled the heavy blue garment up over her lower body before wriggling her arms and shoulders into it. Once it was secure, she pulled her tactical webbing over her shoulders and attached her body armour. She double checked the catches and powered up the electronics. Now sweating she welcomed the suit's cooling circuit kicking into action. She retrieved her helmet. Putting it on, she ran a systems check before removing it and attaching it to a utility loop on her webbing. Satisfied that the suit was operating correctly, she checked her sidearm and holstered it on her hip.

Mira glanced around the cabin and promised to tidy up when she returned. It may be small but it was home.

A faded Union Jack and Namibian flag adorned the bulk-head above her bunk, below them was a mosaic of two and three dimensional photographs; thirty years of memories clinging to the wall of an ageing cruiser at the edge of human-ity's realm. She walked to the vibrant, haphazard collage and removed a crumpled two-dimensional picture of a young wo-man standing on the Seattle waterfront. The girl had tanned skin and brown eyes. Her smile was devoid of cares. Mira placed the photo in her utility pocket. She spun on her heel and left the cabin, her professional mask falling into place.

The *Berlin's* corridors were lit by dim red light emanating from concealed panels. The ship was in her night cycle. Combat vessels operated at a full state of readiness at all times yet maintained the practice of delineating time into day and night. Navy studies had found it enhanced the mental well being of the crew. The fleet worked to Greenwich Mean Time. Every ship and station would operate the same procedures at the same time, regardless of where they were in the galaxy.

Mira checked her wrist computer. It was just before 2am.

She walked past the bank of elevators and ducked into a stairwell leading to the hangar deck. It was a roundabout route but the movement would loosen her taut muscles and the kinetic energy she generated would give a boost to her suit's battery pack.

After six flights of steps she cut through the engineering section. The roar of super-heated plasma flowing through the overhead pipes was deafening. If the reactor was the heart of the ship, those pipes were her arteries, and the pulsing vibration of the deck her heartbeat. Old ships like the *Berlin* were almost alive, their unique quirks and personality known to their crew and passed on generation to generation. These great lumps of metal were as much a vibrant organism as the humans who rode aboard them. Mira had only been with the *Berlin* for two patrols yet she understood the affection long serving crew felt for *Old B.*

She arrived at bay three in a more upbeat mood than she expected. A marine at the guard station saluted and waved her past. She returned the salute. It occurred to her that the higher the rank one attained, the more salutes it garnered. Mira had every respect for the Navy's traditions but found the constant formality increasingly tedious.

A low rumble came from a tug's star-drive while faint jets of vapour vented from the vessel's cooling system. The ugly craft comprised a boxy fuselage with a pair of Honda XF4500 ion engines attached to a network of aluminium struts. *Berlin* carried three tugs; this one bore the number two in pitted red paint on its stubby nose.

Captain Marcus Adams stood at the foot of the entry ramp,

talking with a pair of marines whose battle armour was dark olive compared to the blue of Mira's suit.

Adam's tall, thin physique hinted at his childhood growing up in the low gravity of the Lunar colonies. His pale skin and slight frame stood in sharp contrast to Gunnery Sergeant Rich Barnes' deep brown complexion and muscular physique. Barnes was a giant of a man with the swagger earned from a lifetime of service. He shared a joke with Adams.

A second jarhead stood behind Barnes. Mira could not remember his name; he was one of the *New Guys*. A head shorter than Barnes he still towered over Mira, who barely met minimum service height. Gunny Barnes nodded to her and concluded his conversation with the captain. Both marines made their way up the ramp and disappeared into the tug.

"Commander Thorn, you are looking like a boss today," Adams said. "It suits you. We should get you off the ship more often."

The captain's voice was deep and resonant. It seemed at odds with his build. Adams had the quiet authority shared by all senior officers. Mira wondered if they learned it on an admiralty course.

"Don't try too hard, Captain. You know my position on inspections. What can I look forward to?"

"This was a straightforward interception. We took out three fighters, two bugged out, one is disabled. Roland will recover it while you poke around on the target vessel."

"What's he carrying?" she asked.

Captain Adams shrugged.

"We haven't been able to raise anyone onboard. The ship is badly damaged. I suspect the communications system is down."

"Or the crew are dead," Mira replied.

"Or that. In which case I'll send in Doctor Garret with a

specialist team."

"Understood. How long have I got?"

"As long as you need. It will be a minimum of an hour to recover and secure the pirate vessel so take your time, enjoy yourself."

"I'll have a ball." It came out more sourly than she intended.

"One more thing Mira." Adams moved closer and dipped his head. "I received your most recent psyche assessment yesterday. You have made significant progress since you came onboard. I want you to know how pleased I am. If you need anything just ask, okay?"

"Thank you, Sir. I appreciate it." She tried her best to sound sincere. Mira figured she was the ship's screwball or sympathy case; which one depended on who you asked. She believed Adams was in the latter group, which was certain to be the minority.

Mira locked his steel-grey eyes with her sole green one.

"I mean it, Captain, your support means a lot." Mira had to admit she was feeling better than she had in a long time. Aside for the odd memory lapse she was convinced the tide was turning for her.

He straightened; his expression warmed. Marcus Adams was one of the old school; he treated his crew like his extended family.

"Good hunting, Thorn. Cheer up. You're the face of the Navy."

Mira marched up the ramp. She stopped at the top and snapped off a salute before the hatch slid closed.

Face of the Navy? she thought. *My mug will hardly make it into a recruiting vid anytime soon.*

Barnes and *New Guy* were already in their seats. As she passed she glanced at the man's name stencilled on his armour.

PFC Ethan Tate, a stylised spanner in a clenched fist told her he was a combat engineer.

Tate was a generic marine. His close cropped hair was on the fairer side of brown, his blue eyes eager and alert. Like Barnes he appeared as if he were about to burst out of his armour at any moment. There was a softness to his features. He appeared almost thoughtful as he clicked his restraints into place.

Mira strapped herself in opposite the marines. Barnes was checking his weapon over. The name Babs was stencilled in red ink on the side of the barrel.

"Are you still naming your weapons, Gunny?" Mira asked.

"Only the ones with personality, otherwise people would get the wrong idea," he replied. He pulled out his sidearm. "You've met Babs; this is Carol." He flipped it so they both could see the name on the butt.

Private Tate looked uncertainly at Barnes.

"Babs is his ex wife, Private," Mira explained.

Barnes grinned.

"A fine woman who I loved most dearly."

"And Carol?" Tate asked.

"She's the reason Bab's his *ex* wife," Mira replied.

"Another fine woman who I loved most dearly." Barnes laughed as the tug lifted off the deck and exited the landing bay.

Mira closed her eye and rested her head on the bulkhead. A headache was growing; the pain drilled through her skull. She reached into her armour for two white pills and popped them into her mouth. She fought back the gag reflex and dry swallowed them. They blunted the pain but did not banish it. Today was set to be a long day.

They covered the 20 kilometres from the *Berlin* to the stranded ship in five minutes. As they approached Mira made her way forward to the cramped cockpit and peered through the viewports.

The pilot pointed to scorch marks on the light grey hull.

"They landed some good hits after they burned his shields away," he said without taking his eyes off the ship.

"It's messy," she observed. "They must have hit him with some high wattage weapons. Military grade kit by the look of it."

"It's only a thin skin hull. Solid ordinance would have torn through it in no time. The pirates knew what they were doing. He was lucky," the pilot added.

"Can you spin us around Roland?" Mira asked. The pilot rotated the tug on its central axis while continuing with forward velocity. The corporate logo on the Kobo's anhedral tail fin was different to the standard Lightfoot Developments motif. This one featured the usual single planet orbiting a stylised star, but carried the tag line that read *'Building the Future, Learning from the Past'*.

"He's attached to their Astro Archaeological Division," Mira said.

AstroArc was a smokescreen the corporations used for acquiring non-human technology. The MegaCorps supplied universities and museums with cultural relics and retained high tech finds for commercial advantage.

"A professional hit like this has to be down to the Blades," Mira whispered.

"Blades? I thought Rhodes was out of the piracy business. I heard he was dabbling in Frontier politics."

"An organised fight with high power weapons. This has all the hallmarks of one of Rhodes' operations," Mira said, continuing to study the crippled starship.

"They targeted the shields and the sublights. They wanted

the ship intact." Roland pointed out of the window with a gloved hand. "Look at the condition of the engines."

The damage was worse than Mira first thought. Sparks and vapour escaped into the vacuum from many ruptured pipes. Xander Rhodes and his Blades had always been a potent threat on the Frontier; they were a match for Navy pilots against larger targets. Although Mira had to admit she had heard little of the Blades in recent years. Roland might be right. This could be the work of a new outfit.

Mira shrugged, finding out who was responsible for the attack was not her problem.

"Take us in on the top airlock, Roland."

Mira floated back to the crew cabin. There was a muffled, metallic *thunk* as the tug connected with the Kobo. Barnes and Tate released their harnesses and floated out of their seats. In single file they propelled themselves to the lower airlock.

Mira cycled the controls to pressurise the lock before hitting the hatch release. She put on her helmet and activated the camera. Both marines followed her lead.

The connecting tube between the vessels was three metres long; the hatch at the far end opened to reveal a featureless grey airlock cubicle.

"Want me to go in first?" Barnes asked.

Mira shook her head. "No, I've got this."

She swivelled to enter the airlock feet first. Unlike the tug the target ship would be operating an artificial gravity field. Landing on her head was a rookie mistake Mira had no intention of making. She passed through the second hatch and into the Kobo; her feet connected firmly with the rungs of the entry ladder. Her stomach lurched as she traversed from zero-g to normal gravity. She took a second to allow the nausea pass.

She drew her sidearm and waited for Barnes and Tate to

descend. Once the airlock was sealed, she contacted the tug pilot who silently disengaged from the vessel.

The marines readied their weapons. Mira operated the latch and the inner door irised open. A blast of warm, humid air filled the airlock. She wrinkled her nose. The smell of burnt wiring and melted components was pungent. Beyond the airlock the ship was dimly lit with flickering emergency lighting. A faint blue mist hung in the air.

Mira shuddered. The atmosphere was oppressive, the air heavy and charged. She tried to push the sense of dread away, but it lingered before fading into the back of her mind.

"The reactor must be offline. The air scrubbers are not working," Barnes said.

Mira stepped out of the airlock and swept her sidearm left to right. The barrel light cut through smoke, revealing nothing but an empty corridor.

"Clear!" she reported.

The flight deck lay to her right and the habitation section to her left. Mira coughed, the acrid fumes catching in the back of her throat. Her eye watered and she blinked it clear.

"Hello?" she called, once she caught her breath.

"Is anyone home?" Barnes yelled from behind her. His deep voice echoed off the steel walls.

"I guess not," Mira said when no answer was forthcoming. If the ship were abandoned they would have to secure the vessel, alert the owners and attach a tracking beacon to the hull. If they found bodies, they would need to gather and catalogue evidence for a potential criminal investigation.

"Gunny, I want you to go aft. Check the habitation section."

She looked at the other marine; she couldn't remember his name... Alan? Edward? No, it was Ethan, definitely Ethan.

"Ethan, let's go forward. We'll try to break into their flight log."

"Yes, Ma'am," he replied.

"What about the lower deck?" Barnes asked. The standard configuration for a Kobo was a twin deck freighter. The upper section contained the crew quarters, the lower was devoted to cargo space and engineering sections.

"Let's secure this deck before we go below," Mira said.

Barnes hefted his weapon and moved aft, whistling tunelessly. Mira looked at Tate.

"After you, Private," she said.

They walked to the flight deck in silence, the thick carpet and padded walls absorbing the sound of their movement.

"It's well appointed for a hauler. More like a star liner than a freighter," Tate said.

Mira glanced around her. The carpet was deep blue and flecked with gold stars, the walls textured with decorative padding.

"I'll take your word for it, Private. I'm on a Navy salary, after all."

Tate looked uncertain, like he'd spoken out of turn. "No... I mean... I was just..." His voice trailed off when he picked up on Mira's failed attempt at humour.

They lapsed back into silence.

As they approached the flight deck, the luxury gave way to a more utilitarian style of décor. Rubberised flooring replaced the carpet and the walls were bare painted steel. The flight deck was well equipped, yet small and continued the stripped down aesthetic. The pilot and copilot's chairs were positioned in a slight hollow in front of a curved viewport. Touchscreen displays and banks of switches surrounded each station. Mira moved forward and gazed into the void. The *Berlin* was visible just off the starboard bow. The warship's outline was picked out in dots and dashes of light spilling from her windows while powerful spotlights lit her slate-grey hull. A ripple of homesickness washed over Mira as she stared at the isolated island of humanity. It was unusual and not unwelcome. It occurred to her that reconnecting to humanity could be a real possibility. She recalled something her therapist had said at their first session: *The journey would be one of small steps. You won't realise you have reached your destination until the day you arrive.* She was seeing the wisdom in that bald, bug-eyed psych's words. Her demons were a long way behind her but she knew she had to keep taking those small steps, lest they catch up and consume her.

"No one is home," Tate said.

His voice pulled Mira back to the now. She shook off the low melancholy that had fallen over her.

She scanned the flight deck. Not only was it deserted, it showed no signs of life. The detritus usually found on the flight deck of a long range hauler was absent. There were no empty mugs or half eaten snacks stashed between equipment. No family photographs or pinups were stuck to the consoles. Either no one had been on the deck or the crew suffered from extreme OCD.

"If anyone was onboard, I would have expected them to be here," Mira said.

She slid into the pilot's chair. It was deeply padded and the seat bolsters firmly gripped her body.

"Perks of the private sector," she said absently.

Mira tapped into the ship's main computer and pulled up the recent log entries.

"He left Tellerman Gateway a week ago en-route for... Tarantella."

"The pirate system?" Tate asked.

Mira continued to drill into the database.

"Harsh," she said. "It's lawless and not what you'd call on the grid, but it's still a legitimate outpost... at the moment, anyway."

The legal status of Tarantella was a subject of debate. A free trade agreement existed between the station's Trade Guild and the Federation. Tarantella was subject to Federal Law, but the lack of Federal presence allowed it complete autonomy.

In recent years the authorities had ignored the outpost, preferring to concentrate on expanding the Frontier. It made sense to Mira; if the government came down hard on Tarantella, they would have to act against countless other rogue outposts on the inner and outer frontiers.

A flash illuminated the flight deck. She twisted in the seat. Ethan Tate wore a broad grin, his hands inside an inspection hatch.

"That should do it," he said. The main lights flickered on, followed by the faint hum of the air scrubbers kicking into life.

"Nice work, Private."

Mira continued to read the system logs. They were straight-forward aside from containing no sign of human interaction.

Then she saw it.

"The ship has been on an automated flight-path since it left Tellerman Gateway. The program was uploaded to the Navi-Comp remotely," she said.

She keyed her com-link.

"Rich have you found anyone?" The link crackled with interference, then cleared.

"Negative, Mira. The upper deck is deserted. This isn't a standard freighter either. I bet it's an executive transport of some sort. You want me to go below?"

"Not yet I want to talk to the captain; something isn't right."

She closed the link and changed channel.

"*Berlin,* Thorn." She waited for a reply.

"CentOps, go ahead Mira," Sue Walton answered.

"It looks like we have a ghost ship. The upper deck is deserted, and the log shows the ship left from Tellerman and has been on auto ever since. I will scope out the cargo space but this ship is beaten up. The drive core is offline and I think the sublights are fuc... non functional. I recommend we bring her onboard."

There was a pause; the captain came on the line.

"Mira, if we bring her aboard we have to divert to the nearest port."

She didn't know quite how to sum up her unease.

"Captain nothing adds up. The ship was on an automated course for Tarantella."

A pause.

"I see."

There was a muffled conversation in the background.

"Prepare the vessel for towing. Roland will be with you in an hour. I'd be grateful if you could update me on the contents of the hold. I need to know exactly what we're bringing aboard."

"Affirmative, Captain. We'll check it out."

Mira swivelled the command chair. Private Tate was still trying to bring the vessel's systems online. He was busy checking fuses and re-inserting them into their carriers. Barnes appeared in the doorway.

She told them the captain had agreed to take the Kobo onto the *Berlin.*

"It's probably for the best. She's taken a beating and we can't really be sure how sound the hull is."

"I guess we check the lower decks and shut the reactor down," Mira said, sliding out of the command seat.

"Looks like you were getting comfortable," Barnes said.

"I was." It had been a long time since she had sat in the pilot's seat and Mira was disappointed the ship was immobile. She yearned for the chance to take the stick one more time.

"C'mon Rich, let's look down below. Ethan, I want you to bring the core functions online. Give priority to the shields. Roland lacks a delicate touch with his towing rig."

"Yes, Ma'am," he said, without looking up.

Mira and Barnes walked aft. When they reached the stairwell Barnes hit the door mechanism. The door did not respond.

"Security locked. Damn it," he said reaching for his comlink. "Hey man, it's Barnes. Can you override the security systems?" There was a pause. A light on the door changed from red to green. Barnes hit the control, and the door retracted.

"Kid's good," Mira said.

"Top of his class in engineering. I don't understand why he enlisted. He'd be a good fit for the fleet." He ushered Mira through the door.

Mira did her best to conceal her surprise. She had known the big man for ten years and the Marine Corps was everything to him. As far as Rich Barnes was concerned there were marines and there was everyone else.

Before they entered the stairwell, Barnes blocked her path.

"You okay?" he asked. "I saw you popping pills on the way over. It's not the first time either."

"I'm fine, Gunny, just a headache. Standard issue painkillers."

He didn't look satisfied with the answer.

"Mira, you need the doctor to check it out."

"Rich, I'm fine. My sickness level is already too high. I don't want to be grounded, but it's getting to where Monica will have to report me. I don't want to put her in that position."

Barnes shook his head. "You know she'd never do that."

Mira did. Doctor Monica Garret was one of her closest friends, correction one of her only friends. It still did not sit easy with her.

"Okay, when we get back I'll get her to check me over." It was a lie. Mira suspected Barnes knew, but he let it go.

"Come on, Gunny; let's see what's down here."

She drew her sidearm and activated the barrel light; it cut through the darkness of the stairwell. As they descended the light level increased as the corridor curved around the central hold. After ten metres they came across the entrance to the cargo area. It was a large hatchway recessed into the bulkhead. Opposite the hold was a similarly sized airlock. Barnes tried the door control. It bleeped, but the hold did not open.

He called Tate. Mira could not hear the exchange.

"He can't open it. It uses deep encryption," Barnes said. "He's trying to access the security system to get a visual of whatever is in there."

"Okay, let's move on. I'll look at engineering with you and then secure the upper deck. We'll be turning the gravity off and I don't want the contents of an un-flushed toilet floating around."

Barnes laughed and led the way. They kept their weapons ready but any real intent was lost.

"So why don't you go home, Mira?" Barnes asked.

"What?"

"You have family back home. You're a veteran and you've earned a pension. So why not?"

Mira didn't know how to answer. Barnes was right. There were many officers in her position who had cashed in their commissions for easy lives in the Core Systems.

"Rich... after the crash I was going to do just that but with all the shit that followed... I need the distance. Besides, I can't cook and the Navy feeds me."

Barnes chuckled; it was measured. Mira saw something in his eyes. It wasn't the normal pity she was used to seeing.

She nudged him gently, with affection.

"Don't worry, Rich, I'm getting my shit together."

The door to the engineering section was unlocked and opened without aid from Tate. The compartment was filled with thick grey smoke. Mira recoiled as the acrid fumes hit the back of her throat. Her visor automatically lowered, and she purged the fumes from her respiration system. She breathed the pure NitOx mix and waited for the nausea to pass. She had puked in a helmet once and once was enough.

"Is there a fire?" she screamed.

"No, the auto system has taken care of it. The air scrubbers are out. The smoke has nowhere to go!" Barnes said.

Mira slipped on the floor. She glanced down to see it was covered in PlastiFoam. The extinguishers had done their job and put the fire out but the remnants posed a serious risk.

Barnes disappeared into the cloud of blue-grey smoke and seconds later it vented away, leaving the compartment clear. Mira checked the air quality, poor but breathable. She opened her helmet. The smell of combustion still lingered in the air.

"A plasma leak," she said.

Plasma fires smelt similar to rotting fish. The pungent aroma overlaid the stench of burnt plastic.

"Your face when you walked in! I thought you would lose it!" Barnes said. A broad grin lit his face.

"Think yourself lucky I didn't have breakfast, otherwise I would have."

Mira looked around the room. Dried PlastiFoam covered

every surface. The consoles were scorched but appeared to be functional. The damage responsible for the flash fire was obvious; broken tubing and burnt cable still smouldered at the far end of the compartment. Without the plasma feed inductors the ship had no sublight propulsion or hyperdrive.

Barnes studied a readout on a data screen.

"This is just one big lump of scrap. The reactor is offline and we're running on batteries," he said. "I can take care of things down here if you want to go topside and see if Private Tate can break into the security system."

"Okay, thanks Gunny." She left Barnes to secure the drive section. The stink of burnt plasma seemed to follow her up the corridor.

Romain Vincent watched as the tug grew from a tiny moving spec of light into an ugly slab of metal and girders. His ship was spinning lazily on its central axis. The drive system had dropped into a fail state and all but life support was functioning. A shudder ran through the hull as the towing harness was attached to his fighter. The tug moved away, pulling the smaller ship behind it. Romain slapped the bulkhead with a gloved fist. It was his third interception with this crew and now destined to be his last.

Why did they have to take this job?

The past four years of Romain's life had been spent working for Xander Rhodes, as one of one of the legendary Blades; the scourge of the Frontier. Unfortunately Rhodes was a prick, a hollow echo of the stories told about him. There were plenty of raids, plenty of liberated cargoes, yet Romain had seen nothing more than his basic wage. When a young crew approached him with the offer of a big payday for a small job he had signed on willingly. Only now he realised he had signed his life away.

Once aboard the Navy ship he would be taken to the nearest outpost, processed through the system and sentenced to a prison facility in a federal backwater. Unlike Eden and Freddie he had no opportunity to amass a fortune that would await him on release. They had shown their true colours and jumped away. All Romain could do was sit in his cockpit and watch as he drew closer to the naval vessel and a certain future.

As the enormity of the situation dawned on him he shivered. His stomach churned into a knot.

Fuck you Rhodes. Fuck you Eden and fuck you Freddie.

An idea formed, *The Dead Man's Hand.* He might just be able to bring his jump drive online long enough to leap away; half a light year in any direction would be enough.

Romain cycled through the ship's manual on his knee mounted datapad. The fighter's cannon used a plasma accelerator to generate energy. If he were to force an overload, then the warship's sensors would detect an energy spike. It would appear to them as if his ship were about to explode and it would if he could not dump the excess energy. He would have to vent heat and plasma into space but if he could route it into the drive subsystem, he could kick-start the FTL drive. It was an old trick often spoken of in seedy Frontier bars and UniNet chat rooms. It was a gamble. The odds were against him, but Romain had always been a man to play the long odds.

The tug moved onto an approach vector for the cruiser's docking bay; as it did so Romain switched his weapons system into maintenance mode and set off a chain of commands that would cause the plasma accelerator to feedback. Warnings flashed on his HUD. He overrode them and waited. A trickle of stone cold sweat ran down his neck. The plan unfolded as the tug engaged reverse thrust and pushed back; it released the towing bar as it did so. Romain was now moving backwards relative to the cruiser. He entered the override code to halt the reaction and used his residual power to flip his ship onto an escape vector. The weapons system did not respond; frantically he retyped the override instruction. The temperature was now critical. The chain reaction was running out of control.

Three seconds later Romain Vincent's pirate career ended in an expanding ball of super-heated plasma.

CHAPTER TWO

MIRA popped another couple of pills as she returned to the flight deck. The pain behind her eye showed little sign of subsiding. Despite her reluctance she decided to visit Dr Garret on her return to the *Berlin*.

Ethan Tate was removing circuit boards from the overhead consoles. He checked them and reseated them.

"Ma'am, I have restored climate control to operational status; we should see the temperature and humidity stabilise. Shields are offline, but available when we need them. I have started diagnostics on the major systems."

"Affirmative, Private. You've done good work. This ship is in a worse state than we thought. We're on battery power and the reactor has scrammed." She tapped her com-link. "Sergeant Barnes, how are you doing?"

The energy discharge from the exploding fighter filled the view port; nano seconds later a secondary explosion ripped through the lower decks of the *Berlin*.

"Fuck!" Mira's mind raced to process the horror unfolding outside the ship. Further explosions blossomed throughout the cruiser's hull as the aftermath of the first tore through the vessel.

"Barnes get up here," she yelled into the link.

"*Berlin,* this is Thorn. Do you read?"

Static was the only response.

Ethan pushed past her, making for an open access panel on the engineering console. He pushed in a rack of circuit boards and flicked a bank of switches. The ship's lighting blinked off and a second later red emergency lights came on.

"I've diverted the remaining power to the shields," he said. "Debris will come this way." As he spoke the Kobo shook and lumps of twisted metal hurtled past the view ports. The shields fizzed under the onslaught of smaller objects. Ethan's action had probably saved their lives. In a detached part of her brain she made a mental note to write him a commendation if they got out of this.

Mira tried her com-link again. After a burst of static a cacophony of voices echoed in her earpiece, then only silence. She watched as explosions flashed through stricken cruiser's hull. Seconds later the main reactor exploded with a stellar bright discharge of energy that tore the ship apart.

Mira blinked. She sat on the deck and tried to steady her breathing.

"What the fuck just happened?" she asked, her voice a hoarse murmur. Ethan replied without taking his eyes off the sight unfolding outside the ship.

"That fighter, it must have exploded in the bay." His voice wavered as he spoke. "A malfunction, maybe a deliberate act. People say insurgents destroy their ships to avoid capture. I thought it was BS but..."

Mira stared at the rubberised deck. Her vision tunnelled to a single black dot as the world swam around her; all she could think of was the eighty crew onboard the ship.

What happened? It was one fighter. Her thoughts coalesced into a semblance of clarity. The *Berlin* was one of the first

Europa class cruisers to leave the Martian yards. The reactor was positioned next to the hangar in a design oversight inherited from the older Atlantic class.

She remembered the loss of the *Oslo*, the first of the Europas. She had been lost over five decades ago. It was a case study on one of the engineering modules in the Academy. One of her tugs suffered an engine malfunction in the hangar. A minor explosion had triggered a chain reaction that destroyed the ship. The Admiralty ordered a design change to the second batch of Europa vessels. Improved bulkheads were retrofitted to the five original vessels. The Navy had disposed of all ships built to the original specification. All except for the *Berlin*.

Barnes and Tate were looking to her for guidance. She was the mission commander and their welfare was her responsibility.

Unable to process anything close to a rational thought, Mira stood and stumbled aft toward the crew cabins. Her nerves jangled and her emotions were running out of control. She leant forward, resting her hands on her knees and steadied her breathing. Her throat burned with an acid reflux from the painkillers. She remained bent over, waiting for the burning to pass, and as it did her training took control of her shattered emotions. Mira spat foul tasting fluid onto the deck, straightened and wiped her mouth.

She waited for her hands to stop shaking before walking back to the flight deck. Gathering herself, she addressed the marines.

"We have to get this ship functioning and help our shipmates," she said.

Is that it, Thorn? Is the fucking obvious the best you can come up with? Think about specifics!

"Ethan you're the closest thing we have to an engineer. We

need enough power to get over there." Mira pointed to the debris field. "Then we need to get this ship jump capable. It's a big ask but we have to try. The drive section is in a mess. We need to fabricate some new ducting and bypass the ruptured tubes."

"I found a spares package; it may be of use," Barnes said.

"I'll check it out," Ethan replied, his voice steady and his emotions held firmly in check.

"Good," Mira said. "Get to it. I want to deep scan the wreck. I'll join you when I'm done."

The marines went aft while Mira focused her attention on the Kobo's sensor suite.

The floor hatch was tiny. Barnes had rolled back the carpet and unfastened the covering plate. Mira stared at the rectangular opening in the steel deck.

"You are fucking kidding me?"

"Small enough for a mouse," Barnes said.

Mira winced. Mouse was her old call-sign from another life; a life that ended in an oily fireball on the Cydonian plain.

She sat and slipped her legs through the hatchway. She looked up at Ethan and Barnes. Their faces were masks of grime, sweat and exhaustion.

"It will be a tight fit even for me, Rich. You're lucky I'm not claustrophobic," she said, lowering herself through the narrow opening. Her feet connected with the deck below and she wriggled her shoulders through.

"Okay?" Ethan asked.

She nodded. He gave her the diagnostic kit; she somehow squeezed it through the hatchway and clipped it to her belt.

"The Engine Management System should be about five metres ahead of you. You will recognise it from the warning notices on it."

They had bypassed the damaged engine and re-routed plasma conduits to the remaining three. Her arms and wrists were sore from the work, her fingers and palms covered with tiny cuts and burns. Mira had been impressed by how well Ethan Tate had used the Kobo's meagre spares package to complete a near rebuild of the injector feed. When the repair was complete Barnes restarted the reactor unit. The ship's electrical system had come back to full operation, but the engines had stubbornly refused to fire. Mira and Ethan shifted their attention to the software running on the engine management system. She had struggled to comprehend the complex engineering diagrams and notes; Ethan had no such problem.

Their hopes now rested on the engine control unit. The FTL drive and the sublight ion engines used a common control system known as the Control Nexus. The Nexus controlled the drive system; crucially it ran the software required to diagnose and fix engine malfunctions. Ethan had an idea the problem was an application fault rather than physical damage. The only chance of fixing it would be to bypass the ship's engineering station and talk to the engine management system.

Mira squeezed through a narrow gap between pipes. They were hot and she flinched as her cheek brushed against one. Her head clanged on the pipe above her. Shock waves of pain rippled through her skull.

"Fuck this shit," she mumbled, blinking sweat from her eye.

Mira lay on her side and pushed herself between a pair of upright pipes; she couldn't move. Her upper body was through but one arm was trapped.

She breathed in and tried to pull herself forward. She moved a few centimetres. She reached out with her free hand and gripped a pipe. It was hot and burned her but she kept hold. She exhaled the air from her lungs and pulled herself free. Mira checked her hand. The palm and fingers were sore and red but she could move it. Satisfied it was nothing more serious than surface burn, she pressed on.

Ahead of her was a grey steel box mounted to the bulkhead. It bore the Sirius Dynamics logo and a warning notice that read:

WARNING HIGH VOLTAGE–DANGER OF DEATH

"I've found it. It wants to kill me," Mira called back. "I'm trying to locate the diagnostic port."

Mira fumbled around the edge of the unit, her fingers finally alighting on the recessed socket. She unclipped the terminal from her belt and extended the ribbon cable. She connected it to the unit with a firm push.

Mira booted the device and clicked through the welcome screen. She waited while it established communications with the drive system.

The initial readout confirmed the information from the flight deck's engineering panel:

Engine 1: READY
Engine 2: ERR 99
Engine 3: FAIL
Engine 4: ERR 99
FTL: OFFLINE / UNAVAILABLE

The fail state on sublight three was to be expected. The whole unit had been reduced to scrap by a laser blast. She relayed the information back to Ethan.

"I'm not showing detailed faults on two and four. I'm just getting code 99. Is there anything in the manual?" Mira asked.

There was a pause before Ethan replied.

"Code 99—miscellaneous or unspecified error," he said. "It's a generic code for a non functioning control system. I suspect three is still showing a fail state because we've taken it offline and the Nexus doesn't know that." There was a pause. "The fail state is preventing the software from communicating with the engines. You'll need to find the shipyard menu and clear it."

"Okay thanks," she said, no wiser.

She cycled the diagnostics tool through page after page of data. Finally she arrived at a 'Shipyard Only' page. It contained a warning to proceed with caution. Mira acknowledged the message and was presented by a page of advanced procedures. Clicking through each she paused at:

16-Remove Engine (s) from Power Group.

"Ethan, I have an option of removing an engine from the power group. Does that sound right?"

There was a long pause. She assumed he was referring to the manual.

"Removing it should clear the fail on three and force a rebuild."

Mira clicked into the submenu and selected engine three for removal. The handset flashed a warning. She clicked OK to continue.

ENGINE REMOVED FROM POWER GROUP—REBIAS Y/N
(CAUTION! RUNNING AN UNBIASED POWER GROUP CAN CAUSE
CATASTROPHIC ENGINE FAILURE)

Mira froze. Her thumb hovered over the OK button.

Was a re-bias and a rebuild the same?

She was the commanding officer, so the buck was with her.

"Fuck it," she said and pressed the button.

The hum from the engines died, and the lights flicked off. The darkness and silence pressed in on her. An eternity seemed to pass with only her breathing for company.

Nothing happened.

Her hands shook as she fumbled the handset. It threatened to fall from her grip. The screen showed a simple spinning timer. She repeatedly clicked *UNDO* to step back to the top-level menu. The handset remained unresponsive. The panic built as Mira's mind went into free fall.

"Oh fuck, oh fuck," she repeated it over and over.

Mira was on the brink of tears when the Nexus emitted five beeps. The lights came back on and the familiar whine of flowing plasma filled her ears. The blind terror lifted and she laughed. The nervous giggle evolved into a full laugh that made her head spin. Once she had regained control Mira clicked the handset back to the status page:

Engine 1: READY
Engine 2: READY
Engine 3: OFFLINE
Engine 4: READY
FTL: ONLINE / AVAILABLE

Mira thumped the bulkhead.

"Yes!" she said through gritted teeth.

"We have power," Ethan shouted. Even over the sound of the engines spooling up she could hear the relief in his voice. "The power group is functioning in limp mode; but we are mobile *and* FTL capable. I guess our duct work is sound!"

Mira backed out of the tight space.

Ethan helped her climb out of the hatch. Mira's relief was echoed in the young soldier's face.

The surviving members of the *Berlin* crew assembled in the main lounge. It was located aft of the bridge. The wide oval room was decorated with neutral colours and deep filled couches. Corridors led in three directions to the guest cabins. Barnes was the last to arrive, running up the staircase from the lower deck.

Mira passed them a grainy image printed from the ship's navigation computer.

"There isn't much left." She paused as the marines studied the picture. "The largest fragment is a section of decks three through eleven. It's around 250 metres long and is still pressurised."

She pointed to a circular arc marked on the printout in red ink.

"Fortunately the ship's artificial gravity generator continued to function. It has created a well around which the larger fragments are orbiting. We got caught up in it and are following the wreck."

Ships ejected their gravity core in the event of a failure. The idea was to keep the wreckage together to allow for rescue. Mira was grateful the fail-safe had functioned as intended and kept the *Berlin* in one place.

"What are the chances of anyone being alive over there? I've seen how explosions rip through a ship. They incinerate everything in their path." Barnes spoke with unconcealed emotion.

"I'll be honest Rich, the chances are slim and going over there will be risky. We have to be certain no one is alive. We owe it to our friends."

"Okay. What are we waiting for?" Barnes replied.

"Ethan and I will go over."

Barnes tried to protest.

"Gunny, I checked the EVA suits. There are only two and neither will fit you. Besides, I'm the only one who has an EVA certification." She omitted to mention that her last and only space walk had been in Low Earth Orbit nine years ago.

Mira explained her insertion plan. She highlighted an airlock on the superstructure as their way in and out. She and Ethan would work through the ship, looking for survivors, compartment by compartment.

"Once we are aboard disengage and hold station. If hostiles show up jump clear. I have programmed a jump path so you won't have to rely on your skills for any more than the basics."

Seconds passed, no one said anything.

"Okay, it's a plan, just don't take any chances in the hull, Mira," Barnes said. He stood and headed for the forward corridor.

Mira tried to pull the EVA suit's gloves tighter around her fingers. It was at least one size too large for her. Ethan's suit was a better fit although he still squirmed as he checked the function of his lamp. They stood in silence, uncomfortably close to each other in the cramped airlock. The Kobo slid closer to the wrecked cruiser. There was a jolt as the docking collar mated with the *Berlin's* airlock. The iris shaped hatch opened with a hiss of air.

Mira pushed herself through toward the hull. She tried to cycle the airlock controls. When the control panel did not respond, so she reached for the manual release key; it was located in a recess next to the hatch. She inserted the key and rotated it. After three turns the mechanism engaged and the outer door slid inward and up. Ethan followed her through and reversed the procedure, manually hauling the hatch closed.

"Thorn to Barnes, we're in."

"Solid copy. I'll be waiting for you when you're done. Stay safe. You have 110 minutes EVA remaining."

Mira closed the link. Ethan floated out of her blind spot. She flinched involuntarily as he appeared in her eye line.

"Are you ready?" she asked. "I have no idea what we'll find behind the inner hatch, so prepare for the worst."

"Yes, Ma'am; this marine is ready."

Mira detected the false bravado in his voice, it echoed her own. Through the sapphire crystal of his helmet Ethan looked like an uncertain boy.

"Call me Mira," she said, opening the second hatch. "I think the chain of command broke when the ship was lost."

Ethan clicked his intercom twice in acknowledgement.

They emerged into a dark corridor. The beams of their helmet lights cut through the darkness. A mist of fluid droplets filled the air.

An object bounced off Mira's helmet. She spun to see a severed forearm floating in the darkness. The skin was scorched black in places, the remaining blood swelling the fingers.

She activated her mag boots. They anchored her to the deck as she caught her breath.

The arm continued to float down the corridor; it was a woman's with painted nails. Mira shuddered, looked away and tried to banish it from her mind.

"Are you okay?" Ethan asked.

Mira caught her breath. "Yes, it just gave me a shock. We should keep our helmets on. We could run into a vacuum behind any of these hatches. Let's play it safe." It occurred to her that the droplets in the air likely comprised a large quantity of body fluids. She kept that thought to herself.

Mira unravelled a three metre tether cord and attached it to a hook on the breast plate of Ethan's suit. She gave him the other end and he clipped it to the back of hers.

"Just in case we run into open space," she explained. "We're not engaged or anything."

Ethan's laughter put Mira at ease.

She flicked off her mag boots and floated free from the deck. She took a moment to accustom herself to zero-g before heading forward.

They floated through the corridor. An eight was painted on the wall adjacent an elevator shaft. Mira orientated herself.

"This is deck eight. The weapons bay is forward of here; armoury is above us, as is the infirmary," Ethan said.

Mira shivered when she realised her cabin was five decks beneath them in the section exposed to space. She wondered how many of the crew had slipped off to sleep at the end of their shift, never to awake; she thought of the severed arm.

Perhaps they were the lucky ones.

They continued to sweep through the ship, moving like ghosts through compartments once teeming with life. The *Berlin* had a crew of 80; yet nothing moved in the darkness, save for loose equipment and personal effects. Occasionally bloated and burned bodies floated out of the shadows toward them. Sometimes they were faces Mira recognised, other times not. Neither spoke as they floated through wreck. The occasional creaking and popping of strained metal relayed through her suit's audio sensors were the only sounds Mira heard in the dead hull. The silence became ever more oppressive, and she felt the need to fill the void. Her usual reluctance to waste time with idle words was secondary to her need to hear a living voice.

"You appear very skilled for a combat engineer, Ethan. Sorry I didn't mean it to come out like that. I mean you seem to know your way around a ship's drive system," she said, awkwardly. There was a pause.

"I've been fooling with engines since I was a kid. I grew up around starships; my dad works for Sirius Dynamics in Houston."

"So why the Corps?" Mira asked. "Fleet would offer you more options, not to mention safety." Mira knew the truth of the saying *Navy does the flying, Corps does the dying.*

"I failed the entrance exam, twice. I'm not so good with written tests."

Mira could sympathise. She had barely scraped the grades for academy entrance and it was only when she began flight training had she seen them improve. A sympathetic instructor had told her that everyone just needs to find their groove. What Mira lacked in engineering knowledge she more than compensated for in Astrogation and the ability to fly a starfighter.

"My only choice was to enlist and fleet doesn't allow enlisted crew to specialise. The Corps does," Ethan said.

"Sirius Dynamics? That explains how you know what the inside of a star liner looks like."

"We did travel a lot when I was young. My dad had a legendary expense account," he conceded.

Mira wondered why he had not followed his father into a civilian business but thought better than to ask. Her parents had a legal background and while her elder sister had qualified as a criminal lawyer both she and her brother had chosen very different paths.

They lapsed into silence before Ethan continued. "Can I ask you a question?"

"Sure."

"You have a Marine Corps Insignia on your armour. I thought you were Navy?"

"Yeah I am. I was attached to VMM-655 during the war. I flew a Cobra out of the Mariner City Barracks. It didn't work out so well." She paused. "Did you hear that?"

The sound came again. A faint crackle in her ear. "I thought I heard a voice on the local channel. It was faint. I couldn't make out any words."

As she listened, Ethan adjusted his comms system. He made a hand gesture indicating he wasn't hearing anything. Mira tried to fine tune her com-link. The voice evaporated into static; she knew it was real but now all she could pick up was the hiss of background radiation. She waited. It came again. The words were unclear, but it was a voice, human and female.

"There! I have it locked." She watched Ethan adjust his link trying to lock into the same narrow band transmission.

"I hear it. I think it's Doctor Garret!" he said, excitement in his voice.

Mira keyed her link. "Monica, come in, please? Doctor Garret can you hear me?" She paused, waiting for a reply. "This is Mira Thorn. I have Private Tate with me. Do you read?" There was a pause, static crackled in Mira's earpiece.

"Mira?" The voice sounded tired, the Doctor's normally crisp English accent blunted by fatigue. "I'm trapped in the infirmary. The door is jammed. There was an explosion. Everyone is dead." She sounded confused.

"Are you injured?" Mira asked. "Is there anyone else in there with you?"

"No, on both counts." Her voice took an echo of its normal personality.

Mira reported called Barnes.

"Doctor Garret made it, Rich. She may locate more survivors with her monitoring equipment."

"Understood Mira. You have 45 minutes EVA remaining."

Barnes was trying to keep his voice steady, but Mira could detect the relief in his professional response.

45 minutes? She wondered where the time had gone

Mira and Ethan pushed themselves along the corridor with greater purpose. A loose fire extinguisher floated out of the darkness and bounced off Mira's shoulder. She stifled a cry born more of surprise than pain, and did not slow her pace. They arrived at the infirmary door and Mira used her mag boots to stand on the deck while Ethan appraised the hatchway.

"The power is out to the lock," he said. "The hull is badly warped so I can't crank it. An explosive entry will be the quickest way."

Mira keyed her com-link.

"Monica, stand back from the door. Ethan will blow it out. Can you locate an emergency respirator? We have an atmosphere but the air quality is poor."

There was a crackle of static.

"I'm ready," Doctor Garret replied.

Ethan pulled an explosive cord from his pack and secured it around the edge of the hatch. He motioned for Mira to stand back as he attached a small remote detonator. Stepping out of range, he triggered the explosive. Mira's ribs shook as the shock wave passed through her. Smoke bloomed around the door. Ethan stepped forward and gave the door a hard shove with his shoulder. It floated clear of the frame and into the infirmary. He grabbed it and placed it out of harm's way.

Monica Garret floated forward; she struggled to stay upright in the weightless environment. Her face was streaked with blood from a head wound she had dressed herself; the needle work was below the doctor's normal standard. Her hair was loose and blonde strands floated like a halo around her head.

Monica hugged Mira. Even through the suit she felt the

strength of the doctor's embrace.

"I thought I was alone," she said, sobbing. "You came for me, Mira." Monica disengaged, struggling to regain her composure.

"I ran a check on the crew beacons. I only detected one," the doctor said as her demeanour shifted back to ship's physician.

Every crew member was fitted with an emergency locator tag beneath the skin of their right shoulder. It was a short range device that allowed location in emergency situations.

"Commander Kite is in elevator 4B. I picked his signal up a while ago but it's been fading in and out."

"Ethan, go to 4B and see if Alex is alive."

"On my way." He pushed off from the deck. Mira remembered the tether and released it before Ethan dragged her through the doorway.

"Mira, I didn't pick you up on the scan nor Private Tate. If you are alive, there could be others."

Mira explained the chain of events that led to her being off ship when the explosion occurred.

"We found no signs of life anywhere we looked," Mira said. "There has been extensive depressurisation and secondary explosions all over the ship. I'm sure we are the only survivors." Mira felt oddly detached at the statement, as if by saying it she could process the loss and accept it.

"We have a ship, Monica. We can get home or at least somewhere."

Her earpiece crackled.

"Ma'am... Mira I mean. I have located Commander Kite. He's alive but out cold. He has a head injury. He has an airway, and no obvious bleeds."

"Alex is alive," she informed the doctor.

She keyed the com-link. "Ethan, do you need the doctor to

assist?"

"Negative; I've stabilised him and improvised a litter. I can meet you by the airlock."

"Okay. We are done here. Head back to the egress point and we'll come to you. Ethan, do not deviate from the main corridors."

Mira closed the link.

"I have no idea what medical facilities are available over on that Kobo so gather up anything we might find useful. We are zero-g all the way back to the hold so weight is not an issue."

Monica removed a green transit case and started packing supplies. Mira assisted as the older woman directed. When she was satisfied the crate was full, Monica used a key card to open her records cabinet. She fished out data cards for Mira, Ethan, Alex and herself and slipped them into her pocket.

"Sergeant Barnes made it out too," Mira said.

"Rich made it?" Monica Garret appeared relieved at the news.

Monica removed the final record card. She tapped a code into the cabinet's control pad and erased the remaining cards.

Mira glanced around the wrecked infirmary. This ship had been her home for the past two years. She had spent many off-duty hours in sickbay drinking from the doctor's unofficial supply of expensive booze.

"Don't forget the Jovian Brandy," Mira said.

"I already packed it," Monica replied from the office on the far side of the room. Mira blinked hard as a silent tear traced its way down her cheek.

Mira and Doctor Garret arrived at the airlock and found an unconscious Alex Kite strapped to an elevator door with electrical flex. His face was ashen, his blond hair matted with dried blood.

Ethan Tate was absent.

Monica knelt over the unconscious officer, inspecting his head and neck before tracing her hands down his spine.

"We could do with getting fluids into him." She checked his pulse. "He'll be back to his normal prickly self soon enough."

Ethan had secured a stack of supply boxes to the deck with magnetic pads; Mira assumed Tate had been raiding the ship's stores, located a deck below.

Mira keyed her com-link to page the ship.

"Rich, come in please."

The Marine Sergeant answered immediately.

"I'm here, Mira."

"We have located two survivors; can you pick us up?"

"Sure, not a minute too soon. I'll feel better once we have put some distance between us and here."

Mira acknowledged and swapped to the local channel. She was about to call Ethan when the circle of light from his helmet lamp swung into view around the bend in the corridor. A moment later he appeared pushing two large crates in front of him.

"Supplies," he said. "These are a pair of plasma guns; we'd normally fit them to tugs. I noticed our new ship has two internal hard points and figured these would be useful."

Mira agreed. She had a destination in mind and the weapons would offer a welcome reassurance.

Ethan pointed to the other crates.

"These are field service packs full of engine spares. The Kobo shares a lot of common parts with our tugs. I also have personal weapons, body armour, ration packs and general supplies."

He lifted a smaller box from the deck. "I thought this would come in handy." Tate popped the lid of the box. It was full of gold bars, each weighing 250 grams. "If we need to pay for repairs."

"Good thinking, Ethan." The soldier had impressed her with his skills and ingenuity. Fleet's insistence on academic qualification was their loss with this young man. She vowed she'd put that right when they got out of this.

Mira's earpiece crackled into life.

"I've docked, Mira," Barnes said.

"Keep the gravity off on the lower deck. Private Tate has been shopping." She looked around at the dead ship. "Come on, let's get out of here."

With the hatch sealed and the salvage stowed, Mira unclipped her helmet and breathed a lungful of the lower access corridor's cold air. Barnes handed her an energy drink in a silver sachet. She sucked down the warm liquid. It took the dryness from her mouth and throat.

The white fabric of her suit was covered in streaks of blood, human tissue, oil stains and other detritus. The Kobo was equipped with a UV decontamination system which sterilised the suit but did not remove the pollutants. Mira shuddered and fought back the urge to throw up. She unzipped the suit and discarded it on the deck.

Mira stood in her underwear. The deck was cold underfoot and she shivered as her cheeks reddened. She let out a humourless laugh.

"Sorry, I had to get that off."

She studied the space suit on the deck. A piece of burnt skin was stretched across the thigh.

Rich Barnes handed her a blue flight suit. He tossed another to Ethan.

"Avert your eyes, Private!" he bellowed. "Even with my

years of service I may not lay my eyes on an officer in a state of undress."

Ethan turned away and unzipped his own suit.

"That's the smallest flight suit I could find," Barnes said as Mira finished dressing. "There's a whole wardrobe of fancy clothes in the main stateroom."

"Thanks, Gunny. It fits fine," Mira replied, putting two rolls into each sleeve to take them clear of her wrists.

"Private, take these suits up to the main deck and put them into one of the microbial washers. Then check on the doctor to see if she needs any help," Barnes ordered

The young marine gathered up the EVA suits and left the hold.

"Don't be too hard on him, Rich. He's done well."

Barnes nodded. "Yeah, he's a good kid. He's coping well with this. How about you? I can only imagine how tough it was over there."

She thought of the severed arm and wondered who it had belonged to. The painted nails meant whoever it was had been off duty. Mira wondered what the woman had been doing when the explosion tore her apart. Maybe she had been on a date or maybe just pampering herself in her cabin. She hoped it had been quick; she hoped it had been quick for all of them. She shuddered at the thought of the bloated and scorched bodies floating the dark, silent tomb that had once been their home.

The wail of the ship's alarm broke the silence.

"What the hell?" Barnes said.

"Proximity alert!" Mira said already running up toward the flight deck. "I programmed the long range sensors to sound the general quarters' alarm if another vessel came into range."

They reached the upper deck and rushed past Ethan. Mira ran straight for the flight deck and jumped into the pilot's seat.

She pulled on a headset and cycled the central multifunction display. Two ships were approaching from the stern, sweeping back and forth. An analysis of their engine signature revealed them to be Hornets, an ageing design popular with pirates and privateers.

Barnes sat in the copilot's chair.

"What have we got?"

"Two ships, fighters, operating a search pattern. They have not seen us." The ship was operating in low-power mode with a minimal heat signature, their sensor trace was blending with the hot debris field. Mira knew that would change when she fired up the engines.

"I'm re-plotting a course to Tarantella," she said. "It's not ideal but I don't think we have any other options." She loaded the ship's automated path. Once she was satisfied she let the navigation computer optimise the plot. The seconds were counting down as the fighters closed in. Mira chewed on her bottom lip as her head throbbed.

The NaviComp chimed when the course was ready. Mira checked the hyperdrive was primed and started the drive system.

"They'll know we're here now," she said. She advanced the throttles and moved the Kobo out of the shadow of the wreck.

The sensor suite pinged, demanding her attention.

"What the fuck?" she muttered.

"Huh?" Barnes replied, trying to peer over her shoulder.

"Another ship! A big one! Where did he come from?"

The new vessel was larger than the fighters. She used the short range sensors to scan the newcomer. They reported it as an *unclassified vessel*.

"He's five clicks away, closing. We should have seen something that big," Mira said. The flight deck came alive with sounds as the ship scanned them. The Kobo's Identify Friend or Foe system replied with their Squawk code. Mira shut off the IFF and pushed the throttles to full. She reached over and flipped the cover on the hyperspace trigger. Without a word she pressed down and the stars stretched into streaks of light. Clouds of energy blossomed outside the viewports and the darkened flight deck was lit by flashes of blue-green light.

"We did it," Barnes said.

Mira sat back in the seat, her arms and legs heavy with fatigue. Her back ached and her head felt like a freight train was running through it.

"Fuck yeah." It was all she could say. A faint smile crossed her lips as she caressed the control yoke. She had been away from the sharp end for too long.

CHAPTER THREE

FLEET Admiral James Foster slammed his glass onto the ancient oak tabletop with such force its contents spilled over the rim and splashed onto the polished wood.

"I have had enough of this. We have been going round in circles for the last nine hours and you people will not listen. How simple can I make this? The Navy needs the new dreadnoughts to make up for the tonnage you have *already* cut. We are down to skin and bones and you want to pick those clean."

The Senate had been called to vote on a thirty percent reduction in military spending and while Marine Corps outnumbered their Navy counterparts ten to one; the big savings came from cutting fleet tonnage.

The fleet had been in decline long before Foster's tenure. The Europa and Africa classes were at the end of their service lives. The Navy needed to commission their successors. Certain members of the Senate had other ideas.

Fifteen years ago Earth Governance had approved construction of eight new dreadnoughts. These advanced warships, named the Norse class, would make the Navy's current generation of cruisers obsolete.

Foster looked at the faces of the three faction leaders sitting at the table. Each representative was separated by an empty chair. Senator David Conway, Commissioner of the Board of Trade and Commerce shook his head and rubbed his temples. Otto Hofner, Secretary of State for the Core Systems shuffled his paperwork. Senator Vanessa Meyer, Secretary of State for the Outer Frontier stared at him with a curious expression on her lined face.

Beyond them sat the 150 voting members of the Federal Senate in a tiered hemisphere. Their role was to listen to the arguments and vote on motions their factional leader submitted for approval. Half the seats were empty as delegates came and went. Foster took it as a measure of how much interest they had in the fleet. He wondered how many would be here if they were voting on changes to their remuneration packages.

At the same time he understood the disinterest in military affairs. The Martian War had dulled the public's appetite for military expenditure. Further complications arose from the lack of a tangible external threat. The security issues facing the Federation comprised home grown insurgency and piracy, both could be managed by smaller frigates or corvettes. Cruisers, carriers and above all dreadnoughts were expensive luxuries in tough times.

The three empty chairs at the table belonged to committee members who had not bothered to turn up, having already exercised their block votes. It seemed to Foster that the absent members had even more contempt for the Navy than the three fools sitting in front of him.

The Admiral looked at the glass and the pool of water surrounding it. The only sound was the faint hum of the air conditioning. It was if everyone in the chamber had taken a collective gasp and were yet to exhale. Foster was embarrassed by his display of emotion. It was in that moment he realised this was a colossal waste of time.

You cannot change closed minds. It was a phrase his wife was fond of and in most things she was right.

Foster had begun his address by discussing strategic planning, technical specification and the projected threat analysis. None of it swayed the committee members away from their default positions.

His whole career had led to this point. He was the most powerful officer in the fleet and was begging for the fleet to be kept functional. One hell of a migraine was pulsing behind his right eye.

The attitudes of the three representatives came as no surprise. They summed up everything wrong with the Federal Senate and EarthGov.

Conway was a hard line corporatist who believed the corporations could do everything better than central government, including the policing of the trade routes. Conway's faction controlled 48% of the remaining votes, meaning that Foster would need to win him over to secure success. Hofner was an ex-fighter pilot with a cybernetic arm earned during the Martian War. The support of his pro military centralists and their 40% was assured. Hofner's faction did not have the leverage to swing the vote Foster's way. That left Vanessa Meyer.

Meyer was a veteran politician who had served EarthGov for the best part of half a century. Her Progressive Socialist Alliance commanded a mere 12% of the vote. Meyer's block combined with Hofner's would be enough but Foster knew she would never side with him.

Foster had concentrated his attention on Conway. Despite his efforts to illustrate the economic benefits government procurement brought to the private sector, it was clear the commissioner remained unconvinced.

Vanessa Meyer leant forward in her chair.

"Admiral Foster, I could not agree more. It feels like we have been round in circles all day, wasting everyone's time. At my age I take a dim view of my time being wasted. One never quite knows when it will run out."

Nervous laughter rippled through the room.

"I have said little in this debate. I have listened to the arguments and I think now would be a good time to state my position." She paused and poured herself a glass of water. "As Senator Conway has stated, the Frontier Company has done a good job maintaining security between the Core Systems and the Outer Frontier. I have to agree there has been a marked reduction in piracy against *corporation* shipping."

A sardonic grin fleetingly crossed Conway's round face.

"Thank you Vanessa, I..."

"Please let me finish, David," she said. Her tone was stern, yet devoid of animosity. She looked back at Foster.

"Admiral, in your extensive briefing materials do you have the statistics for the attacks on *non* corporate shipping; independents and such like?"

Foster sat frozen for a moment. An aide passed him a datapad. He read and digested the information. It appeared the senator had just offered him an opportunity. He grasped it as a drowning man would a rope.

"Senator Meyer, the data shows on some routes the level of piracy has remained consistent, however on the popular trade routes we have seen increases of between 200 and 500 percent in the period until August. This mirrors an increase we have seen over the past 12 months."

"Preposterous!" Conway said. "What is the source of those figures?"

Foster suppressed a grin, he would enjoy this.

"This is based on Frontier Company data, Sir. Our own data

estimates a 750% increase at the upper end."

Vanessa Meyer thanked him and looked to Conway. Foster sat back in his seat. He was keen to see where the veteran politician would take this.

"So you see David, this illustrates a point you are unwilling to embrace. Frontier is funded and operated by Quantum Infinity and Regina Enterprise; it contracts services to all but one of the large corporations.. It will defend their interests. It is good business sense. The Frontier Company views non-corporate shipping as all cost and no profit." She took a sip of water.

Conway interjected.

"With respect, Vanessa, there are many safeguards built into the legislation. The Frontier Company must act in a socially responsible manner and offer protection to all shipping regardless of their flag."

"David, who the hell will enforce your safeguards on the Outer Frontier?"

Foster watched the back and forth between them with interest. He detected a shift in power and wondered if things may move his way, from the most unlikely of quarters.

"Admiral Foster, you know I am not a friend of the Navy and I could not be described as pro-military. It is my belief the Navy and Marine Corps have been used too often to settle disputes that could have been handled by dialogue. My opposition to the ongoing oppression of the Martian democracy should be evidence enough." A flutter of indecipherable comments rippled around the chamber. She waited for it to subside.

"I am sure you are aware I supported the downsizing of the fleet during the economic disaster that characterised the last president's administration. At the time I asked your predecessor why we should spend trillions of dollars of taxpayers' money on weapons when there were children on the Frontier starving." She paused for a moment and looked him straight in the eye.

"It is my belief it is not the role of the private sector to protect the security of our citizens. I also believe the fleet has been cut too far in recent years; so much so we have seen the growth of both the Frontier Company and Damien Lightfoot's own militia. We cannot have privately funded warlords holding daggers to the throats of the Federation. It is our job to stand up to them and show them we, the elected representatives of 105 billion citizens, are the protectors of their lives and liberty."

Foster could not believe what he was hearing.

Meyer summed up.

"So, Admiral, I am pledging my block vote to the continuation of the Norse programme. I propose that the existing vessels continue in service and the hulls under construction be completed. I also propose an amendment that halts non-essential disposals of serving vessels. This will stem the rot. Additionally, I propose the commissioning of a full strategic review to address our future defence and exploration requirements."

Foster was stunned at her words. He composed himself. "Thank you, Senator. I am grateful for your understanding and support."

Hofner spoke up next.

"My position is clear; I second Senator Meyer's amendment and pledge my block vote."

Conway sat in silence. He blinked and tossed his datapad onto the table.

"I believe this session is concluded. Admiral, you are excused. I propose a brief recess before the vote is cast." Conway eyed the other two senators. His voice was calm yet his movements taut. Anger blazed behind his dark eyes.

Foster stood and nodded to Meyer. He wondered what his

new ally would want in return. Politicians always expected payback and why would Meyer be any different?

An hour later Foster sat alone in the lobby, watching as politicians, civil servants and journalists mingled through the busy space. Senator Meyer and her aide appeared through the throng. The senator said something to the young man and he disappeared into the crowd.

"Admiral Foster, my staff told me I would find you here," she said. "Please, walk with me."

Foster stood. The senator took his arm. They walked toward a glass wall overlooking the city of Strasbourg. An arched doorway opened onto an ornate balcony dressed with abstract sculptures. Foster drank a lungful of freezing air. Fresh air was a luxury seldom appreciated by non-spacefarers, a premium commodity to those used to breathing a recycled oxygen-nitrogen mix.

"Senator I would like to thank you for your support. We need those new ships. To say I was surprised is an understatement. It had been my plan to get Senator Conway onside. I never considered you an ally. I apologise."

"I'm a politician, Admiral, that makes me both a liar and a cheat. I may be your ally today and your worst enemy tomorrow," she replied. A smile warmed her face. Her blue eyes sparkled with a youth undiminished by her years.

"Unlike Senator Conway, I lie and cheat to make sure the people I represent get a fair deal. I want a system that works for everyone, not just the corporations. Regardless of my anti-military views I believe our citizens deserve protection from a politically accountable defence force." She looked out over the snow-covered city. Her breath formed clouds in the air.

Foster understood. He took his oath of service seriously. He believed the role of the Navy was to serve and protect every citizen from threats internal and external.

"Admiral, a woman of my age in my position hears many things. Some of which is hard fact, the rest of it is rumour, gossip and idle tittle tattle. Over the years I have learned that the latter should not be dismissed, but should be looked upon as a resource. The first time I hear something I take little notice, the second time I take an interest. The more I hear it the more I am inclined to believe it to be true. I have heard a lot about David Conway and the Frontier Company. Men like him are fuelled by greed and that makes them a danger to us all."

"As a military man I deal in facts," Foster said. "I prefer to leave the rumour and gossip to the spies and politicians. No offence intended."

"None taken, Admiral. I would expect no less." Meyer laughed. "Enough of this. Please school me on your new dread-noughts."

"They are multi-role vessels, capable of ship to ship operations, surface bombardment and troop insertion. They do everything our current cruisers can do and more."

Foster tried to keep it brief. Meyer listened and asked probing questions. Foster felt his respect for her grow. Unlike most of her kind she knew when to open her ears as well has her mouth.

"The lead ship, the *Valhalla,* has been on the Frontier for eight months under the command of Jon Flynt."

"I know him," Meyer said. Foster could not conceal his surprise. Meyer picked up on it. "We met at an event to commemorate the end of the war. I was sorry to hear about his wife and daughter."

Meyer was up to speed.

"The *Asgard* is nearing completion. We hope she'll start

space trials in three months. *Loki* is not far behind. We laid down the other five vessels two years ago but work was suspended due to budgetary restrictions," he said with a heavy emphasis on the last two words.

"I would like to visit one of them when possible," Meyer said.

"I can arrange that. *Valhalla* is scheduled to return to the home system in the next month."

Meyer thanked him.

"One more thing, Admiral, in a straight fight are these vessels a match for a Frontier Company ship?"

Foster found the question puzzling. Was the senator asking for a comparison or was she interested in how they would match up in an engagement?

"Combat is complex. Many factors will affect the outcome. We call them force multipliers; they include elements such as surprise, location and even crew morale." He thought for a moment trying to find the right words. "On any day a Norseman will kick their arses and take names."

Meyer clapped him on the arm. "That's all I need to know, Admiral."

With that she bid him farewell and walked back into the Assembly building.

Foster took a final look at the city and the crystalline blue sky above it. He was tired, yet satisfied, especially after seeing the results of the vote on giant holo-screens. The motion would have to pass through the Office of the President but it was a formality.

He made his way to a bank of elevators and called one. He pressed the key for the rooftop shuttle pads.

As he waited for the doors to close, he caught sight of Conway standing on a balcony engaged in an animated discussion with an old man in a dark suit. The man rested his weight on a cane. He appeared to be doing most of the talking while Conway listened, looking to all intents like a chastened schoolboy. The stranger paused and fixed his gaze on Foster. His stare was cold and impassive. Foster shuddered as the elevator doors closed. He closed his eyes as the elevator rose but his unease did not settle until he boarded his shuttle.

Clouds of sadness and exhaustion hung in the air of the Kobo's lounge; it mixed with the faint odour of sweat and combustion. Mira gazed at the assembled faces; they shared the same haunted expression. It was now, when they had little to do, that the enormity of the day's events weighed on them.

Mira thought of her last exchange with Captain Adams and of Sue Walton's ever cheerful voice. She thought of the nameless marine at the guard station.

And then there was Roland, the thirty-year-old tug pilot. Mira knew he had a wife and a young son at home in Paris. He had once told her he planned to cash in his commission, leave the Navy and open a bar on the Left Bank.

She wondered how many other dreams had perished with the crew of the *FSS Berlin*.

Mira held her breath and tried to hold her shit together.

Rich Barnes produced a bottle of Lightfoot branded whiskey he had looted from somewhere. He poured a glass and offered it to Mira. After a hesitation she took it and drained the contents in a single gulp. The liquid burned her throat and churned in her empty stomach. She shuddered. She did not resist when Barnes refilled her glass. He offered the bottle to anyone who wanted it; only Ethan declined.

"I'll start with the good news," she said. "The ship is operational and our envelope is stable."

"What's the bad news?" Barnes asked

"Fuel and air supplies are low, not critical, but enough to be a cause for concern. At current performance levels we have five days of fuel and four days of air."

Mira let the information sink in. No one commented further, so she continued.

"I have continued on the same heading to Tarantella. It is three days away so well within our margins. We'll be able to make repairs or charter a ship to a Federation outpost." She took care to form the words and spoke slowly, the booze was taking effect.

"Double T is home to every pirate in the sector. Xander Rhodes practically lives there," Barnes said.

Mira took it as an observation rather than a criticism.

"It's not ideal. There are several industrial outposts in range but I doubt they have the facilities we need. We don't have the fuel to make it anywhere more civilised," Mira replied. "I saw the state of the hull when we came over and I wouldn't trust it to hold up for an extended voyage, even if we had the range."

"Tarantella it is then," Barnes said.

"What about long-range communications? Can't we call for help?" Monica Garret asked.

"The antenna is trashed. Assuming we could fix it we would have to spacewalk, and that's a day of work." She paused. "Providing we have no additional problems we will get there with air and fuel to spare." She stood and pressed the creases out of her flight suit. She swayed but only she noticed.

"Rich, tomorrow I want you to get into the hold. Ethan hacked the security cameras but there is no coverage down there. That concerns me." She looked at the Doctor, who perched on the arm of one of the deep filled couches.

"Monica, how is Alex doing?"

"He's sleeping. He'll be fine, but I want to keep him sedated and monitored overnight. I can do without his whining until tomorrow. He is a terrible patient at the best of times."

They were all trying too hard to be their normal selves. Only Ethan Tate seemed vaguely at ease; he sat on the floor with a bottle of water. His eyes gave him away as he stared into nowhere.

"Ethan, you did good work today. We owe our lives to you."

He blushed.

"Tomorrow I want you to fit those cannons. I have no intention of flying into a shit hole like Tarantella without some iron in my pocket."

Barnes gave a belly laugh. It was subdued but his amusement was genuine.

"Spoken like a true marine," he said. "I always said you were wasted in the Navy."

Mira responded with a shrug.

"Tonight I want everyone to rest. It's been a tough day and tomorrow we move on."

She said her goodnights and went forward to the flight deck. She needed her own space and the peace that came with it.

Mira scanned the multifunction displays. The critical subsystems were in the green. It was an outcome she would not have expected when she first laid her eye on the ship. She drew a deep breath. The air was still stale. The scrubbers had not yet reached maximum efficiency and the smell of burnt plasma persisted on the flight deck. Despite a slew of minor faults she was grateful for this battered ship and the faint hope of salvation it offered.

A ping sounded in her headset. She shifted her attention back to the ship's consoles. The engineering pad was showing a yellow advisory.

"What are you?" she mumbled.

The drive system was displaying an unusual resonance fluctuation in the power output profile. As she watched, the system stabilised. She cleared the alert and continued to study the data. The power remained steady.

Just a passing event, Mira thought as she flagged it on the diagnostic system. A few transient events were to be expected on a healthy drive unit. On a unit as damaged as the Kobo's she was surprised there were not more warnings.

She sat back in the pilot's chair and opened a packet of reformed protein chips.

Being at the sharp end of a starship was like coming home. The Kobo had a very different configuration to the Cobra assault ships she had flown during the Martian Conflict. Yet when she laid her hands on the yoke she was transported back to those low level runs across the red plains, dodging SAMs and arriving at the drop zone in a cloud of flares, chaff and adrenalin. She rocked the seat back, closed her eye and drifted off to sleep.

Mira awoke, disorientated, her thoughts jumbled and incoherent. She sat up. The seat tilted forward. Her half finished bag of chips fell to the floor. She sensed someone behind her. A harsh voice whispered indistinguishable words in her ear. Mira sprung out of the seat, propelled forward by its self righting motion.

The flight deck was deserted. She shivered. She could not shake the foreboding that gripped her. She clenched her fists and regulated her breathing, pushing the panic away.

Movement in the corridor caught her eye. She tensed.

"Mira," Monica Garret said. "Is everything okay?"

The Doctor appeared in the doorway.

Mira sniffed and laughed. "I... must have been dreaming. How long have you been there?"

"I have just arrived. I was talking to Richard, finishing the last of the booze and scoping the ship out."

She walked in. Mira sat in the pilot's chair.

"I knew I'd find you up here."

"Someone needs to monitor the systems."

"Someone does. It doesn't have to be you *all* the time." Monica produced a key card and gave it to Mira.

"What's this?" Mira asked.

"The key to the main stateroom. I found it in the lounge along with the largest stash of holo-porn I've ever seen," Monica replied. "Mira you've been awake for eighteen hours. You need to rest."

Mira tried to protest.

"I'm not listening. You look dreadful. Get some sleep. I'll take over up here."

She slid out of the chair, bent and picked up her chips. Standing, she placed a hand on Monica's shoulder.

"Do you know what you are doing?" she asked.

"Not really. I'll work it out. Trust me, I'm a Doctor."

"Just call me if you need me," she paused at the door. "You said you found porn?"

Monica laughed. "Probably not your taste, all ripped guys in leather. I watched a couple just to make sure. I thought the lighting was excellent."

Mira made a face and went aft. Her back ached and her left leg dragged. She cursed herself for falling asleep in such an awkward position. The damn headache persisted.

She walked through the lounge. The lights were low and her footsteps muffled by the deep pile of the carpet. Barnes lay stretched out on the couch, snoring, a bottle at his side. A glass lay next to it on the floor. Mira knelt, picked it up and placed it on the arm of the chair. She continued toward the habitation section. Her stateroom was at the far end of the corridor.

Mira paused at the door. She was uncomfortable as if she were in someone else's home. The experience on the flight deck still troubled her. She shook off the paranoia and swiped the card. The door slid open and she stepped inside.

The room was spacious with a high curved ceiling. The neutral coloured walls were covered with drapes and framed reproduction artwork; mostly 21st and 22nd century pieces. The furniture was retro styled, chrome and black synth-leather dominated, a large bed the centrepiece. Mood lighting from discrete light bars cycled through blue and purple. The décor would not be Mira's choice but it sure as hell eclipsed the tiny cabin on the *Berlin*. The air in here smelt fresh. It carried a vague scent of lavender, more noticeable after the damp stench of the flight deck.

As she walked in, her fingers lingered on the synthetic marble top of a long dressing table. She caught sight of herself in the mirror. Her face was drawn and creased. Her scars angry on her pale skin. She looked as if she had aged twenty years in the space of a few hours.

She stripped to her underwear and walked into the bathroom. The black marble tiles were cold underfoot. Her feet left sweaty footprints behind her that evaporated almost as soon as they had been laid down. She took off her underwear and discarded it in a disposal chute; she would need to improvise tomorrow but the ship appeared to be well stocked with clothes.

Mira programmed the shower and stepped in. She set the temperature as high as the safety system would allow and stood beneath the nozzle, letting the hot, powerful stream blast the grime and stress from her being. When the drying cycle was complete, she stepped out. The tiles were even colder. She opened a locker beneath the counter, and rummaged around looking for toothpaste; she found it. Something else fell out and skittered across the floor. She reached down and picked up a straight razor, its blade housed in an ivory and gold handle. The razor was old, the ivory faded to yellow, but the gold kept its lustre. Mira opened it and rotated it in her hand. She studied the way light reflected off the silver-blue blade and enjoyed the way reflections danced along the viciously sharp edge. A comforting black veil clouded her rational mind. A familiar shiver of anticipation rippled through her body as she crossed a point of no return.

The first cut always felt the same, a sudden searing pain as the blade bit into her forearm. She gasped and held her breath as blood welled up in the wound, exhaling as it flowed; the tension, fear and sadness flowing with it. She repeated the process twice more before sinking to the floor sobbing. Blood ran down her arm and pooled in a dark puddle on the marble tiles.

Sometime later she dressed her wounds. It was a familiar process. Her arm throbbed, but at least she felt something.

After cleaning the floor she placed the razor back where she had found it. The part of her that did not need or crave the pain would have thrown it in the waste chute but she couldn't do it. She was not strong enough to fight her dark need.

Mira walked back to the bedroom and crawled into the bed. Ordering the lights out, she pulled the silk covers over her. She lay awake, staring into the darkness until a heavy cloak of sleep enveloped her mind, smothering her troubled thoughts with its folds.

CHAPTER FOUR

NIGHTWOLF dropped out of hyperspace and her powerful sub-light engines pushed her toward the wreck of the naval vessel. The 4G of acceleration was easily contained by the warbird's inertia control system and barely perceptible to her occupants.

Karl Manson strode onto the flight deck. His metallic blue armour glinted under the running lights.

"What am I seeing, Lyle?" He placed his cybernetic hand on the pilot's headrest and squeezed the foam, the faint whir of the servomotors audible on the silent flight deck.

Lyle studied the head up display.

"The wreck is a fleet cruiser," Lyle said. "I assume it's the one that scared off Eden and her crew. Fuck only knows what happened though; that was a big ship."

Manson peered over the pilot's shoulder. Lyle's hands were shaking. Manson took a small amount of satisfaction in intimidating the slightly built man.

"An Africa or Europa class ship," Manson said. "The Navy puts all its old shit out here. I need to have a chat with our Eden. This little detail seems to have slipped her mind."

Lyle paused for a moment as further information raced across his display.

"I think you'll be more interested in what you're not seeing

Karl," Lyle said.

Manson snorted.

"I'm detecting four distinct jump signatures: a pair of small craft and an unknown vessel." Lyle licked his lips.

"The fourth is faint and several hours older. That one comes from a Kobo class freighter."

"Our ship?" Manson whispered. The Kobo was supposed to be on an automated flight path. Once the freighter was ejected from hyperspace, it could not have continued without human intervention.

"Can you track it?"

Lyle typed on one of the many touch screens.

"I think so. It'll take me a few minutes... Yeah there is enough wake to analyse. I'll be able to tell you how far if nothing else."

"Good, do it. I'll talk to Eden. Let's see if she is feeling a little more cooperative."

Manson strode off the flight deck. He descended a steel stairwell toward the after section of the ship. As he walked, he added up the additional cost of this job. All the costs he would incur because a squadron of inexperienced low life pirates had interfered in his business. He was sure they would still clear a good margin but what had started as a simple tag and bag operation had deteriorated into a game of hide and fucking seek.

Manson was the President of the Thirteenth Chapter of the Blue Knights, a mercenary company operating out of Zeta Reticuli. The Knights were a tough organisation, known for their violent methods and high client satisfaction rates. For dirty operations requiring plausible deniability, the Blue Knights were the go to guys for the MegaCorps. That was until recently.

The stranglehold the Frontier Company had on trade and security was squeezing the Knights' market. Frontier out-sourced their dirtier jobs to the Knights but corporate work had all but dried up. The organisation was a hungry animal, and it was Manson's job to keep it fed.

Times were lean and getting leaner. Manson blamed his own superiors as much as the corporations. Felix Jenner, the Senior President had grown rich and lazy. A growing number of chapter presidents were hungry for new blood at the top. Karl Manson was determined to be that new blood.

He arrived at the brig. Victor "Snaggletooth" Rybov leaned on the bulkhead, smoking a hand-rolled cigarette.

"Fuck me, Snaggles," Manson said. "What do you put in those things? Shit?"

Rybov stared back with his single human eye and a red cybernetic implant wired into his optic nerve. Rybov was without doubt the oldest member of the chapter, possibly the whole organisation. His face was scarred, held together with titanium and PlastiSkin. Both his arms were augmented with implants and one hand was completely robotic.

"An old recipe, Karl. It's a mix of herbs that kinda chills me out or perks me up, depending on how I blend it."

Manson nodded to the door.

"They spill any more?"

Rybov shook his head. "The boy is pretty much dead. As for Eden... she's a tough bitch."

"I'll see if I can't loosen her tongue. Have Foxy and KK come down." He punched the door release.

Two chairs were fixed to the deck. A young man sat slumped in the left one, his head resting on his naked chest, cold blood dribbling from his nose and eye sockets. In the right chair was a woman. Manson estimated Eden was in her mid thirties. Her hair was dirty blonde, her skin fair. She stared at him, hatred burning in her dark, bruised eyes.

"Eden, Eden, Eden," Manson said as he paced the perimeter of the room. "I wonder if you know where we are?"

She continued to glare and said nothing.

"We are back to where this whole sorry saga started. We expected to find a Kobo. You know what we found instead?"

"Your dick in your mother's mouth?" the woman spat.

Manson slapped her with the back of his hand.

"No need for that kind of talk. I thought we were getting along." He moved back and continued to pace.

"What we found was a big fucking mess. A fleet cruiser blown into little pieces. You know anything about that?"

Her eyes widened.

"I told you before," she said. "A cruiser showed up. He destroyed three ships. Me and Freddie jumped. I don't know what happened to Romain."

"Was Romain carrying anything that could inflict that level of damage?"

"We were flying Hornets. Our load-out was energy weapons. You've seen my ship."

Manson had; he knew she was telling the truth. Something else had happened, and it had been after she bugged out. He changed tack.

"I have a problem. That Kobo was supposed to be mine, except you and your crew got there first. My orders were to capture the ship and bring it to my client. Now I have no ship and a potentially dissatisfied client. That makes me sad because I pride myself on gold star customer satisfaction."

He knelt in front of her.

"What the fuck is so important about that ship?" he roared into her face. Her resolve snapped, her lower lip twitched, and she stated to sob.

"I... I don't know," she said, her voice hoarse. "We knew Rhodes had a vessel on an auto heading for Tarantella and Romain said he only cares about high value cargo these days. We figured it could be our chance to make a big score. So we tracked it and dropped it. We were disabling it when the Navy arrived. It all went wrong from there." She sobbed.

"We detected a jump signature from a Kobo. Did you have anyone else working for you? Someone waiting to take it back to whatever rock you live under?"

Eden shook her head. She was broken, resigned to her fate.

Manson wasn't done yet.

"You don't know anything." Manson stood, shook his head and walked to the door.

"I've told you everything."

"You have. I still have a use for you."

He opened the door. A merc stood in front of him.

"Where's KK?" Manson asked Rob "Foxhound" Gray.

"Victor needed help in the weapons bay. KK volunteered."

Manson snorted.

"His loss then. You complain you don't get any R&R, well fill your boots." Manson gestured toward the girl. "Make sure you clean up afterwards."

Foxhound smirked and swaggered into the brig. Manson closed the door as the girl screamed.

The day started early for Ethan Tate. After four hours of restless sleep he woke with a start; disorientated by his surroundings.

He had selected a cabin forward of the lounge and galley. It was the smallest the Kobo offered. It was functional and tidy, decorated with a bland mix of brown and creme. He assumed it was a crew cabin rather than one of the more luxurious passenger berths. He rose stiffly and pulled on his fatigues. They fitted him well, unlike the rest of the crew who were a size out in either direction.

On the *Berlin* he would have begun his rotation with a run or at least some exercises in his cabin; today he had other plans. He rubbed his hand over his close cropped hair and massaged the stiffness from of his neck as he left the cabin.

He stopped. The air was alive with static. The atmosphere was heavy. The ship was so badly damaged any number of components could cause the ionisation. It was unlikely to be serious. He added it to his checklist and continued to the hold.

The loss of the *Berlin* still dominated his thoughts, but it was manageable. Today was another day. Time to move on. He wondered how the others were holding up. Ethan worried about the commander. She had got them this far yet he could see the doubt in her eye. He wondered what he could say or do to reassure her, to let her know he and the others believed in her. He resolved to speak to her later. For a fleet officer Mira Thorn was approachable, even likeable.

He made his way along the curved corridor through a blast door and toward the hold. Two weapons crates rested next to the airlock. He unpacked the plasma cannons, confident he could get them mounted faster than with the help of the sergeant. Rich Barnes was a good soldier but by his own admission did not understand weapons tech.

Show me where they are and I'll shoot them. I don't need to know how a gun works to fire it! Barnes was an old school sergeant who put his mission and his men first. Ethan respected that.

The cannons were housed in lightweight packing cases. They had two metre long barrels which shone lustrous blue under the lights. A separate module contained the control system and the accelerator reservoir. A tangle of connectors hung from the rear panel. Despite an outwardly simple design, plasma cannons were complex weapons and Ethan understood the care they needed during installation. One missed connection or a poor union joint and the ship would be filled with enough super-heated plasma to incinerate everyone onboard.

He lifted the control section into place and connected the reservoir to a feed from the drive system. One by one he attached the control cables into the wiring loom. He double checked the installation diagram printed on the crate's lid to ensure he connected with the data processing feed and sensor inputs. Once Ethan had the weapon fitted, he ran a diagnostic routine on his hand terminal that confirmed the weapon could communicate with the Kobo's systems.

Ethan loaded the second cannon onto a wheeled dolly and dragged it around to the other side of the ship and repeated the process.

As he hooked up the last of the connections Sergeant Barnes arrived.

"Now, that is a thing of beauty," Barnes said. He clapped a giant hand in Ethan's shoulder

"Thank you, sergeant. Does it need a name?"

Barnes laughed.

"Looks like Nancy. What do you think on the other?"

"Jenna, after my sister. If you met her you'd know why."

Barnes took a marker pen from his pocket and scrawled the girl's name on the barrel. He gave Ethan the pen and set off for the port side.

"You, holding up okay? Yesterday isn't something we train for," Barnes said. It was unexpected and out of character for the sergeant.

Ethan thought for a moment.

"Yeah, it's difficult. I guess we keep our heads down and keep moving. Time for grief is later. Right now we have to survive."

A thoughtful look crossed Gunny Barnes' face. For a moment he appeared lost, unsure of what to say.

"You?" Ethan prompted.

Barnes made no reply. Ethan changed the subject.

"The commander, she's the one the Martian vets talk about, isn't she?"

"The Queen of Cydonia? Yeah that's her. Two hundred and two combat missions. She was awarded the Star of Terra and The Martian Heart. Three pilots came out of the war with both and two were posthumous awards. Did she tell you? She doesn't like to talk about it."

Ethan told Barnes he'd seen the unit designation on Mira's armour and put two and two together.

"So now you know. You're sharing a ship with a pair of legends!"

Ethan could see Barnes was trying hard to be his normal self but the harder he tried the more of his pain he exposed.

"She's not what I expected. She's not like other Navy officers either."

Barnes studied him. "Remember, Private, inside every fleet-brat there is a marine struggling to get out." Barnes became serious. "She has been through a lot, not just the crash... wait a minute... you..." Barnes continued to laugh as he spoke. "That would be against so many regulations and you are so not her type."

Ethan felt the burn creep around his neck and into his cheeks. He liked the commander but Barnes had it wrong.

Didn't he?

"Let's see if we can break into the hold," Ethan said, grateful for an excuse to change the subject. He reached for his tool pack, some items he'd brought from the ship, others he had pilfered from the Kobo's engineering section.

"Glad I could cheer you up, Gunny," he said.

"Oh man you have. Come on let's get this open; see if we can impress the Queen of Cydonia."

Victor Rybov nodded to Foxhound as he left the brig. The young merc was zipping up his coverall and wearing a foul grin on his face.

"Still life in that one if you want a go, Vic," he smirked. "Mind you, a man of your age should take it easy. Don't want the old heart packing in do you?"

Rybov snorted.

"You have work to do," he said. "Get your lazy arse to the armoury. I need the weapons cleaned and prepped. This ship is going to shit."

Foxhound sauntered down the corridor, whistling. Once he was out of sight Rybov opened the door and walked into the brig. The girl lay on her side, naked and curled into a ball, her body wracked with sobs. Rybov went to the young man and checked for a pulse. He shook his head and walked over to the girl. She flinched when he rested his hand on her shoulder.

"Take it easy," he said. "I need you to listen, Eden." She didn't respond. He shook her. "I said I need you to listen. The ship is going to jump. If you want to get out of here you have to go now."

She pulled herself into a sitting position. Her face was drawn and bruised, her eyes laced with anger, hatred and despair.

"Is this a trick?" she asked, her voice a whisper.

"No, no trick. Get dressed and when you get outside turn

left and keep going down. You'll find your ship in the hangar. You have 20 minutes."

"Freddie?"

Rybov made no reply and handed her a crumpled flight suit. She pulled it on, sniffing and trying to compose herself.

"Why are you doing this?"

Rybov paused before he answered. "Manson pushed things too far. He's supposed to be a professional. Maybe I'm getting too old for this. Maybe I've discovered I have a conscience. Fuck it, I have no idea. Shut up and get dressed." He reached for a stun baton looped into his webbing and gave it to her.

"Hit me with a wallop of that. Make it look convincing." Eden took the baton, she studied it for a few seconds before shoving it into his chest. Rybov's muscles locked as his nerve endings caught fire. Everything went black.

Admiral "Aussie" Jon Flynt strode onto the flight deck of the *Valhalla*, still fastening his tunic. His greying hair was unkempt, his eyes bleary from sudden waking.

"Talk to me, Mr Lambert. The distress beacon, is it one of ours?"

"Sir! It's the *Berlin*," Jason Lambert, the Executive Officer, reported.

Flynt considered the information carefully. *Berlin* was Marcus Adams' ship and home to one Mira Thorn, a girl who was the closest thing to family he had left. The distress buoy would only be deployed in the event of a catastrophic failure. He swallowed and gathered his emotions.

"How far from our position, Mr Lambert?"

"Three light-years. We can be there in an hour."

Flynt sat in the command chair in the centre of the flight

deck.

"Is anyone else responding?"

"Negative, Admiral. We are a long way out," Lambert replied.

Flynt swivelled the chair to face the astrogation station. Protocol dictated he issued orders via his Executive Officer, but he preferred to engage his crew directly.

"Mr Cole, I want the most efficient course you can plot and I want it in sixty-seconds."

Jeff Cole responded without looking up from his console.

"Yes, Sir!"

Flynt suspected the young astrogator had plotted the course before he had issued the order.

"Miss Clark, when the plot is confirmed I want you to get us there at maximum FTL."

"Admiral, we have never exceeded eighty percent on the reactor," Samantha Clark replied.

"Well, now is the time, Sammy. I know the ship can handle it."

"Aye, Sir," she responded.

"Plot is confirmed and optimised," Cole reported.

Flynt stroked his beard as the power built. A vibration passed through the deck. It would be imperceptible to anyone who did not share his familiarity with the vessel.

He glanced around the bridge and was met by earnest young faces. Even Lambert, the XO, had thirty years on him.

You're 63 years old Jon, why are you still doing this? he asked himself. The answer was simple: *because this is all you have left.*

He stood.

"I'll be in my office," he said. "You have the deck, Mr Lambert."

He walked to the space behind the bridge that served as an office, briefing room and rest area. He brewed a strong coffee and ordered the lighting to twenty percent. He sat behind his titanium desk. The chair adjusted to his posture. Flynt lifted a silver framed two-dimensional photograph he kept on the desk. Ruth, Amy and Mira smiling for the anachronistic chemical film camera Amy insisted on using.

Flynt remembered the day vividly. Mira Thorn had announced her decision to leave the fleet; Amy had been pissed and he and Ruth had spent most of the afternoon trying to keep the peace. 24 hours later Ruth and Amy were dead. He and Mira were united in grief yet unable to connect, communicate or see a life beyond the Navy. Mira had left before the funerals, blasting out of Seattle Galactic on a fleet shuttle bound for the Jupiter Anchorage. He had followed soon after. His destination was the Martian Orbital Yards and Project Norseman. Flynt closed his eyes, hoping for the best, fearing the worst.

56 minutes later the *Valhalla* collapsed her faster-than-light envelope and entered normal space. Flynt emerged from his sanctuary. His eyes were greeted by a three dimensional projection of the debris field hanging above the strategy table.

"Brief me, Mr Lambert," he said. His voice carried no hint of his feelings.

"Catastrophic failure, Sir. Preliminary readings indicate it is the *Berlin*. The emergency systems have activated, and the debris is orbiting a gravity well. The debris field is six kilometres in diameter."

"Scan for activity. I want to know if anyone is alive out there," Flynt said as he studied the projection.

"Sir, the energy distribution pattern shows the explosion occurred approximately 36 hours ago," Jeff Cole added.

"What about composition? Do you have any clues what

happened to her?"

"Nothing conclusive, Admiral. It looks like a core explosion. I suspect an accident." Cole studied the raw data as the sensors acquired it; drawing what conclusions he could.

"Admiral!" Samantha Clark shouted from her station on the other side of the bridge. "I am detecting a message encoded under the distress beacon's signal. It's a short range transmission and uses level one fleet encryption."

"Play it, Sammy," Flynt replied.

Sam leant forward, flicking her brown hair clear of her face. There was a crackle on the speaker system followed by an automated timestamp and the electronic burble of the de-encryption algorithm.

"This is Mira Thorn, service number 66-773-4037 of the FSS *Berlin*" Mira sounded tired, emotional and alive.

"The ship has been lost in an explosion of unknown cause. Besides myself there are two survivors. We have an FTL capable ship. Due to concerns about the stability of our vessel it is our intention sweep the wreck for survivors after which we will seek a suitable repair facility. We have been involved in an insurgent interdiction and will therefore not disclose further details of our status. Thorn out." The message repeated. He motioned for Sam Clark to shut it off. There was silence on the bridge.

"Mr Cole, I want a full scan of the wreck site. You are looking for life signs and ship wakes. I want an idea of where they could have gone."

Flynt made his way to the centre of the bridge and the situation planning table. He tapped in a sequence of commands and a three-dimensional map of the sector appeared above it.

"Mr Lambert, show me all human outposts in this sector." A series of red dots appeared on the map.

Flynt studied them looking for a clue that would tell them

where they had gone. Baikonur Station or Tellerman Gateway would be ideal destinations but were both a long way from the wreck site. Mira had said they needed repairs. There were several hundred industrial platforms in range, most of which lacked long-range communications or dry dock facilities.

"Tarantella would be a good bet, Sir," Samantha said. "It's the largest outpost in this sector and suitably close."

"I agree, Sammy," Flynt replied. "Commander Cole, I want the wreck logged and a recovery operation started."

Flynt walked to the forward holo-screen. There was little left of the *Berlin*. He wondered how Mira and the others had survived and how they had come across an FTL capable ship. He would have plenty of time to ponder those questions later.

"Use bays seven and eight as a makeshift morgue. I want all of our available shuttles working on recovery duties. We leave no one behind."

He returned his gaze to the forward view screen his relief at Mira's escape was tempered by thoughts of Marcus Adams.

Jon Flynt had lost another friend.

Karl Manson opened the door to the brig and strode in.

"What the fuck?" He took a second to appraise the scene. Victor Rybov lay on the floor, unconscious. Freddie sat tied to the chair as dead as Manson had left him. Eden was gone.

"What the actual fuck?" he repeated.

He walked to Rybov and kicked him hard in the ribs. The old man moaned and coughed, opening his single eye. The implant alongside it glowed red as he stirred.

"What happened?" Manson demanded.

Rybov sat up and looked around him before standing.

"I came in to take care of the girl. Foxy had his fun and left her breathing."

"And she overpowered you? Did you see the size of her?" Manson's rage burned like a comet passing close to a star.

Rybov picked up his shock stick.

"She pulled this out of my webbing and gave me a big belt."

Before Manson could reply his com-link beeped.

"What?" he yelled into the device.

"Karl," Lyle said. "I need you up here. One of those fighters just launched from our hangar."

"Target it and blow it out of the sky," he snarled.

"Karl, we have a bigger problem." Lyle's voice was rising. He only sounded that way when something rattled him. "A Navy ship has just dropped into the sector. It's a big one."

Manson lumbered toward the door.

"Follow me," he said to Rybov. "We'll straighten this later."

He keyed his link.

"How big is big? A cruiser? A destroyer?"

"It's a dreadnought, Karl, a fucking dreadnought."

Manson cursed the mission. The profit was becoming squeezed, and he was surrounded by morons. The Navy had arrived to take care of their own. The *Nightwolf* would have to lie low until the dreadnought jumped.

Manson knew with every second that passed the Kobo would be further and further away. Whatever happened, the job would have to be completed, even if they ended up working for free.

Today was turning into one huge shit storm.

Flynt studied the incoming data stream. The *Berlin* had been ripped to shreds. Of the two largest sections only one remained pressurised and the scouting party had yet to report any survivors.

He took a moment to study the video stream being transmitted from his scouts' helmet cameras. The EVA team were traversing deck eight.

"Hold on, can you get them to check out that airlock?" he asked Sam Clark without taking his eyes from the vid-screen.

The camera panned back and a metallic voice came from the bridge speakers.

"The lock has been manually cranked," the scout said. "From the outside, someone has been in here."

"Mira..." Flynt whispered. She had not abandoned the wreck. He wondered if she had found any survivors.

Nineteen bodies had been recovered and many parts. The flight data recorder had been secured and its contents were being uploaded to *Valhalla's* main core.

"Admiral!" Sam shouted from across the bridge. "I'm detecting a ship wake, inbound, a fighter no IFF beacon."

"Weapons," Flynt replied. "Target that vessel. Do not fire unless ordered."

"Aye, Sir."

With a click of his hand remote Flynt brought up the inbound vessel's trace. It was small, a single seat Hornet. The fighter was following an erratic flight path.

"He's on a heading that will bring him to us," Lambert said. "The weapons and shields are offline."

"No hostile intent." Flynt sat in the command chair and studied the trace on the holo-display. "He's running from someone. Open a channel, Sammy. Let's see what he has to say."

Sam hailed the fighter using a multi-channel page. A few seconds later the response was broadcast through the bridge comms-system.

"Fleet vessel, my name is Eden Holzman. I am in a lot of trouble. I need your help." The woman's voice trembled as she spoke. Flynt had heard similar voices countless times. A human close to breaking point, already shutting down. He motioned to Sam to open the open the com-link.

"Eden, my name is Jon Flynt. We are at your service. Please slow your vessel."

"Navy, I have escaped from a Blue Knights ship. It's still out there. When they realise I have gone, they'll come after me."

"Understood Eden. I still need you to slow down." Flynt looked toward Lambert. "Prepare for her to dock."

"Eden we will bring you on board. My XO will transmit a vector on this frequency. Follow it to the bay. Do not try anything stupid. We have a lot of guns and right now most of them are pointing at you."

"Thank you," came the reply.

With the channel closed Flynt stood.

"Mr Cole, have a detachment secure the ship and escort Ms Holzman to an interview room. Sammy, scan the wider area for the Knights' vessel. Regardless of what you find the recovery of the Berlin is our priority."

Flynt studied the plot. The Hornet was a popular choice for pirates. He wondered how much this Eden Holzman might know about the fate of the Berlin.

CHAPTER FIVE

LIGHTS flickered in the dark hold, casting the cold steel space with an ethereal glow. Mira was surrounded by long range cargo canisters. She was aware of a presence in the darkness, yet all she could see was the racks of pods.

The sound of popping metal drew her attention to the starboard bulkhead. A hole the size of a penny appeared in the wall. Air was being sucked through it. The edges of the hole expanded and a perfect ring of ice formed around its edge.

She ran to the bulkhead and put her hand over the breach; it stemmed the airflow. The cold of the vacuum burned her palm.

"Rich! Ethan!" she yelled. No one responded.

The hole grew larger, turning into a crack. She placed her other hand over it. Still the crack grew.

I have to seal the hold. I have to save them.

A voice answered her, it sounded familiar; yet she could not place it.

You will save them but you will die.

It was her voice, somehow overlaid with another.

Are you prepared to sacrifice all you are for them?

Mira tried to look behind her but could not take her eye off the crack as it spread from floor to ceiling. Air roared past her, escaping into the void.

She pulled her burnt hands away from the bulkhead and fought the airflow as she staggered toward the open hatch. She fell to her knees. It took all of her remaining strength to drag herself to the manual closing mechanism.

Mira pumped the handle and the door began to close. Through vision fogged with tears she could see her friends in the corridor. Rich Barnes and Ethan Tate were dressed in their armour. Monica stood next to Alex Kite. Other figures stood behind them, indistinct, hidden in the shadows.

Ethan stepped to one side. Amy Flynt pushed past him and stood in front of the young marine. He continued to look past her as if the girl were not there.

Amy spoke in her mind.

Mira, you have to save them, when the time comes you will know what to do, Amy said over the roar of escaping air.

With a final effort Mira closed the hatch and collapsed onto the deck.

Seconds later the bulkhead split apart and she was sucked into the black, starless void.

Her com-link roused her. Its beeping insistent and repetitive.

"Lights." The stateroom's lighting gradually came up to full brightness.

A cold sweat broke in her body as her panic rose. Where the hell was she?

The com-link rested on the polished marble top of the dressing table. It continued to bleep, its red light flashing, demanding the call be answered.

Mira picked it up and pressed receive.

"Hello?" she said, aware of the uncertainty in her voice.

"Mira," Monica Garret said.

Memory flooded back, losing the ship, the Kobo, Tarantella.

She held her breath and then slowly exhaled.

"Hey Monica," she said. "What's up?"

"I'm on the flight deck. I'm seeing a warning on the drive system. It's an advisory, but it's logged it three times overnight. I think you should take a look."

"Okay, I'll be right up."

She closed the link and placed it back on the counter. Another lapse, this was different. Mira had become accustomed to forgetting small details like the names of newly met people or where she had put things. She had never lost periods of time or forgotten events.

Stress, she thought. *It's been a tough few hours.*

Her left arm throbbed. She inspected the dressings. Two were holding up but the one covering the deepest wound was stained with blood. She weighed up the options of treating it herself or asking the doctor for help; she opted for the former. Monica had always been there to dress her wounds and suspend judgement. So much time had passed since the last incident she didn't want to burden her friend with her shameful secret. Monica had been through too much in the past 24 hours and did not need to be dealing with Mira Thorn's pointless shit.

She removed the dressing. It was stuck to the wound and needed a painful tug to free it. She sharply drew breath as air hit the weeping laceration.

The wound was bad, deeper than she had intended. Mira had underestimated the sharpness of the blade and her own lack of practice.

Maybe her Shadow Sister, the dark passenger who rode shotgun in her subconscious, had wanted her to go deep.

Mira pulled the field medical kit from her webbing and located a tube of SteriGel. She applied the thick translucent substance into and around the cut. She gritted her teeth as the gel oozed into the flesh. SteriGel was an analgesic and antiseptic.

Once the gel dulled the pain, Mira applied three adhesive sealing strips and a new dressing. She tossed the old one into the garbage chute and flexed her arm.

Say what you like about bleeders, we make damn good medics.

Mira composed herself and walked to the bathroom. She splashed water onto her face and rubbed her temples. Her head pounded.

She took another couple of painkillers. The more she took, the less effective they seemed to be. Mira thought about the stash under her bunk, they were the ones that worked. They were also the ones that made her into a junkie. She was over it now but there was no way Monica Garret would ever consider giving her the strong stuff.

Mira dressed in her flight suit and looked around the stateroom for her boots, as she retrieved them her eye widened, she smiled. Over the back of a chair was a battered leather jacket. Age had faded and cracked the brown leather and there was a small tear on the left elbow. The jacket had a smokey, earthy smell that transported Mira back to the old nineteenth century chairs in her father's study back home. She lifted jacket from the chair; it was heavy and supple. Without thinking, she pulled it on. The fit was on the large side but she instantly fell for the old garment's embrace.

"If I take you I guess it's an act of piracy," she whispered. "I'm good with that, if you are." For a moment everything in the universe seemed right. Mira jogged, stiffly, toward the flight deck. She passed Ethan Tate on the way. He was emerging from the lower deck, his face covered in grime.

"Ethan?" she asked, halting her pace.

"Ma'am, Mira." He sounded tired and frustrated. "I have the weapons installed on the internal hard points. They are ready to calibrate."

"That's great, Ethan. Thank you."

"We are having problems breaking into the hold. Sergeant Barnes is considering cutting his way in."

Whatever was in there was important to the ship's owners. Unless it was an oxygen plant or enough fuel to take them to a fleet outpost, the mystery contents were of diminishing concern.

"Waste no more time, Ethan." She paused for a moment. "I could do with you and Rich heading down to engineering and checking the repair over. Monica has reported a power drain. It's probably nothing but let's be on the safe side."

"Okay, will do. There is some heavy ionisation going on down there; it might be related."

Mira watched him go back below and continued to the flight deck.

Monica Garret sat in the command chair, a mug of coffee in one hand and a cigarette in the other.

"Monica, what is that?" Mira asked as she arrived.

"It's a Wayfarer King Size. I found a pack in the lounge. I gave up 15 years ago. Hey ho we all have vices that are hard to shake."

We do, Mira thought, the dull ache in her arm reminding her of her own.

"Here look," Monica said. She extinguished the cigarette on the remains of the empty carton; it was full of ash and butts. Mira leant over Monica's shoulder. The smoke from the remnants of the cigarette caught in Mira's throat and made her eye water. She was grateful when the air scrubbers took care of it.

The engineering console showed the same power drop and rebuild she had witnessed the previous night.

"It happened three times," Monica said. Mira tapped into the diagnostic log and sure enough the same event was recorded roughly two hours apart.

"We lose power and the reactor compensates, then it bleeds away. I've seen nothing like that before," Mira said. "A power loss should be a consistent drain and the system would identify where it was in the wiring loom. This looks as if electrical energy is just evaporating."

She studied the data. Each power drop was gradual.

"Is it serious?" Monica asked.

Mira did not know. The envelope was stable, and the ship continued to operate within established limits. The power drop was not significant enough to be noticeable, other than by the monitoring systems.

"I don't think so. I'll set up the engineering console to log it. In the absence of an identifiable cause we should look for patterns. Maybe something is periodically turning on and drawing too much power."

She studied the trace, hoping to learn something; her train of thought was broken by Rich Barnes.

"Mira, Monica," he said. "You need to come back here."

"What is it, Richard?" Monica asked.

"Commander Kite is awake. He is in the lounge and he is pissed off."

Monica put a hand on Mira's shoulder.

"I'll handle Mr Kite. You carry on up here."

They swapped places and Mira flicked the remains of Monica's cigarette away from the console. She opened an applet on the engineering subsystem and began a diagnostic routine on the drive system.

Raised voices were coming from the lounge as Mira approached. She had spent an hour on the flight deck monitoring the reactor and testing the targeting system of Ethan's cannons. Calibration options were limited while the ship was FTL, but she was able to check the weapons were integrated with the sensor suite.

Mira was excited to see Alex. She would need to brief him on the plan and make sure he was familiar with the ship. She slowed as she approached the lounge and it became apparent the argument was heated.

She could make out Barnes' deep voice. She could not hear what he was saying, but she recognised the familiar sound of controlled anger. Monica's voice chipped in from time to time. A third voice belonged to Alex Kite. He sounded hoarse and raspy.

"...She is unstable, a flake. We have no idea what losing the ship will have done to her..."

"She got us this far, Alex," Monica said.

"It wasn't hard was it? Find a ship and fix it. A monkey could have come up with that plan..."

Alex's voice trailed off as Mira entered.

"Hello Alex," she said. "Monica told me you would need two days rest, at least."

Alex fixed her with cold grey eyes. He coughed, wheezing slightly with each breath.

"She is not happy, but I have work to do."

"Are you aware of the situation?" she asked. "The *whole* situation?"

Alex nodded. Sadness and anger battled on his bruised face.

Barnes excused himself and left. A look passed between the

big man and the doctor.

"I understand we're going to Tarantella," Alex said, once Barnes had left.

"Yes."

"Do you think that's wise?"

"It's the closest port. If we are careful the local pond life should leave us alone."

Alex grunted and shifted his position; his breath hissed between gritted teeth.

"The place where this ship was heading before it was attacked?" He shook his head in dismay. "That's not what I call a good idea."

"We have limited air and fuel supplies. If I could have found somewhere else in range, I would have done so," Mira replied. She tried her best to keep emotion out of her voice.

"Was it your decision?"

"Yes. We discussed it, I called it. You were out cold."

"And who put you in charge?"

"I'm the senior officer, Alex." Mira spoke with a confidence she wished she felt. She hated interpersonal conflicts but she would not back down; Alex was out of line.

"Thorn, this is not personal, you have a certain reputation..." His words trailed off.

"I do?"

A certain reputation? Of course, the ship's freak, the one-eyed veteran who was only onboard because it was easier to promote her than discharge her?

Unstable, unpredictable, prone to mental episodes, she had heard all about her reputation, more times than she could remember.

Alex clenched and unclenched his fists.

"Your mental health issues are well known. We've all heard

rumours about you. I'm not being judgemental. PTSD is an occupational hazard of the job. I just want to be sure we have the most stable person in command."

"That is enough, Mr Kite," Monica snapped. Her cheeks flushed red and a tiny vein in her forehead pulsed. Mira had seen Monica angry in the past, but she had never seen Monica this angry.

"I am the only person on this vessel qualified to decide who is fit for command. You might not like it, but Commander Thorn is as fit for duty now as she was on the *Berlin*." Monica paused and glanced in Mira's direction. "And rumours are just rumours. I know the *facts* and putting it bluntly there were members of the *Berlin's* command staff with far bigger issues than her for lesser reasons. Need I remind you, Mr Kite, there are a few things in *your* medical history you would rather not have discussed. I don't want to hear any more on the subject."

Alex flushed beneath his bruises.

Mira saw something in Alex she had seen in all of them. He was lost and traumatised. He had the thousand-yard stare of someone passed over by a death that had claimed everyone they knew. Survivor's guilt. She was intimately familiar with the condition. Healing would come with time, but recovery was a long road littered with corpses.

"Alex, I need you to help me. If I make a bad decision I need someone I can rely on to call me on it. We are in this together, all of us. The chain of command as we know it does not apply now. It's not about pips, stars and medals. It's about survival."

Alex Kite scowled. "I'm sorry, I don't accept you have what it takes. You are a reckless loner who only got your position because you have a few medals and..."

"Alex Kite! Wind your neck in now," Monica yelled, getting to her feet.

Alex's face was a blotchy and red, his body tense. Something inside Mira snapped.

"And what Alex? What else could you possibly add?" Mira spat the words through clenched teeth. She braced for his answer.

"Everyone knows you were given preferential treatment because you were fucking an Admiral."

Mira tensed. Her hands curled into fists. She tried to fight it, but the rage boiled inside her. She launched herself at him, raining down ineffective blows that Alex easily deflected. Over the roar of blood in her ears, Mira heard Monica calling for Barnes.

She landed a punch on Alex's cheek and he staggered. She pulled back for another but before she could throw it she was lifted off the ground.

"That's enough, Mouse!" Barnes said. He held onto her and she squirmed trying to get free.

"You think you are fit for command?" Alex yelled after her.

"Fuck you, Kite. I should have left you in that elevator!" she spat back.

Barnes threw her over his shoulder and carried her out of the lounge.

Mira stopped struggling and Barnes deposited her on a stool in the galley.

"The way you two were carrying on I think we should put Private Tate in command; he keeps his head down and does his job. There is no drama with the kid."

"Sorry, Rich. He was being a dick. I was being a dick too, I guess." Mira shook her hand; it ached where it had connected with Alex's cheekbone.

"That was one hell of a punch, saw the old you back there.

Last time I saw that right hook was when you laid out Laurel Bates, back on the *Illustrious,*" Barnes said, chuckling beneath the words. He gave her an icepack, and she pressed it against her knuckles.

"Striking a Superior Arsehole. I was grounded for two weeks for that. Fair play to Bates, she came clean about her role in that one. If she hadn't, I would have been flying ice freighters in the outer system."

"Maybe that wouldn't have been a bad thing. You wouldn't have gone to Mars."

Mira trembled. She looked at the floor then to Barnes, who was busy brewing coffee.

"I was out of order. Alex has a head injury. I could have hurt him... or worse."

Barnes gave her a cup. She took it with both hands.

"He was way out of line. One minute he is ranting about the chain of command and the next he's breaking it. He can't have it both ways. No one is thinking straight right now."

"But it's what people say though, isn't it?"

"You know me, Mira, I don't pay attention to gossip. Those who matter know the truth."

Mira knew her assignment had been the subject of many rumours. Nothing altered the fact she had worked hard to be certified fit for duty. She still had problems, some of them public, most of them not. She had never expected to be accused of screwing her way up the ranks and onto the ship. If that were the case she would have set her sights somewhat higher than deep patrol on the *Berlin.*

She sipped the coffee, relishing its bitterness. Barnes always brewed it with a pinch of salt.

"I heard it from time to time, from junior arseholes. Like I said I take little notice," he said, eventually.

"You should have told me. I know you and Monica mean well. I know you both try to look out for me, but I can take care of myself."

He nodded.

"We are your friends. It's what friends do."

"Sometimes I need space, Rich. I need to make mistakes. I need to toughen the fuck up."

"I get it, we'll back off a bit. Just so you know, back there," he pointed toward the lounge. "That was for Alex's safety."

Mira cradled her cup.

"So what now?" she asked.

Barnes sipped his coffee and peered at her over the rim of the aluminium mug.

"We need both of you to land the ship, I think you should give each other a wide berth. I say we operate a two watch system until we need to put you both in the same room. Time will sort things out. Kite's not so bad, he'll come round in time."

Barnes stood.

"It's been a hell of a couple of days," he said. "Got time for a hug?"

For Rich Barnes, she always did.

CHAPTER SIX

THE marine on guard duty stepped aside as Jon Flynt approached the brig. Flynt returned his salute with a simple nod. Flynt liked to run a tight ship, one where people concentrated on their duties, not formalities. It was a concept the marine detachment had yet to grasp.

A woman in a crumpled and bloody flight suit was sitting at a desk with her head resting on her crossed arms. She looked up at him with puffy bruised eyes.

"Are you Admiral Flynt?" she asked through swollen lips.

"I am and you must be Eden. I have a medical team on their way. Are you able to tell me what happened?"

Eden told him how her crew had planned to intercept an unmanned vessel on a heading to Tarantella.

"Xander Rhodes had his people bust it out of Tellerman. We thought if the cargo was valuable to Rhodes, we'd lift it for ourselves. Freddie is... was always saying how all we needed was a big score to set us up as a proper crew. He wanted people like Rhodes to take us seriously."

Flynt waited while Eden took a sip of water.

"We pulled the target vessel out of hyperspace and disabled it. That cruiser arrived and took out Kandi, Markie and Fritz. Me and Freddie jumped clear. I don't know what happened to

Romain; he was right behind us when we went FTL."

"And the Knights?"

"Bastards. They dropped us out of hyperspace about three light-years from here, worked us over really bad. They were hard on Freddie, then on me..." Her voice cracked. She took a sip of water. "We told them everything, and they brought us back here. I thought I was done for. An old guy with a fucked up face let me escape."

"Okay, Eden, thank you."

The door slid open and two Navy medics stood outside.

"I'll let my medical staff tend to your wounds. After that we'll sort out accommodation for you."

The woman struggled to stand, shaking off the medic who offered to help. She was holding herself awkwardly and winced with every movement.

"When can I leave?" she asked.

"Anytime you want," Flynt replied. "You are not a prisoner. I suspect you'll need a few days to recover, until then we'll extend you every courtesy the Navy can offer."

Eden stared at him, disbelief in her blue eyes.

"You're not going to bust me? Isn't that what you fleet people do?"

"What for? We have no evidence. It looks like you are just another victim. Everything we spoke about..." Flynt shrugged. "Was off the record."

"Thank you," she said in a hoarse voice, before the medic led her away.

Flynt's com-link beeped. He opened the channel.

"Mr Lambert," he said.

"Admiral, we have just detected a vessel, a Vigilant class warbird. The drive signature identifies it as a vessel associated with the Blue Knights."

"Thank you, Mr Lambert. I'll be right there." It added corroboration to Eden's story.

Vigilant class ships were old yet competent warships designed for planetary defence and in-system security. Sirius Dynamics had built close to a thousand for newly established Federation star systems. Many had found their way into the hands of mercenary companies who favoured their compact size, powerful weaponry and a high level of automation.

Flynt left the brig and made his way to the bridge. With the recovery operation still underway the last thing he needed was an engagement with a mercenary crew, not that an ageing light combat vessel could hope to match the *Valhalla*.

"Admiral on the deck!" A marine guard announced as he entered the bridge. It was another formality he could not abide, yet he grudgingly admired the marine's adherence to protocol.

"Mr Lambert what have you got?"

Jason Lambert lifted his gaze from the scanner.

"Lieutenant Clark picked up an encoded burst transmission. It is at the edge of our sensor range."

He walked toward Flynt and activated the holo-display.

"He is running in low power, low heat mode."

"He knows we're here so why risk a burst transmission?" Flynt whispered.

The mercenary vessel was still some way out. A less advanced warship would be unable to detect her. It made the transmission more unusual as any vessel within a 100 kilometre radius would pick it up.

"What do you want to do, Admiral?"

Flynt thought for a moment.

"How long before recovery is complete?" he asked.

"Two hours, there isn't much to recover," Lambert replied.

Flynt understood. The force of the blast and the decompression had been fierce.

"Keep an eye on him. When we're done we'll rattle his cage."

"Aye Sir," Lambert said.

"Admiral, we have an initial idea of what caused the explosion. The *Berlin* was recovering a pirate vessel and a Kobo freighter. There was an explosion in the hangar," Sam Clark said from her station.

"The fighter," Flynt said. "Eden said one of their crew had not followed them when they jumped."

He wondered if he should have let the woman in the brig off so lightly, then again busting minor league pirates was a waste of naval resources. He was coming up with a game plan and figured Eden Holzman might interest one of the players.

Karl Manson picked up a portable power converter and hurled it across the *Nightwolf's* flight deck.

"Fuck me dead!" he screamed. Lyle and Foxhound made no reply. Kenny Kane, KK, stepped aside as the heavy object bounced off the bulkhead and came his way.

"Karl, you need to calm down," Rybov said. He had seen many of Manson's rages. From the look in his eyes this could escalate into a fist fight or worse.

"Vic, you don't tell me what to do." Manson gradually calmed and regained control.

"How long can we maintain silent running?" Rybov asked the pilot.

"Twenty minutes, that is the absolute maximum. After that the reactor will shut down."

The internal atmosphere of the ship was already hot and uncomfortable. Silent running involved reducing the ship's systems to minimum functionality and withdrawing the external heat sinks. Trapping the heat generated by the drive system and onboard electrical systems reduced the vessel's heat signature by 80%. It could only be maintained for a few hours before the ship's systems failed.

"Karl we have enough range to jump clear. We know our ship is heading for Double T. We won't be far behind," Rybov said.

Manson continued to prowl the flight deck like an angry dog.

"No!" Manson's eyes were wild, his face flushed with blood. "That bitch is out there and I want to blow her to dust. We wait until the Navy ship is gone."

KK had been silent until now. He was tall and lean. Aside from a cortical implant above one ear he was un-augmented.

"Boss, I tracked her wake. She headed straight for the dreadnought. She's probably onboard telling them about us."

Manson stared the younger man down. His eyes were like burning coals set into his skull. Rybov reached for his stun stick, just in case.

"I ran up a contingency plan," KK continued. "In case we need to intercept the payload at Tarantella, we have the fuel and it's paid for."

Manson continued to stare.

"Karl, if KK is right, the effects on our margins will be minimal. It'll be a hit but nothing we can't recover from the client," Rybov added.

Manson stopped pacing and sat in the command chair.

"Okay," he said. "We go to Double T. I want a contract on her head."

He pointed at Rybov.

"You make that happen, Vic. When we dock, you put a fucking price on her head so big every bounty hunter on the Frontier will want a piece of her."

No one said a word.

"You got it, Boss," Rybov replied.

Manson sucked down air, calming himself.

"Lyle," Manson said. "Plot a course and get us out of here."

Rybov took his hand off of the stun stick. Lyle swivelled in the seat.

"It'll be five minutes before the drive is charged Karl," Lyle said.

Manson looked in Rybov's direction.

"Vic, bring the weapons on line, get the shields up. KK turret control, Foxhound you are on the main battery."

They moved to their positions. The ship's lights came on and the engines returned to their usual throbbing rumble.

Rybov moved up next to Manson.

"What was the transmission you sent, Karl?" he asked. "That Navy ship knows we are here for sure."

Manson breathed in and out slowly.

"It's a need to know thing, Vic. Right now you do not need to know."

"When my arse is about to be handed to me by the Federal Navy, I have a right to know."

Manson pulled Rybov to one side.

"Our client is hands on, Vic. On this job we don't take a shit without his permission. I had to update him as this is a big deal. It was embarrassing. I am having to eat a lot of shit. So back off."

Rybov nodded. "Okay, Karl, just level with me in the future. I am not the enemy."

Manson leant closer.

"You'll know what you need to know, Vic." He looked past Rybov at the two younger men. "You tell them nothing and get the weapons online."

He abruptly turned away and slumped into the command chair.

On the bridge of the *Valhalla* Sam Clark shouted a warning. "Sir, the mercs are underway. They have raised shields and powered their weapons system."

It was a complication Flynt did not need. "How is the recovery operation progressing?"

"On schedule we should be concluded in the next hour," Lambert replied. "Shuttle three is in the bay prepping for launch. One, two and four are unloading."

Flynt nodded. The timing was useful. He didn't want vulnerable shuttle craft in the firing line if the ships were about to slug it out.

"Instruct three to delay launching. Secure the bay and prepare to engage that ship."

"Aye, Sir." Lambert relayed the order to the flight control section.

"Bring the main battery online and raise the shields." Flynt moved to the tactical table. "Mr Cole, move us onto an intercept vector, as swiftly as you like. Miss Clark, open a channel."

There was a pause.

"Channel is open, Admiral."

"Blue Knights Vessel. Admiral Jon Flynt, *FSS Valhalla*. Power down your weapons and halt for inspection. You have 60 seconds to comply. Please acknowledge this message. You will receive no further warnings."

The seconds ticked down with no response. The vessel was accelerating away at a sustained 2G. Flynt hated the delay but protocol had to be followed.

When the timer clicked down to zero he gave the order.

"Target his drive section and fire at will."

"Sir!" Sam said from her station. "I am detecting an envelope."

The ship's trace vanished from the short range sensor display.

"Can you analyse his jump signature, Sammy?" Flynt asked, trying to keep his voice level and his anger in check.

"Negative, Sir. He must be using a trace diffuser," Sam said. She looked disappointed and didn't take her eyes off her console as she tried to pull something positive from the sensor array.

Flynt sat in his chair, composing his thoughts.

"Let's finish securing the wreck. Mr Cole, plot a course to Tarantella, maximum FTL."

He watched the crew go about their business, feeling tired, old and useless.

CHAPTER SEVEN

VANESSA Meyer completed her press statement and thanked the assembled journalists for their time. The scrum on the steps of the senate building dispersed. The news crews either stowed their equipment or moved on to their next victim. Meyer did not mind giving interviews. It was part of her job and it connected her with people across the Federation.

The senator was relieved as the last reporter moved on. The marathon session had worn her out. As usual, she had skipped too many meals and not drunk enough water. Sticking one to David Conway the previous day had made it all worthwhile. Meyer had watched the session on holo-vid and taken satisfaction from the look on the Trade Commissioner's face.

She turned to Ben Jones, her aide of four years.

"Are we ready to go, Benny?" she asked. "It's dreadfully cold out here."

"Yes, Ma'am," the young man replied. "It will be tight if we are to catch the diplomatic shuttle to Luna. I am sure we can still make it."

Ben was tall and of medium build. His fair skin contrasted with his unruly mop of brown hair.

"Let's get moving. I don't want to get stuck on a shuttle with that awful bore Hofner, or worse still David Bloody Conway."

Ben glanced around him, checking for journalists who may have overheard her unguarded remarks.

"Benny, don't worry." She gestured to the senate building. "My thoughts on this shower of shit can be found all over Uni-Net. I have long given up caring what people think of me and what I say. Take me to the car and let's get underway. You can brief me on who I am seeing and why when we board the shuttle. Until then I want to enjoy the evening."

She hooked her arm around Ben's and walked down the steps. They pushed their way through the crowd. When they arrived on the sidewalk, the car had departed.

Meyer fought back an initial flare of anger as she rounded on the transport marshal. Ben intervened.

"Where is Senator Meyer's transport?" he asked.

"I'm sorry, Senator. Nathan Forrest said he had to get to the spaceport as a matter of urgency," the marshal said. "I have ordered another. It will be here in three minutes."

"How does that affect our flight?" Meyer asked Ben.

"We can still make it, Senator."

She stared at the marshal. "The next time you have a car reserved for a senator, a senator's aide or even his or her bloody gardener I suggest you do not give it to a prick like Forrest. Not everyone is as understanding as I am."

"Yes Ma'am," the marshal replied, avoiding eye contact.

"Bloody Nathan Forrest. What's he doing here, anyway?"

"Strangely enough he came to lobby Conway to do what we have just voted for. He's very pleased with your change of position," Ben replied. "Although he is not so happy that you did so to provide support for the Frontier."

Meyer laughed.

Forrest was the leader of the Earth Independence Movement, a minor Earth centric faction who argued the Federation was a drain on resources that could be better used on the homeworld. Forrest peddled a populist message that had been gaining strength since the Martian War. Despite Forrest's charismatic leadership style the EIM did not hold a single seat in the Senate. It never stopped him lobbying those who did, with irritating frequency.

"Don't tell me. 'Fleet's role is to defend the homeworld.' Same old same old?"

Ben nodded. Meyer was about to comment further when the replacement car arrived.

Meyer let the young man help her in.

Once she and Ben were strapped in, the car rose into the air and flew toward the spaceport on an automated flight path.

Meyer gazed out of the window. The sun was setting and the snowy skyline was afire with vibrant red and orange hues. Sunlight glinted off windows and cast long shadows over the busy streets.

"You know Ben, I miss the Earth," Meyer whispered. She truly did; every time she left for the outer colonies she did so with a heavy heart.

"You could still work from here, Ma'am; most of the representatives do."

"Nonsense, you know me better than that. I belong with the people I represent. Most representatives only visit their people to ask for their votes. My lot included. How can someone sitting at a desk down here know what it is like to survive, let alone make a living on a Stage One Colony?" She paused. "I've been thinking about retirement." She enjoyed his shocked expression.

"Senator, you still have much to offer."

She pulled her gaze from the window and toward her aide. Ben was an idealist, a young man full of faith in democracy and the political process. Even her cynicism could not dull his passion. It was why she employed him. Ben had the potential to be a voice of reason in an ever more polarised galaxy.

"Ben, I only have so many years left. Even someone as young as you must understand nothing can last forever. It's times like these that make it worthwhile."

"We made a real difference, Ma'am."

"We did. Most of all we stuck it to Conway's cronies." She turned to the window with a mischievous smile. The air car banked and descended. The lights of the spaceport passed beneath them.

The car pulled up on a landing pad outside the diplomatic terminal. The doors opened and a young woman in a diplomatic corps suit stepped forward to help her out. She wore a gold name badge that identified her as Zoe Sinclair. Her chestnut hair was immaculately sculpted. The little make up she wore accentuated her delicate features.

"Senator Meyer, welcome," she said. "I'm sorry to inform you that the transport you were scheduled to fly out on has left the gate."

"I suspected as much, damn you Forrest."

The girl looked puzzled but continued. "The next diplomatic transport leaves for Luna in three hours. I can get you onto a commercial flight that leaves in twenty minutes. Mr Forrest is also on that flight. I can arrange for seats close to him if you would like me to..."

"No!" Meyer and Ben replied in unison.

Meyer sucked down a lungful of cold air.

"That is satisfactory, but nowhere near Forrest." She glanced down at the girl's badge. "Zoe."

Zoe was about to say something when her words were drowned out by the roar of a departing spaceplane. Meyer suspected it was *her* spaceplane.

A brilliant white flash lit the night in cold monochrome. Seconds later the rumble of an explosion reached her ears. An expanding fireball turned night to day. A rain of flaming debris fell to earth, causing secondary explosions when it hit the ground.

The realisation of what had happened dawned on Vanessa Meyer. She reached out for Ben's shoulder as the sounds of sirens built in the distance.

Mira carried a mug of hot chocolate into the Kobo's darkened lounge. She sat on a couch, pulling her stolen coat around her. She relished the warmth of the mug, enjoying the smooth sweet taste of the chocolate. It was comforting and took her back to happier days.

"Entertainment," she said. The multimedia system chimed in response to her voice.

"Play music, any genre, relaxing."

The system chimed twice in acknowledgement. Samuel Barber's *Adagio for Strings* swelled through concealed speakers.

Her watch had finished twenty minutes ago, and she had vacated the flight deck before Alex arrived.

Mira finished her drink and lay down; closing her eye she let the music flow over her. The couch moulded to her body, caressing her in a warm comforting embrace. Her breathing deepened, and she floated as sleep gently claimed her.

"Mira." A voice startled her. She snapped upright.

"Alex!" she mumbled.

"Sorry, did I wake you? May I come in?"

"Of course. It's okay. I've been feeling a little jumpy. I guess it's stress."

He sat on a couch opposite and paused, listening to the music.

"*Adagio for Strings*," he said.

"I guess. I'm not much of a classical person."

"Nor am I. I had an expensive education," he replied. "I wanted to apologise. I'm sorry I questioned you in front of the crew and I am deeply sorry for what I said after that."

He appeared genuinely contrite, almost crestfallen.

"It's okay Alex and I should not have hit you. I am sorry."

His hand went to his cheek. He grinned.

"I've had worse. I would have hit me for what I said. Don't sweat it."

Mira chewed her bottom lip.

"Really, it's fine," Alex said. "Look at this. Tell me what you think."

He gave her a datapad. She studied the information: a series of graphs illustrating the power distribution throughout the ship.

"This is the event we've been monitoring?" she asked.

"I'm worried about it," Alex replied. "You see as the power builds back it looks like it is just restoring itself to normal output?"

"Yeah, I see. But that's not the case?"

"Check out the reactor output over the same period."

Mira did as Alex asked. The graph should have been a straight line, instead it showed a steady increase over time. The current output was running at 117%. She evaluated at the graph, unable to believe what she was seeing.

"That's unsustainable. How did we miss it?"

"Easy, it's not an obvious fault. The reactor is increasing output because it is trying to compensate for a cumulative loss. Something is using energy at an ever increasing rate."

The reactor was operating beyond its maximum threshold to maintain power to the ship's systems. It was a process drive engineers referred to as *Thrashing*.

All shipboard reactors had an element of spare capacity, usually a 5% margin. If the safety margin was exceeded, an emergency system would be triggered to shut the system down.

"We had to remove the protection circuit to bring the ship on line," Mira whispered. "Why didn't I see this? This ship is a ticking bomb."

"Whatever is causing the drain is not part of the ship's systems. I can't tell you what it is, but I can tell you where it is," he said.

Alex held her gaze.

"It's in the hold."

Mira leaned against the bulkhead, doing her damnedest not show any outward signs of anxiety. She stood silently next to Alex as Ethan examined the hold's blast door.

Rich Barnes arrived with a nonchalant swagger. Mira saw through his act, just as she was sure he could see through hers. They were all tired and all trying to conceal their worries about what lay behind the door.

"Nice coat," Barnes said.

"It was in my cabin. I stole it," she replied. It felt good to confess the crime.

"I wish all the pirates I met in this job were as honest as you. How's the kid doing?"

A diagnostic tool hung from a port on the bulkhead. It was cycling through an infinite combination of codes to break the door's combination. It had been running since their first attempt to access the hold. It had yet to secure a single digit of the access code.

Ethan gave a disappointed shake of his head.

"If we have not cracked that code by now, we are not going to. We need to consider a more invasive way of getting in. Are you sure you want to go ahead?"

Invasive meant cutting through the metal or blasting the door out of the frame. Even with a vessel in full working order it would be a risky business.

"I don't see we have a choice. Alex has run the math, and he thinks the reactor will be at a critical point in eight hours. We have to stop the drain or drop out of FTL," Mira replied.

Or explode and have our dust scattered over a thousand light-years.

"Are we sure the drain is in there?" Barnes asked.

"I have run a diagnostic. There is a power distribution node in the hold and it is running flat out," Alex replied. "Mira double checked me, there is no mistake."

"I guess someone left a loader on charge. Damn commercial space jockeys, ill disciplined and sloppy," Barnes said. "What do you recommend, Private?"

Ethan looked up from his datapad.

"The door withstands vacuum exposure. It is embedded into the bulkhead and is 300 mm thick. Going in explosively will take a substantial charge."

"Too risky," Mira observed.

Ethan took a marker pen from his flight suit pocket and drew black squares on the door.

"The locking mechanism is located here, here and... here." He pointed to the marks on the door. "I found a heavy duty cutting tool in a storage locker in engineering. I can cut these sections out and we can use a much smaller charge to bust the mechanism. It should just slide open once the bolts are out of the way."

"Sounds good, Ethan. What about risks to the ship?" Mira asked.

"I can't say it is risk free. We're using explosives in a confined space... but yeah I can do it safely."

Mira agreed with his logic.

"Alex? What do you think?" she asked.

"Best option we have. How long will it take?"

"About an hour. It's not tricky, but I'd rather take a little time to cut it right on my first attempt."

"Okay, let's do it," Mira said. "Alex, can you help Ethan with the cutting equipment?"

He agreed. Mira was surprised at his readiness to undertake such a menial task with an enlisted marine, especially when he could have delegated it to Barnes.

Mira walked to the door and contemplated its featureless surface. She reached out and put her hand on the cool metal.

"You feel that to?" Barnes asked.

The question startled her, but she knew what he meant. Something felt wrong down here. The air was charged. She felt it when she stepped onto the lower deck, no she'd felt it the moment she stepped on the ship. Now it was deeper, more intense. She had put it down to stress and the constant headache that hammered in her skull.

"Just nerves, Rich. We don't know what we'll find in there so our minds are playing tricks..." She stopped as static electricity cracked from the door to her fingers.

She stepped back and whispered to Barnes. "I think you should get Babs. Just in case."

Rich Barnes made for the upper decks. Further up the corridor she heard Alex and Ethan returning with the cutting equipment. Their voices were loud and upbeat. Alex laughed at something Ethan said.

For a moment she saw them interacting as nothing more than humans, a pair of space jocks sharing a laugh. A disturbing thought occurred to her.

Maybe Alex Kite was human after all.

Smoke from Ethan's final cut was vented by the air scrubbers. It left a faint odour in its wake.

Ethan removed a small amount of explosive putty from a utility box and packed it around each part of the exposed mechanism. He inserted a small trigger cap then attached all the wires to a remote terminal.

"We're ready to go," he said.

For the first time Mira detected a hint of Texas in his otherwise anonymous accent. She wondered why he suppressed it then she remembered the ribbing she received over her own English-South African hybrid tones.

"Good work, Ethan. When we get back, I will talk to a friend about getting you a fleet commission. I'll need someone to act as a reference for you." She glanced at Barnes.

"Count me in," he said.

Ethan flushed.

"Thank you, Ma'am. I appreciate it."

"Shall we?" Alex ushered them toward the upper deck.

Mira stood at the top of the stairwell and counted them out. Once Ethan came through she sealed the lower deck. If the charge misfired or there was sudden decompression, they would be safe up here.

Barnes gave Ethan a rifle.

"Whenever you are ready Ethan," Mira said.

"Fire in the hold!" He pressed the button.

The only sign the charge had detonated was a telltale blue light flashing on Ethan's handset.

"Successful detonation," he confirmed.

She opened the hatch and they entered the lower deck. Mira's chest tightened; her headache intensified. The atmosphere was dense, the air impossibly heavy.

A faint blue haze hung in the air as they approached the hold. Scorch marks spread across the door, their epicentre at each of the blast sites.

"Alex," Mira said. "Are you able to help me with the door? I would rather these boys keep their weapons ready."

"Sure," Alex said, taking a step forward. He halted and ran a hand over the back of his neck.

"Are you okay?" Mira asked.

"Yeah... I guess. It felt as if someone walked on my grave. The hairs on my neck are rigid."

Mira and Alex pushed on the door and with some effort it slid upwards.

Barnes and Ethan raised their weapons, clicking off their safety switches in unison.

Mira stepped nervously into the darkened cargo hold. She blinked as she tried to see beyond the pool of light around the hatch.

"Lights!" she said, hoping they were voice activated. The hold remained dark. She fumbled behind her looking for an environmental control panel. Her fingers connected with the switch and the hold lights flickered into life. She fought back rising panic as she was transported back to her dream.

The hold was stacked with unremarkable long distance cargo canisters. It was the object in the centre that held her gaze.

"What the fuck is that?" she said.

A black ovoid rested in a cradle. She estimated the circumference at its widest to be close to two metres. The object was obsidian black. It was seamless and had no obvious purpose.

"It's not attached to the ship's power grid. How can it be draining our systems?" Ethan asked.

"The air in here is charged," Alex replied. "It's siphoning it without a physical connection. It's causing the ionisation we're feeling. I have no clue how that must be working."

Wireless charging was standard for datapads and consumer grade electronics of human origin, but the range was short and voltages low. Mira could only guess at how the curious object could draw power from the ship.

"Are we sure that's where the power is going?" she asked.

"There is nothing connected down here," Alex said. His voice faded.

All their voices sounded distant as Mira's fascination with the object grew. A barely conscious attraction and the desire to interact with it drew her forward.

Barnes put a hand on her shoulder; she shook it off and walked to the cradle.

"You sense that, Rich?" she asked. Her voice was little more than a murmur

"Something, maybe...I don't like it. It's like Alex said, the air full of static. It feels like a storm is about to break."

A shiver ran down Mira's spine. Her head pounded; her pulse quickened. Every hair on her body rose as she approached the alien object.

She walked around the cradle. The ovoid was opaque, yet had depth, like an ocean at night or the endless void of inter-stellar space. Mira placed her hand against the surface. It was warm to the touch. The colours deep within the material shimmered beneath her fingers. She withdrew her hand as her fingertips tingled. The surface where she had touched was alive with shifting colours.

"It feels like a sea shell," Mira whispered. "Are you scanning anything from it?"

Ethan answered. "Nothing of note. The thermal signature is no different to the background. There's no radiation of any sort."

"Be careful, Mira," Barnes said. His voice was uneasy.

"It's okay, Rich. I don't think it's dangerous."

She guessed the object must have some kind of ornamental or ceremonial purpose. There was nothing about it that appeared hostile, yet it seemed to be aware of her.

Swirls of colour swam from the depths and danced over the object's surface: blues, greens and the occasional flash of purple.

"Are you guys seeing this?" she asked. Mira smiled as the colours swam before her eyes.

"Seeing what?" Barnes sounded anxious. "Come on, Commander; step away. You are worrying me now."

"It's beautiful, Rich. They're so alive."

"Mira!" Barnes yelled. He sounded ever more distant as the object drew her in. Distant voices spoke to her in a tongue she could not understand. Staring into the lustrous surface was like staring into infinity, deep, silent and complete. Mira was losing herself to the darkness. It was not an unwelcome sensation. It was as if she were becoming part of something bigger, abandoning her worn out body and floating free in a limitless continuum.

She leant against the ovoid. It flexed against her. A charge ran through the surface and through her whole being.

Mira was at peace, warm and secure. It was the same reassuring comfort of a lover's embrace, a candle in the darkness or a kiss in the rain. She closed her eye and breathed deeply. The pain in her head faded, her fatigue melted away. She was light and detached, as if she were high, yet fully coherent.

The world around her dissolved to nothing, leaving only Mira and the darkness. There were voices in the void; they faded in and out as if carried on the wind, hundreds, maybe thousands of them. They meant her no harm. They needed her and she needed them.

Every muscle in her body went into spasm. Her nerves caught fire as the world rushed back into hard focus. Her body reeled and she staggered away from the object. A searing pain burned through her skull into the centre of her brain. She screamed, but no sound came from her paralysed throat.

The Kobo's hold solidified around her. The packing cases and loading equipment lit by harsh overhead lights that hurt her eye. Blue discharges of energy arced from the ovoid to the bulkheads. Mira stumbled away from the object, lost and alone once again. She dropped to her knees and pitched forward onto the deck. Her world went dark and silent.

CHAPTER EIGHT

THE sun warmed the girl's skin as she walked along a tree lined boulevard. Spires of glass and gold towered above her. Strange airborne vehicles zipped between the towers like insects. It was spring; the trees were in bloom with sweet-scented purple blossom. The sound of a thousand conversations blended with the burble of ornamental fountains. The girl was surrounded by life in all its chaotic vibrancy.

The realisation those around were not human jarred the girl's consciousness. The figures who moved through the city were tall and thin. Their skin was light blue.

They were Pharn. She was Pharn. This world was Arethon.

The knowledge was not hers. It originated elsewhere: a mysterious object in the hold of a broken freighter, light-years and millennia from this place.

You can call the object an Ark. It is a lifeboat of sorts, like your ship, a voice whispered in her mind. The voice in her head was not her own.

You hear our voice. These are our bodies, our eyes, our lives. You live through our memories. We took your words from you, so we may speak in your tongue. We thank you for this gift.

Mira Thorn stared in wonder at city around her. The beauty

of the architecture defied classification. It appeared almost organic as if the spires had grown from the earth beneath them. They were woven from black fibres impregnated with gold alloy. The green glass was curved to impossible angles and refracted the warm, yellow light into a myriad of colours.

Blistering heat of an explosion burned through her as fire filled the sky above the city. The towers crumbled; their glass liquefied and ran like emerald tears.

People were burned to dust and blown away by a searing gale.

Somehow Mira remained as the roar of the explosion faded and the dust settled. She lost track of how long she had stood on the scorched ground. A new sound reached her ears: the strange rhythmic pulsing of a star-drive. It grew louder; she covered her ears and cowered close to the ground. A shadow passed over her.

A gargantuan black starship moved over the ruined city, arcs of electricity sparking from its hull. Streams of smaller craft followed it. They were flattened black ovoids with curious projections jutting from their leading edges. Blue energy flickered around their spines. The ships emitted a sound like nothing she had ever heard. A screech that reminded her of an animal in pain, desperate, forlorn and terrifying.

The ships passed by and she continued to walk through the ruined streets. The remains of buildings crumbled to dust and became one with the bedrock.

Go. We are joined. We have a common understanding, the voice said.

My ship, Mira replied; her mind spoke for her. *You are damaging my ship. It will fail.*

We have what we need. Go back Mira Thorn. You have seen our past; help us make our future.

The shadow of night fell as the vision faded.

Mira Thorn gasped and sat up. She blinked as the world came into focus. She lay on the bed in her cabin with medical monitors attached to her forehead. Voices could be heard in the bathroom, the conversation animated and loud. Rich Barnes and Monica Garret were discussing something. She checked her sleeves. They were rolled down. Mira hoped neither Rich nor Monica had noticed her self-dressed injuries.

She disconnected the monitors and made to stand. Her headache was gone and her back free of pain. An alarm sounded on the monitoring equipment and Monica appeared in the doorway.

"Stay right where you are, Commander Thorn."

"I'm fine," she said. "How long was I out?"

Monica looked at her wristwatch. "Two hours, there or thereabouts."

Monica sat next to her. She checked her pulse while Mira relived her encounter.

"She called it an *Ark*," Mira said. "A lifeboat."

"Who? What? Back up a minute Mira," Barnes said.

"I saw something. The girl who acted as my guide was so young, so alive and full of excitement for life. It was as if I was there but... I don't think what I saw was in real time. I think she was telling me a story."

I was her. I want to be her again.

"I'm not mad," Mira said. "Am I?"

Monica removed the monitors. Mira winced with each painful tug.

"You called it an *Ark*. That implies it is occupied," Monica said.

"I guess they're small people," Barnes said, without humour.

His tone carried an undercurrent of disbelief.

"No, it's not like that. It's a repository for... something. I don't know if it is shared memories or an archive of knowledge."

"You know the Navy has similar archives?" Monica said. "It's classified information. There are digital vaults containing DNA of humans and other earth species. They store it as a method of recreating us if we became extinct." Monica laughed. "I know it's nonsense, but they were given government money to do it. Right now all the data required to recreate humanity is floating in deep space. Just in case a future alien species is dumb enough to do it."

Monica concluded her checks.

"I think we should space it," Barnes said.

"No," Mira replied. "Whatever it is it tried to communicate. We can't. I want to help them."

Mira thought about the empty longing she experienced as the vision ended.

They've been out here so long,

Barnes remained unconvinced. "Aside from what it did to you, the ship's systems went crazy. We had power spikes and general malfunctions all over the place. It's not safe."

"Rich, I don't know what it is but they are trying to communicate. If something is alive inside, we can't space it."

Monica intervened.

"Mira is right. It's not our place to decide. Once she disengaged from her Ark, the power stabilised. Last time I checked everything was fine down there. Alex tells me the power drain has gone, and the reactor is steady at 87%."

Mira pulled on her boots and laced them.

"Where do you think you are going?" Monica asked.

"The flight deck. I want to check the drive system." The

fatigue and pain were all but distant memories, her headache a minor irritation.

Barnes excused himself.

Monica waited until the big man left. "I want you to rest. You were unconscious for two hours. That's long enough to require 48 hours of observations."

"Monica I am fine... I feel good."

"Humour me."

Monica Garret stood and walked to a low cabinet in the corner of the room. She rooted around inside and produced a bottle of brandy and two glasses.

"I scoped out the stateroom and liberated one of these last night. Not bad for something with a corporation brand on it," she said as she filled both glasses. She handed one to Mira and sat.

"I need a drink. We have had an exceptional few days. You know I don't like to drink alone."

Mira took the glass. There was a moment of silence until the Doctor prompted her. "Talk to me, Mira. I've known you long enough to know when you are holding back on me."

"Truthfully I feel better than I did when I woke up this morning. I had a bastard behind my eyes but it's gone. Whatever that thing did I'm grateful. There is something..."

Monica sipped her brandy and nodded.

"I'm listening."

"Monica, I'm losing my mind." She took a drink. The doctor was right; she needed it. "I've been forgetful. I've been losing things. I have to write notes to myself on a datapad."

"How long has it been happening?"

"A month, maybe six weeks. It is as if I'm going back to where I was in rehab."

"You said you had a headache? How often have you been

having them?"

"It came on before we left the ship. It was strong, like a migraine. I had two in the past week."

Monica Garret took Mira's hand.

"On your last scan I found an anomaly. A faint shadow on your frontal lobe. It could be something, but it's most likely nothing. Our equipment on the *Berlin* was not up to date or that serviceable. I do not want you to worry. It is far more likely to be insignificant." She paused.

"Brain injuries such as yours are unpredictable. The processes that heal can be erratic and it is possible for patients to experience effects long after the injury. This is probably a transitory problem. You have been stable for the best part of four years."

"Or it could be permanent? It might get worse?" Mira said in a flat tone.

"It could. I would say the odds are against it. Aside from that single scan everything has been fine. It could be a chemical imbalance I can deal with using drugs." She reached into the pocket of her flight suit and gave Mira a wafer of tablets.

"I made sure I brought a supply from the ship."

Mira took the strip. They were Tetrazine, a low level stimulant she had been using since the crash.

"Given the strain of the last few days take double the dose. There isn't much else we can do out here."

"What about the headache?"

"You say it started recently?"

"As I was boarding the shuttle. It went after my adventure in the hold."

"I know you enjoy inspections, probably just stress."

Mira popped two pills and swallowed them with a slug of brandy. It was smooth and warm.

"You should avoid alcohol with those," Monica said.

Mira froze. The doctor laughed.

Tell her about the cutting Mira, her mind screamed. She ignored the inner voice. She couldn't lay that on her friend, not now, not ever.

"Mira, we will get you checked out. After this I'll be able to order all the tests I want and no one will complain. In the meantime don't worry." Monica stood. "Take a rest girl. We are still a long way out and Mr Kite can cover for you."

Monica finished her drink and placed the glass on the counter top. The clink sounded louder than it should have in the quiet cabin.

"We are all grateful to you, Mira, even Alex. Without you we would have all died with the *Berlin*."

Mira made no reply. Monica excused herself.

She sat on the bed and recalled the feelings she had experienced during the dream, *the memory*.

Mira felt it again, a fleeting sadness. It gripped her heart deeper than anything she had experienced before. It put her own pathetic existence into perspective.

Tears came, slowly at first then an unstoppable torrent.

She cried until her eye ran dry. When the emotion passed she stood and almost on autopilot walked to the bathroom.

Mira found the razor where she had hidden it. She gazed at the ancient ivory handle with its gold frame. She dropped it into the waste chute. Her hand hovered above the purge button. Her fingers trembled and seconds stretched into a minute as her resolve wavered.

She hit the button and blew the razor into the dump tank. The tank would be vented into the vacuum when they collapsed their faster-than-light envelope, and that would not be soon enough for Mira Thorn.

David Conway watched as his luggage was offloaded from a government air car. It comprised two diplomatic transit cases and a titanium suitcase. The porters placed the transit cases on an anti-gravity sled. Conway checked the seals were intact. He carried his personal case himself.

He shivered in the cold morning air and pulled his overcoat tighter as he walked over the marble-tiled plaza into the VIP terminal.

Zoe Sinclair greeted him at the entrance.

"Senator Conway, your vessel is on the apron ready to depart. Aside from your diplomatic bags and your personal one do you have any additional luggage?"

"Does it look like it? Let's get this done as quickly as possible. I am keen to be underway."

"Certainly Senator. As I am sure you are aware, we are taking the utmost care following the incident yesterday."

She unclipped a personal scanner from her belt.

"May I?"

Conway raised his arms. Zoe completed her scan quickly and waited for Conway to place his case on the scanner. A green light showed it had passed the security check. His diplomatic cases passed through security with no scans and were escorted directly to his ship by a pair of Homeworld security officers.

"So I take that all is in order, Ms Sinclair?" he asked.

"It is, Senator. I am sorry for the inconvenience. Unfortunately, we are operating under emergency protocols until further notice."

"Tell me," he asked. "Have there been any breakthroughs in the investigation into the accident?"

The incident had thrown the political elite into a state of shock. Three senators and 105 civilians had died in the worst terrorist atrocity since the Seattle Metro attack two years earlier. All flights out of Europe had been halted for 24 hours. They only resumed this morning with limited services. Conway's private vessel was the first departure of the day.

"No, Sir, not yet. The Federal Crime Agency and D37 suspect it was not an accident. Naturally, Earth First are the prime suspects. They've been remarkably quiet in recent years and I think they lack expertise to carry out such an attack."

"You are an expert in such matters, Ms Sinclair?" Conway asked.

"No, but..."

"Then perhaps you should leave conjecture to those better qualified to make such assertions?"

"Of course, Sir," she replied.

"I suspect we will get to the bottom of it eventually," he said, lifting his bag from the scanner.

"Has Senator Meyer left yet? I would imagine the situation would have left her quite shaken."

"She is booked to leave on diplomatic transport later today."

"Be sure to give her my regards."

Without a further word he made his way through the empty terminal toward the gate.

He was met by a steward at the gantry. The man ushered him aboard the ship. After stowing his luggage he settled in the deep synth-leather seat and waited for the ship to be pushed back from the gate. Conway hated the constant delay that characterised space travel.

The com-link on his seat's arm beeped. He idly opened the internal channel. The copilot's voice came through the speaker mounted in the headrest.

"Senator, we are on schedule to depart as planned. I have just received a priority one coded message for you. Would you like me to forward it to your terminal?"

Conway agreed, removing a small flat device from his pocket. He swiped the screen of his mini datapad and entered his secure communication app. A sea of characters danced on the screen before coalescing into a readable message.

The mission is compromised due to external factors. The package is now in the possession of a third party. I have tracked it to Tarantella.
Do you want me to proceed with recovery?
KM.

Conway pondered the message. It was light on detail but carried enough to infuriate him. He typed a message of his own. His fingers bashed each word into the touchscreen in a staccato rhythm.

Manson,
The recovery of the package was the easy option. We have a contingency in place. It carries certain risks and considerable fallout which I will have to manage. I require you to proceed to phase two of the operation. I am transmitting coordinates and an operational plan. Rendezvous with the Frontier Vessel Ariane as directed and proceed from there. You will receive compensation for the additional risk and work required. This will be in line with our agreed rates.
Do not recover the artefact and do not fuck this up.

He re-read the message and pressed the send key. The glass screen flexed beneath his thumb and a warning beep sounded. Conway closed his eyes and composed himself.

He could deal with Tarantella. The assets he needed were

already in place.

Conway typed a second burst message. Once the encryption algorithm had completed he sent it via a secure connection to Frontier Fleet Operations.

He slipped the datapad into his pocket and pressed the service button. He needed a drink.

In Conway's world success often had to be dragged from the incompetent hands of others and he never underestimated the ability of his underlings to fail.

Mira staggered under the weight of the crate. She cursed herself for not having the forethought to use an anti-grav sled or at least a cargo dolly. She dropped the box of scrap and broken components onto the deck of the engineering bay with a satisfying crash.

She yawned and checked the time. It was close to midnight. Her watch had finished six hours ago, and she spent the intervening time clearing the engineering section. Somehow the events earlier in the day had left her alert and too awake to sleep.

Mira wiped her hands on her flight suit and walked back toward the hold, knowing she would find a dolly there.

She hesitated at the blast door. Her hand hovered over Ethan's improvised control panel. She entered the access code one digit at a time. The panel turned green and the door slid open. The lights were still on and the Ark sat in its cradle. Everything was just as they left it. She stared at the object, almost expecting it to react to her presence. It remained inert. No colours danced beneath the surface. It appeared ordinary under the xenon lamps.

Mira took one step then another toward the object. She stood before it and placed her hand on its surface. It had the familiar seashell texture yet the heat and vibration were absent.

"What are you?" she whispered.

She walked around the object, never taking her eye off it. She completed two circuits and stepped back, regarding the ovoid with a cool gaze.

"Not in the mood for conversation, I guess."

The object remained impassive.

"Whatever you are, if you want to tell me something you need to be clearer. I'm just a simple human. I can't find your world. Humans have never heard of Arethon."

She smiled at silent black ovoid.

"I brought you some food."

Mira started at the sound of the voice.

Alex Kite stood in the doorway, his face in shadow. Mira could not read his expression.

"Alex!" she said. "You scared the crap out of me."

"I wanted see how you were doing." His voice was uncertain. The cockiness was gone; his tone was natural and genuine.

Mira studied him. "Scare me like that again and I might give you another slap," she said.

Alex walked into the hold.

Mira smelt curry and her stomach growled.

"Mind if I join you?" he asked.

"Pull up a shipping crate; make yourself at home."

He did. Mira took the container and a plastic spoon. Alex produced two bottles of Lightfoot branded beer from his pockets.

"Rich told me you were a beer drinker. The doctor told me I should stick to water. This is a corporate own brand, which ticks both boxes," Alex said.

Mira unclipped the lid of the container. Without ceremony she ploughed into her dinner.

"Rich has been cooking?"

Alex nodded, unable to speak through a mouthful of food.

Rich Barnes had a reputation for producing meals out of only basic rations. Freeze dried curry was his signature dish.

"He's a talented man, our sergeant," Mira said.

Silence pressed in. Alex's face was swollen and bruised. One mark looked more livid than the rest.

"Did I do that?" she asked.

He answered a nod and a dismissive shrug.

"Sorry."

Another awkward silence.

"Alex, can I ask you something? You know what you said about how I got on the ship? Is it what they all thought?" she asked, not knowing why she wanted to know.

"Mira..." Alex twirled his spoon and shuffled on the packing crate.

"Come on, I'm curious."

"There were a few of the guys, mostly new intake officers. They were passed over for promotion and were looking for someone to blame. It's getting harder to move up the ranks and some people find it easier to find a scapegoat than to address their own shortcomings."

Mira gave a sad laugh.

"I get it. For clarity though it was an Admiral's daughter, and it made it harder to get on a Steelside." She broke eye contact as sadness gripped her heart in a sudden, vice like embrace.

Alex inhaled deeply as if building up to an announcement.

"I caught an STD, on three separate occasions," he said. "That's the embarrassing thing in my records."

Mira was both shocked and amused and didn't quite know how to react. She would never have expected it from a clean-cut guy like Alex Kite.

"So I guess we're equal now?" he added tentatively.

"We're cool, Alex, you sly old dog!" She gave him a playful shove.

"It's why I had that skin reaction on the inspection I covered for you. Please don't tell Sergeant Barnes."

Mira laughed harder before composing herself. "Don't worry; my memory is so bad I'll have forgotten by the time we land."

They fell back into a comfortable silence. Mira could not decide if it were the beer or the conversation but she was relaxed in Alex's presence.

The difference a few days can make.

"It seems different down here. The air is better. That thing still gives me the creeps, but it is not as threatening. What happened when you touched it?"

Mira explained the events as she experienced them. "It was probably just a dream; like you said I have a reputation."

"So this Arethon, did it tell you where it was?"

"No. I saw images, like back story. It was as if we had no common language until we had interacted for a while."

There was not much else to tell, but somehow she felt different.

Alex sealed his spoon in the container and set it to one side.

"For what it's worth," Alex said. "I am grateful you came back for me. There were members of the crew who would have jumped away leaving me and the Doc to die."

"You would have done the same for me, Alex."

"I'm not so sure. It's times like this when you find out who you really are."

Mira drained her bottle; Alex matched her.

She studied his face, his blond hair, square jaw, perfect

teeth and an easy smile. Alex was the type of officer that marines called a fleet-brat: young, handsome and talented. She could not recall ever speaking to Alex socially and wondered if their frosty relationship was as much born from her own prejudices as it was any fault of Alex.

"So now you are down here... Do you fancy helping me dump the scrap?"

"Show me the way but take it easy. I have bruises on my bruises."

"We'll make a fine pair of cripples then."

She stood and offered a hand to Alex. He took it and she pulled him to his feet. He winced.

Mira squeezed his hand.

"Are we good Alex?"

"We are, Thorny."

Jon Flynt was roused from his thoughts by Jason Lambert confirming the completion of the recovery operation. He had been sitting silently at his desk, reviewing the data gathered from the wreck site.

"How many?" he asked.

"39 complete bodies. We have tissue samples of many more," Lambert answered, his tone flat. His face conveyed no emotion.

Identifiable remains would be vital to the families left behind. A dead crewman qualified for a death in service payment to the next of kin. Those who could not be accounted for would be declared missing in action and their families would only benefit from deferred pension rights.

"We also recovered the magazine. It appears to be one *Shipwreck* torpedo short."

A missing torpedo was a complication. It was not the sort of ordinance the Navy would want falling into the wrong hands. The *Berlin* would have been loaded with 120 such weapons and stealing one would make little sense when so many more were accessible. The obvious implication was that it had been fired, but the logs showed no record.

"Sir?" Lambert asked. "Do you want me to continue the search for the weapon or jump the ship?"

"No, leave it. Prepare to jump but wait for my order. Would you be kind enough to send Miss Clark in?"

"Yes, Sir."

A minute later the door opened and Samantha Clark entered. Sam was in her early twenties, young but experienced. She had raw talent and learned quickly. With her dark hair, blue eyes and flawless skin she was undeniably pretty. Sam was forever fending off the advances of the ship's contingent of horny marines; something she did forcefully, but with humour and good grace.

Flynt had poached Sam from Jen Dixon's crew on the *Kenya*. On the *Valhalla* she managed comms and helm duties and was capable in both disciplines. He had already decided she would permanently transfer to the dreadnought.

"Sammy, come on in. Take a seat."

Sam sat opposite. She clasped her hands together and perched on the edge of the chair. She gave one of those half smiles reserved for those in authority with unclear motives. It was a smile Flynt saw a lot.

"Don't be nervous. It's me who should be worried," he said. "I need to ask for a favour."

"Of course, Admiral. What do you need?"

"Don't be so eager to agree. You don't know what it is yet. I need to send an encrypted burst message."

"That's not a problem, Sir. I can configure a Hyperspace

Relay Channel and link it to your console."

"I need more than just the HRC. The transmission cannot appear in our comm logs. The only people who can know about it is you and I. I can't order you to do it, so I'm asking you. I will take full responsibility should anyone at Fleet ever find out."

Sam laughed. "Is that all, Sir? No problem. I can drop the communication system into service mode and backdoor it over the emergency relay. When I bring the system back on line, it will overwrite the log entry."

"Perfect. Can you organise it before we jump?"

She nodded.

"If you don't mind me asking who are you sending...?" she cut herself off.

Flynt studied her. A grin played on his face. He saw few officers like Sam Clark. Trust and loyalty were qualities all too lacking in Officer College graduates. They were the two qualities Flynt valued above all others. He thought of Mira Thorn; she had both albeit tempered with insecurity and doubt.

"It's going to Xander Rhodes. If our people are going to Tarantella, he will be able to help."

Sam stood. "I can see why you would not want any trace of that, Sir. It will take me a few minutes to organise things. I'll patch it through to your terminal. Is there anything else you need?"

"No, Sammy. That will be all. Thank you."

She stood and left the ready room.

A few minutes later his com-link buzzed. Flynt hit the receive key.

"You are good to go, Admiral," Sam said.

Flynt opened his terminal and typed a message.

CHAPTER NINE

A cool breeze chilled Mira's bare skin as the sound of gentle waves roused her from a deep, dreamless slumber. The sun painted the eastern horizon red. *Sailors' warning,* she thought as her mind drifted in and out of REM sleep.

The previous evening she discovered the cabin was equipped with an Enviro-Sim. It was a high-tech piece of equipment that projected images on the walls of the cabin. The illusion was enhanced with scented and directional air circulation.

Mira rolled onto her back and drifted into a fitful half sleep.

She dreamt fleetingly of the city of glass and gold.

Mira shivered into full waking, cold sweat soaking her sheets and her skin burning. She rose from the bed and made her way to the bathroom. She poured a glass of water and popped two of her painkillers. She followed up with her usual medication and waited for the nausea to pass.

Mira focused her attention to her wounds. Two were healing well. The third was inflamed and dark spokes radiated from the weeping wound.

"Oh fuck me," she whispered. She would try to steal antibiotics from medbay, failing that they would land in a few hours. Strong bio meds would have to be a priority.

She washed and dressed. The fever lessened its grip as she made her way to the flight deck.

Alex was sitting in the copilot's chair. She assumed he would fly the approach. Alex continued to work when she entered.

"Alex?"

"I thought you should bring her in," he said, without looking up from his checklist. "I've seen your face when you are up here. It would be sad not to see a smile out of you occasionally."

She thanked him and slid into the pilot's seat.

"You know I'm not certified to do this?"

Alex pointed to the yellowing bruises on his face.

"Neither am I but I'm sure that between us we count as one qualified pilot."

Mira reached for the yoke and stopped. Her hands were shaking.

"Are you okay? You look like shit."

"Yeah, I'm fine. Nerves. It has been a while."

Alex continued his checks. Mira picked up her datapad and worked through her assigned tasks. They worked in silence except for the procedures requiring cross checking.

"Fly a rough approach; you don't want to look like a fleet-brat. Fly it like you stole it," Alex advised.

She was unsure if he was serious. His expression remained earnest.

"Fleet-brat? Just for that you do the call," she said

Alex flicked the internal comm channel to open.

"Ladies and Gentleman, this is your copilot speaking. We are about to commence entry to normal space," he said in a ridiculous parody of a commercial captain. "Please return your cabin attendant to an upright position and fasten your seat belts. I will not be thanking you for flying with us because I know you had no choice."

Mira tried to suppress a giggle and failed.

"You are such a dick," she said.

Alex laughed. Mira thought she saw the faintest of blushes beneath his bruises.

There was something different about Alex, something different about them all. Mira had felt it too, more so since she flushed the razor.

And since I touched the Ark.

She dismissed the thought. Every time she slept she travelled to that city of gold and glass, walked its streets and felt the warmth of the alien sun on her skin. It was as comforting as it was disturbing.

Counting down from five, she collapsed the envelope. The energy waves outside the viewport evaporated and were replaced by the infinite expanse of normal space. The Kobo shuddered and a metallic creak reverberated through the hull. A jarring vibration followed it.

"What was that?" Mira asked, struggling to hold the yoke steady.

"Something broke. All the vitals are in the green. Let's worry about it when we dock," Alex replied.

An alarm screeched.

"Fire!" Alex yelled.

"What? Where?"

"It's on the lower deck, engineering section. We have an internal plasma leak," Alex said.

Mira reached up and hit the fire extinguisher controls for the entire lower deck. She punched the console when the activation light failed to illuminate.

Think Mira! Get it out before it kills us.

"I'm venting. Shut down the feeds to the engines." She

rotated the airlock control and opened the lower deck hatches. The ship shuddered as the atmosphere rushed out.

Decompression alarms rang out over the fire alarm and the ship lurched as jets of super-heated hydrogen were spat into space. It was as if the ship were fitted with uncalibrated retro rockets.

Mira fought the controls while Alex silenced the alarms. A tense few seconds passed as Alex checked the inboard sensors.

The lights flickered. Mira floated against her harness as the gravity failed.

Silence.

The ship lurched, and the engines restarted. The lights came on and gravity returned. Mira was slammed back into the seat with such force that the deep padding could not deaden the pain.

A cry escaped her lips.

"The fire is out," Alex reported. "Locks are closed. We are still losing pressure down there. We must have sprung some leaks."

Mira thought of the dream, how she pressed her hand over the hole in the hull and watched the crack spread from beneath her palm.

She checked the engineering panel. The atmospheric control tab was highlighted with a red exclamation mark and showed a steady loss of air from the system.

She keyed the intercom.

"Rich, we had a problem on the lower deck. The fire is out but we are showing a sustained pressure loss. I need you and Ethan to patch us up."

"Okay will do," came the reply.

"Is it worth it?" Alex asked. "We'll be docking inside an hour."

"We hope. If they hold us in a traffic pattern or can't bring us aboard, we'll choke."

She scanned her console and saw more red highlights than green. They had lost engine four, leaving them with two functioning sublights. A shudder ran through the hull as she increased power. The yoke shook. She advanced the throttles. The ship settled and forward velocity increased.

Mira had no clue how they were still in one piece or how the Kobo kept flying.

Rich Barnes plugged a temperature sensor into the port on the service hatch. He and Ethan Tate stood at the service hatch behind the flight deck. The display showed an air temperature of -14 Celsius.

"It's cold," Barnes said. "The fire is out and it's too warm to be open to space."

He cranked the manual release handle and opened the hatch. The smell of rotten fish and burnt cable rushed out to greet him.

"It was a leak," Ethan said from behind him. "Oh man, that's disgusting."

"Plenty more where that came from." Barnes descended the ladder to the lower deck. The access corridor was pitch black.

He activated his helmet lamp as Ethan followed him down the ladder.

They made their way aft. The bulkheads were scorched black. Everything combustible was burnt to ash. Barnes' boots crackled over the melted plastic that had fused with the floor.

"If Mira hadn't sealed the lower deck, we'd all be dead," Ethan said.

The plasma fire had flashed through every compartment, burning everything in its path. He shuddered when he thought of the consequences of the fire reaching the habitation section.

"It is attention to detail that keeps you alive, Private. When Mira was in a drop ship, she could push it faster, lower and wilder than anyone else because she made sure the little details were covered. She's the only person I know who takes being called a control freak as a compliment."

"You like her." It was a statement of fact rather than a question.

"We have history. Mira Thorn pulled my ass out of the fire more times than I can count and, contrary to rumours, I can count well into triple figures."

They walked on. The hold door was buckled and bent. The remains of transit cases littered the corridor. Barnes peered into the cargo area.

"What the hell?" he murmured. The object was still sitting upright on its pallet. Blue light flickered around it. As Barnes watched it faded.

Something whispered in his ear.

"What?" he said.

Ethan gave him a puzzled look.

"I thought..." he said. "I thought I heard something. Just jumping at shadows I guess."

"It's not burnt," Ethan said, pointing at the object. "The floor is untouched around it as if it repelled the fire."

"It has not moved either. That decompression should have seen it fly out the airlock with the rest of the junk down here." Barnes gave a puzzled frown. The object had considerable mass but not enough to resist an explosive venting.

"I still think we should have spaced it."

"Would we have been able to? I mean what would it do if we tried?" Ethan replied.

Barnes tried to shake off the unease that clung to him. He

forced a laugh as they continued toward engineering.

"There," Ethan pointed to four fist sized holes in the hull. Atmosphere was venting through them. The moisture in the air was freezing and leaving a characteristic white vapour trail streaming into each breach.

"There is a service box by engineering; go grab it while I check the rest of the bulkhead."

Ethan jogged off. Barnes inspected the area. The breach was limited to four visible holes. One had the shape and profile of Ethan's improvised door latch.

Ethan returned with a service kit. He opened the case and unrolled a kevlar weave blanket. He cut it into 4 roughly circular pieces using a cutter stored in the box's lid.

Barnes assembled the adhesive kit and applied the bonding compound to the area around each hole. His hands were numb with the cold and he constantly altered his grip.

With the adhesive in place Ethan placed the patches, allowing Barnes to complete the seal with a hardening compound. When it was done Barnes stepped back dropping the sealant gun to the deck. He flexed his sore and blistered hands.

"Not the most attractive repair I've ever seen, but it'll hold." He keyed his com-link. "Mira, we're all good. You should see the pressure stabilise."

"We're green here. Thanks, Rich."

He closed the link.

"Come on, let's check out engineering." Barnes kicked the service box out of the way and gave the repair a final visual check.

The door to the drive section was blown out of its frame. The compartment was a mess of broken ducting and burnt machinery. Ethan inspected their makeshift repair.

"We got away with it. Our repairs are holding. We're going

to make it."

Barnes reached into his webbing and produced a pocket datapad. He opened the holo-cam app and pointed the device at the ducting.

"One for the collection," he said, photographing the repair. "When I tell folks about this, they'll think I'm exaggerating. This will prove me right."

"Sergeant, before we go back up... I've heard stories about the commander's final mission. What really happened? It's not what you think. I saw a picture of her being cut from her ship on our database and was curious to know more."

Barnes considered Ethan's request. It was not his story to tell, but one he wanted to tell.

"Mouse was on a standard ferry run out to one of our forward operating bases on the plain. The war was winding down and the Dawn's forces were scattered."

"A marine unit was out in the dust, low on air and ammo. They had injured guys and needed urgent EVAC. She volunteered. The extraction went by the numbers, no drama, no enemy contact. On egress a shoulder launched SAM took out most of her ship's control surfaces. She kept the bird in the air long enough to reach Columbus." He paused, doing his best to contain the emotion.

"Before she started the descent, her commanding officer came on the comm and gave her permission to eject. Corps places more value on one pilot than a ship load of grunts. It's a fair point, they cost more to train."

"She refused?" Ethan asked.

"She did. Then a General comes on and orders her to punch out. You know what she told him to do?"

"Go fuck himself?"

"Word for word, Private."

Barnes' voice trembled. "Thirty marines are alive today because of her. The Corps does not forget shit like that."

Barnes blinked twice.

"She was the best damn pilot in the Corps, let no one tell you different. I was there that day, so I know."

Barnes pulled his emotions into check.

"Come on, Private; let's get topside, just in case we spring another leak."

As they passed the hold, Barnes stopped. He took a final look at the dark ovoid. Once they were docked, he would not care if he ever laid eyes on it, or this ship ever again.

Mira balanced the ship's ion drive against the gravitational pull of the star. She brought them in on a fast approach and was happy to let gravity take the strain off the engines.

As they drew closer to the station, the short range communication system sparked into life. A voice came through her earpiece.

"Unidentified Starship, Tarantella Traffic, please state your intentions and identify." The voice was male and sounded bored.

"Good morning, traffic," Mira said. "Commercial vessel registration..." She scanned the console for the ID plate. "... GX-53212. We are requesting docking. We require dry dock facilities. Ideally the cheapest berth you can offer."

There was a pause.

"You and everyone else," the controller replied. "Stand by."

The link went dead with the stone cold silence of a terminated transmission. Mira did her best to keep her panic in check.

"53212; permission denied; we have no available bays. Proceed to Pier 876."

"Damn it," Mira muttered, no bay meant no repairs. She

tried again.

"Control, understood. Our condition is critical. We have severe hull damage; we're leaking atmosphere and I'm having a terrible day. We could do with that dry dock. Control we are in your hands and would appreciate whatever help you can give." She hoped she sounded desperate enough to convince the controller. If all else failed she had more than enough grounds to declare an emergency. At any normal port an emergency status would guarantee an inboard landing. At Tarantella they were far more likely to shut the doors and let you puzzle it out for yourself.

After an eternity the flight controller came back on line. Mira thought she heard a voice speaking in the background.

"53212 proceed to bay 32. Payment will be required within 24 hours of landing. It would appear you have friends in high places. Traffic out."

Alex appeared as puzzled as she felt.

"Affirm, traffic. Thank you, we appreciate it. Have nice day. 53212 out." Mira closed the link.

Mira followed a vector sent to the flight computer by the traffic controller. As they drew closer, the station grew from a tiny speck of light into a giant structure of metal and rock.

Tarantella station was built into the mined out shell of an asteroid. It orbited a dwarf star at the centre of a failed system. Instead of forming planets the accretion disc had coalesced into clumps of rock, ice and heavy metals. Over millennia gravity had marshalled the proto-planetary material into a ring orbiting 180 million miles from the stillborn star.

Humans had arrived 150 years ago and the mineral wealth was now all but exhausted. The resources were extracted, refined and used to build the wealth of the Core Systems. A handful of small mining corporations still operated out of

Tarantella, extracting the last of the system's resources.

The station occupied an elliptical orbit 185 million miles from the star. Once the largest industrial facility in the system, it now operated as an off grid trading post. A favoured haunt of pirates, smugglers and mercenaries. The station management covered its costs and turned a profit by charging commissions on every transaction that took place in the system.

"What a hole," Alex muttered.

The surface of the asteroid was covered in steel structures, some newly built, others relics from the outpost's mining past. The lower half of the station was man-made, a metal structure jutting into space covered with solar panels, heat exchangers and habitation tubes. From a distance Tarantella looked like a giant deformed mushroom.

Mira followed the traffic pattern and the controller gave them final clearance.

As they closed on the station Mira was surprised by the number of vessels anchored to external gantries. Her eye was drawn to what appeared to be a Frontier Company heavy cruiser. Its silhouette dwarfed the Maersk super-freighter on the next pier.

"That's the *Scarlet Angel*," Alex said, following her gaze.

"The what?" Mira asked. The ship's name was familiar but she couldn't place it.

"Xander Rhodes' starship."

Mira gazed at the ship. The design was similar to the Navy's *Africa* class only with greater length and beam. The name *Scarlet Angel* was emblazoned on the side in vivid red letters accompanied by a lewd illustration of a winged, semi-naked woman.

He stole that ship from right underneath the Frontier Company's nose; the guy can't be all bad, she thought.

Mira refocused on flying the approach.

Traffic control contacted and confirmed final docking instructions.

"53212 you are cleared for final. Please try to keep your speed and course constant. My teenage daughter can fly a cleaner approach," the controller said. Mira shot a glance to Alex. He laughed and started his part of the landing procedure.

Mira retarded the ship's throttles and steered onto the downrange leg of the approach. She aligned the heading indicator with the projected glide slope. She trimmed the ship's attitude and alignment.

Her speed and heading did not deviate from the landing system's projected course. The Kobo crossed the threshold of the hangar positioned in the centre of the aperture. The ship juddered as they pierced the energy seal.

Mira set the battered freighter on the pad with precise grace.

"Not bad for a one eyed under-achiever," she said. She powered off the engines and disengaged the plasma feed using a bank of switches on the overhead console. The ship shook and fell silent.

"That was an okay landing, Thorn, eight out of ten," Alex said. He winked at her.

She was buzzing.

That felt good, she thought as she commenced the shut down procedure.

It took a further ten minutes for her and Alex to power down the ship. Once done Mira stood and pushed the creases out of her flight suit, her wet palms leaving faint marks in the material.

"Feels like I've never been away. Thank you, Alex."

He casually saluted as she walked toward the habitation

section.

Mira replayed the approach as she walked. She could still fly a ship as well as she ever could. If the Navy would not let her do it, perhaps she should find someone who would. There was always the option of going private. She had a property on Earth she could sell and Navy pension to cash in.

Possibilities, she thought as she rode the wave of optimism.

Ethan, Monica and Sergeant Barnes greeted her. Relief and happiness erasing the stress and fatigue from their faces.

"We did it," she said as all three of them embraced her. A lump formed in her throat and she didn't know if it was the relief of being on a station or the emotion radiating from her shipmates.

When they had calmed, Mira composed herself. It was time to be Commander Thorn again.

"I have been considering how we handle this," she said. "This ship is done for."

The fire on the lower deck had been the deciding factor. She had yet to survey the hull but expected damaged or lost outer plating.

"So we book onward passage?" Alex asked, joining them in the lounge. "It should be easy enough. I spotted a Maersk freighter moored on a pier. They run regular services to all the main outposts."

"And we have plenty of funds," Mira added.

They sat in silence.

"Alex, I want you and Rich to pay the docking fees and book passage for everyone on an outbound vessel."

Alex cleared his throat.

"Can I make a point?"

"Go ahead," Mira replied.

"Look at yourselves," he said. They looked at each other

dumbly. "You all look like fleet personnel or worse still company haulers. Step outside dressed like that and every hustler on the station will be on you like flies. Worse still abduction is a real possibility; a naval officer fetches a high price in certain circles."

Mira inspected her pressed flight suit, pristine sky blue with the Lightfoot logo emblazoned on the breast pocket. Ethan Tate still wore his khaki under-shirt with *FMC 456–C84 Berlin* in black lettering surrounding the Navy Crest.

"You're right," Mira said, a giggle escaped. "I've already been called a fleet-brat once today, and that's one time too many. I have no idea what the other cabins hold but there is a huge wardrobe in the stateroom jammed with all sizes and styles."

Mira watched as her tired shipmates left on a quest for less conspicuous clothing.

"Alex!" she called to him before he followed the others. "I need to talk to you."

Alex looked at her, suspicion in his eyes.

"When you book tickets, you only need four."

He gave her a puzzled look.

"I'm not coming with you."

"What? What are you talking about? You can't stay here."

"I don't intend to, at least not for long."

"Mira what are you going to do? You can't just walk out on your commission."

She rested a hand on Alex's arm.

"Alex, that object in the hold, it showed me something important. It wants me to take it somewhere. I don't know how to explain it. It's a compulsion. I don't have a choice."

"You always have choices. This Arethon, you don't even know if it exists."

Mira had searched the ship's local datastore and UniNet archives for references to the Pharn homeworld. She had found several mentions in obscure Verani texts but no clues to its location.

"It exists but I don't know where. Xander Rhodes may know more; I'll talk to him."

They stood in silence.

"I'll stay with you," Alex blurted.

"Alex, don't be ridiculous. You have a career to go back to." She paused. "My time is over. I need to find something new. Maybe this is the new start for me."

"You're crazy, Thorny. I can't work you out at all."

"I'm still trying to work myself out. It's not easy but I'm getting there. Days like today help." She stood on tiptoe and kissed him on the cheek.

"Thank you, Alex, for everything."

He smiled. He could not hide the sadness behind it.

"You're welcome."

Alex stood in silence for several seconds before following the crew into the central corridor.

Mira sat on a couch and stretched her arms behind her. They had beaten the odds. This battered and patched up freighter had brought them to safety.

She relaxed and drifted.

A voice whispered in her mind.

Arethon, Mira, we will open the way. We need more energy.

She bolted upright. It sounded as if someone were next to her yet she sat alone.

CHAPTER TEN

CHLOE Song winced as Franz Kramer slammed his fist into the metal barrier. The sound of the impact echoed off the rough-hewn walls of the tunnel.

"Frustrating isn't it, Mr Kramer?" she said. The young archaeologist sat on a packing crate under a light strip, typing rapid fire commands into her oversized datapad.

"What?" the overweight company executive snapped. His eyes were ringed with dark circles. His round face was gammon-pink with anger, fatigue and exhaustion. His hair and moustache were dirty grey, almost the same colour as the tunnel's walls. Kramer was a man used to working behind a desk, not at a drill head.

"When we are so close to a breakthrough, but unable to move forward," she said.

Chloe was an Outlander, born to parents of Korean descent. Like most graduates from her background she had to work twice as hard as her peers to progress her career. She was the expeditions intern. After a string of fill in jobs this was the first placement in her chosen field of astro-archaeology.

It was how the galaxy worked. Too many colony kids chasing too few corporate jobs and the access to the Core Systems that came with them. The system was harsh, but Chloe liked to think it rewarded those prepared to put in the effort.

She stood and stretched her long limbs. Her flawless olive skin and slight build made her look younger than her 23 years.

"It's how digs go," she said. "You make all of your progress in the first few weeks, then everything slows down when you get close to your objective. Look how quickly we got this far into the mountain. I think we got this tunnel dug quicker than it's taken the company to respond to our requests."

Kramer snorted.

Chloe handed him her datapad. A three-dimensional molecule spun on the screen.

"The key to success is what you do in the dead time," she said.

Kramer studied the screen.

"The sub-atomic structure of our wall," she said, doing her best not to sound smug.

"How did you do this?" Kramer spluttered. "We haven't been able to get so much as a sample of the material."

"It wasn't easy. I used a pair of atomic microscopes to scan through the wall at gradually increasing depths. From the data I wrote an app to identify the molecular joins. I gathered the data three days ago and have been working to decode it ever since."

Kramer rotated the pad back and forth. He activated projection mode and a representation of the molecule hovered in the air.

"It looks extremely complex. What is it?"

"An unusual alloy. It's a smart metal and has no human manufactured analogue. The material is a multi-bonded so you can't cut or drill through it with traditional equipment," Chloe explained.

"So any heavy equipment the company is sending will be useless?"

"I'm afraid so. I think there is a way we can do it; we'll need Zack's help." Zack was the team's engineering specialist. He was a dour and practical man from Alabama who specialised in drilling for minerals on asteroids. His ability to make impossible things happen was the reason the Lightfoot Development Corporation had hired him for this mission.

"He's back at base. You can brief me about your idea on the way."

Chloe packed her personal items in her backpack. She tucked her long black hair into her collar and pulled a red woollen beanie over her head. It was a kilometre walk to the tunnel entrance. The passage had a gradual slope. Kramer panted as they walked; his weight and the high gravity of LDC-132 conspired against him. Between laboured breaths he spoke. "How much are they paying you for this job?"

"Nothing. I'm interning and I'm grateful for the experience."

"Not any more," Kramer said. "You've come up with a better lead than the people I am paying. From now on you're on the payroll, grade one. It's not a fortune, but we'll talk again if we break through."

"Mr Kramer, I don't know what to say... thank you!"

Like most Outland graduates Chloe had accumulated a mountain of debt. The grade one salary would start to clear it. It would still take forever but a start was a start.

They stepped into the harsh dry air of LDC-132 and a fierce gusting wind blasted sand into their faces. It was dark and the sky overcast. In the distance the arc lights of the base camp lit the low cloud with a harsh electro-chemical glare.

They made a run for the giant Land Rover Universe parked on a rocky bluff above the earthworks. Chloe arrived first, opened the door and climbed in. Kramer clambered into the driver's seat and caught his breath. He started the motor and engaged the drive. He turned the six wheeled vehicle to the North and headed toward the camp. Chloe outlined her plan.

Chloe stood at the head of the briefing table in the command centre of the containerised base camp. The wind howled outside and sand scraped against the corrugated steel sides of the structure. Kramer had called the team together as soon as they had returned, leaving Chloe little time to prepare her presentation. While the other team members sat in their pristine overalls, Chloe delivered her briefing with grit in her hair and her clothes covered in red dust. Her analysis was met by a wall of aggressive silence from Peter Jarman, Saskia Hart and Zack McArdle. Franz Kramer stood in the corner of the room, drinking coffee from an aluminium mug.

Jarman was the first to speak, his tone condescending.

"So what you've discovered is the wall comprises an exceptionally tough material and we can't drill through it. I'm sorry Chloe, but that much we already know." Jarman was the team leader and worked on the principle of his way or no way. He swivelled in his chair to face Kramer. "What we need is a full team of diggers, all of whom Franz has sent packing."

Kramer sipped his coffee. Chloe focused her attention on her datapad, finding something of interest to investigate. There had been a growing animosity between the two men since Kramer arrived.

"Peter, they were dispatched to another site for reasons that go above your pay grade. It's not open for discussion. Miss Song's findings are," Kramer said, his voice amiable, his eyes anything but.

Saskia Hart intervened. She was a 45-year-old academic with a background in field archaeology and linguistics. She wore a headscarf that held her rusty brown hair out of her dark eyes.

"It is good work, Chloe," she said. "Especially as metallurgy is not your field. I have to agree with Peter. I don't see how it changes anything."

"This is the key to cutting through!" Chloe was exasperated. She had spent her last six weeks fetching and carrying for these arrogant fools, now she was offering them a breakthrough and they could not see it. She glanced at Kramer who gazed impassively at her. This was her battle.

"Look everyone, sorry, it's late and I should have made it clearer," she said. "The technique I used to scan the wall can cut into it."

Zack cleared his throat. He was scribbling on his datapad with a silver stylus.

"I see how we can use this," he said in deadpan southern drawl.

Jarman and Saskia swivelled in their chairs to face him. Zack activated the holo-projector and the contents of his pad filled the air above the table. He had sketched the molecule and converted it to a three-dimensional model; it rotated above the table. Four out of the eight internal bonds highlighted in red.

"The molecule is cross linked to its neighbours using these bonds. It's where the strength comes from," he explained, pointing to the highlighted bonds. "It's clever because of the balance. If you break a bond, another forms."

"Which is why you cannot cut it," Chloe said. "Whatever we cut reforms. It is an alloy capable of healing itself."

"Exactly, it's in a constant state of flux. We're wrong to think of it as a solid. It behaves more like liquid carbon," Zack said. "If we break these bonds simultaneously, we should be able to cut through using a conventional fusion lance."

He highlighted each set of linked bonds.

"How?" Jarman asked.

"We reverse the molecular scanners and use them to drive a charge into the wall at the correct frequency. We then apply a cutting tool. The bonds will be unstable and we can break them," Chloe answered. She liked Zack but was angry at how Jarman addressed the engineer over her.

"It won't be easy," Zack said. "But we can do it with equipment we have. The lance need not be powerful. This is fine work, Chloe, damn fine."

Kramer wandered over to the table and stood next to Chloe. She took it as a subtle display of support.

"How soon can you bring the equipment online, Zack?" he asked.

Zack frowned. He pushed his cap up and studied his hand-written notes.

"I have everything I need. It's just a matter of getting it prepped. Maybe four hours to lug everything up there and assemble the rig. The breakthrough time will depend on how thick the material is."

"It's 1000mm thick, plus or minus 10mm," Chloe said. "Sorry I should have mentioned it in my briefing."

"It'll be at least eight hours cutting through. It could take up to 48 hours to make the aperture wide enough for access," Zack said.

"Large enough to access with heavy equipment and to re-move large artefacts?" Jarman asked.

"I'd factored that in. My rig can auto cut an aperture up to six metres on each edge. The most we can cut out of the wall is three metres by four metres and I have calculated for that."

Chloe studied the faces in the room. Saskia shuffled papers while Jarman drummed his fingers and stared out the window. She couldn't understand why they were so angry; she'd handed them the breakthrough.

Company politics, she thought. She had made them look bad in front of a company vice president simply by doing what they could not.

Kramer put a hand on Chloe's shoulder. She shivered and did her best to conceal it. She did not dislike Kramer, but he was a company exec and she an intern. She was sure it was a simple act of support. It could, and probably would, be interpreted differently by the rest of the team.

"You've done well and you look tired. Get some sleep," Kramer said. "Zack, I want you to get started right away. I want to be back on site at first light."

Chloe wished them goodnight and made for the door, followed by Zack. The engineer held the door long enough for Chloe to exit, before letting the wind slam it closed behind them.

"Oh man, that was worth it," Zack was laughing. "Jarman's face was a fucking picture."

Chloe frowned. "I hope I've not just ruined my future. They're both senior members of the company."

"You have Kramer on your side. As long as you keep him sweet you'll be giving those corporate fucksticks orders inside a year." Still laughing, he strode off into the night, his frame silhouetted against the white glow of the camp's perimeter lights.

Chloe watched him go. The wind whipped her hair across her face. For a moment she thought she heard raised voices from inside the command block. She tried to dismiss the nagging feeling of unease as she trudged toward her tiny bunk room in the habitation block.

Nightwolf shook as she dropped out of FTL in the depths of interstellar space.

"Karl?" Rybov said. "This isn't Double T."

"Well observed, Snaggles, well observed," Manson replied. He lounged in the command chair on a raised platform on the ship's small flight deck. He had stripped off his armour. Skin ink and scars littered his organic arm and chest in a random pattern of art and damaged tissue.

"That transmission you were so worried about? Seems our client was glad I sent it. We have a change of plan; a *very* lucrative change of plan."

"So what are we doing in the middle of butt fuck nowhere?" KK asked from the doorway.

Manson was about to reply when Rybov snapped.

"Watch your mouth, KK."

Manson dismissed it with a wave of his hand.

"We are meeting with the client, or at least his envoy. You know, I think it's nice when a client comes to visit our workplace. It shows commitment, right KK?"

"If you say so, Boss," KK replied.

"I'm detecting three envelopes, Karl," Lyle reported.

Outside the forward view port two large vessels dropped out of hyperspace in flashes of white light.

"Two forward, one aft," Lyle reported. "Frontier Company vessels. They are opening a channel."

The sound of the transmission header came over the flight deck speakers before a voice cut through.

"*Nightwolf*, this is Admiral Gabriel Parker, FRONCO Vessel *Ariane*. Your prompt arrival is appreciated."

"We aim to please, Gabe," Manson replied. "I understand you have a package for me."

"Correct. I have a shuttle prepped to deliver the package. Is this acceptable?"

Manson agreed. He stood and pulled a shirt on.

"I trust there was no problem accommodating the additional costs this will incur?"

"Fifty percent of the additional fee will be transferred to your account once you take delivery. You will receive the rest on completion."

"I'll meet you in our hangar, Gabe." Manson closed the link. "Lyle, send him a vector. Snaggles, you and Foxy load up and follow me down."

Both mercs fell in behind their captain and followed him off the flight deck to the elevator. Foxhound was giving Rybov repeated sideways glances and the old man was getting increasingly irritated. Manson decided to see how far it would go. Sometimes a little infighting kept the boys sharp. It took a firm hand to make sure things did not get to out of hand.

They stepped into the elevator. As they descended Rybov grabbed Foxhound and slammed him against the wall. The younger merc tried to push back, but Rybov had him pinned.

"You got something to say you little shit? Just say it!" Rybov snarled through clenched teeth.

Before Manson could intervene Foxhound reached into Rybov's webbing, pulled out his sidearm and pushed it into the old man's stomach. This was shaping up to be an interesting scrap.

Manson let the two men stare at each other for a few more seconds.

"Knock it off *now!*" he said, calm authority colouring his tone. They glared at each other for a second longer before stepping back.

The elevator came to a stop; the atmosphere remained tense and toxic.

"Foxy, disappear. Vic you're with me." They stepped out of the elevator. Manson glanced back at Foxhound who stood in the centre of the elevator, staring Rybov down. The door slid closed.

"So what was that about, Vic?"

"He's been getting out of line, won't follow orders and doesn't like being pulled up for it. He's a cruel little fuck and a bad fit for this crew."

Manson studied Rybov for a moment.

"You think he was out of line with the girl? That was my idea, remember that."

"He's unprofessional. You told him to clean up, he left it to me. I ain't his bitch," Rybov spat the words out.

Manson laughed.

"You're pissed because you lost face when that girl shocked you cold and Foxy is needling you about it. Fuck me Vic, suck it up and move on."

Foxhound reminded Manson of a younger version of himself. The young man had cocky swagger and couldn't care less attitude that would take him far. Victor Rybov was experienced and fearless but was getting soft in his old age. Something would need to be done. Maybe it was time the old boy retired.

When they arrived at the hangar's airlock the green pressurisation light was already on. Rybov punched the release and opened the door. Manson strode in. Rybov trailed behind.

A Mantis class shuttle in Frontier Company livery rested on the pad. At the foot of the access ramp stood a uniformed officer flanked by a pair of armoured Shock Troops. Between them sat a transit case.

Manson approached and stretched his arms in a welcoming gesture.

"Admiral Parker, Gabe, welcome. I'm sorry our little ship

lacks the grandeur of your own, but she does a job."

"Mr Manson," Parker acknowledged. He offered his hand. Manson took it, squeezing hard.

"The package is in the case. You will also find a data card containing the target details."

"May I?" Manson asked, gesturing to the transit case.

One of the Shock Troopers entered a combination and snapped open the latches. He stepped back to give Manson an uninhibited view.

Inside was a chrome sphere, 400 mm in diameter. Around the centre line ran a ring of indicator lights.

"You are familiar with the operation of a Mass Sink?"

Mass Sinks were weapons capable of opening a point of singularity which would collapse the surrounding space on itself. These intricate and expensive weapons were designed for use against large targets such as stations, planets or even stars. They had been outlawed over 100 years ago.

"The bigger the object you trigger it in, the bigger the bang," Manson said.

"Correct, Mr Manson. To gain full effect a sub-surface blast will be required. The geography of the target makes it relatively easy. Our intelligence shows the Lightfoot team are close to breaking into the subsurface chamber. This will be your easiest route in," Parker said. "We have provided you with an alternate location should it be necessary. We have a contact on the surface and I have given them your contact details; they will advise further."

"What about configuration? Is this thing primed?"

"You have full and remote timing options. We only have one so no mistakes."

Manson's anger flared. He didn't take orders from Frontier Officers. He checked himself.

"There will not be any mistakes, Gabe. Make sure your boss is ready with my other fifty percent." His tone was ice. After an uncomfortable pause Manson smirked. "Trust me, we're professionals."

Gabriel Parker responded with a curt nod and boarded his ship. Manson and Rybov lifted the crate and carried it out of the hangar.

"So what's the target, Karl?" Rybov asked.

Manson's mood lifted as he watched the preppy Frontier Admiral board his shuttle.

"Ever been to the Cygnus Vale, Vic?"

Rybov shook his head.

"Well, that's where we're going. Damien Lightfoot's portfolio is about to take a knock."

Vanessa Meyer strode into the Vice President's office, ignoring his secretary and the pair of Homeworld Security officers guarding the door. She had arrived on Luna three hours earlier. This was her first port of call after she booked into the Tranquillity Hotel.

Daniel Santiago looked up from his paperwork with a surprised expression on his face.

"Vanessa!" he said. "It's always good to see you, but a little notice would be helpful."

Santiago's smile was as genuine as his surprise, his polished teeth starkly contrasting with his copper skin and bushy black moustache.

"Dan, save me the bull. You know why I am here." She rounded on his staff. "You lot, get lost. What I have to say is not for your ears."

Santiago gestured to a round conference table on the other side of the room and stood. Santiago was short and of stocky build. His brown eyes were bordered by thick eyebrows and ill disciplined black hair. He was showing the earliest signs of grey at his temples.

"Shall we?"

Meyer strode to the table and pulled out a chair. She sat.

"The shuttle bomb, you know it was meant for me don't you? And like me you probably have a good idea of who planted it." She placed her hands on the edge of the table and tried regain control. Santiago walked to his drinks cabinet and poured two large glasses of Bourbon.

Sitting, he pushed one across the table to Meyer. She caught the crystal glass and fixed the Vice President with a stare as cold as the ice in the whiskey.

"We know it was meant for somebody on that flight and we have taken precautions to ensure the safety of all government personnel. Many groups have claimed responsibility: *Earth First*, *Martian Dawn*. I am sure if you give it enough time my mother's sewing circle will throw their hat in. Events like this bring out every nut job in the Core Systems."

"That's bullshit and you know it. The day I vote against a motion key to corporate interests the spaceplane I am booked to fly out on has an accident?"

Santiago shuffled, his posture was hunched, his movements taut.

"Vanessa, we've known each other a long time and I owe my position to you. Trust me, we are working on this. The Corporations are capable of many things but the assassination of a senator?" He sipped his drink. "I doubt they would be so bold."

Meyer studied Santiago and wondered what had happened to the radical, fire breathing politician. The man who had rejuvenated the city of Buenos Aires after the riots of 2343. The man who had become Argentina's President and then director of the Pan American Trading Block. His term as vice president in the coalition had been disappointing, lacklustre and self serving.

"What do you make of David Conway?" she asked.

Santiago frowned.

"David? He is ambitious and well connected. He is tipped for the Presidency in two years time. Surely you don't suspect him of involvement?" Santiago laughed, halting as Meyer continued to stare at him.

"What about his connections to Regina? You know he is in their pocket?" she said.

"You need to be careful with accusations like that. Like I said, Conway is well connected."

"You don't deny it then?"

"Almost every member of the Senate has connections to one or other of the MegaCorps. Running for office does not come cheap. I won't deny it, questions have been asked about his relationship with Regina and The Frontier Company."

Meyer was making progress. She sipped the bourbon, not caring for its sticky sweet taste.

"Daniel, I want you to put him under surveillance, do some digging. He is connected to the attempt on my life and a lot more."

"You have evidence?"

"No, but I would not be asking if I doubted he posed a threat to the Federation."

Santiago fidgeted. "I can't help you with this, Vanessa. I cannot use government assets to spy on the Commissioner of the Board of Trade. It's not ethical, and it's illegal. I am sorry, my hands are tied."

Meyer drained her glass. "I see. At least I know where I stand."

Santiago had never been afraid to break rules. His career had been built on gambles and brinkmanship. Now he was in a position where he had more to lose than to gain. A man so close to the top was always under threat; taking the safe choice was the surest tool way to ensure survival.

They sat in silence. Meyer stood and pushed the chair back.

"Thank you for the drink," she said. "If you'll excuse me I need to go to my hotel. I have an early flight to the Frontier."

Santiago stood.

"Vanessa," he said. Meyer could sense something in his voice.

"There are forces at work here that go beyond EarthGov and the Senate..." He paused and licked his lips. "I have my own issues to contend with. I suspect there are moves being made to destabilise this office."

"Daniel?" She studied his face. Nervous fear danced in his eyes. He had a slight tick that was always noticeable when under pressure.

"Please don't worry. I have people on it... I will do what I can. Please trust me and do be careful what you say." Santiago wrung his hands as he spoke.

His manner changed abruptly as if he had forgotten himself or spoken out of turn.

They said their goodbyes.

Meyer walked into the lobby. Ben was waiting for her. She took his arm and directed him toward the double doors. When she opened them an old man was waiting to enter. His dress style was unconventional. In one hand he carried a cane. He gave Meyer a peculiar smile as he ushered her past. She shivered and quickened her pace, unsure of why the stranger had unnerved her.

"I have seen that man before," Ben said as they moved

through the ornate gardens. "He is often in the Senate building... with Commissioner Conway."

There was a familiarity about the stranger, yet Meyer could not recall seeing him before. Then again she saw scores of different faces every day. She struggled to remember even the most recent.

She slipped into her own thoughts. The dome lights were glowing into life as The Moon slipped into darkness.

"Ben," she said. "The Office of the Vice President is compromised."

"He's on their payroll?" Ben asked, his voice an incredulous whisper.

Meyer shook her head.

"No, it's more subtle. I think Conway has something on him. Maybe that man has something to do with this."

"So what now?"

"Time to explore other avenues, less official ones," she said. "Conway does not play by rules, so why should we? I have a plan. It could be career ending so I wouldn't blame you if you wanted to go home."

"Of course not. I trust your judgement, Senator."

Meyer stopped and breathed in the night air. It was artificial, but Armstrong was a green city and the smell of blossom coloured the Nitrogen-Oxygen mixture.

"Thank you, Ben. Let's go back to the hotel. I will need you to arrange transport for us," she said.

Ben agreed. He reminded her so much of a young Daniel Santiago and she knew her aide would one day make her proud. Just as the Vice President once had. She could not help but wonder what had happened to Santiago since he became part of the government machine.

CHAPTER ELEVEN

THE outer hatch slid into the hull with a clang. Alex hit the controls for the access gantry and it extended outward to a steel platform running around the hangar. The ship rested on a pad in the smallest bay Mira had ever seen. The air was cold. She zipped her jacket to the top and buried her head into the collar.

"You don't get much for your money, do you?" Barnes observed.

"Don't knock it. We have a bay and, judging by the number of ships outside, I think it's a good result," Mira said. "Fuck me, it's cold."

"That stateroom has softened you up, Thorny," Alex smirked.

"Yeah whatever. Go do your job, Kite," she replied. "And don't call me Thorny again."

Alex waved and jogged across the gantry with Barnes.

Mira silently said goodbye as they left.

"Alex!" she called after them. "This station has quite a reputation; try not to make it four times, okay?" She laughed as he blushed and continued on.

"What was that about?" Ethan asked.

"Just a private joke, Ethan," she replied. "Come on let's check this bitch over before I freeze my tits off." Her teeth chattered as she spoke.

As they approached the stern, the extent of the damage became clear. Sublight three had been torn away by the force of their hyperspatial exit, leaving a gaping hole and a mass of torn metal in its place. The mounting brackets had sheered, allowing the entire engine to tear free.

"I suspect that's what caused the fire," Ethan said. "The reservoir would have ruptured and dumped the residual plasma into the ship. We were lucky."

Mira had walked through the lower deck corridor and surveyed the devastation. Like Barnes, she struggled to believe the repair had held. She stopped short of entering the hold, happy to avoid the Ark for as long as she could.

"If you think that's bad you will love this," Tate said from the far side of the hull. Mira trudged to where he was standing. The sound of her boots on the metal deck echoed around the hangar.

The hull sheeting on the starboard side of the ship had ripped and torn away from the stern quadrant. The inner pressure hull was exposed. Yellow warts of sealant sprouted from around the steel where the auto repair system had patched small punctures.

"We're lucky the pressure hull didn't breach. She can't jump like that; she'll be torn apart," Ethan said

"She's dead," Mira said. Part of her was relieved. It supported her decision to send the crew off on another vessel.

After mouthing the words *thank you* to the ship, she turned to Ethan.

"In case I don't get a chance, I wanted to give you this." She handed him a small data card.

"I promised you a referral to the Academy. Rich has seconded it. I hope you don't mind but I referred you under a battlefield commission with an extra help requirement. They'll give you all the support you need."

"Mira, I don't know what to say. Thank you."

"You earned it, Ethan." She pointed at the broken ship. "That would not be here if it were not for you." She blinked and tried to hold it together. "I need you to do one more thing for me."

"Sure."

"Wipe the flight logs with a deep format."

"Of course."

He was about to go back to the airlock. He paused, waiting for her to follow.

"Go ahead, Ethan. I have things I need to take care of on the station. I'll see you soon." Mira hated lying to him but she did not want to burden him with the truth.

She watched as he disappeared into the hull. Despite the cold, she was sweating. A deep shiver ran through her. Finding medication was her priority. Once she had, she would consider the best way to catch the attention of Xander Rhodes.

Alex Kite stood in line at the currency bureau and tightened his grip on the case. He was grateful for the chain fixing it to his wrist. He felt as if everyone was scrutinising him and weighing his worth.

If they only knew how much is in this case... he thought.

Barnes appeared through the crowd, carrying a pair of disposable beakers. He gave one to Alex and popped the lid off his own.

Alex inhaled the coffee's aroma, enjoying the rich roast. The taste delivered on the promise of the smell; it was hot, sweet and just what he needed.

"That's not all." Barnes produced an orange from his pocket.

"When was the last time you had fruit?" Barnes tucked his cup into the crook of his arm and peeled the orange. He gave half to Alex.

"My credit disk took a hammering to get that, so enjoy." Barnes smiled as juice ran down his chin.

Alex took stock of his surroundings and chewed on the fruit. It was small and watery, indicating it was hydroponically grown. It did not matter; it had a sweetness he had not tasted in months.

"Where do you suppose all these people have come from?" he asked. "I came through here a few years back and there was nothing like this population."

"I asked the coffee shop guy," Barnes said. "Most of these people are from the Outer Frontier. There is talk of colonies going dark out there."

"MegaCorps? Pirates?"

Barnes shrugged. "No one knows for certain. There are plenty of strange tales about weird alien ships. Some are blaming the Verani," Barnes said. "C'mon man, you're next." He gestured toward a vacant cashier's window.

The transaction was simple. Alex exchanged four bars of gold for 150,000 credits loaded onto an untraceable disk. The cashier did not react at the amount nor the Navy stamp on the bullion. The rate of exchange reflected the no questions, no paperwork service.

They pushed their way through the crowd and located a station admin office. A woman with purple hair and nails sat behind a scruffy steel desk. She was browsing the station's bulletin boards on a battered terminal.

"I want to pay our docking fees," Alex said.

The woman didn't look up.

"Bay 32," he added.

The woman closed her BB app and swapped to a different screen. She tapped in the bay number.

"30,000 for a week," she said.

"Steep. Do I get a discount for early payment?" Alex asked.

"Space is a premium here," she replied. "In case you hadn't noticed."

Alex handed over the credit disk. The woman inserted it into a reader and processed the transaction.

"You know, if you have free cargo space you can always ship some of that lot to the Core Systems; you'll make your fees back and turn an easy profit. You will be doing the station a favour."

"How so?" Barnes asked. "Surely more people coming through means more trade?"

The woman snorted.

"The ones with money leave; those without stay. They're a drain on our resources. We can't cope with this many people. Rhodes is playing a dangerous game letting them come here."

"I guess they must come here for a good reason. From what I hear colonies are being attacked," Alex said.

"That's what they say. I guess they've just found out life on the Frontier isn't what they thought it would be. They're just fucking freeloaders looking for an easy life."

Alex thanked the woman and they left.

"Nice attitude," Barnes said, shaking his head in disgust. "We should check out the departure schedules, find out who is going where."

They walked into the Medina. Tarantella assaulted Alex's senses with a cacophony of voices speaking in every human tongue. Hawkers shouted and buyers haggled. Trade was conducted beneath garish neon signs that flickered and buzzed above every shop and market stall. The sights and sounds were overlaid by the stink of humanity and the aromas of street food.

Alex was drawn into this chaotic, potent mix of noise and smells.

Something was bugging him. "Sergeant, I need to ask you something."

Barnes nodded.

"Thorny said something about being involved with an Admiral's daughter. It was Amy Flynt wasn't it?"

"It was. She was planning to fold her commission and start a new life. When Amy died Mira signed on with the *Berlin*."

Alex ran a finger over the stubble on his chin. "I thought she was just fucked up because of the war. I did not know she was coping with that too."

"Alex, Mira was never fucked up. She was lost and trying to find her way home." He paused for moment, as if searching for the right words. "Thing is, this last few days have brought her back to us. She's becoming the Mira I met a long time ago, maybe a little older and a lot wiser."

Alex had seen it too. Losing the ship had changed them all. The reclusive, timid and unpredictable Thorn had been replaced by a confident officer and one hell of a pilot. Alex admired how she had brought the ship in once she stopped hooning it. He wondered if that Thorn had been there all the time and he had been too much of an arsehole to give her a chance.

"She isn't coming with us," he blurted out.

"What?"

"Mira, she wants to take that Ark thing to Arethon."

Barnes stared at him in disbelief.

A hand tightened on Alex's shoulder.

"Take it easy, man," a voice said from behind him.

Two men in tan station security uniforms appeared either side of the sergeant's shoulders. One jabbed a laser weapon into Barnes' ribs

"Come with us gentlemen. Please don't make a scene," the man holding Alex said. Alex nodded to Barnes, and they allowed themselves to be led through the crowd to a transport tube.

"Where are you taking us?" Alex asked.

"Sorry, they don't tell me any more than they need to. Stay calm and everything will be fine."

The man hit the call button and the capsule arrived after a few seconds. Alex glanced at Barnes, who winked.

The sergeant swivelled and drove his shoulder into the first of his captors, knocking him to the floor.

Alex grabbed the man holding him between the legs. He squeezed hard. The man bent over in a spray of saliva, a high-pitched scream spilling from his throat. Alex brought his knee up and drove it into the man's nose. It made a soft crack. Barnes had floored his second captor, the first was rising to his feet, a shock stick in his hand.

"Rich!" Alex cried. Barnes swivelled and grabbed the weapon beneath the charged end, he wrestled it from the guard's grasp. With a fluid motion he tossed the baton to his other hand and drove it into the guard's chest. The man shook, fell to his knees and then to the deck. A dark wet stain spread from his groin.

"Hold it!" another voice shouted.

Alex whirled to see a fourth man holding a laser rifle; the business end was pointed at them. The man was muscular. Unlike the others he was not wearing a uniform. Instead was dressed in a simple white t-shirt over a pair of olive combat pants. His close cropped hair showed the earliest signs of grey.

"Gunny Barnes, as I live and breathe," the man said lowering his weapon.

"Martinez? Man, it's been like forever."

Martinez stepped forward, and they embraced in a giant man hug.

Events moved quickly and Alex struggled to make sense of their situation.

"Once the bromance is done could someone explain what just happened?" he asked.

"Alex, this is Juan Pablo Martinez. He's a marine."

"Former marine," Martinez said.

"No such thing JP. Once a marine, always a marine. This is Alex Kite. He's a fleet-brat, but he's okay."

Alex scowled.

"I'm sorry about this." Martinez pointed at the groaning men picking themselves off the floor and limping away to lick their wounds. "Out here I spend half my time dealing with fuckwittery of the highest order." He shouldered his weapon and watched the station security men leave.

"Listen Gunny, I was sent to collect you. My boss wants to talk to you guys. Those goons work for the Trade Guild. I don't know what they were playing at."

"Your boss?"

"Yeah, come on I'll fill you in on the way."

"What about the rest of us?"

"They are probably sipping cocktails at the top of the station. It took a while to locate you. As soon as I heard two newbies had changed a lot of gold, I knew where to look."

Alex glanced uncertainly at Barnes, unsure if he should trust the newcomer.

"It's cool, Alex. I trust him."

Martinez led them to the transport tube and entered a security code. The pod sped toward the upper levels of the station.

A voice crackled in the girl's earpiece.

"Tish, are you reading me?"

"Yeah."

"Where are you? Do you have eyes on the target?"

"In the Medina, Level 4 and yes. Now shut up and leave it to me, okay?"

She closed the link and walked through the crowd. It parted as she moved silently and purposefully. Traders and shoppers stopped to stare at the tall, lean figure in glossy black armour striding through the masses. The locals, used to such sights, looked but saw nothing.

Tish had followed her target from Bay 32. She was distinctive, black haired and wearing an eyepatch; a peculiarity in a galaxy where cybernetic implants were the norm.

The woman appeared sick. She meandered through the Medina, lost and nervous. Tish wondered if she should intervene sooner rather than later. The quicker the woman made it to the transportation tubes the cleaner this would be.

She spotted movement out of the corner of her eye. Something was wrong.

A pair of station security operatives pushed their way through the crowd. After a quick appraisal Tish decided they were heading for the same target.

Sprinting through the crowd, Tish grabbed the woman and dragged her toward a transport tube.

"What the fuck?" the woman screamed.

The woman tensed and threw her weight in the opposite direction trying to break free. Her single eye stared at her, full of defiance. Tish knew the look; the woman was preparing to run or fight. Micro calculations were being run through her mind quicker than her green eye could blink.

"Come with me. I am here to help. I don't want to stun you,"

Tish said. Her voice was distorted by the helmet speaker. Even to her it sounded harsh and intimidating. It was supposed to subdue a target but this time it had the opposite effect. The woman shoved Tish in the chest with all her weight. The movement so sudden it caught her off guard. She staggered. When she regained her footing, the woman was sprinting away.

Tish spun around, the security operatives were upon her. She pulled out a stun baton and drove it into the closest man's shoulder. He shook and fell to the floor. The second, realising what had happened, took a step out of range and keyed his com-link. Tish whirled on the spot, her sleek leather boot connecting with the side of his head. He fell unconscious to the floor alongside his colleague.

Tish dropped to her knees and paused to regain her balance before leaping to her feet.

"Sorry fellas," she said as she ran after her target.

Mira ran. She had not seen where the woman in armour had come from but knew she was in trouble. She had an uncomfortable sense she was being followed since she entered the Medina district.

She thought she was just being paranoid. Alex's advice on abduction had spooked her and she told herself she was jumping at shadows. Her fears were confirmed when she spotted the security operatives tailing her; it was then the woman in body armour had stepped out the crowd.

Mira ran on, pushing her way through the throng. Her vision blurred as her eye streamed and her monocular view made it hard to judge distances. She rounded a corner. Her lungs were burning and her energy falling away. She slowed her pace, hoping she had done enough to elude her assailant.

Mira stopped and glanced behind her. She saw no sign of

the security team nor the armoured woman.

What was she? A bounty hunter? A member of a crime syndicate... What the hell was I thinking...

She ducked into the doorway of a boarded up shop. The stench of rotting food and urine was overpowering. She rested her hands on her knees and breathed. Infection coursed through her bloodstream and her strength was failing. She fought back the need to vomit.

"Mira Thorn?" the distorted voice of the armoured figure barked.

The woman in body armour stood at the mouth of the alcove.

"Please, I am here to help you. Don't run, I can't help you if you run." The woman held up her hands, showing them to be empty.

"How do you know my name?"

"It's a long story. There are people on this station who wish you ill; I am not one. You look sick. Do you need a doctor?"

Mira thought about lying. "I need anti-infection meds. I have a wound that's gone bad." She slurred as she spoke.

The woman removed her helmet. She was young, her skin station-dweller pale with a faint line of freckles splashed over the bridge of her nose. Her eyes were deep blue, almost unnatural in their hue. Most striking of all was the river of flame-red hair that flowed from under her helmet.

"I'm Tish. You have questions and I'll answer the ones I can. First, I will get you some help." The girl flicked her hair clear of her face and keyed her com-link.

"It's me. I have met a friend. She needs medical attention so I am taking her to Norm's."

There was a pause while she listened to the reply.

"No... No, it's fine. It's not serious... No it's unnecessary..."

she said. "Look, it's just a girl thing. Okay?"

Tish closed the link. A smile warmed the girls face. "That will keep him off our backs for a while."

"If you are here to help, what's with the whole cyber-ninja thing?" Mira pointed at the armour. "It's not what I would call welcoming."

"Xander insisted, he's a little over protective."

"Rhodes?"

"The one and only, as he likes to remind us. Can you walk on your own?"

Mira smiled weakly and pushed herself off the wall. She swayed, and the world blurred in and out of focus.

Tish moved forward and grabbed her around the waist. Mira was impressed by the speed of the girl's reactions and her strength.

"I thought not. Come on, it's not far. I'll get you sorted and afterwards we'll give you some answers."

The doctor, a bald man in his fifties, finished stitching and redressing Mira's wounds. The inflammation was still present, but the lividity had faded. Like the infection, Mira's fever and the constant nausea had abated. The medication the doctor administered was fast acting. Mira estimated it was an hour since he gave her the shots of blue tinted serum.

"I'm feeling good," she said.

"You won't get biotics that strong in the Core Systems," the doctor said. He was talkative and enthusiastic about his work. "They are unlicensed and they are extremely effective."

"Are they safe?" Mira asked.

"Totally fine. They are unlicensed because they work. The corporations don't like it. They make their money out of repeat customers."

Mira had read that theory on UniNet.

Tish watched from the corner of the room. She had stripped out of her body armour and wore a pair of impossibly tight synth-leather lace up jeans with a matching vest top. A pendant in the shape of a silver sword hung around her neck. Mira was transfixed and hoped the girl had not noticed. Tish was taller than Mira. She leant against the bulkhead in a way that combined with her outfit to accentuate the gentle curves of her toned body.

The doctor gave Mira a strip of pills before heading for the door.

"Two every eight hours for three days. If anyone asks you did not get them from me."

He winked and wished her good luck as he left the treatment room. Mira heard him cheerfully greet his next patient.

"Thanks Norm," Tish said. She pointed to the dressings on Mira's arm.

"Did you do that yourself?"

"I don't see what that has to do with you," Mira snapped. Guilt stabbed her in the gut. It wasn't this girl's fault. She was about to apologise when Tish smiled, her blue eyes alive under the treatment room's bright lights.

"It's okay. I understand." She walked to Mira and revealed her forearms. They were covered in small faded scars. "Before I came here, my life was shitty."

"I'm sorry... Tish. Yeah I did it. I thought I was getting better..."

"Sometimes you need to bleed?" Tish reached out and put her hand Mira's shoulder. "I understand."

She gave Mira a glass of water. "Are up to walking?"

Mira's strength was returning, so was the headache.

"Yes."

"We can catch a transport tube to the upper levels when you're ready. You look a lot better now. I am so glad you didn't puke. I hate puke."

Mira laughed and slid off the bed. She winced at a twinge of pain in her back.

Tish took her hand. Mira hesitated.

"Everyone needs someone to hold their hand sometimes," Tish said. "Come on. I'll take you topside."

They walked through Norm's waiting area and into the Medina.

Tish was right. In a place as strange as Tarantella, it felt good to have a hand to hold.

They arrived on the upper levels after a short tube journey. Tish was a pleasant travelling companion. There was something about the girl's easy going nature that drew Mira in. Tish was at ease with herself in a way Mira always wanted to be.

"So, who were the goons following me?"

"Station security. They work for the Trade Guild. We noticed a spike in the internal comms traffic as soon as Xander authorised the bay."

"Why? What is their interest in the Kobo?"

"They have been causing us problems for a while. Their interest in your ship caught us by surprise. We secured the hangar with our people when we found out. Xander thinks one of MegaCorps may want the ship and requested the Trade Guild intervene."

"Are we safe?" Mira asked. Her stomach flipped. She knew what was in the ship; she had sensed its power. It was an asset a corporation would go to great lengths to acquire.

"You and your ship are safe," Tish replied. "You are under Xander's protection and that counts for a lot out here."

Mira stopped.

"What about my crew?" She had not given them a second thought since she left the hangar.

Tish squeezed her hand. "They are fine. We picked up two in the Medina and the other two on the ship. Don't worry Mira, you can trust us. We may be pirates, but we're honest."

For a second Mira locked eyes with Tish. She glanced away as the carriage came to a halt.

They stepped out of the pod and Mira followed Tish into the corridor. Dim red lighting reflected off alloy walls in the narrow passage.

"Where are we?" Mira asked.

"The upper levels; Xander's quarters."

An ornate spiral staircase led upward. Tish led the way and Mira emerged into a second corridor. Her boots sank into deep black carpet. The steel walls were hidden behind silk drapes. Tish led her into a circular room at the far end of the passage.

They were in a tower on the upper surface of the asteroid. The room was dark, illuminated by directed spotlights and starlight. A wall of glass ran around the perimeter. Mira released Tish's hand and walked toward it. Her eye widened as she drank in the view.

"It's beautiful isn't it?" Tish said.

She was right. It was breathtaking. The silver accretion disk was punctuated with dark spokes of dust. The underside was occasionally illuminated by energetic discharges. The disk stretched as far as Mira could see. In the distance the dwarf star shone like a diamond in a silver ring. It reminded Mira of the view from the long decommissioned Saturn Orbital Station. This ring dwarfed the Saturnian micro system by multiple orders of magnitude.

"We depend on the belt for water and mineral supplies. The system may not be economic for the MegaCorps, but it gives us what we need."

"You are self sufficient?" Mira asked.

"We have levels devoted to agriculture. Our water comes from the belt and mineral refining is a given. We still import a few products; but it's a lot less than you would expect."

"Mira Thorn," Xander Rhodes said from behind her. Mira could not be sure if he had been in the room when they entered. He was tall and narrow-faced. His long blond hair was loose; a bandanna kept it out of his face. He wore a simple black silk shirt over a pair of synth-leather jeans. His beard was tidy and trimmed to a point. It was a shade darker than his hair. He looked nothing like the mugshots the Navy had on file.

"Welcome to our station. Come, join me." He gestured to a semi circular couch. A low table had been laid with finger foods. Mira looked at him and slowly walked over. He handed her a large glass of wine and motioned for her to sit. Her stomach growled at the sight of the food. She could not remember when she had last eaten.

"I take it all is well now? Are you feeling better?" he asked.

"Yes, thank you." She glanced at Tish, who responded with a gentle smile.

He offered a plate of sandwiches. She took one and ate quickly.

"Where are my friends?" she asked through a mouthful of food.

"I set them up with accommodation," he said. "It turns out your Sergeant Barnes is an old pal of one my guys. The charming Doctor Garret and Private Tate were also cooperative." He grinned at Tish. "From what I hear you gave Tish quite the runaround."

"I told you the body armour was a dumb idea, Rhodes," Tish said. She slipped onto the chair next to Mira and helped herself to some wine. She took a sip and gazed at Mira over the rim of the glass.

"It's made on the station," she said. "We grow the grapes in hydroponics and the water comes from the belt."

Mira raised her glass. The wine was ice cold, sharp, but not unpleasant.

"I owe you my gratitude. I thought we had lost that ship," Xander said.

"So what's your interest in it?"

"I guess I owe you that. Some of what I am going to tell you will sound far fetched."

Compared to my experiences with the Ark? Mira thought. *I find that a little hard to believe.*

"The Kobo you arrived on was busted out of Tellerman by one of my people. It was on a layover for refuelling before proceeding to Mizarma," he said. "My operative programmed the ship to fly here on autopilot. We were planning to intercept it at the edge of the system, take what we wanted and send the ship back to Lightfoot."

He paused as if waiting for Mira to reply when she didn't he continued.

"That was our plan until Eden Holzman and her crew intercepted the vessel. They operate out of an agri-colony in the region you encountered it."

"We thought it was you who intercepted the vessel," Mira said, thinking back to her initial survey of the damaged ship. It seemed like a lifetime ago.

A shadow crossed Xander's face.

"Eden was one of the best... she was one of us, but she decided her future lay on a different path. We went out separate ways a few years back."

He blinked twice as if the mention of Eden's name meant

something.

"Everything worked out though. You found the ship, and it led you here," Xander said. "It was quite an achievement. That ship is a mess."

He had so far avoided the big bucks question.

"So what do you want with the Ark?" Mira asked.

She noticed a look pass between Tish and Xander.

"You know what it is?" Xander said, his grin frozen in place.

Mira responded with a slow nod.

"How?"

"I had some kind of interaction with it. It called itself an Ark."

Xander slapped his thigh. "Now that is unexpected!" he said. "We know a little about it but we thought communicating with it would be tricky."

"It started the interaction. It was a stream of images and sensations at first, words came later. I felt like it was manipulating me, initially anyway."

Mira struggled for words. It was difficult to explain without a common reference point.

"No that's not right. It was as if it were... getting to know me and learning how it could communicate."

"Tell me about what it shared with you; leave nothing out," he said, his eyes taking on an excited zeal.

Mira told him of the dream, the vision, the voices she had heard. Something else occurred to her.

"I feel better when I am close to it. I have a lot of old injuries, a lot of pain. When I interacted with it, the pain went away. When I left the ship it came back." She rolled her shoulder; it clicked and a lightning bolt of pain shot down her left side.

Xander sat in silence. He stoked his beard. "For the past

eight years I have been dealing with the Verani Government, primarily the Political Caste. They have, sorry had, a representative on the station. It was he who told me of the Ark and suggested I acquire it."

It took a moment for the statement to sink in.

"Wait, you have contacts in the Dominion? EarthGov has no official ties with them. Why you?"

"All in good time. Let's worry about the Ark for now," Xander said.

He placed his glass on the table. "How familiar are you with the *Verani Creed*?" he asked.

The Creed was a standard reading requirement for naval officers. Like most religious texts Mira found it ponderous and full of inconsistencies. Like almost every cadet she had skimmed over it.

"I've read it. I always thought it was bollocks. What has it got to do with the Ark?"

"I can only tell you what we learned from the few translations of the text we have and the information our contact shared with us," Xander replied.

It appeared to Mira as if Xander was gathering his thoughts as a parent would before explaining a difficult concept to a child.

"The Creed tells of a great war fought by *Those Who Came First*."

Mira was familiar with the three pillars of the creed: *Those Who Came First, Those Who Were Left and Those Who Came After*. The Verani considered themselves to be *Those Who Came After,* the chosen heirs to an ancient legacy of knowledge and technology. Earth scholars interpreted the text differently believing *Those Who Came After* referred to all sentient life in the galaxy. No one had any clear idea who *Those Who Were*

Left were. Most assumed it was the remnants of the combatants and possibly the authors of the Creed.

"Our Verani contact referred to that object as an Ark, as you do. He believes it houses the consciousness of a people called the Pharn. Their homeworld is in the Cygnus Vale; they call it Arethon."

The realisation that what she had seen had happened and the voice in her head had been real was almost impossible to process.

"I saw the end of everything," she whispered.

Tish refilled Mira's glass. Her hand lingered on Mira's thigh. A tingle ran through her. Tish smiled as Mira glanced in her direction.

Xander steepled his fingers lost in his thoughts.

"The Pharn were once flesh and blood like us. Somewhere along the line they transcended into a post physical state. The Verani talk of these Arks as repositories of consciousness. They are scattered throughout the Vale and beyond. Lightfoot acquired that object a while ago, from sources unknown. It must have reached out to you for a reason."

"They want to go home," Mira said, remembering the feeling of empty longing, the intense home sickness.

"If they want to return home, I can only assume that they somehow have a presence on Arethon or some way of reconnecting with their kin. This will be important to the Verani, which means it's important for humans too."

Xander shook his head and gave a dry laugh. "There is only one problem with returning them to Arethon... No one knows where it is."

They lapsed into silence

"It has communicated with me. Perhaps we can instigate a communication with it. The Ark could guide us? It has the ability to absorb and use electrical energy. It nearly killed the Kobo by syphoning the reactor. There is something else..." She paused. "Before I left the ship a voice said *We need energy.*" She shuddered at the memory of the inhuman voice whispering in her ear.

Xander made no reply.

"I want to see this through, Xander... I have to. All I ask is for you to get my crew home."

Xander snapped out of his reverie.

"That's easy. Aussie Jon is on his way here."

"Jon! How?"

"Me and Jon have an understanding. He assumed this would be your destination and called me. That's how we knew who you were." He stood. "I need consider the options. Working with the Verani is like walking a tightrope. We could upset them by taking the Ark back to the Vale. We could upset them if we don't."

He excused himself with a slight bow. He was about to leave when he stopped in the doorway.

"Tish, why don't you take our guest to the hangar? Show her what we've been doing out here."

Tish stood and offered Mira her hand. Mira accepted and allowed Tish to pull her upright. She stumbled into her and stood for a few awkward seconds.

"Come with me. I have something that will blow your mind," Tish whispered.

"More than being communicated with by ancient post physical beings in the hold of an unmanned freighter?" Mira laughed at how absurd it sounded.

"Wait and see."

Tish activated the elevator door with a key card and ushered Mira inside. She tapped in a code and it descended.

Mira could not help but stare at Tish. The pirate girl picked up on her gaze and responded with a flick of her hair.

She wondered about Tish's alignment.

It's been a while since you saw someone in those terms, Thorn, she reflected. *And now is not the time,* she reminded herself.

Awkwardness forced her to break the silence.

"So what is the connection between Xander and Jon?" Mira asked.

"They've known each other for a while, six or seven years. They were on the Verani homeworld at the same time."

Mira knew Flynt had been part of an exchange program during a time when relations between the Federation and the Verani Dominion had been better. She did not know he had visited their homeworld; as far as Mira could remember the people who had could be counted on the fingers of one hand. Jon Flynt had never mentioned it. She wondered what other secrets he might be hiding.

"What was Xander doing there?"

"He's been on good terms with them for a long time. We found a starship with some cryogenically frozen clerics on board. It had no power and had drifted through the buffer zone. We picked them up and took them home. They've treated him as one of their own ever since."

This was all news to Mira. Navy Intelligence classified Rhodes as a retired pirate and part time activist, not as a confidant of the Verani Dominion.

Navy Intelligence, the definition of an oxymoron, she thought with a slight smile.

"So what now, is he their errand boy?"

Tish responded with an easy laugh and a smile that lit her face.

"Yeah, I guess that's about right. He takes care of their interests outside their sphere of influence."

Another thought occurred to Mira. "Are you and him together?" She blurted it out before she could stop herself.

"No! That would be just so...urrrgh," Tish replied, feigning a shudder.

"Sorry... you seem close."

"We are. He adopted me when I came to Double T. I was just a kid. I was hustling in the Medina when station security picked me up." She looked away. "He took me in and gave me a new life."

The elevator came to a halt. Mira stepped out into a corridor hewn from the asteroid. The walls were uneven, dark grey and shot through with minerals. Cables and pipes were surface mounted to the rock. A blast door was set into the wall.

Tish leant with her back to the door, one knee raised, her booted foot resting on the wall.

"So what's your story, Mira?" Tish asked. "Why are you so sad? What gives you the need to bleed?"

Mira never spoke of her dark habit, not even with Monica.

"Tish... I," she faltered.

"It's okay. You don't have to say anything. I thought as one bleeder to another..."

Mira could feel her gaze, her blue eyes boring into her, caressing her soul.

"I crashed my ship on Mars. That's how I ended up looking like this." She gestured to her scars. "I lost my flight rating and thought everything was over for me. It was okay; I met someone who helped me start over." Mira reached into her pocket, her fingers grasping the crumpled paper of the photograph. She took it out and gave it to Tish.

"Amy Flynt," Mira said.

"Jono's daughter?" Tish asked.

"Yes."

"She's pretty. Jon doesn't talk about her."

Mira tried to speak but words did not come. They stood in silence.

"She meant everything to me and some terrorists took her away because they thought Outlanders were queuing up to take Earth jobs."

She wiped a tear away, another took its place.

It wasn't just the thought of Amy, it was the loss the ship and the trauma of getting here. Too much had happened in too short a time. She was lost, alone and abandoned.

Tish stepped forward and held her. There was no uncertainty or hesitation in the movement, just warmth. Mira let her hold her until her sobs stopped. She composed herself, sniffed and wiped her face

"I'm sorry," she said. "It's been a bad week. I don't normally share that." *Especially with people I've just met.*

"It's okay," Tish said. "You should let things go. Hold on to the good and cut loose the bad. Otherwise it will drag you down. Trust me, I know."

Mira sniffed and smiled. She looked at the deck. Her cheeks burned.

"Mira Thorn, you have a pretty smile. You should smile more often," Tish said, reaching for the door control.

"You're a pilot?"

"In another life... yeah. I guess I still am."

"In that case, what I'm going to show you now will definitely make you smile."

The doors opened into a cavernous hangar. It took Mira a few seconds to digest what she was seeing, such was the scale of the ship it housed.

They stood beneath the pointed nose of a starship. It was like no vessel Mira could have imagined. The ship was long and streamlined. The point of the nose thickened into a slim fuselage that fanned out into a pair of delta wings. Each supported six Rolls Royce Void Spirit star drives, the same sublights used on the *Valhalla*. Rising from the stern were a pair of anhedral tail fins, each one bigger than the Kobo she had flown in on.

"Fuck!" Mira whispered. Her go to cuss word did no justice to how she felt. Tish was right; she was smiling.

"Where did you get it? What is it?" She could not get the words out coherently. Mira remembered how she felt when she walked onto the deck of the *Illustrious* during a squadron launch. This came close to that adrenalin fuelled sense of wonder. Her heart pounded. A million questions formed in her mind. The sadness of talking about Amy was burned away by this technical wonder.

"We built her. Her sub frame comes from a modified Verani Corvette. The Verani supplied a lot of tech and we bought, scrounged and stole the rest. It's taken us four years. It took me a year to get the design formalised."

"You designed her?"

"Me and one of Xander's friends from his pirate days."

"Sorry, I didn't mean to sound surprised."

Tish shrugged it off. "They tell me I have that Aspergers thing. I'm obsessed with little details and I kind of see how things work. We used contractors to put her together. She turned out okay. There are a few things we'd do differently next time."

"At the wreck site we detected an unidentified vessel. Was it her?"

"Xander and Luke were looking for the Kobo. They found you but you jumped before we could open a channel. Xander suspected you would come here and Jono confirmed it."

"The ship came out of nowhere. I never saw it until we were scanned."

"That's the stealth system. Up close you'll see her. She's nearly invisible in the IR and EM spectrums."

Mira had to admit it was impressive. Tish led her into the hangar and spoke excitedly as they walked.

"FTL is capable of a compression factor of nine-point-eight, but we've only achieved eight so far. Four decks, including a shuttle bay with space for up to four drop ships; we only have one."

"A compression factor of almost ten? The fastest vessels in the fleet have a maximum of seven."

FTL speed was measured in compression factors of 100. The drive system created a pocket of hyperspace called an envelope which surrounded the ship. A starship could not travel faster than the speed of light but the envelope could.

The more energy a vessel could supply the envelope, the faster its relativistic velocity. Most commercial ships were lucky to achieve a compression factor of 5. Most warships operated to a maximum of 7.

Mira did not know what the *Valhalla* was capable of, but it was unlikely to match the speed Tish claimed for this ship.

"She can undertake a planetary landing in up to five times gravity. That was difficult to achieve with her big arse," Tish added.

They climbed a stairway and arrived on a gantry running parallel to the ship. The vessel carried no standardised identification or registration number. The name *Nemesis* was emblazoned on the side of the vessel in red letters.

"The spirit of divine retribution," Mira whispered.

"Our world is unbalanced. The corporations exploit everyone and everything. Xander wants to address that imbalance. He sees this as a way to fight back. I'm not sure the Verani will let him; they have their own agenda. I don't always trust them."

Mira looked along the ship's length, admiring the sleek lines and seamless joins in the plates.

"Why are the Verani helping you? I have never heard of them sharing technology with humans."

"That's Xander's deal. He agreed to work for them if they provided him with the technology to do it. After a while they became more demanding. Y'Barri, their representative, told Xander he would need to take the ship into the Vale. He did not say why."

"Why can't they go themselves?" Mira said.

"Their religious caste will not let them. They are worried they will start a new age of destruction. We don't figure in their creed so they want humans to do their dirty work."

Tish's com-link beeped. A general alarm wailed. It was interspersed with an automated announcement telling civilians to head for their nearest secure area or remain in their accommodation. Tish listened to her link. Her eyes widened.

"Come on. We have to get to Central Ops," Tish said.

"What's happening?"

"A Frontier Company ship has just entered the system," Tish replied, taking Mira's hand and dragging her toward the blast door. Mira glanced back at the Nemesis. She still had many questions, all of them secondary to her desire to fly it.

CHAPTER TWELVE

THE transport tube came to a halt and the door slid open. Tish ran ahead. Mira followed several paces behind.

"This is Central Operations. We are in the core of the asteroid," she said as they emerged out into a brightly lit corridor. Security operatives and damage control personnel rushed past, their faces hidden behind the smoked glass of their helmets.

"Just how much control does Xander have over this place?" Mira said as she followed.

"He owns the station but leaves the day to day running to the Trade Guild and an elected Mayor. They're all a bunch of scumbags, just interested in making money. Xander handles defence and all non trade related external relations. He has a presidential role. It is a tense relationship."

They arrived at a blast door guarded by a pair of security operators. They stepped forward, blocking Mira's path.

"She's with me," Tish said. When they failed to move she took a step forward. "Just get out of the way. If there is a problem, take it up with Xander."

A look was exchanged, and they stepped back, dispelling any doubt Mira had to Xander's authority.

Mira found herself in a long oval room. She estimated there were fifty people manning consoles. Xander Rhodes stood at the centre before him a situational map of the system. The atmosphere was frantic. People dashed from console to console; information was shouted from operator to operator. The departure board was alive with vessel ident codes, all stacking up to leave the station.

"It's the same every time a fleet vessel enters the system," Tish said. "All the rats run."

Xander gestured for Tish to join him. She squeezed past the traffic controllers coordinating shipping movements. Mira tagged along like a lost child.

"It's a Frontier heavy cruiser," Rhodes said. "He's about two hours out. No communication as yet."

"What does he want?" Mira asked. "This system does not fall under their mandate. Hell, it barely falls under Federal control."

"I assume they are here for your ship. I was expecting some corporate fall out, but this is an outrage."

"You expected this?" Mira said, unable to conceal her shock.

"I was expecting heat from Lightfoot or some mercs. That object must be important to some big players."

What have we gotten ourselves into? she thought as the red blip on the situation display edged closer.

Xander barked orders to the flight controllers.

"Xander, what do the Frontier Company want with the Ark?" Mira asked.

"I suspected another party is pursuing a similar aim. I don't know why," he replied. "Please, let me sort this out, we will talk later, okay?"

She agreed.

"Good, we've powered up the defence grid and we have about thirty fighters under our direct command; we can probably count on another ten. The *Angel* is preparing for departure and we have... well you've seen what we have," Xander said. He sounded far from optimistic. Mira understood his fears. Frontier cruisers were heavily armed behemoths mounting a formidable main battery. A single vessel could overrun a colony world and Tarantella would be no match.

"I suspect this is just sabre rattling," he said. "They want to intimidate us into handing the artefact over."

Mira was not so sure. She knew how FRONCO operated.

"Xander, Frontier do not sabre rattle. They are not constrained by the same rules of engagement we are. If they want the Ark, they will take it."

Xander fixed her with his cool grey eyes.

"But," she continued. "You can't give them what you haven't got."

"You want to take it off the station? We don't have the time to load it onto another ship."

"So we'll use the Kobo."

"It's risky. I guess we can program it to fly out on auto."

"It will be too easy for Frontier to intercept her. I'll fly her," Tish said.

"No," Mira replied. "Let me do it, I know the ship better than you."

Xander ran his fingers through his hair.

"I'm not comfortable, Thorn. When I saw your vessel come in I was surprised the ion curtain didn't break it in two."

"Xander, she's a tough bird and I don't need to push her hard. It will be a Sunday afternoon drive. We don't have time to discuss it. I have to go now."

Xander did not reply immediately and when he did his tone was confident.

"Tish take the *Nemesis* out. Rendezvous with Mira at the old solar station and transfer the Ark. Depending on how things change here, we'll decide on where to go after that."

"What about my crew?"

"They'll go with Tish. It's the safest option. This is not their fight. It's not yours either, Mira Thorn. I am grateful for your help."

She suspected it was more her fight than Xander knew.

Ten minutes later Mira was zipping up a flight suit. Unlike the lightweight corporate hauler's outfit, this was a military spec garment, olive green and reinforced with carbon fibre armour. Mira was impressed. It was a good as the suits the Navy used. She checked the collar and noted the same labelling.

Once she had hooked up the NitOx supply, she pulled her borrowed leather jacket over the top. There was something comforting about the garment. Mira did not know if it was the aged scent or the way it wrapped itself around her small frame. She would not give it up without a fight.

Tish gave her a helmet. They walked in tense silence to Xander's quarters.

Her crew were waiting.

"Mira? What's going on? The station is going crazy." Alex's eyes flitted to the window where the shipping movements were plain to see.

Mira spoke rapidly, filling in the blanks in the chain of events and outlining the plan as it stood.

"Tish and some of Xander's people are leaving. I want you guys to go with them."

"What about you?" Monica asked.

"Xander thinks this ship has come for the Kobo. I'm going to fly it out of here. We'll meet up and transfer the artefact to one of Xander's vessels."

"Mira, the Kobo is unsafe," Barnes said. "Ethan told me

about the visible damage. We don't know what the substructure is like."

"Rich, that's why it's me flying it. I know it's limitations."

"I'm coming with you," Alex said. "Can you fix me up with a suit?" he asked Tish.

"No," Mira said. "I can fly it and there is no point in risking both of us."

"Mira, the workload in that cockpit is unmanageable for a sole pilot. If I'm with you we have a greater chance of success. It is regulation anyway. Navy insists on two crew on all ships that require it."

Mira wanted to argue but Alex was right. If she failed, and the ship was destroyed the Ark would fall into Frontier hands or be lost. She knew she wouldn't be able to fly and operate the improvised weapons system on her own.

"Okay, Alex, you win. Tish can you give him a suit?"

Tish left the room and came back a minute later with an armful of flight suits.

"One of these should fit," she said.

She sized Alex by eye and selected one. "You are about Luke's height. Try this one."

She gave Mira a data card. "RV coordinates."

Monica wolf whistled as Alex stripped. His face reddened. Mira was grateful for the distraction.

Martinez arrived. Sweat glistened on his forehead.

"The ship is ready, Tish."

"Juan, take Monica, Ethan and Richard down. I'll join you shortly," Tish replied.

Mira noticed the tone of Tish's voice had changed. She sounded like a starship officer, clear concise instructions, issued with authority. Her shipmates left with their heads bowed, shoulders slumped. Monica stopped and raised her hand. Mira mirrored the gesture. She hoped it wasn't the last time she would see them.

Tish was at her side.

"If anything goes wrong, see they get home," Mira whispered.

"Xander won't let you down. Come on I'll take you to your ship. I know a shortcut."

The journey to Bay 32 took five minutes. The station thoroughfares were all but deserted, save for a few homeless refugees and patrolling damage control teams.

The Kobo was how they left it, resting forlornly on the pad. The damage looked far worse than Mira remembered.

"Tish," Mira said. "We can take it from here. Get your ship underway."

"Okay." She tapped Alex on the arm. Without warning, Tish hugged Mira.

"For luck. I'll see you at the RV."

Mira stood rooted to the spot. She'd only known the girl a few hours. She made a decision and hugged back.

"Thanks Tish, for everything." The size of the task she faced dawned on her. She realised this might be the last hug she might ever have.

They watched Tish run over the gantry and out of the hangar.

"Come on, Alex. Let's get out of here."

"She likes you, Thorny," Alex said. Mira shoved him in the ribs. He winced and grinned.

"Come on. You're in the hot seat," he said, heading into the vessel. Mira checked her combat computer. The Frontier Cruiser would be in weapons range in an hour and twenty minutes. At least time was on their side.

Her headache cleared, and her thought process seemed to

sharpen.

Never underestimate the power of the adrenal glands, she thought as she strapped herself in.

They pre-flighted the Kobo as quickly as they could using the emergency checklist. Mira held her breath as she fired up the engines. She let out a relieved sigh as they came online and maintained a steady output.

Mira lifted the Kobo off the pad and used the manoeuvring thrusters to flip it through 180 degrees. The yoke vibrated. The ship was shaking itself apart. Mira pushed the master throttle to maximum and blasted through the ion curtain into the void. The vibration in the controls peaked and dropped away. The freighter was back in its element, freed from the confines of artificial gravity and atmosphere.

The space around Tarantella was chaotic. Outbound ships crossed and recrossed their flight path. Off her starboard side a pair of cargo vessels come close to a collision. Ahead of her the *Scarlet Angel* was already underway, her powerful ion engines accelerating her away from the station. Mira cursed her limited field of vision as she tried to track the surrounding starships.

"Don't worry," Alex said. "I have it covered."

He was leaning forward, craning his head to get a clear view of every corner of the viewport.

Mira pushed the data card Tish had given her into the Navi-Comp and a trace appeared on the head up display. She aligned with the direction pip and increased their relative velocity.

"The traffic should mask our exit," she said, checking the IFF transponder switch was in the off position. She rested a finger on it to be certain.

"Where are we going?" Alex asked.

"There is disused solar power plant in close stellar orbit. We'll be able to transfer cargo under the cover of the solar wind."

Mira scanned the displays. It was as a sound plan in principle, but first they had to get there.

Xander Rhodes stood in front of the tactical display, the burble of radio chatter a constant drone in the background. Even he was surprised by the number of vessels deserting the station. He didn't blame them. A few years ago he would have been the first to board a ship and blast out.

Central Operations was not his usual domain. Despite his tenuous governance of Tarantella, he never took part in the day to day running of the infrastructure. Then again it was not an everyday occurrence for a hostile warship to come knocking.

"Xander, all of our assets are deployed and the defence grid is powered. Will the *Scarlet Angel* be under your command?" Dan McKenzie, the duty Ops Manager, asked.

"She's yours to deploy as you see necessary," he said. "I have another vessel that is otherwise tasked. Once her mission is complete, I'll hand her over to station defence."

McKenzie issued the orders.

"Incoming transmission on the public channel," a comms officer shouted from the far side of the room.

"Put it through." Xander picked up a headset and put it on.

"Tarantella Station and specifically Xander Rhodes. My name is Virginia Cochrane, Commanding Officer of the Frontier Company Vessel *Ardent*. Deactivate your defence grid and stand down."

Every eye in the Operations Centre was fixed on him.

"Captain Cochrane, this is Rhodes. You have no jurisdiction in this sector. We are not affiliated to the Federation or the Frontier Company. Your presence in this system is undesirable. It is having a detrimental influence on our right to free trade and our right to self determination. You do not have permission to approach. Please leave the system as soon as your FTL drive is charged. I must inform you, we will defend our station robustly should you attack."

He closed the link.

Silence.

"Dan," Xander called the Ops Manager over. "What is the current threat assessment?"

"We have superior firepower and they will have to fight their way through. We will take damage and casualties."

"To what level?"

"Moderate to severe."

The cold reality took a bite out of Xander's soul. There were 50,000 people on the station, with refugees it was likely to be twice that figure. At the end of today some of them would be dead and it would be on him.

His musings were interrupted.

"Xander we have detected two additional hyperspatial envelopes." McKenzie said.

"Two more Frontier vessels have entered the system, a second cruiser and a carrier."

Xander exhaled. *A carrier? How badly do they want that thing?*

"Open a channel to Cochrane."

"Channel is open."

"Captain Cochrane, please state your business. You and your friends are pissing me off."

There was a hush before Cochrane responded.

"You have a vessel belonging to Lightfoot Developments on your station. Surrender the vessel and its cargo and no further action will be taken."

"Your intelligence is wrong. We have no Lightfoot vessels on board. We have no contracts with LDC." He changed tack. "Even if we did, The Frontier Company does not represent Lightfoot, so again, I ask under what authority are your vessels here?"

"We are obliged by the Centauri Treaty to act against inter-solar piracy. You have 30 minutes to surrender the vessel or we will use appropriate force."

Xander found a chair and sat.

"The carrier is launching fighters," McKenzie reported.

"Engage at will," Xander said.

On the holo-display a line of green triangles representing the forty strong station defence force took up a holding position while the *Scarlet Angel* moved to flank the lead cruiser. He needed the *Nemesis* but feared even that would not be enough. There was one more ace up his sleeve. He only hoped he'd live long enough to play it.

An alarm flashed on the Kobo's short range sensor panel.

"We have two fighters in sensor range," Alex reported.

"Are they heading our way?" Mira asked, her eye not leaving the pilot's station displays.

"Not yet. They are on perimeter patrol,"

"Alex, power up the weapons. We're in no position to fight but they may force our hand."

The power dropped as Alex diverted energy to the weapons systems. It was barely perceptible as the gravity field's inertial dampening system isolated Mira from sensing the loss of performance. Instead she detected it through the yoke and the throttles as they became less responsive to her touch.

The ETA displayed in the bottom left of the Head Up Display increased from 10.30 minutes to 11.03. The solar power plant was visible on the navigation screen and Mira assumed the *Nemesis* was already there, masked by her stealth system.

Once the ship was trimmed and in even flight, she turned the conversation to their host.

"What do you make of Rhodes, Alex?"

"First impressions?" Alex said. "Not what I expected, whatever he's done in the past he genuinely seems to care about the people on the station," Alex replied. "I think he sees himself as a 24th century Robin Hood. You know what bothered me? He doesn't seem to have many people. The Navy believes he has 2,500 Blades. The station could only muster 40 fighters to defend it?"

Mira thought about it. She had met Tish and Martinez and that was it. Station security were a separate entity operated by the Trade Guild. She wondered just how many people Xander Rhodes really had on his side.

"Maybe they are on the *Scarlet Angel*. Right now, there is only Tish and Martinez on the *Nemesis*," she said. "He is working with the Verani, to what extent I don't know. They've helped him build a ship far more advanced than anything we have."

Alex didn't have time to reply as the ship's sensor array lit up.

"We have just been scanned by a targeting system. Two vampires inbound at speed." Vampire was Navy terminology for a hostile fighter. "They must have detected our drive signature and worked out who we were."

Mira weighed up their options. The Kobo was down on power and no match for the manoeuvrability of a fighter. In their favour they were packing a pair of heavyweight plasma cannons. All she had to do was get them pointing in the right direction.

The ship shook as an energy blast hit the shields.

"Shields holding," Alex said. "That was a warning shot. They're testing us out... They are pinging us to open a channel."

"Ignore them, Alex. We shoot and then we run. *Nemesis* is out there somewhere. Let's hope Tish sees what is happening."

Mira pulled the ship into a sharp turn, flipping it onto an attack vector. The hull creaked under the strain.

"I'll line them up, Alex. You crack them off. For our sake don't miss. We won't get another chance."

The improvised targeting system locked onto the fighters and a pair of moving diamonds appeared on the HUD. They were being lazy. Their formation was loose. Mira knew FRONCO operated an uprated version of the Navy's Typhoon. Even if the Kobo were fully functional, it would be outclassed by one let alone a pair of fighters. The Frontier pilots also knew it and it made them sloppy. That was their first mistake. Their second was to assume the hauler was unarmed.

Mira pushed the throttle as hard as she dared. She took a sideways glance at Alex.

He had his head down, using the navigation system as a gun sight.

The fighters let off four bolts of energy. The first two flew wide; the second pair rocked the ship when they impacted the shields.

"Shields are down to 35 percent," Alex reported. "They are not rebuilding."

The distance closed to three kilometres. Mira lined up on the lead fighter. A tracking pip traced the direction of the Frontier Vessel.

"He has no idea we have iron," she murmured. "Alex is that close enough for you?"

He made no reply as a pair of high energy plasma slugs flew from the underbelly of the Kobo.

A fireball bloomed ahead of them.

"Yep, that's close enough," he said.

Mira pulled the ship around and advanced the throttles. The second fighter registered what had happened to his wingman and moved in onto an aggressive vector, increasing his speed as he did so.

"We won't have surprise on our side now," Mira said. They were a long way from the rendezvous point and heading further out.

The divergent course opened distance between the wounded freighter and the inbound fighter. It was temporary but it might buy them enough time.

Two blasts burned the shields away, a further two slammed into the hull.

"Mira, we are breached! Lower deck."

"Fuck this!" she screamed as the engines died and the ship tumbled out of control. The console in front of her exploded, showering her with sparks and pieces of hot alloy.

The lights went off, leaving only their suit lighting to illuminate the flight deck. Mira went light in her harness as the artificial gravity failed.

"We've lost power!" Alex said. "The reactor is thrashing, but we have no power. We're in a lot of trouble."

"Check the relays, have they scrammed?"

"Negative, no faults in the drive system, wait, I'm detecting a huge load sucking energy out of the ship."

Mira was certain she knew the cause.

"Alex we are done here. We have to get the Ark off the ship. We fix a transponder to it and hope the *Nemesis* can pick it up."

"And us?"

"We bail with it and hope for the best."

Mira shivered when she considered the risk. The flight suits and helmets gave moderate protection in a vacuum but their air supplies were limited. She was certain if they stayed with the ship they would be dead within minutes. Bailing was the only option left.

"Doesn't sound like much of a plan," Alex said as another blast rocked the ship. "But it's better than no plan. Come on, Thorny, let's go."

Alex closed his visor and released his harness. Mira unclipped her own and pushed herself out of her seat.

She activated her mag boots and they ran from the flight deck. Alex opened the stairway, everything that wasn't fixed was sucked into the vacuum below. Moving as quickly as their mag boots would allow, Mira and Alex made their way through the curved corridor. The walls were blackened from the fire. A black fog of loose debris swirled in the air. Mira pushed her way through the twisted hold doors. The Ark rested in its cradle as immobile as ever. Energy arced from its surface and it pulsed with blue and purple light. Alex strapped himself to the pallet. Mira hit the explosive release on the cargo ramp; it blasted clear of the hold. Vertigo gripped her as the stars spun in the aperture.

The Ark shimmered as if it were phasing in and out of reality.

"Can you see that, Alex?"

"I'm doing my best to ignore it!"

She pushed the object toward the ramp. It didn't move. With the gravity off and the atmosphere gone the object should have budged yet somehow it defied Newton. Mira did not know if she was imagining it, but space appeared to be flexing around her. There was something else. She could sense a presence probing her mind.

"Move you fucker! We're trying to help!" she screamed. It

shifted toward the ramp so suddenly she nearly lost her grip. She fumbled for a tether line and attached it to the cradle. The line tightened with a painful jolt and the object spun out of the hold. Mira tumbled for several seconds until the suit's stabiliser fired and righted her.

They were in open space. The Kobo rolled away from them in its death throes. A bolt of energy struck the ship, and the reactor gave out, exploding in a white fireball.

The death of the ship lingered on Mira's retina. In the darkness all she could hear was the muffled sound of her own breathing.

They floated in the debris field. Explosions flashed silently in the distance. Mira had lost track of time. She guessed it had been close to an hour since they bailed out.

Mira's breath formed ice crystals on the inside her visor and she could no longer feel her fingers or toes. The suit either did not have heating circuit or its power had failed.

"I hope they get through it," Mira said.

"They will. Did Rhodes tell you any more about that thing?" Alex asked.

Mira craned her head to look at the object. It was still lit from within by random flashes of light. She still had and odd sense it was alive. A chime sounded in her ear, a warning that her suit's oxygen supply had entered its reserve stage.

She told Alex everything she had learned of the Ark and the post physical race living within it.

"Alex, I don't think I will make it," Mira said, when she was done.

"Mira! The ship will be here soon. It's just a matter of waiting and conserving air." Alex did not sound convinced.

"No, hear me out, after the first night on the ship I had

this... dream. I think the Ark was trying to communicate with me but at a simple level. It was before I connected with it, so it was trying to manipulate my mind. At least that's what I think."

She told him about the dream of covering the holes in the bulkhead with her hands before being sucked in to space.

"A voice kept saying *if you save them, you will die*," she laughed. "I guess it was prophetic."

More explosions bloomed and faded in the distance. The battle had a surreal and deadly beauty from this distance.

"Maybe this is what they intended. We saved them. Perhaps it's down to Rhodes now."

Mira shivered and stared into the void.

"You know my parents would approve of your Ark," Alex said, seemingly at random.

"Huh?"

"They were religious, Neo Catholics," he replied. "They would like the Ark. It sounds like purgatory. You know, where all the lost souls go?"

"I never had you down as religious."

"I never was but when you're a kid, you do as your parents do. At least I did... until it all went wrong." His breathing sounded laboured as he spoke.

"I used to be an Altar Server," he said. "One day, when I was about twelve, I was standing at the front of the church. I got diarrhoea." He giggled. "Man, it was the worst. I stood there with it flowing out from under my robes and over my shoes. People in the pews were screaming and running for cover. I was the only person left in the whole damn church. Just me standing in a puddle of wet shit, laughing my face off. The other kids called me Alex Shite for months. Fuck my life. It's been one embarrassing moment after another."

Mira laughed, knowing her oxygen was out but not caring.

"I can beat that," she said. "When I was seventeen, I went back to London to visit my Grandmother. I was out sightseeing and I remembered I'd left a beast of a vibrator on the bed. I stood in front of Westminster Abbey in a state of near panic. You see, Nan would make my bed every day and I knew I was busted."

She replayed the moment in her mind. It banished the cold, just enough.

"When I got home, she did not say a word. I ran upstairs, totally horrified. When I got to my room Nan had made the bed. She put the vibe on the side table with a little note asking me if I could get her one the same."

Alex joined her in laughter.

"How old was she?"

"Seventy three!" Mira's head spun. The cold lessened as her brain began to shut down.

"Your grandmother sounds sweet," he said, his voice distant.

"She was. Maybe I'll see her soon. Amy too."

Alex made no reply.

Mira thought of Tish and wondered if there could ever have been something between them.

Guess I'll never know.

The chime sounded in her ear, this time ringing every 3 seconds. She fumbled for a control on the side of her helmet and silenced it.

"Alex, my air is gone."

"Same here."

He pushed himself towards her and held out his hand. Mira took it and squeezed hard.

"Sleep tight, Thorny," he said.

"You too, Alex."

As Mira's oxygen ran out her vision tunnelled until only a tiny circle remained. The darkness closed around her in a cold embrace.

CHAPTER THIRTEEN

XANDER watched in dismay as the last of his fighters was destroyed. Only the Scarlet Angel and the station's defences stood between him and defeat. The battle had not been one sided. The Frontier Cruiser Ardent had suffered extensive damage and limped to the edge of the system. It was little compensation. The carrier had responded by launching a second wave of fighters. As they headed for the station, Xander knew there was little he could do to halt their advance.

As the *Ardent* withdrew Xander had received a further message from a Frontier Admiral named Parker, again requesting surrender. Xander had been tempted.

His thoughts were interrupted.

"TT Ops, *Scarlet Angel*," Luke Rhodes called in.

"Go ahead, Luke," Xander said.

"Do you want me to pursue the *Ardent* or return to a defensive position?"

"Luke," he said. "I need you to come back. The people here are depending on us."

"Understood. We'll do what we can."

The link clicked closed with a finality that broke Xander's heart.

A shudder ran through the station as the first salvo of fire hit.

"We are engaging enemy fighters," Dan McKenzie said.

Another shock wave shook the station. Xander called up the damage report on the holo-screen. Fires were reported through the lower levels, mostly on the cargo handling decks.

"Mr Rhodes!" one of the traffic coordinators shouted from the far side of the room. "There is another hyperspatial envelope. A large vessel is entering the system."

Xander detected the change in mood. Another ship meant the battle was certainly lost.

"Mr Rhodes, it has a Navy transponder. It's a dreadnought. He's transmitting on the open channel."

"Put it on speaker," Rhodes said, his face broke into a grin.

"...Flynt of the *Valhalla,* designation DC-001. Commander of the Frontier Battle Group, stand down and explain yourself. This system does not fall under your jurisdiction."

There was a pause.

"Admiral Flynt. Gabe Parker, Frontier Admiral in Charge. We are conducting anti piracy operations. The situation is in hand." Parker's voice was unruffled and silky.

"The hell you are, Parker. Stand down this instant or you will be engaged!" Flynt roared.

"Way to go, Jono," Xander whispered. No one heard him. They were all frozen, listening to the exchange.

Calmer now, Flynt continued.

"The Navy has seniority in all operations. Stand down and get the fuck out of this system before I open up with the biggest broadside in human history!"

There was a pause.

"You do not have authorisation, Admiral. My forces will hold the line."

"Do you want to take that chance?" Flynt responded, his

voice devoid of emotion, his tone leaving no doubt about his intentions.

"The dreadnought is charging his main battery, Xander!" McKenzie reported.

Time slowed as the seconds ticked by.

"Fighters are withdrawing!" A cheer went up in the Ops room at Dan McKenzie's report.

Ten minutes later all three Frontier Vessels built envelopes and jumped out of the system.

A second, heartier cheer rippled through the room. Relief was clear on the assembled faces. Xander studied the damage report. The station had fared better than he expected but fires still burned in the cargo docks.

"What about casualties, Dan?" he asked.

"I'm getting reports of 1000 plus dead. That will increase."

Xander was stunned.

"Xander, the fleet vessel has opened a secure channel. He is requesting to speak to you."

"Patch him through."

He pulled on a headset.

"Xander Rhodes, I told you that one day you would need the Navy," Flynt said.

"You did Jon, thanks. You cut things close."

"I prefer fashionably late. I have my medical team on standby. Do you require help?"

"I'll have the flight operations people send you a vector. We should have a pier big enough for you. We have casualties and our own medical staff will be at full stretch so I appreciate any help you can offer."

He closed the link

"Xander, it's a fleet vessel!" McKenzie said through gritted teeth.

"He saved our arses, and he has medical supplies. Let him dock and arrange for the Admiral to meet me in my quarters."

Xander cast his gaze around the ops room. The faces that stared back wore a mixture of fatigue and relief. One young woman burst into tears; two of her colleagues comforted her.

"Thank you everyone," he said. A faint ripple of applause followed in his wake as he strode from the Ops Room.

"Mira." The voice spoke in her mind. It was the same voice as had spoken in the vision.

She panicked. Her world was black.

"Who are you?" she asked, her lips did not move.

"We are Pharn," it replied.

"You are in the Ark?"

"We are the Ark."

"What do you want?"

"To rejoin the collective. Time is short, shadows are gathering. We must return to Arethon."

"I don't think I can help you. Things are not looking so good for me. I think I might be dying. You told me I would."

"This time is not your time. You will survive this. Your species mates will save you. We will sustain you until they arrive."

"What about Alex?"

"This term is meaningless."

"The other human."

"The other is not relevant."

"He is my friend. He is relevant."

Silence.

"If you can save me, you can save him. Otherwise I will not help you."

"We absorbed energy from your ship to make this communion possible. The rate of absorption has damaged this unit. Entropy will soon see the Ark fail and we will be lost. We will sustain the other human until it is unviable for us to continue."

"What do you need me to do?"

"Take us to Arethon."

"I don't know where Arethon is. No humans do."

Charts flickered in her mind, a tiny world orbiting a main sequence star. She recognised the Cygnus Vale but not the location within it.

"We have given you what you need. Will you save us?"

"Yes."

"We will save you, Mira Thorn."

The voice fell silent. Mira's consciousness faded into darkness; she was no longer alone.

Mira opened her eye, squinting against the light. Her head pounded. She had suffered ferocious hangovers in the past but nothing before had come close to the steam hammers pounding in her skull. Her visor was down. She was shivering. Her chest tightened as claustrophobia gripped her.

Her visor opened and Monica Garret leant over her.

"Keep calm, Mira. We have been increasing your oxygen level. Keep still and let your body recover."

"Alex?" she asked.

"We have him. We are doing our best."

Her eye focused. She was in a large, brightly lit landing bay. The walls were steel-grey.

"*Nemesis*?" she said.

"Yes, stay still. Richard is here. I need to attend to Alex."

Barnes swam into her field of vision. "We picked you up just in time," he said.

"What about the Ark?"

"We just brought it aboard. It's safe."

Mira pushed herself upright and propped herself up with her elbows. Her vision swam and her head throbbed. She glanced sideways. Monica was working on a lifeless Alex Kite.

"Rich, what's happening?" she asked.

"Alex did not respond as well as you. His lungs were already damaged and his air ran out before yours."

Martinez pumped an airbag over Alex's mouth. His face was blue. He remained unresponsive. Monica drew up a shot and hit him with it.

His arm twitched. He coughed. Mira staggered to her feet and ran to him. She held him tight.

"Alex!" she cried.

He coughed. There was a faint haze of blood in his spittle.

"It's okay, Thorny," he rasped. "I told you they would save us."

"Alex is struggling, Mira. I need to get him to the infirmary. His lungs took severe damage on the *Berlin* and it is affecting him now."

"Will he be okay?"

"He will have a rough few hours but he will be fine. Trust me."

Alex took her hand and squeezed it.

Mira dragged herself to her feet. Ethan and Martinez loaded Alex onto a gurney and carried him off.

The Ark stood on the deck, still attached to the pallet. The iridescence had ceased to flash through the surface. The strobe Alex had mounted on the framework continued to pulse. It throbbed in time to the thuds behind Mira's eye.

"Rich, I have to get to the flight deck."

"I'll show you the way. This ship is astounding. Even a grunt like me can appreciate it."

Mira had been keen to get aboard the vessel but never expected to board in quite such a dramatic fashion. She shivered, yet to feel the benefit of the ship's environmental system. Her hands were still blue, her fingertips and knuckles showing signs of bruising. She flexed her fingers, trying to work out the stiffness.

"Are you sure you are okay? When we brought you aboard, your oxygen was out and you were close to being a popsicle. You should take it slowly, Mira."

"I'm fine, Rich. This is important. I need to look at the charts."

He led her to a central corridor. The paint smelled new. The rubberised flooring had none of the characteristic scuffs and nicks that arose from heavy use. As they walked, Mira noticed that several of the wall panels were removed, exposing wiring and subsystems. At one point she had to step over a thick power cable running across the floor. It broke out of one wall panel and connected to another.

"Tish told me they are still ironing out problems," Barnes said. "She seems quite a character; easy on the eyes too."

Mira nudged him with her elbow. The sudden movement sent a ripple of pain through her head, but it was worth it.

"You are a dirty old man, Richard Barnes."

He chuckled. The easy going sound coaxed a smile from Mira.

"Less of the old, if you don't mind. Don't say you hadn't noticed."

"I hadn't noticed," Mira lied with a smirk.

When they reached the flight deck Tish swivelled in the pilot's seat to greet them.

"Mira! I'm sorry we took so long..."

"Don't worry, Tish. We made it. What's happening? Is the

station safe?"

"Frontier bugged out when Aussie Jon showed up with the biggest vessel I've ever seen. The station was damaged and there are casualties. We are twenty minutes out."

Mira nodded to the copilot's chair.

"May I?"

"Of course you can."

Mira settled in and pulled on a headset.

"Tish, can you give me access to your NaviComp? I want to see the Vale."

"Okay, why there?"

"It's complicated and weird. I need to prove I'm not full of shit."

Tish flicked switches on the central panel and the console in front of Mira lit up. She pulled up charts and adjusted the zoom factor. She didn't know what she was looking for, so she flicked through star maps in sequence.

Click, Click, Click, Click, Click.

"Mira?" Barnes said. She barely heard him.

Click, Click, Click.

She arrived at a familiar pattern of stars and zoomed in. A typical system with a main sequence star. The system comprised four gas giants and three rocky worlds. One was in the centre of the Goldilocks Zone, the narrow band where conditions would allow life to flourish.

She studied the screen looking for the identifier.

LDC-132.

"That's it," she said.

"What?" Tish asked, leaning over to see the screen.

"That's Arethon."

Mira stared at the screen. Somehow everything became real. The compulsion to take the Ark to this lonely world in the

Cygnus Vale was strong, an inexplicable, irresistible pull. It was like her need to cut or perhaps the magnetic draw of a new lover.

She would need a ship and this one would do just fine.

Nemesis pulled into the hangar and came to rest on the pad. The roar of her sublights and vertical lifters shook the rock of the asteroid as she touched down.

Jon Flynt watched as the vessel berthed. He did his best to conceal a smile that betrayed his awe at the ship.

"So you finally got her into service." His gaze did not falter from the *Nemesis*.

Xander clapped a hand on his shoulder.

"Don't tell me you had doubts, Jono. It has nearly bankrupted me on three occasions, but we still knocked her out quicker than your fleet yards."

It was a point Flynt had to concede. Xander and his rag-tag group had conceptualised, designed and built the ship in the same time it took the fleet to agree funding for *Valhalla's* weapons system. Then again Xander had used every piece of Verani tech he could get his hands on. Flynt studied the vessel; her sleek silhouette spoke of her heritage.

"How are things with our blue skinned friends? I noticed Y'Barri is not on the station."

"There have been changes on their homeworld. The military caste has swapped their allegiance to the religious caste. The political caste has become marginalised for now. These things happen from time to time, their culture is fickle and prone to instability. To be honest, I don't know who is worse, our government or theirs."

He paused and gave a dismayed shake of his head.

"The religious caste are preparing for what they call the second age of destruction. They are pulling their support for me and fortifying their homeworld. Y'Barri requested I retrieve the Ark and take it to the Vale. Clerical Governance shut him down before he could tell me what to do with it."

"And you think Mira has the answers?" Flynt asked.

"Possibly. She has communicated with it and in Y'Barri's absence she is all we have."

Flynt continued to stare at the *Nemesis*, lost in thought. The *Valhalla* was the most important vessel the Federation had ever produced, and she had just been made irrelevant by a ship constructed by a bunch of outlaws on a disused mining platform. They were living in strange times. The political affairs of the Verani Dominion were important, but a long way from the now.

"So," Xander said, finally breaking the spell of the *Nemesis*. "Thorn, can I trust her?"

"I do," Flynt said.

Rhodes frowned. "You're biased. She's part of the establishment, a naval officer."

"So am I and you trust me."

"Sometimes," Xander replied.

"I've known the girl for ten years. Mira is like family. She's never been one to conform to anything. After her crash she got worse. I guess my daughter was a bad influence. When Amy died, Mira went back into the black because she did not know where else to go."

I did the same thing, Flynt thought.

"And the others?"

He stroked his beard.

"Monica Garret and Rich Barnes will stick by Mira whatever happens. The other two are unknown quantities. Kite is a fleet-brat so I fully expect him to jump aboard the *Valhalla* when we truck out."

The *Nemesis* powered down. She vented exhaust gases that were ejected by the hangar's extraction system. Her running lights and strobes went off as the airlock slid open.

Martinez led the way, followed by Tish.

"She's grown up since I last saw her," Flynt said.

His chest grew tight, and a lump formed in his throat as Mira Thorn stepped out of the ship. She saw him and ran forward, coming at him as if she were on a fleet fitness check.

"Jon!" she said and launched herself into his arms. She held on to him for what seemed like an eternity.

Mira shook. Every human emotion coursed through her in a split second.

"Jon!" she repeated.

"Mira, it's good to see you. When we found the *Berlin*; I feared the worst."

Flynt held her. Mira detected the familiar tension in his embrace as if he were holding something back. Jon Flynt had always been the same, warm yet distant. Mira put it down to a life in the fleet. He could shake a man's hand one minute and send him to his death the next.

"That's probably not how I should greet an Admiral," she said, her voice cracked. "I'm sorry I left so soon. I couldn't stay."

"I'll give you guys time," Xander said, turning and walking toward the ship.

Mira watched him walk to Tish, who spoke animatedly to him. Behind them Ethan and Barnes were helping Alex cross the gantry. He shook them off. He raised his hand. She returned the greeting.

"Are you up to walking?" Flynt asked.

"Sure."

They walked toward the stern of the *Nemesis*. Mira fought to stay focused on Flynt and not be distracted by the giant vessel.

"Impressed by her?" Flynt asked.

"I can't get my head around it. These people are not a government or a corporation... but look at her." Mira pointed at the ship.

"Xander has always been well connected," Flynt said. He changed the subject. "How have you been Mira?"

She dragged her attention from the *Nemesis* and gathered her thoughts. Her default position would be a lie, a smile and a re-enforcement of her self denial. This was Jon Flynt, and she owed him more.

"It has been hard, Jon. I've OD'd twice, cut myself more times than I could mention. I was hooked on painkillers for a long time but..." She put her hand on his arm. "Just recently things have got better. Losing the ship finally put my pathetic life into perspective."

"Ready to rejoin humanity?" he asked.

"Maybe, if humanity will have me." She was keen to move attention off herself. "How about you?"

"I'm tired and I'm old. I'm coping. The Norse project has helped me come to terms with the loss and I have made some new friends along the way. I have young crew and they have an infectious enthusiasm for life." Flynt stopped walking. The old sparkle was there in his eyes, yet a fleeting sadness haunted his face.

"I wish you had got in touch. I wish I could have spared you some hurt," he said.

Mira didn't know how to respond. There were times when

she drafted a letter only to delete it before sending it. Even Jon Flynt could not have prevented her falling into a self destructive spiral.

She changed the subject.

"You have a lot of secrets, Jon."

"A fair point. We live in difficult times Mira and, if the Verani are right, they could to get tougher."

The Verani kept popping up. Like most humans Mira had never laid eye on the elusive aliens, yet here she was in a hangar with an admiral and a space pirate both of whom seemed to share privileged access to the highest levels of their government.

"So tell me."

Flynt leant on the gantry railings; Mira huddled next to him. Below them the *Nemesis* sat on her pad. Xander's crew set about refuelling her and conducting post flight maintenance. There were far fewer people than there would be on a Navy dock, but they worked at a pace and to a system that offset their numbers.

"Have you ever wondered about our galaxy?" Flynt asked. "How we seem to be the only ones in it?"

"There is a lot of life aside from us. You're just looking at it from a point of view of sentience," Mira countered. "All life is life. I dunno perhaps having the smarts is hard?"

"You sound like my daughter and it's a fair point, but look at the progress we have made. Go back a thousand years and we were a vulnerable, infant species standing on the shores of a cosmic ocean. A pandemic or natural disaster could have wiped out humanity before we'd discovered the combustion engine.

"Go a step further: assume a big enough meteorite had hit the earth in 1000AD. Humans would no longer exist. If that happened tomorrow humanity would prevail."

Mira understood the concept. It was called the survival imperative. It was the reason why humans established the first Martian colony back in 2069. Mariner Base had become Mariner City and was now home to three million people.

"Resilience, we have spread to the stars. We are no longer bound to a single location," she replied. "We have found ruins and artefacts all over the galaxy and no sign of those who built them. If an alien civilisation had blossomed in this part of the universe then they should still be around, unless..."

"Something removed them," Flynt finished the sentence for her. "It is extremely difficult to eradicate a space faring species. The Navy has run numerous models and found it nearly impossible. The universe is stuck with us... for now."

Mira told Flynt of the vision, the city of emerald glass and gold. She told how she watched its destruction.

"It wasn't a dream, Jon. When I was in space the Ark spoke. I know where Arethon is. We call it LDC-132."

"A Lightfoot Corporate world... or prospect at least," Flynt replied.

Corporations sought viable worlds and registered their claim for future development. As far as Mira knew none of the large corporations operated in the Vale. Aside from the legal restrictions imposed by the Vega Treaty, the region was considered a stellar wasteland.

"You know, there is a section in *The Creed* that talks of a cycle of destruction? Life starts, life flourishes, life is destroyed. Repeat."

Mira remembered those verses.

"And those who are left prepare the way for those who come after," she said. "Do you think the Ark contains those who were left?"

"Maybe. The problem is we only have the Verani Creed and

like most religious books it has more to say about the organisation of their society than it does historical events."

Mira tried to piece it together; if the Ark contained those who were left, it would explain why the Verani were interested in it. It would confirm them as *The Ones Who Came After*. Such an artefact would strengthen the power of the religious caste. Her knowledge of Verani politics was sketchy, but she knew enough to understand the power struggles at the top of their society.

They're not much different to us, I guess.

She caught Flynt staring at her, an odd smile on his face.

"You still chew your bottom lip when you think." He laughed. "Mira, don't sweat it. You look tired. The Creed is mostly bollocks. It would appear to hold truth, but it's not written by or intended for us. It's a tool for Verani clerics to hold on to power."

It all was all so distant and remote. Mira would have dismissed it all out of hand had it not been for her connection to the artefact. None of it made any sense. It was like an un-winnable game being played out over millennia by players she could not see or understand.

"But why, Jon? Why this cycle? What's it for?"

"Why do we suffer Mira?" he replied. "You have suffered so much in recent years; why keep going? Why not just stop?"

"The thought crossed my mind; I tried more than once."

He ignored her and continued. "I have an idea that we suffer because we have to. Suffering makes us fight. Suffering makes us become who we are meant to be."

Mira thought about it. She was still here; she had prevailed.

I'm still the same sad loser I always was, but I'm working on it.

"So the cycle is a kind of evolutionary thing, survival of the fittest?"

"It is as good an explanation as any. A species rises, grows strong. What happens when it meets its match? There is only one winner, the strongest. The cycle of destruction, natural selection via conflict."

They fell silent.

"Jon I'm not going back. I will do what they asked of me. I'm taking the Ark home, back to Arethon."

He put an arm around her. "I can't help you," he said.

"I know."

Returning the Ark may not yield answers, it may just present more questions and dangers. It was an uncertain future, an exciting future.

Mira took the stairway down to the hangar's main deck and toward the ship's access ramp. Tish was waiting, her flight suit unzipped and the arms tied around her waist. Her synth leather vest top shimmered under the lights. Despite the chill air of the hangar her alabaster skin glistened with beads of sweat. Her face lit up as Mira approached.

"Hey," Mira said. "Thank you again for coming for us."

"We would have been there sooner but their fighters were all over us before we could engage the stealth system. Xander is aboard the ship. He wants to talk."

Mira glanced uncertainly at Flynt.

"You can trust him Mira, just talk to him."

She took a step toward the ramp and realised Tish was not coming.

"Just head forward. He's in the main crew lounge; you can't miss it. What he has to say is for your ears only, apparently," Tish said.

"Okay, will you wait for me?"

"Of course!" She beamed.

Mira climbed the ramp and entered the ship. The only sound was her footsteps as she walked through the bright corridors. The vessel was powered down. It was almost too quiet. Starships normally pulsed with life and noise; the throb of the engines provided a background to the sounds of humanity. To Mira an idle vessel was nothing more than a lifeless mausoleum of technology.

She found the crew lounge. Xander Rhodes was sitting on a red synth-leather couch. He glanced up from his datapad.

"Mira Thorn, you have had a most eventful day," he said. He gestured for her to take a seat. She perched on the edge of the opposite couch.

"It has been one of those weeks. You know how it is."

He gave her his datapad

"Look at this."

She scanned the plot. It showed a timeline of the battle. The flight path of the Kobo was highlighted from the moment they left the station until the *Nemesis* picked them up.

"We were in open space for a long time," Mira observed. The timeline showed 124 minutes elapsed from their ejection until pickup.

Xander sat forward.

"That interested me. Your suit only had an air supply for 60 minutes."

"What about reserve?"

"That includes the reserve. Operational time is 45. They are not designed for EVA, just for internal pressure loss."

"The Ark said it would sustain us."

"It seems to like you."

"Why me? I'm not special."

"Everyone is special, Mira. It took a long time for me to understand that. We all contribute our best to make the universe better."

"I'll do what it wants. I'll take it to Arethon. Tish said you built this ship to go to the Vale. Let me take it there."

"I hoped you would say that. We'll take a few days to get our crew together and we'll head out. It will piss off the Verani and violate Federal Law, but you can't please everyone all the time."

Mira stood. Xander sprung to his feet and put his hand out.

"Welcome to the Blades, Thorn; even if it is a temporary arrangement."

After a slight hesitation she took his hand. His grip was firm and his eyes full of childlike excitement.

CHAPTER FOURTEEN

THE Mercury class diplomatic vessel touched down in a cloud of Luna dust. The ship was a sleek, efficient, almost Art Déco design. The hull was polished silver alloy. The four star drives concealed in sleek nacelles beneath the swept wings. Mercury class ships were the smallest vessels in the EarthGov Diplomatic Fleet, with accommodation for a single representative and their staff. What the Mercury lacked in size it compensated for with speed.

Vanessa Meyer seldom used government vessels; she preferred the scheduled services of Virgin Galactic.

EarthGov had not confirmed the attack on her shuttle as an assassination attempt, but had insisted government staff and representatives were to use DipCorps vessels. Such a restriction would normally have angered her but on this occasion it offered her certain benefits.

"Ben, the flight crew," she said. "Are they aware of our destination?"

"Yes, Senator. As you requested, they are cleared to level one. They didn't so much as blink when I told them where we are going."

"Good, let's get aboard."

As she walked toward the boarding tunnel a man dressed in

a light blue suit approached her. He wore a badge identifying him as a member of the Vice President's staff. Ben stepped between them, blocking his approach.

"Senator Meyer!" the man said. "I'm glad I caught you. The Vice President asked me to give you this."

He gave her a thick brown envelope sealed with a holographic seal of the Vice President. Meyer ran her thumb over the stylised representation of the Milky Way.

"Thank you Mr…"

"No names…" he said, already turning to leave. "Vice President Santiago said he hoped you would find the contents of interest. He also asked me to give you a message."

She raised an eyebrow.

"He said whatever happens, you know the truth about him and not to lose faith. Aside from that he wished you safe passage." The man shrugged. "He said it would make sense in time." The man excused himself and rushed away.

The Mercury lifted off the pad and broke free of The Moon's gravity. It turned onto a heading toward Mars where a gravitational slingshot would propel the vessel back through the inner system and around the sun. The second slingshot would push them onward to the realm of the gas giants. Protocol dictated that vessels could only build their FTL envelopes when beyond the orbit of Neptune. It made for a tedious start to any interstellar journey.

Fortunately Meyer had something to occupy her.

She opened the envelope and slid out a folder containing several documents. A note in Daniel Santiago's handwriting lay on top.

Vanessa,

I apologise for what you may have seen as a lack of interest or consideration today.

There is a concern that a certain individual has a vested interest in the Frontier Company and their activities.

I have information our mutual friend authorised FRONCO to conduct a military operation against the Tarantella station. Such authority resides with his office but it is subject to Admiralty authorisation. Neither he nor Frontier have sought clearance from Admiral Foster.

It is unlikely the Admiralty would sign off on such an operation, due to the potential for civilian casualties.

We are unsure why this action is being taken, however we have an indication it may have something to do with a Lightfoot vessel heading for Tarantella.

Perhaps more disturbingly we have evidence that the subject has had dealings with a chapter of the Blue Knights. This also seems to relate to the Lightfoot corporation and their activities in the Cygnus Vale, notably a world known as LDC-132.

My operative has information stating that the Blue Knights are en route to LDC-132; their intentions are unknown. This information is credible but unverified.

Our friend has been the subject of much research by my office and the enclosed dossier provides all we have on him. The information is sensitive and carries a security rating of Red Ultra.

This situation is fluid, and the information is scarce. Please be careful Vanessa.

Yours

DS.

Meyer folded the note.

"Ben, would you be a dear and pour me a drink? A large one."

Meyer took out her datapad and typed a message. She hit send and Ben presented her with a glass half full of her favoured Martian Brandy.

"I hope this gets to you in time, Xander," she murmured.

Ben raised an eyebrow at the mention of the name.

"My... an old friend, Ben. One who thinks he has an opt-out clause from Federal Law. In his defence he has a good heart."

She finished her drink as the Mercury transitioned to FTL.

CHAPTER FIFTEEN

THE transport tube came to a halt at the top of the station with a hiss of compressed air. Xander stepped out and made his way through the darkened corridor to his quarters. He hummed to himself; it was a tune he'd heard Tish streaming to her datapad.

It had been a tough day. Xander had never expected to engage a Frontier battle group, nor had he expected a Navy dreadnought to come to their aid. It paid to have friends in strange places.

He had been reluctant to admit it, but he had been impressed by Flynt's dreadnought. It carried a formidable weapons system, backed up by serious armour. His own *Nemesis* was a technological wonder but it would struggle against a Norseman. He reminded himself they were different tools, designed for different roles. The *Nemesis* was a rapier, the *Valhalla* a two handed battle axe.

As he approached his quarters, the silence pressed in on him. A dull ache burned in his skull and fatigue clouded his thoughts. It was an unusual feeling for a man who always tried to be on top of his game.

He had read the damage reports. The death toll stood at 1,287 with another 302 injured. The cargo docks were badly damaged and would take weeks to repair. The reduced cargo capacity would impact trade and that would seed unrest. The time ahead would be a challenge, but people here were strong. They would bury the dead, tend to the wounded, make repairs and carry on.

A large man in an ill fitting business suit was staring out at the belt with his back turned to Xander. He held a glass of whiskey in one hand, the bottle in the other.

"Oliver?" Xander said.

"Xander, this is a special room you know. Back in the old days I always planned to have my accommodation here."

"I hear you're not doing so badly for yourself," Xander replied.

Oliver turned from the window and waddled to the centre of the room.

"Xander, things are not right on Tarantella," he said. "People are worried and as your friend I thought it wise to bring their concerns to you."

"Oliver, that's kind. I have things under control."

"That is as may be, but as a friend I owe you my candour."

Xander motioned to the couch. Oliver sat and poured himself a top up. There was a hiss of air as the foam cushions accommodated his weight.

Oliver placed the bottle on the table and took a mouthful of whiskey. His jowls and chins shook as he shuddered through the burn.

"I hope you don't mind me helping myself. This is a fine blend."

"Knock yourself out. Your concerns?"

"Not *my* concerns Xander, the Trade Guild's concerns. They feel the refugee crisis is getting out of hand. We don't have the infrastructure to support a humanitarian mission."

Xander regarded Oliver with a cool stare. The man seemed

to gain weight every time Xander met him. Oliver was right, they had a long history together and right now that was the only thing keeping the conversation civil.

"They have nowhere else to go, besides it is good for trade. Most of them are just passing through."

Oliver gave a hollow smile that never made it to his eyes.

"If only that were the case. The shippers are charging ever increasing fares for onward passage, leaving more of these unfortunates stranded here."

Xander knew what was being said on the station's news channel and the local UniNet node; his open door policy was leading to resentment from residents. He knew the station had limited facilities, but was not prepared to close the door on those in need.

"We can arrange onward passage using some of my ships and once the *Angel* is repaired, we can move even more people to the Core Systems."

Oliver laughed.

"Xander, do not be so naïve. The Core Systems don't want them any more than we do. They're *Outlanders* they have no documentation and no right of access."

Outlanders were tasked with establishing new non corporation colonies. Entry rights to the Core Systems were surrendered in exchange for a relocation package. Movement restrictions extended to their descendants. When the Frontier expanded, the population of Outland Colonies were accorded full freedom of movement, but were disbarred from residency in the Sol System. It was a crude attempt at population control; it was as outdated as it was barbaric.

"Xander, we live in difficult times. We have a high population that is not contributing to the wealth of the station. Our cargo facilities are damaged following an attack by a Frontier battle group and now you have a Navy dreadnought anchored to one of our piers."

"We saw off the Frontier Company and I lost good people," Xander hissed. "My fighter squadron is wiped out, so don't come in here and lecture me, Oliver. My people paid for this in blood while your precious Trade Guild were boarding ships and making for the nearest Federal outpost."

There was a pause. Xander studied Oliver. The straight cut of his suit was deformed by the rolls of fat beneath it. He had to remind himself that despite Oliver's comical appearance he was a powerful and dangerous man.

"Xander, we are grateful. The Trade Guild is split. You know there is pressure for a change in leadership?"

Xander laughed.

"I own this station."

"You do, but you also have debts. Building that vessel of yours was not cheap and hangar fees alone are extreme."

"If my finances were your concern, which they are not, you would know I can meet my commitments."

Oliver frowned. The expression was forced and laced with faux concern.

"I have no doubt you can, Xander, at the current terms. As I say these are turbulent times and many in the financial community are seeking to minimise their risk. Many are looking for safer places for their money. Debt can become unaffordable if uncertain conditions prevail."

"Are you threatening me, Oliver?"

The fat man feigned hurt. It was a theatrical parody of indignation that infuriated Xander. It took all of his control not to punch Oliver in his fat, sweaty face.

"Xander, I am speaking as a friend. This is only what I have heard. The last thing you want is for your creditors to foreclose.

You would lose the station, *The Scarlet Angel* and that thing you have been building in the central hangar. All I am saying is that if you were to relinquish control quietly, you could walk away with your assets and dignity intact. The Trade Guild will continue with the day to day running of the station. Everything will continue as normal. No shots would be fired." Oliver spat the words out. They were full of venom.

Xander was left in no doubt about his position. He tried to disguise his feelings as a satisfied smirk crossed Oliver's pudgy features.

"Oliver, when I acquired this station it was a derelict scrap pile with a three figure population. The Trade Guild only exists because I built this place into what it is."

"As I say, we are grateful to you, but back then you had more to offer. Today you have few people and no ships. If you'll excuse my candour, you brought a damaged ship onboard that endangered the whole station. Some of us are concerned you have become a liability."

Xander glared at him.

"I'll leave you to think things over, Xander," Oliver said, placing his glass on the table.

Oliver heaved himself out of the chair and waddled to the door. He paused and surveyed the room as if measuring it up. "Oh and one more thing."

"What?"

"You have our gratitude for the contribution your people made to the defence of the station. The destruction of your forces has left us... disadvantaged," Oliver said.

"I'll see what I can do."

"No need, Xander. The Trade Guild has made alternative arrangements for our security, with a third party."

Xander hated Oliver's games, the way the man had to draw

out every sentence for dramatic impact.

"With whom, Oliver?"

"The Frontier Company. We are expecting their envoy tomorrow." With that Oliver turned and left.

Xander opened a comm-channel.

"Martinez, I want the *Angel* to hold station. Repair as many systems as you can without dry dock. I need her ready to jump at short notice. Make sure the *Nemesis* is fuelled and don't offload the object. If you have anything you can't live without I suggest you find it and load it onto the *Nemesis*."

Martinez acknowledged and closed the channel.

Xander walked to the window, poured himself a drink and gazed into the void.

Tish's apartment was decorated in bright shades of orange and yellow. It was compact and spread over two levels. The upper section was a living area, with a sleeping area accessible by a flight of steps. There was a sense of order to everything, books were stacked neatly, surfaces were uncluttered. Even the cooking utensils were categorised by size and purpose.

"I thought you could crash here. Sorry it's a little untidy."

Mira could only dream of her living space being this organised.

"Thank you, Tish. I will. Don't go to any trouble. I'm happy couch surfing. It's a nice place," Mira replied. Even she could hear the fatigue in her voice. The encounter with the Ark and her near death experience had left her exhausted.

She walked around the perimeter of the apartment while Tish busied herself in the kitchen.

A bookcase covered one wall. It housed volume upon volume of text books and manuals. It took Mira a moment to understand the filing system. Books were organised by category, then by subject, then by author. Many were recognisable from the academy reading list: *Neville's Star Drive Dynamics (2312)*, *Shuster & Hussien's Studies in Atmospheric Performance (Second Edition 2318)* and *Bond's Compression Space Travel: A Study of the Implementation and Operation of the FTL Envelope (2320)*. Mira had never seen them in printed form. Other volumes were specialist studies in ship design while some had titles in the distinctive script of the Verani. On the top shelf were an array of bound folders with handwritten titles. Mira pulled one down and flicked through it. Each page was covered in handwritten script, neatly presented and spaced. The text was interspersed with diagrams and equations.

"You have quite a library," she said, as she replaced the folder.

"I like printed books. Xander has his crews pick them up for me. I have digital copies of everything, even my own notes. I like things I can touch. I'm weird."

"You're not weird Tish. You remind me a little of someone I used to know."

Mira sank into one of the oversized couches. It moulded to her body. The stress of the last few days drained away. Fatigue and loneliness were quick to fill the vacuum.

Amy had loved printed books, but then again Amy was born in the wrong century. Mira thought back to her apartment, full of old cameras that worked using a chemical film and music encoded to plastic laser discs. Tish was very much an inhabitant of the 24th century. Her preference for paper struck Mira as contrary.

"What do you want to drink?" Tish called.

"Do you have any beer?"

Tish appeared a moment later with two bottles. She tossed

one to Mira who caught it in one hand.

She checked the label. *Belt King - brewed amongst the stars for added strength. Best served at absolute zero!*

She cracked it open and took a long pull. The beer was cold, fizzy and stronger than she expected. Thoughts of the *Berlin*, the Ark and everything else slipped from her mind. Mira took another mouthful, savouring its bitter taste.

Tish crashed down beside her, rousing her from her thoughts. The girl was animated, radiating an infectious blend of happiness and excitement. *Oh to be young again*, Mira thought. *Fuck it you're thirty. You've just forgotten how to enjoy yourself.*

She realised she didn't know where her friends were.

"Tish, where is everyone?"

"Don't worry. Monica took Mr Alex to Norm's to fix him up. Richard and Ethan were going back with Jon. There was someone he wanted to bring over."

They had been good shipmates and Mira would miss them.

"Am I inappropriate?" Tish asked.

Mira looked at her, struggling to understand what she meant. Tish appeared forward and somehow innocent at the same time. Her outward appearance seemed at odds with her library and her modest apartment. Tish had mentioned Aspergers. Mira had a cousin with the condition and could see echoes of him in Tish.

"No... I'm not sure what you mean but no..."

"I worry. Xander says I over-share and sometimes say or do the wrong thing. He says I'm too forward with people I like..." She paused. "Was I wrong to ask?"

"Tish, you have nothing to worry about. You have a personality and there is nothing wrong with that."

Colour flushed in the girls cheeks. "Doctor Norm told me I

would sometimes struggle to make sense of some things people say or do."

"Do you?"

"Sometimes."

Mira clinked her bottle against Tish's. "So do I Tish, so do I."

Tish moved closer. "But you're so smart... An officer in the Navy..."

"Apparently I have ADD," Mira said. It was not something she had spoken of since an awkward visit to a doctor's office 20 years ago. "I'm supposed to be impulsive. The old me, the before the crash me, was. I used to get into trouble a lot. The only time I would feel calm was when I flew."

They fell into a comfortable silence. Mira broke it. "So what's your story? Were you born on the station?"

Tish folded her long legs behind her. Her blue eyes sparkled amongst the fading freckles. "No, I've been here for about 10 years," she said. "I grew up on the streets of Halesburg. You've probably never heard of it. It's the primary city of a mining colony called Stanley's Hope."

She was right, Mira hadn't.

"I don't know what happened to my parents. I don't really know how old I am. I lived on the streets hustling to survive. Begging is easy when you're a little kid, not so easy when you get older. I got to an age when I learned there were other ways to get by. It was a spaceport. There was no shortage of low life scum looking to get their ends wet for a few bucks."

Guilt gripped Mira's heart as she thought of her own carefree childhood under African skies. Tish's story was not unusual for the Frontier, but hearing it first hand from someone who lived it was something altogether different to reading about it on UniNet.

Mira hesitantly slipped an arm around the girl's shoulders. Tish rested her head against her and put her arm around Mira's waist.

"You don't have to tell me this, Tish," Mira said. "It must have been hard."

"It's okay, It's all in the past. I don't have regrets; there is no point. I survived. I did what I had to. It's the way of things out here. You survive because tomorrow will be better."

Tish told Mira how she was being always being busted for trying to stow away on outbound ships. Despite how tough her life had been, she still laughed at some of her stories.

"One day I got lucky. The ship took off and was FTL before they found me. They brought me to the captain. He looked me up and down and told me he would drop me at their first port of call. He told me I would have to earn my keep. I worked hard on that ship, mostly just cleaning the accommodation section. One engineer showed me around the drive system. That was when I got interested in ship design." Tish paused. "I never found out the captain's name but I owe him my life."

"When you got here, Xander took you in?"

Tish sipped her beer.

"Not right away. I was in the Medina, turning tricks. Station security busted me and he got involved. He took me in and sent me to school. I've been here ever since. My life here has been good." A nervous frown crossed her face. "Sometimes I feel different... lonely, like an outsider. There has never been any-one... Well, you know, important."

Tish paused and changed the subject. "What about you? I mean I know the sad stuff there must be good to balance it," Tish asked, her voice a whisper. "Where do you come from?"

"Where do I start? I was born in Hammersmith, in London," Mira said. She told Tish of how her parents had moved the family to Africa when she was five years old.

"My parents were lawyers for the Pan-Africa Mining Corporation. We lived on the Cape for a while. My dad had enough of corporate law and bought an energy farm in Namibia. I loved it there. I was kind of wild, always busting out of class to go on adventures. Once I hitched all the way to Dar Es Salaam." Mira laughed at the memory. "Dad grounded me. He was ready to send me to boarding school back in England."

Tish listened wide eyed. "Those places sound exciting. So far away. I've seen holo-vids of Earth. I would love to go there. Will you take me?"

"I will, Tish. When we're done with the Ark I'm going home for a while. I need to think about where my life is going."

"Can I ask you something?"

"Sure."

"You and Mr Alex, you seem tight."

Mira thought about it. She was surprised how close she had grown to Alex. He was different away from the ship. He was still a colossal dick, but his heart was in the right place. Maybe it was their near death experience or maybe everyone was different away from the Navy.

"He's a good friend. Closer than I ever thought he could be."

"Oh." Tish tensed.

"He's just a friend, Tish; one I didn't expect to have. There is nothing more to it. I don't... I prefer... I mean..." Mira's cheeks burned. She was out of practice at the whole being human thing.

"I know what you mean," Tish said, her cheeks glowed. She rested her head back against Mira's shoulder.

They sat in silence for a while. Mira listened to Tish breathe, enjoying the closeness of a warm human being. Eventually she drifted off to sleep.

Mira awoke to Tish shaking her. Her face was alive with panic.

"Come on Mira, we have to get to the upper levels. Xander told me to pack my essentials and meet him topside. Things must be bad."

Mira processed the information.

"Huh? What? You're leaving?"

Tish threw several items into a backpack, including an ornate copy of the Verani Creed. She scanned her bookshelf and pulled several volumes off and packed them alongside it.

"I guess, maybe. I don't know. He said the Trade Guild is moving against us." She scanned the apartment as if ticking off a list or maybe saying goodbye. "He always said it might come to this."

Tish opened a cupboard and removed a small hand pistol, a Heckler and Koch 100 watt energy weapon. She slipped it into her pack.

"Do you need me to carry anything?" Mira asked.

Tish shook her head.

"Most of my stuff is on the *Nemesis*. Come on," she said, heading for the door.

Mira followed Tish into a corridor. Tish led the way toward a T-junction. Two armed security personnel rounded the corner and blocked their passage.

"Get out of the way," Tish said.

Mira sized them up. They were in partial armour which protected key areas, but left others exposed. Their hands hovered close to their weapons.

"Tish, I need you to come with us," the first said, his name badge read Harman. He looked at Mira. "You are free to go about your business, Miss. I suggest you consider leaving the station."

He leered at Tish. "Your standards are falling. Are you fucking freaks now?"

The second man sniggered like a twelve-year-old boy standing tall alongside the playground bully. Mira had heard worse over the years. She controlled her breathing and kept her expression neutral.

"Okay, I don't want any trouble," she said, stepping forward. She moved between the guards and stared at Harman. When his eyes locked to hers she drove her hand forward and grabbed his balls, squeezing them as hard as she could. The guard's eyes bulged and his face turned purple, he dropped to his knees, struggling for breath. Mira kicked him in the side of the head, knocking him unconscious.

Tish pushed the second guard into the wall with her shoulder before kicking his feet from under him. She punched down on his windpipe. There was a brutal pop and the man clawed at his throat for breath.

"One of the more useful things I picked up on the streets. You fight dirty, Mira Thorn. You'll make a good Blade," she said. "Let's go!"

They raced through the corridors of the station. Tish stopped at a door in the bulkhead marked 'Maintenance Personnel Only'. She punched a code into the lock and pushed the door open.

Mira found herself in a narrow, dark stairwell. She shivered in the damp cold air. The sound of dripping water echoed off wet walls.

"This is part of the old ventilation system. No one comes in here. It's the safest way up," Tish said. "I hope you're fit."

They began the ascent. Their boots clanged on each step as they ran.

When they arrived at the top Mira was panting. Sweat matted her hair. Aside from a slight glow in her cheeks, Tish barely looked like she had climbed three kilometres. After a short run through service corridor, Tish opened a door, and they emerged into the familiar hallway leading to Xander's rooms.

"No guards up here," Mira said. "I thought this would have been the first place they would come."

"They don't want a direct confrontation. They are trying to isolate Xander. They want to put him under pressure so he walks away. That's how they operate. They're cowards."

Mira and Tish made their way to the observation lounge.

Rich and Ethan stood cradling weapons; between them was Monica, Alex and a woman Mira did not recognise. The new-comer appeared to have been subjected to a recent beating. She was dressed in a Navy issue flight suit, devoid of rank and insignias.

Martinez and Xander stood on the other side of the room, having an animated conversation. Mira could not make out what was being said.

"Eden!" Tish hissed. "What the fuck?"

Tish made toward her, her stride purposeful and her head down.

Rich Barnes stepped between them.

"Take it easy," he said. "Your man will explain everything, once we get off this rock."

Mira joined them.

"Where's Jon?" she asked.

"The Admiral has gone back to the *Valhalla*. Things are going south and he didn't want to outstay his welcome," Barnes said, handing Mira a laser rifle.

"Why didn't you go with him?"

"Jon told us what you were planning. We wanted to help," Monica replied.

For fuck's sake Jon! Haven't these people been through enough?

Tish continued to glare at the woman she had called Eden. Xander interrupted them.

"Tish! Come over. You too, Mira."

Rhodes was wearing a long leather duster, under it Mira could make out ammunition belts and lightweight body armour. He looked more like an outlaw of the Old West rather than one of the New Frontier.

"Xander?" Mira asked. His face was sallow, his eyes blood-shot. He smelled of whiskey. When she first met him he appeared to be completely in control, right now he looked stressed and close to panic.

"Listen, we have to leave. The Trade Guild is staging a coup," he said. "We're safe while Jon is moored here. When he jumps all bets are off. So we leave before he does."

Tish told Xander about the events outside her apartment.

He pulled Tish close.

"I'm sorry, kid. I should have told you what was happening."

Tish broke away, wiping a stray tear from her cheek.

"Why is my crew still here?" Mira asked.

"They volunteered. We don't have enough people to crew the ships. Jon will leave them MIA until the job is done. We'll rendezvous and you all go back to the fleet. He has a cover story in place."

Mira accepted the explanation; now was not the time to argue. Tish was still agitated.

"What about her?" Tish pointed at Eden.

"Same reason. Eden had a run in with some Blue Knights. She has offered to crew for us in exchange for a crack at them. Ten minutes ago I received a message informing me those same Blue Knights were heading for LDC-132. Now if we're all done, I suggest we get out of here before the Trade Guild grow a pair big enough to knock on my door."

Mira turned to her crew. "Come on! Xander is in charge!"

Xander rolled back the carpet and exposed a hatchway. Beneath it was a dark shaft. A corroded steel ladder disappeared into the darkness.

"It's about a kilometre down, then a half hour run to the hangar."

Mira looked at Alex. He was tired and haggard, with fresh bruises under his eyes.

"Xander what about Alex?"

"Martinez, you take care of Mr Kite."

"I'm okay," Alex said. "Just give me a weapon."

Barnes fell in beside Alex and Martinez. The three of them climbed into the opening, one after the other.

Only Mira and Xander were left as Tish climbed into the shaft.

"Xander, what's happening? I heard you had 2,500 Blades at your command."

"Don't believe the hype, Mira Thorn. I have about 200 people in my organisation, maybe another hundred who I trust enough to contract for me. I scaled down when I bought this place. I was earning more than enough to get the *Nemesis* project underway and keep the Trade Guild happy."

"Are they powerful enough to oust you?"

"On their own I doubt it. They may control station security and trade, but that's a very different job to keeping the whole machine from breaking down. The problem is overnight I learned they have a new ally. The Frontier Company made friends with them following their attempt to take the station by force."

"FRONCO would destabilise the station to get their hands

on the Ark?"

"Frontier and whoever is a backing them." He gave a hollow laugh. "The short version is: I'm fucked."

He pointed to the hatch. "We have to move. Station security have been trying to break into the hangar. It's a reasonable assumption to think they are after the Ark. We'll talk more when we are underway."

Mira lowered herself into the shaft. It was tighter than she expected. After a final glance up, she started her descent into the black heart of Tarantella.

CHAPTER SIXTEEN

Mars orbit was the most congested sector of human space, eclipsing even Earth's volume of raw tonnage. This was the gateway to the stars; a staging post for outbound traffic to the Frontier. All the corporations maintained cargo hubs above the red planet. The Frontier Company operated all but three.

Traffic movements were relentless. For every vessel breaking orbit another two entered. Endless lines of freighters were stacked by overworked traffic controllers into long queues waiting for service at their destination ports. Ships could be held in the traffic pattern for days and even weeks.

The traffic stack was an irrelevance for anyone on a diplomatic shuttle. David Conway's spaceplane dropped into an approach orbit and bypassed the holding queue. The ship's wings bit into the thin atmosphere and began to glow as the red surface sped beneath the ship at four times the speed of sound. After three orbits the ship roared into Mariner City's spaceport.

Conway drummed his fingers on the armrest while he waited for the ship to power down. The seatbelt light went out and his steward approached. The young man lifted Conway's case from the overhead locker.

"Is there anything you require, Senator?"

"No, thank you, Stephen." He took his case and made his

way to the hatch.

"Have my diplomatic bags shipped to the Curiosity Hotel. I will be staying overnight. Be sure to have the ship ready for the return trip."

"Of course, Sir."

Conway crossed a walkway encased in transparent plexiplate. The red landscape surrounded him. In the distance giant funnels of dust spiralled into the air and danced toward the western horizon. Ahead of him the primary dome arched upward. It was bluish green from the outside, from the inside the chemical composition gave the illusion of a blue sky to the dome dwellers who lived beneath it.

The arrivals zone was deserted, save for a few business travellers and three cleaning bots tracing their predetermined path over the granite floor. Armed security personnel out-numbered the inbound passengers five to one. The security presence was not the only reminder of the war; one wall was scorched black and covered in pits from shrapnel. It stood as a stark reminder of the conflict that had killed so many Martians and brought the galactic economy crashing to its knees. Wilting bunches of flowers lay in front of the wall as a tawdry memorial to the fallen.

Conway cleared customs with a flash of his diplomatic identity card and called a cab to take him to his destination.

The computer controlled vehicle darted through busy streets that could have belonged to any Federation world, save for the distortion brought about by the dome. The car dropped through an underpass and left the primary dome. An illumin-ated sign above the roadway read 'Dome 4 - Industrial and Fabrication'.

Conway took out his data assistant and sent an encrypted burst message. The reply came back in an instant.

I am waiting for you at the agreed meeting place.

Be here in 15 or I leave.

After clearing the freeway, the car threaded its way through an industrial zone. It came to a halt outside a tired, characterless factory unit. A grimy, worn out sign proclaiming it the home of *Mars Lifting Inc, Sub Orbital Lifting, Anywhere Anytime. Best Rates in Mariner City and Beyond!* A comic book sketch of an obscenely curvaceous girl adorned the sign. She wore a pink space suit and was giving the viewer an exaggerated thumbs up. A local artist had made their own contribution to the artwork with the addition of a spray painted penis curving upward toward the dome.

Conway swiped an untraceable credit disk over the cab's meter and the door swung open. He disembarked, straightened his suit and walked through the main entrance.

He entered a warehouse. A few empty packing crates and worn out lifting equipment were the only contents.

"Von Hagen?" he called. A figure moved on the overhead gantry.

"Mr Conway." The figure stepped out of the shadows and revealed himself to be a thickset man, pushing sixty yet well toned. He wore a simple set of overalls and chewed on an unlit pipe. His hair was grey, his face wide and had the pasty complexion common to Martians.

The leader of Martian Dawn was distinctly unremarkable.

"Come up, let's talk." Von Hagen beckoned Conway to follow.

Conway climbed a steel staircase. Von Hagen was already at

the end of the walkway. He disappeared into an office of corrugated metal suspended from the ceiling by thick cables.

Conway followed, his shoes clanging on the steel mezzanine. The office was like every other grubby industrial office in the galaxy. Faded Playboy calendars hung from the walls along with notices and order schedules. The only furniture was a pair of blue steel desks, littered with yellowed paperwork. A tired Delphi branded terminal sat on each one.

Von Hagen was sitting in a decrepit chair, his feet on the desk, his hands crossed behind his head.

"Take a seat," he said. He gestured to a rough blue chair with holes mended with duct tape. Conway sat without hesitation, not taking his eyes off Von Hagen.

"What are you staring at?" Von Hagen asked. His voice was more puzzled than aggressive.

"The great Max Von Hagen. The man who won the Martian War of Independence." Conway laughed. "You're not quite what I expected."

"That's why I am still alive, Mr Conway. Being unremarkable is the best way to survive in plain sight of your oppressor."

"You won't find any argument from me on that point," Conway replied. "Tell me Von Hagen, how does it feel to have won that very bloody war yet still lost the peace?"

Von Hagen tensed. The veins on the sides of his neck flared. Conway made a mental note. Knowing how your associates operated was essential if you ever needed to put them in their place. Von Hagen relaxed, letting the remark pass.

"It's a long game, Mr Conway. The fact you are here confirms that we are not done yet."

"I am here because you requested I be here, and it's *Senator* Conway," he corrected.

Von Hagen chuckled. "I don't recognise your government,

so out here with me you are just plain *Mister Conway*."

Conway blinked. Von Hagen was a sharper prospect than he had expected; caution would be necessary.

"To business then." Conway popped his case open and removed a data card. He tossed it to Von Hagen who studied it before tucking it into his top pocket.

"On that card you will find all the information you need to conduct the operation," Conway said. "I will leave the final planning to you; after all you have the experience, contacts and local knowledge."

"What about hardware?"

"It is in hand. I have two diplomatic bags being offloaded from my ship as we speak. They'll be shipped to any address you require. One of them contains a second data card containing operational codes, frequencies and passphrases. I have arranged a fake identity that carries Triple A privileges."

Von Hagen scribbled a note on a scrap of paper and gave it to Conway.

"There," he said.

They sat in silence for a moment, getting the measure of each other.

"Do this properly and you'll have your independence inside of a year. If it goes wrong, well that'll be on you."

"I understand," he said.

Another awkward pause.

"See yourself out, *Mister* Conway."

Conway stared at the rebel leader a moment longer. He stood and left without another word.

He stepped out onto the street and used his datapad to hail a cab. Before boarding it he sent a message to a courier company to collect and deliver the diplomatic bags to the address Von Hagen had supplied.

He screwed Von Hagen's note into a ball and was about to toss it away. He stopped and chastised himself for his recklessness. He tucked the ball into his suit pocket.

Conway took a final look around the industrial area. The dome was low overhead, and the buildings followed its contour. Mariner and all of Mars was such an unpleasant place. He wondered why anyone cared enough to fight over it.

After a seemingly endless descent, Mira stepped off the ladder. She caught her breath and opened and closed her hands several times to work out the stiffness. Rich Barnes was waiting. Babs was slung over his shoulder.

"Tish has taken everyone down. I thought I would hang back for you two. I dunno about him." Barnes pointed at Rhodes. "But I know you can't shoot for shit."

"Let's hope we don't have to find out," she replied.

The sound of laser fire echoed down the corridor. Barnes rolled his eyes and shrugged. He readied his weapon.

"I guess I spoke too soon."

"Security must have worked out what's happening," Xander said.

Barnes dashed through the blast door, ducking under the partially lowered shutter. Mira unslung her weapon and checked the charge. Xander produced a pair of chromed high calibre pistols from beneath his duster.

"Xander? Projectile weapons?" Mira asked. "Are you serious?"

"I'm a traditionalist, besides we're below the surface. It's all rock behind these walls. Come on let's move."

They followed Barnes through a wide pentagonal tunnel toward the sound of the gun battle. The crack of laser weapons grew louder. Discharges flashed in the darkness ahead of her.

Her footfalls echoed on the decking. She glanced down to see the bare rock of the asteroid beneath the walkway, confirming Xander's assertion of their depth.

"How long is this tunnel?" Mira asked.

"About three clicks," Xander replied.

She picked up her pace and rounded a corner. Ethan, Martinez and Eden were crouched behind a stack of cargo canisters. Monica was doing all she could to prevent Alex joining the fight. Ahead of them Mira counted ten station security operatives. Ethan stood and fired a burst of laser fire. A guard fell backwards, a glowing hole in his body armour. The sound of the man's scream reached her ears a few seconds later.

Mira ran to Ethan's cover and aimed her weapon. A bolt of energy flew above her head and into the steel bulkhead.

"Shit!" she screamed, slamming herself to the deck. She peeped over the transit case and managed to get off a couple of blasts. She did not know if they hit anything.

There was an ear-splitting roar. Mira glanced behind her. Smoke rose from the barrels of Xander's hand cannons. Incoming fire intensified, and she hunkered down. She shook as the dark tendrils of fear and panic infiltrated her consciousness.

Mira steadied herself. She rose to a crouch, and took aim at a security operative. She pulled the trigger to the first position. Time dilated as if she had crossed the event horizon of a black hole. She held her breath and squeezed the trigger to the second position. The weapon was recoilless but still vibrated with the discharge. Her target dropped to the floor, his face burned away and his weapon falling from his grasp. Mira ducked back into cover as adrenaline banished her fear demon.

"Where is Tish?" she asked.

"She was right where you are!" Ethan yelled.

Mira called the same question to Martinez. He shook his

head and continued to return fire.

No matter how many of the guards they dropped the incoming fire never seemed to abate. Mira lined up another shot. She missed, as did Barnes. Martinez downed two. Their places were taken by more troops.

An energy bolt fizzed past Mira. She heard a cry from behind her. Martinez spun and went down, clutching his shoulder. Monica broke cover and ran to him. The big man groaned and tried to stand. Monica applied a sterile dressing while Alex scooped up the rifle and fired.

"Xander, there must be another way!" Mira screamed "There are too many…"

A blinding flash lit the tunnel. A rush of hot air knocked Mira to the deck as the roar of the explosion rolled past her. She covered her head as dust and rubble rained down. Something wet landed on her arm; it took a moment for her to realise what she was looking at. With a shudder she brushed the severed finger away.

A hush fell. The only sound was moans coming from the tunnel ahead. After a laser blast they stopped; the silence pressed in. Mira shook her head, trying to clear the ringing from her ears. She peered over the packing case. Thick white smoke boiled in the tunnel, it thinned as the extraction system stirred the air. The artificial breeze carried the stench of burned flesh.

Mira stood, her weapon raised; the others were doing the same. A figure appeared through the smoke.

Tish walked toward them. Her strides were long, her pace unhurried, bordering on cocky. She carried her pulse rifle upside down over her shoulder, her finger still on the trigger. In spite of the swagger there was a look of sorrow and confusion on her face.

"I stole an incendiary grenade from right under their noses," she said as she reached them. "I knew some of those guys." She sniffed and sat on one of the transit cases.

"How did you get over there?" Mira asked.

"Under the floor. I crawled behind them and tossed the grenade. It was brutal."

"What the fuck did you expect?" Eden snapped. Her tone was hostile and angry. "Toss an incendiary in a confined space and people will fry. We are lucky you didn't take us with them."

Mira shot her a look.

Eden walked off, cursing under her breath.

Mira took Tish's hands. There was a familiar look in the girl's eyes, the haunted stare that comes when death is personal and too easy; when you wonder if part of you has died along with the target.

Xander knelt next to her and put a hand on her shoulder.

"You did well kid. You saved us. Don't worry about Eden. She has her own issues right now."

Tish composed herself.

"This was an advance patrol. I think they were chancing their luck. We should move. They will have called for reinforcements." Tish stood and slung her weapon.

"Glad you're on our side," Barnes said as he walked past to take up point. Martinez staggered to his feet, took his weapon back from Alex and joined him.

Tish smiled. It was a weak substitute for the real thing, but it didn't matter to Mira.

"Can you walk with me?" Tish asked. "I don't want to walk through it on my own."

"Sure," Mira replied. She reached out and took Tish's hand without thinking. "Sometimes, everyone needs someone to hold their hand." she said.

The smoke had all but cleared. Ahead of them were a dozen twisted and burnt bodies. Some were burned to just bone and tendon. Mira had once landed in a rebel position that had been hit with an orbital strike. That had been tame in comparison to the surrounding carnage.

"Close your eyes, Tish. Let me lead the way."

"No," she said. "I did this. I have to live with it."

One body had been blown against the wall and sat as if taking a rest. The man's exposed flesh and been burnt black. Steam rose from his eye sockets as his internal fluids continued to boil.

Despite her growing fatigue and back pain, Mira broke into a run.

"Come on, Tish. Let's get to your ship."

They fell into line at the rear of the column, neither of them looked back.

Martinez pointed to a floor hatch and Barnes spun the release mechanism to open it. He lowered a mirror through and spun it in a circle.

"Clear," Barnes said. He jumped through the opening. He landed on the metal gantry with a clang.

One by one they climbed down. When it came to Mira's turn she dangled her legs through. It was a long drop even for someone the height of Barnes. She counted to three and slid her body through the hatch. She gripped the edge and hung there before releasing her grip. She landed gracefully on the gantry. It did not prevent the flare of pain in her back; she bit down on her lip until it subsided.

Tish clattered to the deck behind her and offered her a hand. She stood and stretched.

"So who is she, anyway?" Mira gestured toward Eden who

was standing next to Martinez, her face unreadable.

"Eden? She used to be a Blade but didn't like taking orders. Last I heard she'd been working as an independent. She poached some of our people. Fritz and Romain were good guys." Tish did not take her eyes off Eden while she spoke.

"No love lost between you two then?"

Tish shook her head. "She and Xander, well you know how it is. He's over it now. I'm surprised he let her back."

"Come on, let's get moving!" Xander shouted from the stairway. They headed toward the lowered entry ramp.

Figures ran into the bay and took cover by the blast door. Unlike those they had met in the tunnel these were armoured Frontier Company Shock Troops.

"How did they get aboard?" Mira screamed, ducking for cover as laser fire fizzed above her head.

"A lot of ships have been coming and going," Xander said. "Get down!" he added, just in case anyone had failed to appreciate the situation.

They want the Ark, Mira thought.

If the Trade Guild wanted Xander gone, it would make sense for them to let him leave. Frontier must have worked out what had happened to the object.

Mira flicked weapon's safety switch off and fired a salvo of blasts as they all opened fire. The ship's ramp was about fifty metres away, the Frontier Troopers another hundred beyond it. They were outnumbered and outgunned. Getting to the ship was their only hope.

"I can get onboard and start her up, if you can lay down covering fire," she said.

Xander studied the scene as if checking the plan in his own mind.

"Tish, Eden and Private Tate, go with Mira Thorn. When

you get there, lay down cover for the rest of us while she starts the departure process."

Mira gathered them together. Tish glared at Eden.

"Take it easy; we have a job to do," Mira said.

Tish broke her gaze. "Okay."

"Tish, we can have it out later if it would make you happy. Let's get this done first," Eden said. She raised her weapon.

"Are you ready?" Eden asked Mira.

Mira nodded and broke cover. She ran forward, firing. Adrenalin and terror surged through her system. Behind her the rest of them opened fire in a cacophony of laser weapons and solid ordinance. The boom of Xander's pistols was unmistakable in the symphony of destruction.

Time slowed. Sounds were muffled and her vision shrank to a tunnel. After an eternity she slid into the cover of the ramp. Eden was close behind. A blast of energy flew over Mira's shoulder. Tish tumbled to the ground and lay motionless.

"Tish!" Mira screamed over the noise of the battle.

Ethan Tate dropped to his knees next to the girl and dragged her to the ramp.

"Mira get on board and start her up. Get us out of here," he shouted.

Mira put her fears for Tish to the back of her mind and ran. Her boots gripped the rubberised decking and propelled her into the *Nemesis*.

Breathing hard, she arrived at the flight deck. Mira powered on the avionics and began the engine start sequence. She tapped into the turret controls and swivelled the weapon to target the area close to the hangar entrance. She squeezed the trigger and released a devastating stream of energy into the side of the station.

The flight deck speaker crackled into life.

"Mira!" It was Xander's voice. "We're all on board. I'm sending Eden forward to copilot for you."

Mira didn't wait. She increased the power to the vertical lifters, and the *Nemesis* rose into the air. Retracting the struts, she reversed the ship out of the bay. The ship was responsive and powerful. It immediately felt like an extension of herself.

Eden jumped into the seat next her and clipped on a headset.

"Martinez is hurt; Tish is in shock and your flyboy is having trouble breathing, so you have me. I'm Eden. I guess you know that."

"Mira," she replied. "Tish is okay?"

Eden completed strapping herself in.

"She took a glancing hit on the leg. It's just a cosmetic burn but it has left her shaken. She's just a kid who talks a good fight. I always told her being good on the range is one thing and being good against the living is another."

Mira flipped the ship through 180 degrees. She walled the throttles as they passed through the hangar's ion curtain. They headed away from the station with a 6G acceleration.

"Xander wants to rendezvous with the *Angel* at the solar plant. I am laying in the course now," Mira said.

"Do you know how to operate the weapons on this thing?" Eden asked.

"No, will we need them? The station lost its defence fighters in the engagement."

"There were Shock Troops on the station. If they are onboard I assume a Frontier fighter detachment must be embarked too," Eden replied.

Mira could not fault the logic. She opened a public channel on the com-link.

"Xander! I need someone to handle the weapons. We might

need to fight our way clear," she said.

There was a pause.

"Martinez is out of action and Tish is in no state to do it either," he replied.

"Do we have anyone else?"

"Yeah, me." Xander appeared in the doorway. He sat at the weapons console. "It'll be just like the old days. I'm hoping we don't need the main battery, that's Martinez's domain. I can control the turrets from here."

"*Valhalla* is underway," Eden reported.

Mira glanced at the scanner; Flynt was moving the dreadnought between the *Nemesis* and the station, a standard blocking manoeuvre that dated to the time of Nelson.

Eight traces appeared on the scanner.

"We have company!" Mira said, pulling the ship onto an escape vector.

"I have it covered," Xander said, his voice calm.

"Vector the shield toward them, Eden," Mira said, without taking her eye off the forward display.

"Flynt won't be able to engage," she added. "So this is down to us."

The *Nemesis* was still accelerating. Tarantella fell behind them, shrinking to a tiny speck of light. The ship's velocity relative to the fighter craft decreased and Mira was not surprised when the first bolts of energy hit their shields.

"Poor effort," Eden said. "They didn't so much as scratch us. You have some pretty tasty shields on this can, Rhodes."

"You like that E?" he said. "You'll love this!"

The ship shuddered as the laser turrets extended and fired. Mira looked to the scanner and the traces of the fighters disappeared one after another.

"The targeting computer had them tracked from the moment they entered our sensor range. They were dead as soon as they launched." Xander pushed his seat back. "I'll take the credit but anyone could have hit the button."

"No more fighters," Eden reported.

They were clear of the station; the Ark was on board and their casualties had been light. Today had worked out just fine.

The solar station came into view. It comprised a cylindrical core with long panels extending from the central hub. The panels captured the star's energy and converted it to electricity to be stored in giant batteries. It had been an integral part of the miner's supply chain. When the miners left, the station had fallen into disuse.

"I've not been here for a while," Eden said as the station filled the viewport.

"What does Xander use it for?" Mira asked.

"It's a supply dump. He stores the things here he wouldn't store on Double T. He's kept it going all these years. I think he knew today would come." She paused. "For what it's worth, I'm sorry about your ship."

"The *Berlin*?"

"It was my crew that took down that Kobo. We kicked it all off. I'm sorry."

Mira stood and put a hand on Eden's shoulder. "It isn't down to you. It sounds like things didn't work out so good for you either."

"Are we cool, then?" Eden asked.

She felt no animosity to Eden; she didn't feel anything right now other than the relief of being alive.

"We're good, Eden. You have the ship. I'm going to check on everyone."

By which you mean Tish, don't you Thorn? her Shadow

Sister whispered. *I can see through you, even of the others can't.*

Eden commenced the docking procedure.

Mira walked aft through the wide central corridor. She wasn't familiar with the layout of the ship and nothing was well signed. After a few wrong turns she found herself in the medical bay.

Monica was tending to Martinez's arm. Alex was trying to assist and appeared more of a hindrance than a help.

"Thorny!" he said.

"Alex, how are you feeling?"

"Better. Doc drained my lungs last night; it wasn't pleasant. I'd rather have my balls dipped in hot oil than go through that again."

"Alex," Monica said, without taking her eyes off her patient. "Just because you have been spending time with Commander Thorn, there is no need to adopt her language. You have a university education; she has a vulgar tongue and mind like a sewer."

Mira smirked. It was fair point.

"Is... Tish down here?" she asked as casually as she could.

"Through there with Rhodes," Alex said. He pointed to a side room.

Mira stood in the open doorway and knocked on the bulkhead. The room was dark. Xander was talking to Tish who sat on the edge of a bunk wrapped in a silver Mylar blanket. She was shaking. Xander was trying to calm her.

Tish had discarded her jeans and vest in favour of a simple flight suit, albeit one decorated with artificial gem stones.

"Xander?" Mira said.

"She has a minor burn. The whole experience has shaken her up. It has hit her harder than I ever imagined it would."

"I'll come back," Mira said.

"Mira don't go," Tish said. "Please."

She stopped and walked to the bunk. Xander stepped aside and left.

"Tish, I thought the worst when I saw you go down."

"I'm okay. It was just a burn. Mira, I've never been this scared. I feel sick."

Tish appeared lost and vulnerable. The confident persona replaced by a subdued shadow. Mira reminded herself that Tish had lost the only home she had ever known, or at least known happiness in.

"I killed all those people; that shot should have killed me."

Mira gazed into Tish's eyes; they were red and damp, but retained their sparkle. Mira found a paper tissue and dabbed the tears away.

"It doesn't work that way, Tish. You did what you had to do. It isn't easy or pleasant. The time to worry is when you feel nothing, or worse still enjoy it."

Mira's stomach flipped. Tish was closer to her now. She did not know how it had happened, or what to do next.

"You're shaking!" Tish said, the colour returning to her face. A mischievous laugh escaped.

Mira blushed. "Shock," she lied.

Tish slipped off the bunk. Somehow Tish was holding her. Mira stumbled over her words. "I'm sorry," she said. "I'm not great at this."

Tish moved closer. She spoke in a whisper. "Out here, in this life, you have to take chances. We could all be dead tomorrow. I thought you were cool when I saw you in the Medina. When I saw you looking at me in transport tube I knew what I wanted. So what if you would only be on the station for days or hours? The future isn't all that important; it's the now that matters."

"Mira!" Alex said from the doorway. "We've docked."

Mira stepped back, breaking Tish's hold. Her cheeks burned and her heart pounded.

"Uh... okay. Thanks Alex. I'll come up."

"Sorry, for barging in, just carry on. I'll be helping Monica. Pretend I was never here." As he left, he tripped over a medical trolley, clattering its contents to the deck.

Tish laughed, so did Mira. It felt good.

"Can... Can we continue this conversation later?" Mira asked, avoiding eye contact.

"We can, Mira Thorn," Tish replied. A sly smile crossed her face. "It doesn't need to be just conversation."

CHAPTER SEVENTEEN

THE Fusion Lance tore into the metal with a screech and burned its way through.

"Damn thing is working," Zack McArdle said in a whisper. It took all of Chloe's self restraint not to jump on the spot and clap.

"I mean I knew it would, but knowing is one thing and seeing it is another," he said. "It was smart thinking Miss Song. I'm surprised I didn't think of it myself."

The featureless alloy liquefied under the heat of the cutter and was collected in a ceramic pipe that removed the super-heated metal from the wall. The slag would be stored for later analysis. Chloe rubbed her eyes, the smell of the molten alloy had an acidic tang.

"We should move up the tunnel, Zack. It smells bad," she said. It wasn't so much the unpleasant nature of the fumes that bothered her; she suspected they could contain any number of toxins and vaporised heavy metals.

"Hell yeah," he said. "The computer will manage the cut from now on. Let's see how the other half are getting along."

They walked the short distance out of the cavern. Outside the wind had dropped but occasional gusts swirled the red dust into funnel shapes that danced across the rocky surface. Saskia

Hart and Peter Jarman stood next to the Land Rover, checking equipment. Kramer was nowhere to be seen.

Saskia called her over. Chloe acknowledged with a wave and jogged toward the giant six wheeled vehicle. As she got closer Jarman walked away.

"Good luck dealing with that one," Zack called over the wind. Chloe suppressed a smile. Her good mood threatened to desert her when she saw the stony expression on Saskia's face.

"The drill works well. If all goes to plan, we'll be through before sunset tomorrow," she said.

"Good," Saskia replied. "You did well to work that out."

"I sense a but." Chloe was in no mood for Saskia's school mistress manner today. When she had been assigned to the team she had looked at Doctor Hart with admiration, taking her every word as truth. Over the last three months Chloe realised Hart didn't have a clue what she was doing and was more out of her depth than she was. Saskia made up for her inadequacy with a condescending manner that bordered on bullying. She had found a natural ally in the egotistical Peter Jarman; both seemed to conspire to make the young intern's life as difficult as they could.

"You should have discussed it with me first and not bothered Mr Kramer. Remember I am your line manager."

Chloe stared coolly at the older woman, who shrank when she didn't fold and apologise.

"I was with Mr Kramer when I made the discovery. It made sense to bring him up to speed."

"We have a way of doing things in science. You should always have your findings peer reviewed. What if you had made a mistake? You would not have just embarrassed yourself. Your incompetence would have destroyed the reputation of the whole science team."

"That's a little harsh, Doctor Hart..."

"Life is harsh girl and in science a reputation takes years to build and seconds to destroy."

Chloe sighed. "Okay, I understand. Next time I will consult with you first."

Saskia appeared satisfied with the answer and changed the subject. "So what is happening now? When do we go to the drilling site?"

"Zack thinks it will be 12 hours before we break through. The lance is creating some nasty fumes, so we should wait up here," Chloe replied. "Zack is hooking up a feed so we can monitor the temperatures and watch how everything is progressing," she added. She knew Saskia was not interested and would spend all of her time locked in the air-conditioned cabin of the Land Rover.

"Just let me know when we break through. If you have any problems come to me first." Saskia opened the door to the vehicle and climbed inside.

Chloe agreed and made her way to Zack's control tent.

Franz Kramer sat at a folding desk in the prefabricated command unit. The wind howled outside and made the corrugated walls flex with each gust. Thin daylight fought its way through a grimy window, bringing little illumination to the hut.

Kramer used a portable terminal to establish a secure uplink to his company drop-box. A new audio message from Damien Lightfoot awaited him. It was dated a day ago; it had arrived in the last hour. A yellow exclamation mark next to the message highlighted it as urgent. Kramer hit the play button.

"Franz, thank you for your recent progress report." Lightfoot's voice carried quiet authority, beneath an Irish lilt.

"The intel division has credible information indicating your team is compromised. You were wise to ship your excavation crew off world when you did. I'm sorry I did not share your suspicions. Our intel does not rule out one of your core team being responsible.

"This is not the only unfortunate news. Your ship was intercepted, and the artefact has been stolen from Tellerman. We believe Xander Rhodes orchestrated the theft. The ship has been lost to pirates en route to him. We do not know the vessel's whereabouts or status.

"I will continue to investigate and will leave the excavation team in your hands. You know the value of the site and how much time and money has gone into this project.

"Good luck. Lightfoot out."

Kramer closed the app. He drummed his fingers on the desk as he processed the information.

Saskia Hart appeared in the doorway.

"Come in, Doctor Hart," he said.

"We are having problems with the drill head," she said.

"In what way? Zack told me it would be a matter of hours, what has changed?"

"Cutting is harder than we expected. The lance is working, but it is taking far longer to burn through than he originally calculated."

"Timescale?"

"Zack is uncertain. He is working on the worst case of three days."

Kramer slammed his fist on the makeshift desk, papers and his terminal jolted into the air.

"Do we have the power to continue?"

"Zack has gone back to base to bring up some additional power packs and a solar generator." She walked over to him and rested her hands on his shoulders. He wasn't sure what to make of it.

"Don't worry, Franz, everything is fine."

He wondered if it was.

CHAPTER EIGHTEEN

THE ancient blast door creaked and clanked as tired servo motors hoisted it into the solar station's bulkhead.

Mira was about duck under the door when Xander stopped her.

"Wait until it is locked in place. The station is old and you would be wise to take care around the bits that can kill you."

Duly warned Mira waited next to Gunny Barnes and Ethan Tate as the door continued its slow ascent on rusty chains. It locked into place with a clang.

"Come on," Xander said. "We had better make this quick before the boys on the station work out where we are. The Trade Guild will not care, but those Frontier troops are looking for the Ark."

"So what's the plan, Xander? I assume you have one." Mira matched his pace.

"The *Angel* is docked on the other side of the station. I'll be joining her along with Martinez. My son Luke will be joining your crew. So will he." Xander pointed to a figure approaching them. "That's Spence," he said. "Don't let appearances fool you. He is the best drive specialist I have ever met. It was him and Tish that made the *Nemesis* a reality."

Spence was a tall, thin man. His hair was long at the sides

and bald on top. He wore a pair of dark circular welding goggles on his forehead. Pieces of equipment were hung from loops on his overalls; they swung like baubles as he walked.

"Mr Rhodes, I've not seen you in a while," he said. He looked around Xander. "Is Tish with you?"

"Spence, it's always a pleasure. Tish is on the *Nemesis*. You be nice to her and respect her space," Xander said. "If you don't my new friend Gunny Barnes will have a few words with you. Are we clear on that Spence?"

"Clear as the day, Mr Rhodes." He looked at Mira and smiled. A gold tooth glinted under the station's lighting.

"What's your name, soldier girl?" His eyes crawled over her.

"My name is fuck off," she snapped. "Xander there is no way I am having him on the ship."

Xander took her to one side.

"Spence is harmless. It's his act. Underneath he's an okay guy. He's also the only person I know capable of managing the ship's drive core. You need him."

"Xander, no. We are carrying an unpredictable artefact into an unknown situation. It could be a shooting war for all we know. I don't want someone on board who is more interested in looking at my arse than they are fighting the ship."

It didn't come out as she intended. Xander dropped his gaze to the deck as he tried not to laugh.

"What difference will it make?" Xander lost his battle and burst into laughter.

"That's not the point..." Mira replied. She mentally conceded that aside from the creeped out feeling Spence gave her, she didn't have a point.

"Mira, you need to think about priorities, see the bigger picture. If it makes you feel any better I've been looking at your arse ever since you came on board." He glanced at Barnes.

"Sergeant Barnes, have you ever snuck a look at Mira Thorn's arse?"

"Occasionally."

"See what I mean? No one cares. Oh and for what it's worth I've seen you sneaking a look at Tish's arse." Xander continued to laugh. It was the most relaxed Mira had seen him since their first meeting.

She flushed, relaxed and joined the joke.

"I get it. Can we move on from my arse now? You know you sound like Jon?"

See the big picture Mira, look beyond the engagement, the battle, the war. That was one of Flynt's favourite speeches from back when she served as a Junior Flight Lieutenant on the *Illustrious*.

Spence was talking to Barnes and Ethan.

"Spence," she said. "My name is Mira Thorn. You can call me Commander Thorn."

"Affirmative, Commander Thorn."

Xander made his way to the three men and began a discussion that ended with Spence leading Barnes and Tate further into the station. He returned to Mira.

"Where are they going?"

"We're moving supplies from the *Angel*. Your magazine is a little understocked."

They stood in silence. Xander was the one to break it.

"Tish," he said. He let the name hang in the air, for a moment.

Mira's cheeks flushed.

"What about her?"

"This is her first real mission. I would rather she didn't go... but she is insistent. I want you to look after her."

"I will, Xander. She is one of the crew."

Part of me hopes she is more than that, Xander.

"Mira, she's a good shot and a good pilot, but she's unbloodied and untested. She needs someone experienced to support her. You saw how she was back on the ship?"

Mira understood, better than Xander could know and she would ever admit. The universe was a cruel place and the desire for adventure was a poisoned chalice. Mira joined the Navy to fly starships, and the universe gave her a war.

"Xander, don't worry. Rich and I will take care of her. She'll be staying on the ship until we work out what is happening on the ground. I won't put her in danger. Trust me."

Rhodes put an arm around her.

"You guys are more than welcome to run with us when you're done. We're just a big happy family. No salutes, no chain of command and one fucking amazing starship. Did I mention a charismatic and dare I say sexy beast of a leader?"

"You must introduce me to him sometime," she replied.

In truth Mira found Xander and his small crew of misfits easy to work with. They worked as a team, but not because of a hierarchy or a political directive. They worked together because they needed to do a job.

The whine of an electric motor drifted down the corridor and the headlights of a munitions truck swung into view. Spence drove while Barnes and Tate rode in the back. Gunny Barnes was laughing. Ethan looked terrified. Behind the cart was a trailer. Mira's eye widened as she realised what it was carrying.

Six SS-880 *Shipwreck* nuclear torpedoes were strapped in cradles. All of them carried Navy ident codes, all from different ships. One carried the lettering C84 - *FSS Berlin*.

"We salvaged it from the wreck," Xander said. "We figured the Navy would not miss one."

Mira watched the cart pass. Sadness washed over her as the faces of her flight deck crew haunted her thoughts.

"What about the others?" she asked.

"Borrowed from various stations. A couple were a gift from Admiral Flynt."

"So much for the fleet's weapons control protocol."

Lax inventory control did not surprise Mira. Most of the logistics staff were civilians. They were poorly paid and had little job security, so any chance to earn a little extra on the side would be tempting.

You can only grind people down so far before they stop caring. She thought. If Navy moral was low, it must be even lower amongst civilian staff.

"Mira!" Barnes yelled. "Check this out! This guy names his missiles!" He pointed at Spence.

Each torpedo bore a girls name - *Amber, Electra, Dina, Veronica, Susan* and *Maria.*

Despite herself Mira found herself smiling.

"You okay?" Xander asked.

"Yeah, I am. Thank you for this, Xander."

He raised an eyebrow. "It has been a pleasure, Mira Thorn. Come on, I'll introduce you to my boy."

He led her through the station. Every surface was old and worn. The only light came from grimy yellow service lamps.

Arriving at the *Angel's* airlock they were met by a young man, his hair blond, his face thin. He was the image of his father. Next to him stood a woman, Mira put her age somewhere in her mid forties. She was beautiful, her skin a lustrous ebony, her face framed with long chestnut hair. Angular cheek bones added to a refined, slightly aloof appearance

"Mira," Xander said. "This is Luke. He's my son and probably the best pilot of the *Nemesis*, despite what Tish would tell you."

Mira shook his hand.

"Hi," she said. "I didn't know Xander had any children."

"Neither did he until five years ago," he said.

"I'm Asha Malik," the woman said. "Seeing how Rhodes sucks at introductions."

"Mira," she replied.

"We've met before, in a manner of speaking."

Mira tried to place her. She would not have forgotten someone as distinctive as Asha Malik. Her voice had a certain familiarity... Mira could not place it.

"I was a traffic controller on Mars High during the war."

"How did you end up out here?"

"By accident. We were civilian contractors, so when the war ended I found myself out of a job. I headed for the Frontier to find my fortune. I found this lot instead. I was on the same star liner as Luke and Martinez and fell into the life when I met Rhodes. Nowadays, I astrogate this bucket." She jerked her thumb toward the *Angel*.

"I was on duty the day you came down. I was your sector controller," Asha said. "They would never tell us what happened to downed crews. I'm glad you came through."

It never occurred to her that traffic operators and ground staff felt the loss of flight crew as much as the squadron. She was lost for words.

"Thank you," Mira said.

Asha stepped a little closer.

"You're welcome, Mouse." Mira recognised her voice, she had heard it many times before.

You're welcome, Mouse. The final words she heard before that fateful last landing.

"Say what?" Xander asked.

"Just catching up with a friend," Mira replied, her voice cracked with emotion.

Asha bid her farewell and made her way back to the *Angel*. Mira was once again touched by the warmth and community among Xander's *Blades*.

Xander's voice roused her from her thoughts. "Luke knows you want to take the Ark home."

"I think you're mad, but I'm in," the young man said.

"You're not alone. Never an hour passes without me doubting my sanity," Mira replied.

Xander hugged his son.

"You're not coming with us?" she asked.

"I have other plans. Some business to take care of. I want to make some new friends," he said.

They stared at each other.

"Good luck, Thorn."

"You too, Rhodes."

They went their separate ways. Mira walked with Luke, swapping their respective experiences of the battle of Tarantella.

"So what do I call you?" Luke asked. Mira was still struggling to process how much he looked like his father.

"Uh Mira? I get called other things, but that's my given name."

"Good, I wasn't keen on Commander. No salutes?"

"No salutes. Come on, show me what you can do with this ship."

The blast door crashed closed behind them.

Mira walked through the ship's central corridor. She was happy to let Luke lead the way. There was a buzz in the air. The familiar, electric tingle every departure generated. The ship lacked the sweaty, human smell of a fleet vessel. *Nemesis* smelled of fresh paint, new plastic and clean air scrubbers. She stopped mid corridor and absorbed the atmosphere.

This is how it should have been in the Navy, how I wanted it to be in the Navy, how it never could be in the Navy,

An uncomfortable revelation hit home. It had not been the crash that had brought her career to a standstill, it had been the wallowing self pity that followed.

Luke paused, turning to face her. "Are you okay?" he asked.

"I'm fine, just enjoying the moment," she replied.

"This ship has a great vibe. I feel it every time we get underway. Come on, I'll take you to the sharp end."

When they arrived on the flight deck Tish was sitting in the copilot chair working through a checklist. Alex Kite sat behind her at the astrogation console. Mira gestured for Luke to take the pilot's seat. Before he got a chance to sit Tish leapt up.

"Lukey!" She hugged him swiftly and went back to her checklist.

"Good to see you, Tish," he said. Luke turned to Mira. "Are you sure?"

"Go ahead. It's your ship after all. Besides, everything I've flown has crashed or blown up."

"What are you doing here?" Mira asked Alex.

"Astrogating," he replied.

"Xander was supposed drop you off with Flynt. You should be on your way back to fleet, not on this... whatever we're calling it."

"Adventure works for me. Do you think I was going to miss out on the chance of seeing this ship in action? Besides, if I turn up at Federal outpost questions will be asked about the rest of you losers."

He had a point. She wondered how Flynt would square this

away.

Same way as always, he'll grin and say: 'I am an Admiral, I can do what I like.'

"Okay, plot a course flyboy."

"This is one hell of a ship, Thorny." Alex was borderline raving. "A lot of what I've seen is stock so familiarisation won't be a problem. She's better put together than anything to come out of Mars in the past 20 years, that's for sure."

"I'm glad you approve, Alex. Xander could make a fortune if he licensed the design to our people," she replied, instantly regretting the *our people.*

"The main reactor is online. I have commenced the engine start sequence. Tish is nearly through her checklist," Luke said.

Tish ticked off the final item on her list and the deck throbbed with increasing power. Tish flicked a bank of switches on the overhead panel.

"All station connections are retracted. Plasma is flowing and the sublights are hot," she said.

"Take us out, Mr Rhodes," Mira said.

After she gave the order the vibration in the deck grew more intense as the engine's power increased. The ship edged backwards, slipping away from the solar plant.

"I'm sending the escape vector the NavSystem," Alex reported.

Luke acknowledged and their relative speed increased as the *Nemesis* slipped clear of the station's micro gravity field. He pointed the ship toward open space and increased the power further. The *Nemesis* began to move forward at an astonishing rate, so much so that Mira was pushed back as the inertial damping system struggled to contain their acceleration.

"How long before we break the mass lock of the station?" Mira asked.

"We will be clear to jump in three minutes," Tish replied, without taking her eyes off the instruments. "Mr Alex, do you have an FTL solution for me?"

"Payback for calling me, Thorny," Mira whispered.

"Affirmative. Your course is laid in; you can jump when ready, *Miss* Tish."

They waited in silence. A green light flashed on Tish's console.

"We are clear," Tish said.

Mira placed a hand on each of the headrests and drew breath.

"Build an envelope. Jump when ready." *Spoken like a proper captain* she thought. *Who am I fooling? This is just standard bridge stuff. A captain has a plan...*

Luke counted down from five and built an envelope. Stars stretched into streaks and were replaced by the energetic clouds and discharges of the envelope.

"How long?" Mira asked.

"Eighteen hours, give or take," Luke replied.

Eighteen hours and an answer.

Vanessa Meyer sat at the tiny desk that occupied one corner of her cabin. A message was waiting in her drop-box. She opened it and flushed it through a decryption filter.

Senator Meyer!

What a surprise to hear from you! It has been a while since we last spoke. Here I was thinking you had forgotten us poor pirates out on the Frontier.

These are not the best of times. Thank you for the warning. Sadly it arrived after FRONCO had launched their operation. We sent them packing thanks to the timely intervention of your own Aussie Jon.

Since the attack my position has become untenable, and I have been forced to leave.

Double T was offering help to displaced persons. The Trade Guild made it clear they have no intention of continuing this policy. I need to find a new base of operations.

I will take a gamble and pay a visit to Damien Lightfoot on Mizarma. He and I have similar interests. He has worlds to spare and that may offer a lifeline to people in need of somewhere safe. I would like to propose we meet on Miz. I am sure that the kind words of a senator would help bring Lightfoot onboard. Failing that, you can always get me out of jail.

Kindest, warmest regards,
X.

Events were moving fast. Meyer wondered what could have precipitated the attack on the Tarantella station. She was certain the local Trade Guild would not make a move against Rhodes unless they had the backing of some serious fire power.

There was a gentle tap on the door.

"Come," she said.

The door slid open and Ben stood in the opening. He was still formally dressed.

"Benny, do you have any casual clothes?"

He shook his head. "Senator, Galactic Network News is running a story you need to see."

"A coup on Tarantella?"

"It is best if you see it for yourself Ma'am," Ben said, still hovering in the doorway.

Meyer activated her holo-screen and called up GNN. The footage showed Daniel Santiago being led out of his office by senate security officers. The ticker at the foot of the screen read *BREAKING NEWS: Vice President Santiago Arrested on Suspicion of Child Abuse. President Schmitt accepts his resignation.*

Meyer listened as the female anchor detailed 18 allegations, dating back 23 years.

"That is a fabrication," she said. "I've known Daniel since he was younger than you, Ben." She shook her head in disbelief. "He's corrupt and a borderline alcoholic, but he's not a child molester."

She sat in silence. Ben gave her a brandy.

"This is shocking. Dark forces are at work here. Has Conway announced his candidacy for the Vice Presidency?"

"No Ma'am, he is on Mars."

Meyer killed the video feed.

"What about you, Senator? Will you consider running? You have the backing."

"Right now I think we should keep a low profile, at least until we find out what is going on. Mark my words, Conway will have that job by the end of the week."

She gave her glass to Ben. "Fix me another and ask the captain to re-route us to Mizarma, as fast as he can get us there."

Meyer watched him go.

A few minutes later the intercom crackled into life.

"Senator?" It was the captain.

"Yes?" she replied.

"I understand you want to re-route to Mizarma?"

"Yes, Captain. Is there a problem?"

"No, Ma'am. I wanted to confirm your intentions."

"Captain, are you questioning my aide's integrity?"

"No, Ma'am... It's standard procedure..."

"Good, because Ben speaks for me. If he tells you to jump, you don't call me and ask how high. Is that clear?"

"Yes, Ma'am!" he replied. His tone indicated he had taken the rebuke in good humour.

Meyer closed the link. She rubbed her temples and walked to the viewport. She stared at her reflection and the energy clouds behind it.

Xander Rhodes sat at an ancient desk with a worn leather top. The oak timber was chipped and scarred. It had once been owned by a 21st century President of the United States. Xander often wondered if the wounds on the desktop had tales to tell. He sipped from the glass of belt whiskey he had been nursing for an hour.

He struggled to shake the melancholy that had haunted his thoughts since the *Nemesis* had departed.

This was one of the rare times when he missed his old life. Raiding ships and outposts, stealing from the corporations; all for his own gain and the benefit of those close to him. It was a simple life, death or bounty. No commitments, no responsibility.

Times change and for Xander that change had been sudden.

Tarantella had been a good setup, a comfortable lifestyle with easy wealth. It had been where he learned about family.

First there had been Tish, the street kid arriving on a battered tramp freighter. She was lost, alone and needed someone to save her. He had taken her in and seen her blossom into a talented, beautiful young woman. Five years ago Luke had arrived from Mars; the son he never knew had. He was already a gifted pilot and warrior when he walked into Xander's office and announced who he was. They bonded almost immediately, without the tension that all too often accompanied estrangement.

Tarantella had been more than just a home; it had been a hard education in how the Federation worked. The egalitarian dream was just a dream; the rich grew richer by keeping the poor in poverty. The system survived by pitting citizens against each other in an endless cycle of petty struggles. It was easy to see, yet impossible to change. It was the reason he had striven to turn the lawless station into something better, and he almost had.

Xander drained his glass. The acid burn of the whiskey was undiminished by the long melted ice. He wondered if he had done the right thing sending the *Nemesis* to the Vale and hoped Mira Thorn was everything Jon Flynt said she was.

The buzzing of a com-link intruded on his thoughts.

"Go ahead Martinez," he said.

"Xander, we're picking up a distress call from Viola Prime. It's a Code Orange."

Code Orange was reserved for planetary emergencies.

"How close do we pass to them?"

"Twelve light-years. Asha says we can be there in three hours."

"Have her plot a course. I'll be up."

Martinez acknowledged and closed the link.

Xander stood, walked to the sink and splashed water onto

his face. He caught sight of his reflection in the mirror. It exposed more of his state of mind than he would have wanted.

CHAPTER NINETEEN

CHLOE Song did her best to suppress her excitement as the lance completed the final few centimetres of the cut. Zack had wanted to pass a micro camera through the slit in the wall and take a peek. Chloe forbade it. She told herself that it was not protocol, but she really wanted to see the look on Saskia Hart's face when they broke in. She wondered who would take the credit for the breakthrough, Saskia or Jarman.

Cutting through had proven to be a bigger challenge than Chloe or Zack had anticipated. After three days of constant breakdowns and improvised repairs they were finally through.

Chloe had slept little, Zack less so. The only consolation had been Saskia and Jarman relocating to the comfort of the base camp.

Zack was stowing the drilling kit when they returned.

"We're through," Chloe said. "It wasn't easy, but we did it."

"Have you opened the breach?" Kramer asked.

"No, we waited for you."

Jarman peered around Chloe, toward the wall.

"Good, you're starting to understand proper operating procedures." Jarman pushed past her and examined the metal. He reached toward the wall and pulled his hand back with a yell.

"Careful," Zack said. "It's still hot."

Jarman glared at him. Chloe covered her mouth to conceal a grin. She could feel the heat radiating from the metal from where she was standing. Jarman's arrogance knew little or no limit.

"How long before we can punch it out, Zack?" Kramer asked.

"I can do it now. It just depends if you want to run a fibre camera through the gap."

Jarman shook his head.

"No need. Chloe can you start your camera running?"

Chloe slipped her headlight and camera in place activated them both.

"We should have a proper camera crew for this," Jarman mumbled, speaking loud enough so that both Chloe and Kramer could hear.

Zack moved into position with a hydraulic ram. He placed two pads onto the cut-out section of wall and another two either side. The inner pads pressed forward on command and after a moment the cut section fell forward onto a metal floor with a loud clang.

A blast of cold, odourless air rushed from the gap.

Zack tested the air quality.

"It's okay. Better than okay in fact," he said.

Kramer made his way forward into the hole. He cast his lamp around. A semi-circular tunnel sloped downward. A series of glyphs decorated the wall. They were faded with age but their style was familiar.

Saskia pushed past Chloe and joined Kramer.

"It's Old Verani," she said.

"Verani?" Kramer replied. "How can that be? This place is older than they are."

"*Old* Verani," Saskia corrected him, her tone acidic.

"What does it say?" Jarman asked.

"Nothing of note. It's just level identification, roughly Level 1, Section 3."

"Great, we've broken into an ancient car park," Zack mumbled.

Chloe laughed. It was as much Zack's deadpan delivery as his observation. Part of her was envious of the engineer; he could say whatever he liked and get away with it.

Saskia glared at her with eyes laden with disapproval.

"Come on let's get in," Kramer said.

One by one the team followed him into the dark, cold tunnel.

Chloe looked back toward the surface and the circle of daylight in the distance. She shivered. Raiding the tombs of ancient Egypt was all Chloe had read and dreamt of as a young girl. On this barren world she faced the reality of entering a structure more ancient than she could imagine. Unlike the Pyramids or the Valley of the Kings, this structure was older than humanity. She did not know if humans were ever meant to find what lay within.

They followed the slope of the tunnel and moved deeper beneath the surface. Chloe walked in silence, listening to Jarman loudly speculate about the tunnel's age.

Chloe played her torch around the inside of the tunnel. The featureless ceiling arched over her head giving no clues to the tunnel's purpose. They had been walking downward for three hours. Chloe's datapad indicated a distance of 12 kilometres and a depth of 15 kilometres below a datum point on the surface. Aside from some markings in Old Verani and what Saskia described as *simple graffiti* the tunnel was anonymous.

"You know what's weird about this place?" Zack asked as he

moved up beside her.

Should she have noticed something? Chloe was a trained, if inexperienced, archaeologist.

"The air... it's fresh," she replied. Chloe had been in some deep excavations on other worlds; they were hot and unpleasant. She checked her datapad, ambient temperature was 14 Celsius with 10% humidity. The air quality rated average plus.

"Something must be regulating the environment," she said. "And we must be linked to the surface."

"Exactly what I was thinking. Kind of made tunnelling into the mountain pointless," Zack agreed.

"If this tunnel runs to the surface, why didn't we see any sign of it on orbital scans?" Chloe wondered. Tunnelling into the mountain had been a time consuming and no doubt expensive process.

"The tunnel is about 4 metres wide. It would be easy to disguise. It would look like a cave or a natural feature. Besides none of the other worlds Lightfoot has excavated has had this configuration and, as butt-head likes to remind us, *it's all about context.*" Zack mimicked Jarman's voice. "I don't know why we didn't do a more thorough scan though. It would have saved us a lot of messing around. What do you suppose this place is, anyway?"

Chloe shone her light around the tunnel.

"I'm not sure. It is functional, not ceremonial. It looks like a service tunnel."

"My thoughts exactly. We are in some kind of industrial or military facility, not a tomb or religious site," Zack said. "Something else, look at the walls."

Chloe looked. The alloy had been replaced by stone, yet she failed to see anything remarkable.

"Concrete?"

"If this were human, we would cut the tunnel and line it with concrete sections. I would expect to see expansion joints, every ten or so metres. This is cut into the rock with incredible precision. The surface is smooth."

Chloe brushed her fingertips over the wall. It felt like glass.

"You sound like an archaeologist, Zack."

"Guess I fell in with the wrong crowd. Shame I can't explain all the Verani graffiti."

"I've been wondering about that," Chloe said. "I'm no linguist but Old Verani differs greatly from the modern version we know. Aside from ceremonial usage it hasn't been spoken for 3000 years. From what we know of their history they have been capable of interstellar travel for only 1000 years."

"So?"

"These facilities date to around 10,000 years ago. That's out of step with their timeline." Chloe was interrupted by a call from ahead of them. They picked up their pace.

"What's that?" Zack said as they caught up with the rest of the team.

In the gloom Chloe could make out an irregular shape. As she grew closer, she saw it was a dead non-human life form.

"I think we can assume it is not a zombie, Saskia," Jarman said. "It's remarkable though."

The dead alien lay prone on the rock floor. It would have stood at least three metres tall on hind legs that were long and articulated in three places. It had two pairs of arms: one pair long and multi jointed, the other much shorter. Each arm ended in a six fingered hand with long clawed fingers.

Chloe found the creature's tail most disturbing of all. It was long; its vertebrae pushed out through its exoskeletal shell like axe heads.

She walked around the corpse. The creature's head was

bulbous and she counted six protrusions she took to be eyes; they were black and lifeless.

"Is that one of them? The ones who built this place?" Chloe said.

Saskia rounded on her.

"Don't jump to conclusions. It is insectoid. I suspect it is a native species from when this world could support life. It most likely made its home here when the facility was abandoned."

Zack walked forward and knelt in front of it.

"It has opposable thumbs," he said.

"And?" Saskia replied.

"Opposable thumbs are what we have. It allows us to grip and manipulate objects. This, whatever he is, could use tools."

There was silence.

"It does not follow that it had the intelligence to do so," Jarman said.

Zack stood and brushed himself down. "You're right. I meet plenty of humans in the same boat."

Jarman glared at him.

"Chloe can you photograph it and log his location. We will need specialists to remove and examine it. Let's move on," Kramer said.

Once Chloe completed the documentation of the bug. She reached out and gently placed a hand on the animal's body. It was smooth and shiny. She tapped it; it was hard like a sea shell.

Chloe stared at the creature, fascinated by it.

"Come on, Miss Song. We better catch them up," Zack said.

She stood and followed the others, taking one a last look at the creature. *We have discovered a new species and no one cares.* She thought. This was not her vision of science. This was corporate tomb raiding.

Jarman, Kramer and Saskia stood at the end of the tunnel. As she approached Chloe noticed the light levels increasing. The area ahead was illuminated by its own light source. It was warmer here and the throb of distant machinery filled the air. The corridor opened into a vast circular chamber at the centre of which a deep, wide shaft descended into the ground. Glowing cable ran around each level and alien machinery protruded from the rock face. A central bridge ran over the shaft leading to a dais in the middle. A crystalline structure was located in the centre. It glowed in the half light. Corridors similar to the one they had descended through led in three directions.

"What is it?" Kramer murmured.

"This has to be an archive; exactly what we have been looking for," Jarman answered, his voice low.

Now who is jumping to conclusions, she thought.

Chloe could not see how far the chamber extended into the mountain. The walls curved as they rose above her. The zenith was lost high above. She estimated the chamber was about a kilometre in diameter and probably as high. Looking over the rim of the shaft made her stomach flip.

The shaft was deep, like the ceiling its true extent hidden in darkness. The abyss was almost hypnotic. She forced herself to step away, fearing the darkness might somehow claim her.

"Where do you suppose the light is coming from? Is this facility still operational?" Jarman asked.

"It would appear so," Saskia replied.

"Fucking geniuses," Zack mumbled behind her. He hawked and spat into the shaft.

"You know what they should consider?"

Chloe looked around her.

"The air," he said. "It's moving, more than it was when we got down here."

He was right. A stiff breeze was blowing from each of the corridors. The air was fresh and cool.

"The machinery we can hear, it must need cold air," she said.

"Exactly, a lot of cold air. The airflow is increasing, so it is responding to us being here," Zack said. "See how the shaft narrows as it goes down?"

"Like a funnel?"

"Exactly. The air will move faster down there than it does up here."

Chloe walked to the closest of the tunnels. It was next to the one they had descended through. It did not take any kind of instrument for her to identify the angle as ninety degrees.

Standing in the arched entrance the breeze was strong enough to ruffle her hair.

The tunnels were smooth... that made for efficient airflow. Something was bothering her about the make-up and layout of the four shafts...

"Girl!" Saskia called from behind her, disrupting her train of thought.

Chloe span and faced Saskia. Her cheeks burned; her eyes narrowed. "I have a fucking name!"

Saskia's face turned the colour of beetroot. "What did you say?"

"I said I have a name."

Saskia stormed toward her. Kramer stepped in her way, he said something Chloe did not hear. Saskia protested and skulked off.

Kramer walked to her.

"Chloe, that was unprofessional," he said.

"But..."

"But understandable. She should not speak to anyone like

that."

Chloe squirmed and rubbed her hands against her coveralls.

"What I need you to do," Kramer said. "Is to continue documenting the chamber. You are the only real scientist here, so I know I can trust you to do it properly. I require a 360 degree holo-map with measurements and composition analysis. When you are done, we'll take a look at the central platform."

She did not know if Kramer was just trying to pacify her but he had a point; she was the only scientist here. She unpacked her equipment.

CHAPTER TWENTY

MIRA sat at the briefing table with Barnes, Luke and Eden. A three dimensional topographical map of the area of LDC-132 occupied by the Lightfoot team hovered in the air in front of them.

"The excavation is about nine kilometres from the base camp," Luke said. He used his hand to pan the map. "It would be logical to assume they will all be at the excavation. An orbital scan will confirm it when we arrive."

Mira was uneasy; so much of the plan depended on assumptions.

"We need to be in and out before these mercenaries arrive," she said.

"I'll take care of them. You do what you need to," Eden said.

Mira fixed her with a cool stare.

"Eden, we deal with the Ark and the Lightfoot people first; everything else is secondary. We need everyone to achieve a successful outcome." She softened her tone. "Look I know you want revenge but you'll have a greater chance of success if you let us help you."

Eden's face was calm and unreadable. Mira once again wondered what had happened to her. What made her hate the Blue Knights so much?

"Okay, when the time comes don't get in my way."

Silence fell across the table.

"Back on topic..." Barnes said. "We were thinking about a rocket drop. Once we secure the area, we bring in the drop ship with the Ark."

"Sounds reasonable," Mira replied. "But you don't sound convinced. What's the problem?"

"You. Rocket insertion puts the body under a lot of strain. Do you think you can handle it?"

"Rich, I'll be fine. Most of my vulnerable bits are either fused or made of metal."

As a teenager Mira had been an accomplished JetSuit racer. The drop suits used by the Corps were a different beast, but the general principles of operation were the same. It had been years since she used a rocket pack either civilian or military. The thought excited and terrified her in equal measure.

"Okay," Luke said. "We have the basics of the plan. If the merc's ship arrives while we are in orbit we always have the option of shooting it down."

"We'll cross that bridge when we have to," Mira said. "Luke I want you to find Ethan and prep the drop packs. Eden I want you copiloting and driving the ATV. Alex will be in command of the shuttle."

They stood and left. Barnes loitered by the door.

"So, when we're done, will you still resign your commission?" Barnes asked.

"It's my time, Rich. Losing the ship brought it all home. It's time for sorry old me to get on with life."

"And a certain girl with red hair has nothing to do with it?" Barnes had a sly grin on his face. "I've seen the way you are with her."

The blush in Mira's cheeks answered for her. Barnes

grinned and squeezed her shoulder.

Am I that obvious?

Before she could reply her com-link beeped.

"Thorn," she said.

"Mira, Alex. Spence just informed me there is a problem with the drop ship; he can't get the avionics online. I figured as you know Cobra's you might be able to help."

"Okay, I'll go down."

Barnes saluted and headed for the armoury while Mira made for the hangar.

Mira entered the hangar and walked along the upper gantry. Beneath her was the ship's Naja, a civilian version of the Cobra assault ship. Her heart fluttered when she saw the ugly craft with its short wings, high cockpit and slab sided fuselage. The stern cargo ramp was lowered and a Rhino ATV was parked ready to embark. Spence was nowhere to be seen.

She descended a metal stairway and climbed the ramp. Spence was tunelessly singing an old song. The only words she could make out were *Viva Las Vegas*. He cut off and mumbled.

Mira went forward. Spence was in the inspection pit beneath the cockpit.

"You have a problem Spence?" she asked.

He bolted upright, startled.

"No, by no I mean yes, since it is you asking, Commander Thorn." He pulled himself up and sat on the deck. "I can't get the avionics to come online. They start up then drop into a fail state and then they won't restart. I give them ten minutes and bingo they start then fail again. It's quite disappointing."

"Does the HUD start without the main navigation system on?"

Spence reached behind him with a long, thin arm and

flicked a switch on the console. The Holo-HUD glowed into life.

Mira immediately knew what to do.

"Try pulling fuses 13,15, and 44," she said. "Power it up, then put the fuses back. Power down and cold start."

Spence gave her a curious look.

"Not sure... No that will not work." He pulled his goggles over his eyes. "I'll try it."

Spence clambered into the cockpit. He opened the fuse compartment and removed the fuses. He sat in the copilot's seat and fired up the system. Just as before it failed.

"See, same problem," he said.

"Replace the fuses and cold start."

Spence did as instructed. The cold start took three minutes. When complete the avionics fired into life.

"Well, I'll be damned," he said. "Where did you learn that?"

"On Mars. We had the same problems on some older Cobras. One of the crew chiefs stumbled on that method. He had no clue why it works, but it does. I had to do that in the field, under fire. It was the longest cold start of my life."

Spence scratched his head. "I suspect a glitch in the keep awake function. This is running the old firmware; it dates back a few years. I should update it, but stolen goods don't come with support plans," Spence said, mopping his brow with an oily rag.

"Thank you, Commander Thorn. I can get back on track now. I had been keeping that glitch from Xander."

Maybe Mira had been wrong about this strange character.

"Mira," she said.

"What?"

"Call me Mira."

"Ah," he replied with a nod. "Call me Spence."

Without another word he slipped out of the copilot's chair

and disappeared back into the inspection pit.

He started singing.

Nightwolf dropped out of her hyperspatial bubble and entered a descending orbit of LDC-132. Periodically she scattered planetary positioning satellites in her wake. As each satellite became active, it optimised its position using tiny rockets. The ad hoc satellite network would provide navigational and communication support to the Blue Knights on the surface.

The ship entered the thin upper atmosphere. Her underside turned red, cerise and white as friction retarded her entry speed. A ten kilometre plasma tail extended from her stern as she raced across the sky. The tail only dissipated as she slowed to a more sedate sub sonic cruising speed.

Once the ship had broken through the cloud layer and the violence of re-entry had passed, Karl Manson released his restraints and made his way forward.

"Talk to me, Lyle."

The pilot was busy with the controls. He knew better than to keep Manson waiting.

"The network is online and the data stream is processing. I am picking up the main base and the excavation site eight clicks to the North. No radio traffic and no surface movement."

Manson studied the monitor. It was harsh terrain but a rover would have no issues traversing it.

"Uhh Karl," Lyle said. "I'm detecting a massive dust storm about 50 clicks South-West. It's inbound on the landing zone."

"Size, duration and ETA?"

"Big, it will be overhead in an hour and last approximately 36 hours."

"We better get down and underground before it comes through."

Manson left the flight deck without another word, heading below toward the crew ready room.

His team sat in silence, strapped into their seats in full battle dress.

Manson leant in the hatchway, supporting his bulk with both arms on the door frame.

"We are landing in two minutes," he said. "We secure the base camp and pacify anyone we find there."

"Once we're done, Vic and Foxy prepare the rover. The weapon is already loaded and needs to be deployed subsurface. My contact down there informs me the Lightfoot Corporation have broken into a subterranean structure. This provides us with an optimum location to deploy the weapon. We go into the mountain, arm the bomb and leave. We take nothing from the site." He studied his team. "Everyone good with that?"

"Yes, Boss," they answered in unison.

Manson did not mention the storm. He figured that was need to know information.

30 minutes later the Nightwolf touched down on the surface. The rear hatch opened and Manson's team stepped into the hot air of LDC-132.

CHAPTER TWENTY-ONE

Viola Prime was an unremarkable Earth like world and a former Regina Enterprise corporate claim. The planet had been designated as an agricultural colony but had been dropped from Regina's portfolio as part of a post recession asset realisation. The company had decided it had enough agricultural planets on its roster.

The tiny world remained deserted until 53 colonist families adopted it and founded an independent cooperative colony with their EarthGov relocation grants. Against all odds the venture succeeded. The population had grown to half a million souls, all of whom enjoyed a standard of living exceeding that of some Core Systems worlds.

When the Frontier had been extended, Regina commenced legal proceedings to remove the colonists and a protracted dispute was dragging its way through the Federal courts. The colonists had the law on their side; Regina had money and a principle to prove. Once the legal options were exhausted, they had the Frontier Company take whatever unofficial action they deemed necessary.

Xander Rhodes stood on the flight deck of the *Scarlet Angel* watching his crew work. Martinez manned the helm, a seat normally occupied by Luke. Four crew members busied themselves with bringing the ship into orbit. Despite the immense size and fire power of the *Angel,* her systems were automated, allowing a total crew of 40 to fly and fight her. Xander had to hand it to FRONCO, they knew how to build ships.

"Xander," Asha Malik said. She was manning the sensor and astrogation suite. "This is weird."

Xander walked over to where the woman stood. She had a puzzled look on her face.

"Weird? Define weird. Martinez painting miniature soldiers in his downtime is weird. Give me some specifics, Ash."

"Comms traffic is non existent. I'm not picking up any background chatter, no emissions at all, except random pings from automated beacons."

"This is a low population system; it could be normal."

Asha disagreed with a firm shake of her head.

"There would be something: radio transmissions or routine comms traffic. I'm not picking up signal bleed on any of the subspace bands, UHF, VHF or S-UHF."

"What about space traffic? They have a surface spaceport here. What about vessel movements?"

"I'm not even tracking satellites."

"Okay, keep monitoring. Take us in Martinez, slow and easy. Ahmed, bring the weapons online."

The weapons officer confirmed the instruction.

Xander resumed his position in the centre of the deck. He watched as the tiny bright dot resolved into a silver disk. Viola Prime revealed itself as a world wreathed in dense white and grey cloud, lit from within with flashes of lightning.

"That's not what I was expecting," Martinez whispered.

"Me, neither." Xander studied the view screen. "Asha, what's going on down there?"

"Surface wind-speed at the equator is 300kph. It slows to

around 100kph around the poles. Surface temperature is.... Whoah, one-hundred and twenty Celsius. Radiation levels within normal limits," she replied.

Xander stared at the screen. Nothing could have survived down there and it explained the lack of comms traffic.

What sort of weapon could have done that? he thought.

"It looks like someone set off a bunch of Nukes," Martinez observed. "When I was in the service, I took part in a test bombardment on Fenos IV. It looked a lot like that when we were done."

"Radiation levels are all within normal limits. This wasn't a nuclear attack. Launch a probe let's see what's going on beneath the clouds," Xander replied.

"Xander!" Asha said. "I'm picking up a transmission. It originates from an orbital source; it's human. Feeding the location to the helm now."

"Martinez, take us there. Asha can you get a message through? Tell them help is on the way."

The ship increased velocity and changed orbital trajectory. The vessel shifted beneath Xander's feet and the gravity subtly altered. They soon came up on the transmission source, a small freighter drifting in an eccentric orbit.

"Asha can you raise the occupants?" Xander asked.

"Negative, the transmissions ceased a few minutes ago. Their power is failing."

"Martinez bring that ship on board. Have Tyler and Haig meet me in the hangar, full weapons load-out."

The pressurisation light took forever to turn from red to green. Xander paced up and down outside the hangar door. He was as impatient for answers as he was curious about those onboard the ship. The light changed to green and Johnny Haig hit the release button, sending the hatch up into the bulkhead.

The freighter was in the centre of the bay, resting on its skids. Kurt Tyler walked up to the hull and operated the manual release mechanism and cranked the main hatch open. There was not enough power to operate the decontamination system and instead of a blast of super-heated steam, cold water flooded onto the deck. A big man in dirty coveralls appeared in the hatch. His eyes were wide, his unshaven olive-skinned face drawn and tired. He was joined by a slightly built woman, similarly dressed. Her hair was black and matted. She shared the same complexion as the man. Behind her were three children: two teenage boys and a girl who could not have been more than five. Her skin was fair, her hair blonde and straight. The girl clutched a broken doll with a shock of black hair and a missing eye. She gazed around the hangar, eyes wide with fear and wonder. Her doll fell from her grip. Xander stepped forward and picked it up.

He knelt next to the girl.

"What's her name?" he asked.

"Susie," the little girl replied.

"She looks like a friend of mine," he said, handing the doll back to the girl. He stood and greeted the man and woman.

"It's okay, you are safe. We are here to help."

"You don't look like fleet. We called for help, but no one came," the man said.

"We're not fleet. We have medical supplies and once we have finished here, we can take you to a place of safety."

The young girl looked up at him.

"Nowhere is safe from the monsters," she whispered.

Xander strode into the infirmary. Norm Leonard was finishing a routine examination of the family.

"Is everyone okay?" he asked the doctor.

"Aside for a little dehydration and exhaustion everyone is doing well," Norm replied. "I'll leave you to it."

"Can you tell me what happened?"

The man looked at the woman.

"Well, Mr Rhodes..."

"Xander."

"I'm Pete Gibson; this is my wife Sandy and my two boys: Jason and Mark."

The teenagers greeted him politely.

He picked up the young girl and sat her on his lap. "This is my little princess, Cathi."

The girl was tired, pale and frightened. Xander produced a Lightfoot branded chocolate bar from the pocket of his duster. The kid smiled and took it, glancing up at her father as she did so.

"What's your story, Pete?" he asked.

"Three days ago the colony was attacked," Gibson said. "At first we thought it was the corporation sending in their heavies to pull us into line."

Sandy put her arm around her husband.

"The ships that attacked us, they weren't like anything we have ever seen," she said.

"How so?" Rhodes asked.

"They weren't human. Verani maybe? They hit us hard, destroyed everything. The attack went on forever. We got off planet before they detonated that weapon."

"The one that destroyed the atmosphere?" Rhodes asked.

Gibson nodded.

"We run a small shipping operation out of Brandon City, well I guess we did. We take agri products out and bring machinery in. Anyway we were prepping for departure when it all kicked off. We were in orbit when we detected a gigantic vessel, heading inbound," Pete said.

"Roughly how big?" Xander asked.

"Bigger than one of the new bulk carriers Frontier have been operating. It was that ship that used the weapon. It knocked our drive system and set us adrift."

"A lot of folk got off the surface," Sandy said. "They didn't seem concerned by outbound ships. It was as if they wanted the planet. That's why we assumed it was corporation heavies."

Pete took a trembling breath. Sandy put a reassuring hand on his shoulder.

"It was lucky we found you when we did. Your orbit was decaying," Xander said.

"We are grateful. If you hadn't come... Well you know."

Xander clapped a hand on Gibson's shoulder. "You would do the same, Pete. What goes around, comes around. Right?"

"Damn straight. Us 'Tier folk look after each other," Gibson replied.

"Why didn't the Navy or FRONCO come?" Sandy asked.

Xander frowned. "The Navy isn't what it was and Frontier is only concerned with corporate assets," Xander said. What little information the Gibson family had provided correlated with everything he had seen in system and heard from refugees on Tarantella.

"I'll have one of my crew show you to a cabin. Once we complete our survey of the system, we are heading to Mizarma. You'll be able to repair your ship while you are on board."

Gibson thanked him and Rhodes bid them goodnight. He walked sullenly to his quarters.

Viola Prime had been scrubbed clean of human structures, yet in the probe's final grainy frame he had seen something else. Giant black roots were emerging from the ground and covering the surface of the planet. The probe had gone dead not long after.

His cabin was lit by a single night-light. A silhouetted figure moved toward him.

Asha Malik placed her hands on his shoulders. "You need to sleep Xander. You look dreadful."

"Somehow I doubt I'll get much tonight."

"Then it's a good job I'm here." She pushed him back toward the bed. Straddling him, she ordered the light off.

The wail of the general alarm snapped Xander from the depths of sleep. The *Angel* lurched and shook under an impact.

"Lights!" he yelled. The stateroom was lit with cool white light as the enviro system responded to his command.

Asha staggered to her feet, rubbing her head. A red mark on her cheekbone heralded a developing bruise. "Xander! What's happening?"

He didn't answer, instead he keyed his com-link. "Martinez! Speak!"

"Multiple inbound vessels, unknown configuration."

He closed the link and pulled his clothes on.

"It has to be the ships that attacked the planet!" Asha said.

Xander agreed as he hunted for his boots.

"Ash, get to the flight deck and gather all data you can; this is an opportunity to learn something."

She tied her hair into a pony tail and ran from the cabin still dressing. Rhodes followed, carrying his boots under his arm.

"Bring me up to speed, Martinez," he said as he rushed onto the flight deck.

"We have fifty inbound vessels. They've been hitting us with energy weapons; nothing substantial aside from the hit that breached the shields."

"So what are they doing?" Xander wondered

"We are being bombarded by sensor pings. They seem to be as curious about us as we are them," Asha said.

The ship was rocked by another blast.

"Shields are holding," Ahmed said. "But that shot drained our reserves."

"Have we got any external views?" Xander asked.

Asha punched a command sequence into her terminal. A 360 degree view from around the ship hovered in the middle of the flight deck. Xander studied the projection.

Small ships zipped through projected sector. Dark shadows, moving quickly with bright propulsion emissions extending from their after sections.

"Freeze and zoom grid 131,168, 43," he said.

The display froze and a small section was magnified. It showed a black vessel, shot through with green and blue streaks. It shimmered in the star light. The ship was a flattened ovoid. Curved spines extended from the sides of the ship and pointed forward. There were no seams in the hull or any of the usual external fittings he would expect to see on a human vessel. There was something organic, almost insectile about the ship.

Xander whistled.

"That's neither human nor Verani. It looks like some kind of bio-mechanical technology. It's way in advance of anything I have ever seen."

Blasts hit the ship in quick succession. A warning siren wailed through the bridge.

"Shields are down," Ahmed said. "We are taking structural damage."

"Ahmed, target the closest vessels and fire at will. Let's see if they can take it back."

A rhythmic shudder ran through the hull.

"Main battery is firing." He studied the sensor reports of the engagement. "The firing solution is unsuccessful. We cannot maintain lock."

"What? You hit nothing?"

"Not a single target," Ahmed replied.

The ship shook under another impact. Sparks showered from an overhead panel.

"Damage report," Xander yelled.

"Hull breach on deck nine. The repair system is handling it," Martinez said.

Xander thought for a second. This fight could only go one way. "Martinez jump us out of here and resume the course for Mizarma."

Martinez built an envelope and seconds later the ship was FTL.

Xander slumped into the command chair. "Asha, I want you to prepare a full analysis of those vessels. I want to know how fast they are; what they're made from and what their pilots had for breakfast."

"I'm on it, Xander," she said.

He thanked her.

Martinez spun in his seat. "We'll make planet fall in eight hours."

Xander Rhodes rubbed his temples and tried to gather his jumbled thoughts.

CHAPTER TWENTY-TWO

KARL Manson strode up the Nightwolf's cargo ramp, pushed past Foxhound and peered into the engine bay of the Rhino ATV. He angrily pulled at connectors and electronic components.

"What the hell is this shit?" he yelled. "No one thought to fire the bastard up before we made planet fall?"

"It has just been overhauled after the Orion Expanse job, rebuilt and..." Foxhound never finished the sentence. Manson swung around and knocked him to the deck with a smack of his cybernetic hand.

"So you assumed it would be fine? If you assume anything you assume the person who serviced it is a bigger arsehole than you are!" Manson made his way toward him. Foxhound scrambled backward trying to regain his feet. Rybov appeared at the foot of the ramp.

"Boss," he said. "You should see this."

"Wipe that grin off your face, Vic."

"Karl you *need* to come out here."

Manson lumbered down the ramp. The air was alive. He was buffeted by the gusts of wind. The storm had intensified since they landed. Rybov pointed to the horizon. The sky was dull red. Clouds of dust danced and flickered, illuminated from within by flashes of lightning.

"I checked with Lyle. It'll be on us in ten minutes."

Manson swiftly turned.

"Get that fucking rover going, Foxhound."

"Karl, even if he fixes it we don't have time to make it to the excavation. We're talking winds of 200kph. The sand will kill the rover in minutes."

"Fuck it!" Manson screamed into the air, his words lost in the strengthening gale.

"We gotta wait it out, Boss."

Manson's thoughts were as turbulent as the incoming weather system. Rybov was right, travelling cross country in the storm would be suicide. It also meant that the Lightfoot people could not leave the dig site. The mission was reset. At least they would be ready to leave as soon as the storm had run its course.

He marched up the ramp, hitting the close button. He took some small pleasure in watching Rybov run back into the ship. Behind him the ATV roared into life, filling the hold with black fumes from its hydrocarbon engine.

Manson loosened his armour and headed back to the habitation section. All he needed to be was patient. It was not his strongest asset, and he felt certain that the odds of him killing someone just for the hell of it had just shortened.

Damien Lightfoot arrived at his office at 9.30 local time, just as he had for the past 50 years. In that time the office had transformed. Lightfoot started his career as a property broker, operating from a room above an accountancy practice in Dublin. As his business grew, he relocated his operations to off-world developments on Luna, Mars and finally Mizarma.

His office was large, minimally furnished, with one wall dominated by holo-screens. The other was a curved panoramic window overlooking down town Delain City and Channing's Bay beyond.

Mizarma was Lightfoot's greatest achievement, a corporate world that had trebled the initial investment in 35 years. Six months ago he handed control of the planet to an elected administration, some 15 years earlier than he was obliged to do so. The only request he made in return was to headquarter his company in Delain. President Lucy Anderson had been agreeable, partly as an act of public gratitude to the founder of her world, but also mindful of tax revenues Lightfoot Developments would pay into the planetary exchequer.

Jane, Lightfoot's PA, had arranged company bulletins on his desk and placed a china cup of green tea next to them. Lightfoot lifted the cup with a frail, trembling hand and walked to the picture window. The warmth of the sun drove the chill from his bones. The surface of the bay shimmered in the sunlight. Pleasure craft cut wakes across the glass like water. He loved this planet. Of 103 developed colonies Mizarma was the only one he ever considered retiring on. Unfortunately a long retirement was not on the agenda for Damien Lightfoot.

At 72 years Lightfoot was a shadow of his former self. His once red hair was thin and white. Only his neat beard carried the last vestiges of colour. In recent years his face had taken on a narrow hawkish appearance. His long thin nose projected from sallow cheeks. His sunken eyes still burned with a lively intelligence and youthful zeal.

Three years ago Lightfoot had been diagnosed with a wasting disease 24th century medicine could only stay. The sickness had taken his strength, but not his resolve. When the doctors had told him there was nothing they could do, Lightfoot took it upon himself to find a cure. Lightfoot Life Sciences had been charged with developing a treatment programme. Lightfoot had often described himself both as an optimist and a pragmatist; the chances of finding a cure were slim but there was always hope.

He drained his tea, returned to his desk and sat. Leafing through the bulletins revealed little more than everyday company news. Mineral finds on three prospect worlds, continued logistical issues in dealing with the Frontier Company and confirmation of the purchase of six naval vessels were the only ones that generated a flicker of interest.

He turned his attention to wider news. The resignation of the Vice President was the lead story. Election fever had gripped the Federation. Lightfoot suspected it was a distraction tool to distance the administration from the alleged crimes of a former favoured son. Three days ago the field to replace Santiago had numbered five hopefuls. Through scandal, blunder and double deals that field numbered but two. David Conway had emerged as a clear favourite; his only challenger the popular, yet inexperienced Senator Annabel Lifeson.

Lightfoot snorted.

"Whoever wins that one will be everyone else's loss," he mumbled.

He scanned the second page news. The Navy had confirmed the loss of the cruiser *Berlin*. It was unfortunate, putting the loss of life aside he had planned to buy the vessel when she was decommissioned.

His desk intercom buzzed.

"Yes, Jane?"

"I have an inbound transmission with a diplomatic ident code."

Lightfoot swivelled in his chair to face the picture window. It was a glorious morning.

"Tell them to contact the department of inter-solar affairs.

We don't run this planet any more."

"I already did, Mr Lightfoot, but the senator was insistent she meet with you."

In a detached part of his mind Lightfoot wondered if Jane would ever use his first name.

"Very well, who is it?"

"Senator Meyer."

"Oh sweet Jesus. Clear her for landing on the rooftop pad and have her sent here. Let's get this over with as soon as possible."

The intercom clicked and fell silent.

Lightfoot closed his eyes and wondered what business a career anti-corporatist could have with him.

Vanessa Meyer strode down the ramp of the shuttle. She looked disdainfully at the junior executive who had been sent to greet her. The woman wore a purple business suit with a severe cut. It was very much on trend for the emerging economies of the Inner Frontier.

"Mr Lightfoot did not deem my visit important enough meet me himself?"

The woman gave a look that combined shock and disappointment. "I'm sorry, Senator. Mr Lightfoot is not in the best of health at the moment."

Meyer softened. "We both know it's about politics. I have every sympathy for Mr Lightfoot but he's wise enough to know he should never bullshit a bullshitter. Come on, lead the way and don't mind me. It has been a long journey."

Meyer let herself be guided to the 105th floor. They emerged into a long corridor. One side was full length glass, the other a semi-organic wall covering that shimmered in the mid morning sunlight. Meyer found the sight of a technician watering the wall with a micro-spray amusing and infuriating in equal measure. Corporate boastfulness knew few limits, even out here on the Frontier.

"This one is it?" she asked as she burst through a closed synthetic mahogany door.

"Good Morning, Senator," a woman sitting at a crystal desk greeted her with a smile.

"Through here is he?" She pointed at a closed door.

She did not wait for a reply.

"Good!" She barged through.

"Damien," she said as she entered the office.

Lightfoot stood and walked around his desk, he extended his hand.

"Vanessa, direct as ever." He glanced over Meyer's shoulder at Jane, who stood in the doorway with the flustered purple-suited executive. "This is Senator Meyer on a good day. Jane could you organise some drinks? Tea for me and…"

"Brandy," Meyer said. "My aide Ben will be with us soon. Could you make him comfortable and feed the poor boy something?"

Jane agreed and disappeared back to her office.

"So Vanessa," Lightfoot said, gesturing to a sofa next to the picture window. "What brings you out here?"

She sat. "Damien, you and I have common interests."

"I find that a little hard to believe. The last time we met you called me a corporate parasite."

"I think the term I used was leach, but I'm glad you got the meaning. I was generalising a little. As corporate leaches go you are not the worst."

"I'm pleased to hear it."

They paused while Jane served drinks. Lightfoot thanked

her.

"Damien, I presume you heard about the attempt on my life?"

Lightfoot told her he had as he blew the surface of his tea. He took an exploratory sip and set the cup aside.

"It took Conway off GNN for a while. You know the Vice Presidency is down to a straight run off between him and that awful Lifeson woman?"

It was news to Meyer.

"She'll be out of the race by the end of the day and they'll have a coronation of Vice President Conway soon after. That's why I am here."

She reached into her bag and slid a folder across the table.

"Before Santiago was set up, he sent me this information."

Lightfoot took the folder and leafed through it.

"A lot of that dossier is speculation, hearsay and conjecture but it supports my belief that Conway is using The Frontier Company for some very unusual tasks. The chain of connections between him and their upper management is conclusive."

"Exploration," Lightfoot said. "I wouldn't be surprised if he is using their resources to scout new colonies to boost his portfolio and those of his inner circle. You know what politicians are like."

"Maybe, take a look at the photograph on page 93."

Lightfoot flicked ahead, he froze. Still holding the folder he asked.

"Where is that?"

Meyer shook her head. "I was hoping you might know; somewhere in the Vale. That image was taken 15 years ago when Conway worked as a lobbyist for Regina. Do you know what it is?"

Lightfoot gave a nod, not taking his eyes from the page.

"It's a spacecraft. It's ancient. We have found similar derelicts, but this one looks to be intact."

"It is. Conway has it on a research station in Saturn orbit. It has the codename *Scarecrow*." She sipped her drink. It had an unfamiliar yet pleasant texture. "Now I have grabbed your attention, let me make a proposal."

Lightfoot stood and walked to the picture window. He folded his hands behind his back.

"I'm listening."

"Conway has done his best to destroy the Navy. I have gone some way to preventing the final blow, but I fear the policy the house voted through will not be implemented. He will be promoted to Vice President and he will block it. I am certain Conway and his Frontier friends are operating under some kind of external influence."

Lightfoot turned away from the window. "That's a pretty strong accusation, but I still don't see what this has got to do with me," he said.

"Damien, you have no love for The Frontier Company. Your reasons are the polar opposite to my own, but we can work together. I know you have been buying up every redundant naval vessel that comes on the market. Scrap merchants from Mars to Tarantella have been cursing your name."

"Frontier refuse to protect my vessels because I won't use their brokerage services. I have every right to protect my interests."

"I agree," she said. "Admiral Foster provided me with a list of vessels the fleet was preparing to dispose of in the next six months. They won't affect fleet tonnage because they are too costly to refit. I suggest you buy all of them."

"Why? My requirements are being met by my current tonnage and planned acquisitions."

"Damien, when Conway is in charge there will be no Navy, just the Frontier Company. That's why I need you, if we are to offer any kind of protection to our citizens."

"Protection from what? Frontier will manage commerce, provide security and open new worlds. The average Federation citizen will see prices increase and maybe some short term shortages but that'll probably be the extent of it."

Meyer gestured to the window. "Something is happening out there. Frontier won't lift a finger to protect Mizarma or any other non corporation world. That's why we have to act."

She finished her drink.

"Xander Rhodes is on his way here," she said.

"Rhodes?" Lightfoot spluttered. "I'll have system security blow him out of the sky!"

"You might want to hear what he has to say. You have a team on LDC-132 at the moment?"

He confirmed it.

"A small scouting expedition is prospecting for fuel sources in the region."

"That would explain why Conway sent a mercenary company out there. The same mercenaries who could not acquire an artefact Rhodes borrowed from you. So please let's sit and discuss this like grown ups."

Lightfoot's shoulders slumped and he let out resigned sigh. He placed the dossier on the table and nodded his agreement.

CHAPTER TWENTY-THREE

Tɪsʜ dropped the Nemesis out of hyperspace in low orbit above Arethon. It took considerable skill to break an envelope close to a gravity well. Mira was impressed.

"I'm detecting an orbital communication and planet-nav network," Tish said, her eyes not wavering from her instruments. "It's not Lightfoot's. Someone else is down there."

"Let's have some surface images. Can you concentrate on the Lightfoot camp?" Mira asked.

A few seconds later Tish sent an image of the base camp to a holo-screen on the navigation console. It showed a collection of temporary buildings, a few hundred metres from them was a large spacecraft.

"A Vigilant, that is no LDC vessel," Mira whispered. It could only be the mercs Eden had encountered.

She keyed her com-link.

"Eden, can you come forward?"

"I'm prepping the rover!" Eden snapped.

"It's important."

A few minutes later Eden arrived. She was dressed in a compression suit and carried a helmet under her arm.

"What..." her voice trailed off.

"Your Knights?" Mira asked.

Eden nodded, not taking her gaze from the monitor.

"Is this going to be a problem?" Mira asked.

"For them, not me." She strode from the flight deck.

"Eden!" Mira called after her. "The mission comes first."

Eden turned. Her brow was furrowed and her eyes blazed with anger. "Mission first. Then keep out of my way, Thorn."

Eden headed for the lower decks.

"You can't trust her," Tish said.

Mira made no reply. She didn't need trust, all she needed was for people to do their jobs, for whatever their reasons.

"What about their network?" Tish said. "I can hack it. They will know we are here if I do."

Mira considered it. Surprising the mercs offered an advantage that was marginal at best. It would still come to shooting.

"Can we use their network without them knowing?" she asked.

"Yes... but why?" Tish asked, with a puzzled expression.

"Can you mess with their navigation? Send them in the wrong direction?"

"I like that idea! They will work it out, but it will buy us time You are an excellent Blade, Mira Thorn!."

Tish bowed her head and rapidly entered code to her terminal. Her hands danced over her keypad, her eyes flicked between holo-screens.

Mira opened a channel to the shuttle. She couldn't quite bring herself to think of it as a drop ship.

"Alex, are we ready to launch?"

"Affirmative," Alex's tone was cool and professional.

"I'll be with you in a few minutes." She closed the link.

"Tish, if you don't hear from us in twelve hours or you detect any kind of energy discharge bigger than a rifle, get the ship out of here and head for Mizarma."

"Not going to happen, Mira. You are all coming back," she said between bursts of rapid fire typing. Tish spun around in the chair, a satisfied grin on her face.

"We own their network! I'll patch the data stream through to the Naja and your personal navigators."

Tish stood and put a hand on Mira's arm.

"We'll have that conversation when you get back." Her cheeks glowed.

"Twelve hours Tish, I mean it." Mira wanted to say more, but the words were not there.

She headed for the hangar. Alex briefed her via com-link on the way. He had run his own orbital scan and besides the mercs vessel, he had also detected a small ship on the surface. Alex had identified as an Aurora, a light transport craft. A dust storm was raging over the drop zone and although it was moving away, they were in a for a rough ride.

Mira arrived at the bay and approached the Naja. Part of her was jealous it would be Alex at the business end rather than herself.

Stop living in the past woman.

She climbed the ramp and entered the ship. Her team were ready, suited and armed. Barnes and Tate checked their load-out over while Luke sat, staring straight ahead, with a calm expression on his face. Mira was puzzled at his lack of reaction.

Barnes slapped Ethan on the shoulder.

"You are a state-of-the-art bad ass, Private. A mean, green, fighting machine. You have learned from the best. We are mobile, agile and hostile. We are the benchmark by which future bad asses will be judged."

Barnes was amped as he took his seat opposite Mira, his energy infectious.

Luke remained unfazed, staring into space ahead of him.

"Luke?" Mira prompted.

He said nothing, continuing to stare. Then he blinked twice, he smiled at her.

"I was meditating. It helps me prepare for stressful situations. My mother taught me how do it."

Mira strapped herself in to her compression seat.

"Perhaps you could teach these two, might shut them up during the drop," she said.

The stern ramp retracted and the lock sealed. Alex's voice came over their headset speakers.

"Everyone strapped in?"

All four acknowledged in unison.

"No funny announcement, Alex?" Mira asked over the com-link.

"Not today," he replied.

"Going down!" Barnes boomed as the ship dropped like a stone from the belly of the *Nemesis*.

A flight instructor had once told Mira the designers of the Cobra had made a decision to take all the noise from outside and put it on the inside. The drop ship's civilian counterpart had inherited the same characteristic. The roar of the three ion engines filled the compartment, making every loose piece of equipment shake. Mira's ribs thrummed as if they were independent of the rest of her body.

Aside from the noise the descent was smooth until they hit the upper atmosphere. The ship bumped and rolled in the thickening air. Mira held her breath and fought back the need to vomit as the Naja bucked and pitched into the troposphere. She wished the ship was equipped with windows. At least they would give her a point of reference. The descent required two full orbits of Arethon, which she knew would take seven minutes. She stole a glance at her combat computer; they were six minutes in.

"Approaching the drop point," Eden informed them. "I am opening the ramp. We're heading into some chop, so stay attached to something solid."

Mira stood and pulled her visor down. She hooked her tether loop onto a rail.

"You okay, Commander?" Barnes asked.

She replied with a thumbs up.

Mira was breathing in short gasps. She hoped the comm system wasn't picking it up.

A new voice crackled in her helmet. Monica Garret was monitoring the team's vital signs from the *Nemesis*. "Calm yourself Mira, breathe."

Mira tried her best. Her nerves were on fire. She was close to panic.

The ramp lowered and the dirty red surface flashed beneath them. Clouds of dust rippled like waves over the rugged terrain. From altitude the storm appeared almost serene. Mira knew differently; she had flown in Martian storms and knew how they harboured a powerful, indifferent violence.

The drop light flicked from red to green. Mira braced herself and deployed her drogue chute. It pulled out into the airstream behind the Naja. The tether jolted her as it tightened. Mira unclipped her anchor hook from the rail.

The acceleration was terrifying. The drogue pulled her out of the bay and into the air.

The ship shrank into the distance. She keyed her com-link.

"Thorn. Out and clear."

Each team member sounded off. Satisfied they had all made a clean exit she cut the drogue loose and activated her descent system. The tiny thrusters mounted on her battle armour fired, levelling her flight path. Once her orientation and alignment were correct her rocket pack activated, propelling her toward the surface at two hundred kilometres per hour. Mira glanced around her. She could see the flares of the others' packs. From here on in the rocket pack would guide her to the drop zone.

The volatile atmosphere buffeted her body. She pitched and rolled in an empire of cloud and wind. It was as exhilarating as it was terrifying.

Mira entered the sandstorm and visibility dropped to zero. Her suit's lights were reflected back from the seemingly solid wall of dust. Sand and grit rasped over her visor and helmet. The crystal glass was tough and should have resisted the abrasive assault, but it still fogged as particles were dragged across it.

The surface approached and Mira's suit righted her, her thrusters fired to halt her descent. She braced for landing and touched down gracefully in a cloud of dust. She unclipped her pack and discarded it on the ground. Faint curls of smoke rose from the motors. The wind was strong, coming in powerful dust laden blasts. She kept her visor sealed.

A shiver ran through her. This was Arethon; a place she had only seen in a dream. She wondered if this had been where the beautiful city of glass and gold had once stood.

The dig site was larger than she expected. Heavy equipment sat idle where the Lightfoot team had dug and blasted their way into the mountain. The sky was clearing; the trails left by the team's drop suits were already dispersing. The exhaust plumes were not too far apart, but her monocular vision made it difficult to judge.

Sergeant Barnes appeared from behind a ridge on the far side of the excavation, his silhouette giant and distinct against the slate-grey sky. He was joined by a second figure. As they approached she recognised it as Luke Rhodes.

"Where's Ethan?" she asked.

"He didn't land with us. I saw him head in over that way." Barnes pointed to the East.

Mira keyed her radio.

"Ethan, come in please."

There was silence.

"Ethan, do you read me?"

More silence.

She punched a channel to the ship.

"*Nemesis* we are down, We cannot locate Ethan. How are his stats?" Mira asked, hoping for a positive answer.

After a pause Monica replied. "He's showing green."

Her voice was distorted. The signal quality was poor. The sandstorm was still affecting the communications system.

Mira closed the link.

"The storm is messing with comms. Rich, I want you and Luke to check out those buildings. Make sure no one is in them. I'll find Ethan."

They agreed.

"The mercs are not here yet," she said. "We have to assume they will be soon. Ten minutes and we go down. Ethan or no Ethan."

They split up. Mira ran in the direction Barnes had indicated, trying to raise the missing man on her com-link.

She crested a rocky outcrop. Ethan Tate struggled to his feet. She ran to him.

"I clipped a rock as I came in," he said.

His black armour was scratched and dull where the sand had scoured it on the way down.

"Is it broken? Can you walk?" Mira asked.

"No, I'm certain it's soft tissue. Give me a couple of minutes," he replied

Mira unclipped an emergency medical pack from her belt

and removed a small syringe.

"Hold still," she said.

Locating a vent in the lower leg of Ethan's suit she pushed it in.

"Better?"

Ethan nodded and stood forward onto the injured leg. He grimaced but was able to stand.

"Better," he said. His voice sounded somehow distant.

Mira's world spun. Nausea gripped her as vertigo messed with her perception. She staggered. Ethan grabbed her and stopped her falling onto the rocky ground. The world ebbed in and out of focus.

"Mira?" Ethan said.

"Wha...Wha..." she stumbled over her words. "Amy... I'm sorry... I'm sorry. I didn't mean it... don't be mad..." she mumbled.

Her knees gave way. She fell into Ethan. Confusion reigned in her mind.

The world came back into focus. Her head pounded. Mira fumbled for her visor release and opened it. She panted, drawing down gritty air. Her hands were shaking.

"I'm okay..." she said, standing on her own. "Just the shock of the descent..."

She was aware of a numbness in the left side of her face. Her fingertips tingled uncomfortably. She took a moment to be sure the sensation had passed and for her hands to stop trembling. They never quite did.

"Mira..." Ethan said. "Are you okay? You called me Amy."

She shook it off, mumbling an excuse.

"Come on Ethan, let's catch up with Rich and Luke."

Mira helped him scramble up a slope. He was able walk by himself once the stim took effect.

"That will get you mobile for now. You'll pay the price to-morrow," she said.

Her mind still dwelt on the incident. *What happened to me... I lost it...* She dismissed the negative thoughts and tried to concentrate on the mission.

They rendezvoused with Barnes and Luke at the excavation. The sergeant reported the camp was deserted. He pointed to a small prefabricated control centre.

"Everything is powered and there is an active data link between the control centre and the excavation. I think they are all below ground."

Mira surveyed the area.

"*Nemesis,* can you see any movement from the mercs?"

"Negative Mira. They are still under the storm," Tish responded.

Mira checked her combat computer. "Let's bring in the Rhino," she said.

Barnes called up Alex.

"Ethan can you move?" she asked.

"Yep, just tell me where you need me."

"Good. You and Luke get area denial devices deployed. If these guys are coming, let's give them a surprise."

Barnes dug two flares into the ground and ignited them. They lit the dawn twilight with a hard red glow. He fired a third into the air.

The Naja arrived, roaring overhead and performing a circuit of the landing zone before approaching the flares on a slow descent. The forward ramp lowered as it approached. Mira blinked, dazzled by the ship's powerful spotlights. The ship touched down and the landing gear flexed under the strain. The Rhino sped from the cargo bay. Once it was clear the Naja lifted off and flew over Mira's head, the sound of its engines lost in the storm.

"Saddle up sweethearts. The bus won't wait," Barnes yelled.

Mira pulled herself into the vehicle and waited while Luke and Ethan laid Viper mines in sand behind them. Several tense minutes passed until they climbed aboard. Their hands and arms covered in fine red dust. Eden gunned the engine and drove them down an improvised access road to the tunnel entrance. A Land Rover Universe and a second set of prefab buildings were located close to the entrance. Eden pointed the rover toward a tunnel leading into the mountain. It was just wide enough to accommodate the vehicle.

After a short drive the Rhino stopped next a metal wall. A neat hole had been cut in the alloy. There was enough space to turn the rover to face outward. Eden had to engage forward and reverse gears several times to complete the manoeuvre.

"End of the line!" she announced from the cab as she shut the engine off.

Mira climbed out and wafted the exhaust fumes away from her face.

"Okay, Luke and Rich unload the Ark and we'll use a sled." She sized up the cut in the wall and judged it to be large enough.

"Rich, I want you and Luke to dig in here. Fall back when you need to. Ethan, you and Eden come with me."

"Don't you want me to stick with the sergeant?"

Mira shook her head.

"Not with that injury. These guys will want to bug out quickly. Don't be so eager for action. I'm sure it'll find us," she replied.

Eden was already unhooking the Ark. It was packed into a large transit pod which sat on top of a zero-g hover sled.

Mira ran to help her.

"Do you know how you want to play this?" Mira asked, once the Ark was secured on the sled.

"No, I'll improvise. Whatever happens I want the one they call Manson. Even if you get the others, he is mine."

Mira and Eden guided the sled through the tight opening. Once they were in the corridor, the extra space made turning the large object easy.

"Let's move," Mira shouted as she pushed the object through the tunnel.

Karl Manson paced around the hold as the cargo ramp lowered. Once it was in position KK drove the ATV onto the surface. Rybov walked down the ramp with his weapon unslung, his armour glinting in the ship's floodlights. The old merc walked around the rover, giving it a final visual inspection.

Foxy loaded the last of their gear and climbed aboard. Manson followed, taking his usual seat at the rear of the vehicle.

They drove into the dawn. KK followed the pip on the nav system.

Manson closed his eyes and dozed. He had developed the ability to catnap during his younger years. Every minute of energy saved when you were not in combat might just save your skin when you were.

He jolted awake.

The rover was still moving. Manson checked his combat computer.

"Where the fuck are we?" he barked.

"On our way boss," KK replied.

"The fuck we are! Stop the vehicle."

He keyed his com-link.

"Lyle send me a directional beacon from the ship."

After a few seconds his computer beeped. He studied the

data on the small screen.

"No one thought to question why we had not arrived?" he asked, trying to keep his voice steady.

No one answered.

"The Plan-Nav was showing the correct direction, Boss," KK replied.

Mansion breathed heavily.

"It has been hacked. Someone has sent us the wrong way."

"Who? No one knows we are here," Rybov said.

Instead of answering Manson called up Lyle.

"Give me a unidirectional guidance wave. Point us at the target."

A few seconds later, a new pip appeared on the head up display.

"Follow that KK. Deviate over two degrees and I'll cut off your fingers and shove them up your arse. Clear?"

"Yes, Boss."

Dawn was colouring the eastern horizon red and yellow as they arrived at the excavation site. It had been a silent, tense and uneventful journey. Manson leant forward and peered through the wind shield. A pair of burned out flares glowed on the ground in front of the artificial incline.

"Someone landed heavy equipment here, Boss," KK said.

Manson could see for himself the telltale signs of recent landing. Dust had been blown into drifts and the ground bore black scorch marks.

The vehicle lurched. The force of the explosion threw Manson into Rybov. The rover ground to a halt accompanied by the sound of tearing metal.

"We've lost the drive axle!" KK yelled as he shut off the motor.

Manson leapt from his seat and clambered out of the

vehicle. Rybov and Foxhound were already on the surface.

"Someone mined the area," Rybov said. "Whoever landed here, knew we were coming."

"For fucks sake!" Manson roared and climbed out. He slammed the door closed with such force it bounced open on bent hinges.

"Vic, get a drone out and sweep. KK what's the status on the vehicle?"

KK shook his head. "Broken, it's not going anywhere."

"We're on foot from now on. Once Snaggles has cleared a path we head below ground. Be alert for traps."

Rybov stood 15 metres ahead of him, controlling a drone. It swept in a pre defined pattern over the ground. It would stop and fire a small blast of energy into the ground when it detected explosives below the surface. It took nearly an hour to clear a path.

Once Rybov confirmed they were clear, Manson stormed to the rear of the vehicle and opened the cargo compartment. He unlocked the case containing the Mass Sink. The weapon sat on a bed of foam, a red light blinking on its surface. He suspected this would be the only time he would ever see one deployed. His lip twitched uncontrollably at the thought of how much destructive power was contained in the polished steel sphere.

He slammed the case closed.

"Foxy," he said. "Load that into your pack and move out."

He strode past Rybov and walked across the cleared ground toward the excavation entrance.

"Come on you maggots! Get your hands off your cocks and pull up your socks. We have a planet to destroy, some killing to do and prizes to win. Move it!"

His troop fell in behind him. Rybov leading the younger guys and not so much as breaking a sweat. For all his faults the old man could maintain as good a pace as his juniors. It was a shame he didn't share their can do attitude.

Mira slowed the sled as light flooded into the tunnel. There were voices in the distance. She assumed they had caught up with the Lightfoot team.

Eden was talking enthusiastically to Ethan about the dead alien they encountered further up the passage. It was the first time she had appeared distracted from her hatred of the Blue Knights.

"Eden, come with me. Let's introduce ourselves. Ethan, bring the cargo up behind us."

They rounded the final turn and entered the chamber. A group of three people stood looking toward a central platform straddling a wide shaft. A girl was taking measurements with a laser measure; she stepped back and raised her hands when she saw them. The measure dropped from her grip and broke apart on the rock floor.

"It's okay," Mira said. "We are here to help."

Eden jerked a thumb toward the shipping canister. "We brought this."

The girl remained rooted to the spot.

"Mr Kramer!" she yelled. One figure turned. His silhouette was huge. Mira stepped forward.

"My name is Mira Thorn, Federal Navy. You have mercenaries inbound. They landed before we did. We do not know what they want, but trust me it won't be anything good."

The fat man made his way over, followed by his companions. Another man joined them. He was thin with lank hair protruding from beneath a ball cap jammed to his head.

"Are you in charge?" Mira asked the girl.

"I am," the fat man said. "Franz Kramer, this is Peter Jarman and Saskia Hart, our lead scientists."

Mira shook his hand.

"This is Chloe Song our junior team member and Zack McArdle our engineer. Mercenaries you say?"

Mira explained the chain of events that had brought them to this arid world.

Ethan stood the cargo pod upright and opened the door. Inside the Ark rested on a smaller sled, its black surface alive with rapidly circling light.

"Is it meant to be doing that?" Chloe asked.

"I think they're excited," Mira said.

"They?" Chloe asked.

"I know what the commander is referring to," Kramer said. "Walk with me Commander Thorn?"

She let the big man take her to one side.

"You have activated the device?" he asked, once they were out of earshot of the group.

"Not intentionally. It reacted to my presence and has been communicating. They tell me they want to rejoin their collective. They asked me to bring them here," Mira replied. She explained her various interactions with the Ark.

"Several of our team reported visions or voices from it but not with the level of coherence or clarity as you describe. Can I ask you something?"

"Go ahead."

"Why are you doing what it asks of you?"

Of all the questions she had asked of herself that was one she was avoiding. "I saw their past. There was a girl... or their equivalent. I saw the end of the world through her eyes. I felt her loneliness in the vision. I think I did it for her."

Kramer stared at her. She did not know what else to say.

"A personal connection, that is unusual," Kramer replied.

His eyes drifted back to the Ark.

"I guess I wanted answers too. I wanted to know who they were, what happened to them. I think they were trying to communicate something else. It was as if by helping them I would help humanity."

Kramer continued to walk toward the platform. Mira fell in beside him.

"We have found several facilities in the Vale," Kramer said, gesturing around him. "They have been little more than holes in the ground. We found this place by chance. One of our remote probes detected a low level energy emission. We had no plans to survey this sector in any detail until then."

He gestured to the cavern around above them.

"Saskia thinks it is a vault; a store of ancient knowledge. Damien and myself have very different ideas, so does our intern."

Mira was one step ahead of him.

"A bigger version of the Ark, somewhere for the souls of the first ones to inhabit," she said

Kramer raised an eyebrow.

"Souls? An interesting choice of word, Commander, but yes. A virtual city... no a virtual universe," he said. "Of course if they were to come here there would need to be some kind of interface to allow them to transfer. Come, take a look at this," Kramer said, leading her to the central platform.

It was ten metres in diameter. The alloy was covered with sand and dust making it slippery under foot. In the centre was a crystalline structure standing a metre high. It was hollow. The concave centre was a perfect fit for the Ark.

"This machine exists for your Ark. As I said we have found derelict facilities on other worlds. We think devices like the Ark were designed as secure vaults, strong enough to survive a catastrophe."

"*The Ones Who Were Left?*"

"Maybe we have all we need to find out"

Energetic discharges flashed in the darkness and a powerful hum built from the depths of the shaft. Mira checked the time. Barnes had not reported contact with the Knights.

"We need to decide what we are going to do, Franz. The mercs won't waste any time getting down here."

She paused and continued to stare into the darkness of the pit. The hairs on her neck rose. Her chest tightened as the air became dense and charged.

"Can you feel it?" she whispered.

"Yes... it has been building since you arrived. I'm going to propose something that breaks all of our standard protocols. Do you want to see how all this works?" Kramer asked. "I know I do and I suspect once the machine is active there is little our mercenary friends can do to stop it."

Mira weighed the options. They were here to bring the Ark home. It was the most logical course of action.

"Okay. We'll bring it over." She ran over the walkway. Kramer followed at a slower pace.

"Eden, Ethan break out the object. We need to move it over there." She pointed to the platform.

"Zack, can you help them?" Kramer directed the lanky man to assist with unpacking the Ark.

"Miss Song!" Kramer said. "Please deploy your instruments and set up as many cameras as you can. Point them at the object."

"Franz!" Saskia said, running toward them. "What are you doing? This is not protocol."

"No, it's practical. Time is short. We are set to learn a lot in a tiny window and you can complain about it or observe it. I think you know which option will be best for your career."

Saskia scowled.

"Mira!" Ethan called. "We are ready."

The Ark had been removed from the transit case and rested in a steel cradle on the anti-gravity sled.

Mira ran to it. The surface of the object was covered in darting colours. A tingle of energy surged through her. She gripped the steering controls of the sled, releasing the brake she pulled the Ark over the walkway. Ethan and Zack steadied it as she manoeuvred it.

Dread and fear gripped her heart.

If you save them, you will die.

She tried to dismiss it. The only threat was the mercs. They could deal with them.

Are you prepared to sacrifice all that you are for them?

I saved them and now I'm saving you, she thought. *I feel fine.*

"Watch out for the edge," Ethan cautioned. She shivered as half her boot balanced on the precipice.

When they reached the platform, she deactivated the sled, and it rested on the ground.

"We need to put it into that receptacle," she said, pointing to the crystalline structure. As she spoke the indentation pulsed with blue light.

Ethan and Zack moved toward the Ark. Almost instinctively Mira stepped forward and lifted it from the cradle. It seemed to have no mass.

"I've got it," she said.

She laughed at the surprised expression on the two men's faces. "It's weightless!"

Energy coursed through her body. Every nerve and every sinew burned with the life force of a million beings. She became the Ark, and the Ark became her.

Mira carried the glowing ovoid to the crystalline structure and lowered it into place. She stepped back and waited.

The Ark glowed, vivid colours swept over its surface. A rumble grew into a roar from deep below her. The structure in the centre of the platform glowed blue then white. The ground shook and a dazzling beam of light erupted from the depths of the pit, through the Ark and on to the top of the chamber. Ethan ducked, shielding his eyes. Mira was at the centre of it. Her whole world was light. Energetic disruptions danced and span around her. She found herself surrounded by countless living beings. They moved like eddies in a stream or pockets of tranquil air in a hurricane.

They danced around her. Over the roar of the machine, she heard their voices. The energy consumed her. It flowed through her body, banishing the pain and sadness from her being.

The noise grew ever louder. The air was energised. It swirled around her. The chamber resonated at a frequency beyond that of human hearing. The ground shook as dust and ozone filled the air.

The spectacle continued for what appeared to be an eternity but in reality could only have been a few minutes. Mira was at the centre of the symphony of light, colour and sound. She could sense the joy of the Ark dwellers as they became one with the machine.

And then it was over. She was alone.

The chamber fell silent. Mira blinked, her eye coming to terms with the darkness.

She staggered, the pain behind her eyes returned, pulsing and intense. Her nose dripped. Blood spotted on the ground, big heavy droplets.

"That's not good," she mumbled.

She tried to walk to Ethan and Zack, but her legs would not obey her.

"Mira?" Ethan called. He sounded distant, light-years away.

Mira stumbled and fell to her knees. She pitched forward onto the hard metal floor.

If you save them, you will die.

She scrambled upright, her breath coming in shallow gasps. Her world was defined by pain and confusion. She tried to focus on her friends. They were distant and receding, like stars slipping beyond the horizon. The left side of her body was numb, the muscles rigid. It was becoming harder to breathe. Pressure in her chest grew, as if her heart were about to explode.

There were others here now, figures, little more than indistinct shapes crowded into the chamber, hundreds, thousands of people.

Someone was moving through them.

Amy Flynt pushed past Ethan. He took no notice and continued to look past her.

The girl held out her hand.

You did what was asked of you Mira. You saved them. No more pain, no more tears. It's time to sleep.

The world flared red before fading to black. Mira experienced a fleeting moment of euphoria, then nothing.

CHAPTER TWENTY-FOUR

EDEN blinked twice to clear the imprint from her retinas. No one spoke.

What the hell just happened?

She did not have time to complete the thought as a roaring gale blew from each of the four shafts. She staggered to maintain her footing.

"What's happening?" Eden screamed.

"This is a huge machine!" Chloe Song yelled in reply. "The corridors are cooling shafts! It's why they are so smooth!"

Eden braced herself against the wind and ran across the bridge to where Mira lay. She knelt, felt for a pulse and found none. She grabbed the handle on the back of Mira's armour and dragged her off the platform.

Panting, Eden lay the body on the ground. Ethan Tate was next to her. He pushed her out of his way. Panic filled in his face. He reached for Mira's wrist computer. He froze.

"She's dead!" he said in a hollow voice.

No one said anything for several minutes. They stood in silence; no one seemed prepared to take charge.

The howling wind dropped to a breeze. The only sound was an electrical hum coming from the shaft.

The light in the chamber was brighter now.

"Listen up. We need to get everyone out of here. We can still be topside before the Knights arrive," Eden said.

"No!" Jarman said. "We don't know what happened here; the machine has become active and it's because of that object." He pointed to the Ark. It still rested on the platform, its surface dull, grey and lifeless.

Tate rounded on him. "That thing killed Mira!"

"Calm down, soldier. We have to focus!" Eden said.

Someone needed to get a hold on the situation. The Ark was delivered; the machine was active. As far as Eden was concerned this part of the mission was complete. This was her chance to seize the initiative.

The sound of energy weapons echoed down the corridor.

"Great," Eden said.

"Mr Tate get these people into cover." Eden keyed her com-link. "Barnes, it's Eden. Can you hold them? We will come to you."

Barnes acknowledged with a double click of his link.

"What about Mira?" Tate asked.

Eden looked at the crumpled body on the floor.

"Use the pod. We take her with us," she said. *I don't know her, but I've left too many people behind.*

Eden clicked to the command channel and was about to call Barnes with further instructions when weapon's safety switch clicked behind her.

Eden froze and turned to face the others. Saskia Hart had one arm around Chloe's neck. In her other hand she held a laser pistol; it was pointing between Eden's eyes.

"Tell your people to stand down!" Saskia said.

"It was you!" Kramer sounded disappointed and angry in equal measures. "You were the infiltrator?"

"Shut up, Fat Man. Everybody on their knees. Hands behind

your heads."

Saskia tensed, her aim unfaltering. "Tell your people to stand down!"

"If I don't? You seem a little outnumbered," Eden said. She dropped her hand to her weapon.

Saskia pointed her gun at Jarman and fired a single shot at his chest. Jarman staggered; his eyes widened as he pitched forward onto the ground a hole burned through his torso.

"There's one less now. Tell them to stand down, or the girl is next."

Eden keyed her link.

"Barnes, it's Eden. Stand down."

"What? Where is Mira?"

"Stand down, we have a situation here."

"Let me speak to Mira."

"Thorn is dead. Stand down."

"What?" The sound of gunfire stopped.

Saskia released her grip on Chloe. She fell to the ground, panting. Eden glared at the older woman.

"I will kill you, just so you know," she spat the words out.

"You are welcome to try," Saskia said. "But the odds are against it. Drop your weapons and get comfortable."

A tense hour passed until Luke and Rich Barnes entered the chamber. They had their hands above their heads. Barnes loped in front, his shoulders down and his head bowed. Four Blue Knights swaggered behind them, their weapons pointed at their prisoners.

"Well, well, well," Manson said. "Eden! Fancy seeing you here. KK you might get a go on this one yet!" he said.

Eden said nothing. She glared at Manson before shifting her cold gaze to Foxhound. He had the same shit-eating grin on his face as always did.

"You'll have to wait your turn. I'm going to kill these two first," Eden hissed at Saskia.

"Brave words," Manson replied. He walked toward the centre of the chamber and took a long look down the shaft. He returned to Eden and grabbed her by the throat. He lifted her off her feet and tightened his grip on her windpipe. She struggled ineffectually.

"Brave words, indeed. No one *has* to die today."

Manson carried Eden to the shaft and held her over the edge. Her feet paddled in thin air and her vision blurred.

He stared at her with cold, dark eyes.

"I squeeze harder and you die; I loosen my grip and you die. I own your life Eden. I will choose how and when it ends."

She stopped struggling and glared at him. Manson tossed her onto the rock floor. She lay gasping for breath.

"Same goes for the rest of you. You'll only live as long as I allow you to."

Manson dragged Eden over to the rest of them. "This is a very unfortunate situation, but if we all make an effort and play nice, I am sure everything will turn out just peachy!"

Manson studied the faces of the Lightfoot team. "I expected to find you lot here," he said.

"The rest of you are unexpected, but life is more interesting if you get a surprise once in a while."

Saskia walked over to him, her brow knotted and her face red.

"They brought the device here and activated the machine. The two events you were supposed to prevent, Manson." Saskia hissed.

Manson glared at her. "Well, we're here now and we've brought the best toys." His voice was laced with fake geniality. "In fact we have quite a show planned!"

Barnes moved up next to Eden. "What happened?" Barnes asked, his voice a desperate whisper.

"She took the Ark over there. The place erupted with light and noise. When it was over, she was sick, bleeding from her nose and ears. Some kind of aneurysm, I guess."

Barnes wiped his eyes.

"I'm sorry. I didn't know her. She seemed okay," Eden said.

Barnes blinked. "We finish the job, for Mira."

Eden had every intention of doing just that.

The Knights unpacked their equipment. It looked like the parts of a crane or gantry. Saskia Hart hovered over them with an aloof arrogance.

Eden glanced at her comrades. Both the fleet soldiers were broken by the loss of their friend. Luke scanned the room as she did. She found it darkly amusing how leadership now fell to a pair of pirates.

Chloe sobbed, and the man with long hair tried to comfort her. The fat man, Kramer, was sitting on his own.

"You," Eden said to Saskia Hart. "Snow White's Mother."

Saskia made her way over, picking her way over the rocky floor with care.

"What's the big deal with this place?"

The older woman gazed at her with disdain.

"You do not understand what is at stake here do you? How could you?"

"That thing has caused me a lot of grief." Eden pointed to the Ark. It had lost its sheen and looked like a worn, eroded stone. "I lost people I cared about trying to steal it. So enlighten me. What are we all dying for?"

A half smile crossed Saskia's face. "There are things in this universe that humanity is not ready to understand, or at least not all of them."

"And you are?" Kramer said.

Saskia walked over to him and crouched.

"You know why Lightfoot has you scrabbling around out here in the dirt?" she spat. "It is not for the advancement of humanity; it's to save his skin. He hopes you will find a cure for his wasting disease, some alien technology that will prolong his life, maybe even a product he can patent and sell to the Federation."

"I suppose your goals are more noble?" Kramer replied.

Saskia stood.

"I serve a higher purpose. There are beings in this universe who would regard humans in the same way a lion regards a mouse. When they return, it will be prudent to be on the right side."

"Beings so powerful they have to use a mercenary company to do their dirty work? Ever think you've been cheated?" Eden mocked.

Saskia stared icily at her.

Manson interrupted before Saskia could reply.

"Listen up campers!" he said. He stopped as he passed Mira's body. He knelt and playfully slapped her cheek. "Look at you, laying down on the job. That's the problem with the galaxy these days, too many slackers!"

There was silence.

He stood over Tate.

"What you didn't find that funny? Too soon? I get it. You had the hots for one eye?" He shook his head. "Man, that's just a little desperate."

He circled them.

"Motherfucker..." Ethan whispered.

Manson laughed.

"I have been called far worse boy, but wind your neck in or

I'll break it."

He stood in front of them and placed his hands behind his back.

"We are almost done here. As everything has gone so well, I am in a pretty fucking happy place right now."

"And that's good news?" Eden said.

Manson nodded. "Well, I was planning on killing one of you, maybe two. You see, I have anger issues. It would probably be you Eden because of our history and your big mouth." He scanned their faces, seemingly judging their worth. "Oh and maybe you."

He pointed at Luke. "Xander's boy, right?"

He walked behind Chloe and dropped to his knees.

"Do you think you could stop crying and pay some FUCK-ING ATTENTION TO WHAT I AM SAYING?"

The girl tried to stop, sniffing and gulping air.

"See it's easy, don't worry, be happy." He ran a hand through her hair.

He straightened. The sudden movement made Chloe flinch.

"This little job is earning me a fuckload of money. So much money I am planning a move up the career ladder."

Barnes tensed. Eden sensed it. She reached for his arm and pinched it. She gave him a hard stare. Manson was trying to rile them. Eden was under no illusions he would kill them without an excuse. It improved their odds of survival not to give him one.

Manson continued with his speech.

"Most people think of me as a murderous bastard, and to be fair that's close to the truth. What they don't understand is I'm a businessman. It's all down to economics. In this game, good business sense is as important as a sharp aim." He flashed a fake smile.

"You lot are of zero value but neither are you any cost. So you keep calm, don't make waves, let us finish our job and you all get to fight another day."

"Yeah right," Tate said.

"Keep a lid on it," Barnes hissed.

"Listen to the big man, soldier boy. I won't warn you again. I genuinely don't want to kill anyone," Manson said, his hand caressing the butt of his pistol. "We do our job, we leave, then you get to leave. Keep quiet and you live." He laughed. "Whether you get off the planet before it cracks open is a different matter. That is very much your problem."

Manson barked instructions to his men.

"I was warned we had a mole. I assumed they would have been amongst the dig team," Kramer whispered to Luke.

"Nice of you to mention that when we arrived," Luke replied.

"I'm sorry but Saskia has been with the company for a long time. She was the last person I suspected."

"So who does she work for?" Eden asked. They were no closer to understanding who wanted the planet destroying.

"I don't know," Kramer said. "Whoever it is let us do the hard work. We led them here."

When the weapon prep was completed, Manson used a hand terminal to program instructions into the Mass Sink. He gave the device to Foxhound.

"Why here?" Tate asked. "Why not just surface detonate the weapon, surely it's powerful enough?"

"It's a Mass Sink. The more mass surrounding it when it goes off, the bigger the bang," Luke replied.

"Which means this shaft goes deep enough for the device to fracture the crust and push shock waves into the mantle. Gravity will pull the planet apart," Eden said. "They must have well connected friends to get their hands on one of those."

"Friends who don't want anyone else accessing the machine," Luke added.

Manson and Foxhound loaded the weapon into a steel cage and attached it to the winch. The weapon began its descent.

Eden wanted that bomb. It was just a case of working out how to get it.

Victor Rybov watched the bomb begin its descent. A large drum of reinforced carbon fibre cable rotated silently beneath the boom of the winch. Manson had insisted on an eight hour window before final detonation. Rybov would have preferred longer, but there was never any arguing with Karl.

The old man could not shake the unease haunting him since entering the chamber. He tried to put it down to being underground. He did not like being under millions of tonnes of rock. In truth his real concern was Manson. The man was becoming more erratic and more violent than ever. He had long suspected Manson harboured an ambition to rise to the top of the organisation and now the possibility was a reality, Rybov was worried. Something would need to be done.

He sauntered to where Eden sat on the rocky floor and knelt next to her.

"Eden," he whispered. "Listen. The bomb the boys are lowering into the shaft has no fail-safe. When we leave don't try to interfere with it, just get these people out. You'll have about eight hours. You understand me? Just get them out."

"Okay," she replied.

"I have offloaded a crate of equipment and stowed it in your transit pod. It might help you."

"Thank you," she said. "Don't be on that ship when it leaves. I can't guarantee your safety."

Rybov chuckled; it rattled in his throat.

"I admire your spirit, girl."

"Vic, are you done chatting?" Manson called from the bridge.

"Yes, Boss." He stood and faced Manson.

"Good, I've got a little job for you."

Rybov sauntered from the captives. He already had an idea what Manson had in mind for him.

The Blue Knights loaded up their gear and marched through the tunnel opening. Saskia Hart stood momentarily under the archway and gazed around the chamber before heading off after Manson and his squad.

A rumble of an explosion filled the cavern and the roof above the entrance collapsed. The dust cleared to reveal a pile of rock and metal blocking their escape route.

Fine dust filled the air and Eden coughed as it caught in her throat.

"Great! Just bloody great!" Kramer yelled as the blast subsided.

"Shut up and listen," Eden said. "There are three other tunnels we can use."

"How?" Kramer yelled, he was pacing, his face red with anger. "We had to cut our way into that one; it's the only way out."

"We had airflow through all four tunnels when the machine came out of hibernation," Chloe said.

"Exactly. Rybov said we have eight hours." Eden was on her feet, heading toward the winch.

"Sergeant Barnes, I want you to lead these people out of here. There is a box of equipment stashed in our pod. See what you can use."

"You're are not coming?" Barnes replied.

"I'm going after the weapon."

"I'll come with you," Zack McArdle said.

"It's not your fight, mate," Eden replied.

"After the war I spent two years deactivating IEDs. I can defuse that Mass Sink."

He had a point. For Eden's plan to work she needed to get the weapon to the surface. Eight hours would not be enough time and the device would certainly be tamper proof.

"Zack! No!" Chloe said. "Can't you do something from here?"

The engineer waved off her protest.

"The winch will be linked to the weapon. If we interfere with it, it will go off. We have to intercept it and interface with the device. We have eight hours, six for caution. If I can't do it, I still have time to get off world."

"You're sure you want to do this?" Eden asked.

"No, but we have to try. I put a lot of work into this job. I don't want someone blowing it up. Besides do you have any idea what a bomb like that could sell for?"

Eden knew but had a different idea.

"What about Mira?" Ethan asked.

Eden glanced to where Mira lay. Carrying a body would slow them down.

"Put her in the pod. We'll bring her out," she said. "I promise." It was not an ill intentioned lie. She had to say something to get the grief stricken kid moving.

Zack ran to the area close to the demolished tunnel and retrieved his pack

"Climbing equipment," he explained as he searched through the backpack.

They walked to the edge of the shaft and discussed their

plans.

From the far side of the chamber Barnes shouted.

"See you topside!"

"Count on it." Eden waved and watched him lead his charges into the tunnel.

"Look down there. The shaft runs straight for about 300 metres then there is a ridge that spirals down. The shaft narrows to a point," Zack said.

"What about those energy discharges?" she asked.

"You know how to duck?"

Zack's deadpan delivery made Eden question if he was serious. A bolt of energy cracked between the walls of the shaft.

"I can duck," she replied.

Zack set up his equipment. Eden slipped into a harness and clipped the thin wire to it.

"Are you sure this will be long enough?"

"Let's find out." He pushed off and rappelled down the shaft. Eden followed.

The descent proved to be easy and they arrived on the ledge with plenty of cable to spare.

The ground appeared to be rock. As she unclipped her harness Eden noticed it was some kind of alloy, covered in dust and rock fragments.

"This place must be old," she said.

"About 10,000 years, so I'm told," Zack said. "Come on." He led the way down into the depths.

They spiralled around the perimeter of the narrowing shaft for an hour. Eden glanced up and could no longer see the chamber above them. Distracted, she slipped, pain flared through her back as she hit the hard alloy floor. Zack took her arm. She scrambled to her feet.

"Careful, it's a long way down," he said.

"Thanks," Eden said through breaths. Her heart was racing.

"Do you need to rest?" Zack asked.

"We don't have that luxury. Let's get the weapon."

They continued downward; the carbon fibre cable holding the weapon was occasionally lit by flashes of energy.

"What's the deal with you guys then? No one had the time to explain up top," Zack asked.

It was a damn good question.

"That thing Thorn called the Ark. My crew tried to steal it and the Navy got in the way."

"So how come you're working with the her?"

"Long story."

"I have time. We've got a lot of walking to do."

Eden told him her tale.

When she finished, they continued to trudge on in silence. Zack stopped.

"It kind of makes sense," Zack said.

"So share your insight."

"This place is a city, not one you or I would understand. The Ark is what it sounds like, a transport vessel." He gestured around him. "Just think how many souls could live here."

"Souls? A little too deep for me, mate."

Then again maybe souls was not such a bad term. Eden believed everyone had an essence, quintessential intelligence that defined who they were. The word *soul* unnerved her with its metaphysical connotations.

"Okay consciousness then. Apply the First Law of Thermodynamics; energy can neither be created nor destroyed. Conscious thought is energy and when we die it has go somewhere. What if it could be captured? You would need somewhere to store it and sustain it, otherwise entropy would step in and *pfft*." Zack blew across his open palm to illustrate the point.

Eden was laughing now. It was absurd...

"Yeah, it sounds dumb, but it's what I'm seeing." Zack started walking again.

"I thought you were just the engineer. That's a complex idea for a grease monkey."

"Chloe, the intern came up with the theory before the mercs arrived," he said. "Your friend Thorn got a raw deal. She helped them; now she's dead."

Thorn's death bothered Eden. Whatever or whoever was in the Ark seemed to treat human life as expendable.

Eden had always been fascinated by alien life. She would spend many hours on UniNet reading articles on non-human intelligent life. Freddie was always hating on her for it. What did he know? Freddie only used UniNet to look at holo-porn.

Eden remembered one piece written by Carlos Vasquez, the scientist behind the common evolutionary theory. It theorised that life-forms evolving under similar conditions would evolve along similar lines. It was thought prime species on Earth like worlds would have hands capable of utilising tools, walk upright and have binocular vision, this being the optimum form to exploit the environment. It was a theory supported by the Verani's humanoid physique.

Intelligence was a different matter. Humans were smart but there was no guarantee those on other worlds would have the same level of innate intelligence or value set. Non-Human life-forms had the potential to view humans as humans would regard cattle and may treat them as insignificant. Human treatment of the great apes in the nineteenth and twentieth centuries was often given as an example of interspecies genocide.

Eden shuddered at the thought.

Maybe we should just let the bomb go off. The galaxy might be better off without this world and its machine.

"Over there," Zack said, interrupting her thoughts.

Ahead of her was the end of the cable and the Mass Sink in its cage. The timer gradually counting down.

"How do we get to it?"

"Leave that to me," Zack said.

Zack unhooked his backpack and assembled his equipment. He attached a tool pack to his belt and fixed a diagnostic computer to his wrist. The last thing he put together was an explosive traversing system.

"Do you carry that stuff everywhere?" Eden asked.

"Yep. You never know when you might need to defuse a planet killer."

"Meeting you was our lucky break."

Zack took aim on the far wall. A red dot danced on the rock showing where the harpoon would hit; it would turn green whenever it crossed a target section capable of taking the strain. Satisfied with the position Zack fired the bolt with a hiss of compressed air. There was a flash on the other side of the shaft as the harpoon drilled into the wall with the aid of a small rocket motor.

Zack removed the handle and chose a spot on the wall behind Eden.

"Stand clear," he said.

He placed the butt against the wall and activated the tunnelling charge. The end of the cable drove into the wall.

Zack tested the wire. He nodded, satisfied it would take his weight.

"She's good," he said.

"You're climbing over there?"

"Yeah, give me the pulley system." Zack pointed to a titanium pulley block. He took it from Eden and clipped it onto the wire before hooking it to his harness. Zack lifted his feet off the ledge. The cable barely moved under his weight.

"It'll do," he said as he activated the pulley's electric motor.

Slowly he edged out over the abyss. He looked down and could see only darkness.

Cool air blew over him from above.

"This facility has an efficient cooling system."

"Great," Eden replied.

"It means your friends will get out. That much fresh air can only come from the surface."

He focused his attention on the weapon. As he approached it he surveyed the job. The cage would be easy to open but he would need to be careful not to let the weapon fall into the shaft.

He positioned himself under the cage and released the catches. The bomb was secured to the inside with three straps. Zack realised he had been holding his breath. He released it with a huge sigh.

He switched his wrist computer into diagnostic mode and extracted a probe from a recess in the side. He connected it to a port on the bomb. He booted up and studied the code. Zack raised an eyebrow at the copyright information in the code's header.

"This was put together by the Frontier Company."

His flicked into the countdown timer. 5 hours and 23 minutes remained.

"Shit," he said. "Bastard has short timed the weapon."

"How long?"

"Just over five hours."

"You better get busy then."

While his terminal communicated with the device, he visually inspected the weapon. The casing was seamless and aside from the diagnostic port he could see no way in. It meant he would need to work on the software alone. He had to admit working on code written by a Martian Insurgent to detonate an IED would differ greatly from code written by the Frontier Company.

Different does not mean impossible. Different job, same tools.

He checked the handset. The auto diagnostic had identified six fail safes; they were highlighted in yellow. He studied the code and disabled each in turn. The lights on the bomb continued to blink; so far so good.

The code was a compact three thousand lines. Zack would need to read through each line looking for hidden traps and tamper controls. He scanned and re-scanned. On the first run through he saw nothing of concern; it bothered him. Starting at the top he scanned again and found something. A simple two line section. It looked like a timer control check; it was a routine to prevent interference with the countdown. He used the handset to remove the code.

Zack wiped sweat from his eyes. The counter was down to 3 hours and 58 minutes.

He continued to examine the code. There was no deactivation sequence or at least none he could identify.

Think man, your life depends on it.

The timer...

There was no need to deactivate the weapon, all he had to do was extend the detonation time. If he could make it long enough, he could get off world drop the weapon in space. With minimal mass to surround it would have a similar effect to a cherry bomb.

"Eden," he said. "I think I have it."

He scrolled to the timer section. It was a standard loop. After the correct number of cycles it would trigger the detonation sequence. He used the editor to assign a value 999 to the counter variable. Taking a deep breath he rebooted the program and cycled to the timer. The screen read:

DETONATION IN 999 HOURS

"Well, that was easy!"

"You did it?" Eden stood and stretched.

"Yep, it can still be triggered either in person or remotely. There is a danger the mercs may do it, but it's slim. They'll be long gone by the time the bomb was supposed to go off."

He unclipped the bomb from its cage. It was heavier than he expected. Making sure he had a firm hold, he activated the pulley and tracked back to the ledge.

Eden took the weapon from him and placed it in her pack as he packed away his kit. When he was done he stood. Eden brandished a shock stick.

"I'm sorry Zack, I need that weapon." She plunged the baton at him and his nerves lit up as he lost consciousness.

CHAPTER TWENTY-FIVE

MIRA Thorn opened her eyes. The Milky Way arched high overhead in a clear desert sky. A cold breeze blew out of the West, bringing the promise of water by dawn. The Benguela Fog had yet to roll in, but the air was cooling and thickening around her in anticipation of its arrival.

Mira stared at the stars with two green eyes.

She sat up and blinked as she became accustomed to the darkness. She lay on the side of a mighty dune. Below her the baked white clay of a long dry marsh floated in a sea of endless red sand. Twisted and blackened acacias sprouted from the sun-blasted ground like skeletal fingers reaching for the stars.

It was the Deadvlei, and she was home.

Mira had not been here since she was seventeen. She and five friends had taken a road trip across Africa, a crazy zig-zag route from Windhoek to Cairo. It was the year before she left for the academy; her last year as a civilian. The night they had spent in the sun scorched Namib desert had been one of the best of her life.

She stood in a fluid movement, unencumbered by pain.

More recent memories came back to her: the Ark, the all engulfing light, the sea of pain and the endless, lonely darkness that followed. How had she arrived here? Earth was hundreds of light-years from the Cygnus Vale.

Movement on the Vlei drew her attention. Someone was walking on the baked clay, a casual, sauntering stroll that was heartbreakingly familiar. The newcomer stopped by a dead tree and waved.

After a moment of hesitation Mira half walked, half slid down the side of the dune.

"Run Mira. The faster you go the easier it is!" the figure shouted. The girl's Australian accent immediately recognisable, dispelling any lingering doubts as to her identity.

Mira ran, exhilarated by the sand shifting beneath her feet. The sound of the Amy Flynt's laughter was carried by the wind and spurred her on. A few seconds later she was running across the dry marsh to where the young woman waited.

Amy was dressed in her torn black jeans and a stretched sweat top; blonde hair curled from beneath a knitted woollen cap. She looked the same as she had on the day they met.

"I told you it was better if you ran." Amy shifted her weight to her left foot and twirled a strand of hair.

Mira caught her breath. "Amy? Is it really you? Am I *dead*?"

"I thought you didn't believe in an afterlife? When you're dead you're dead, right?"

"I don't but... I can't explain this. This place feels real... I don't understand. What's happening?"

"It feels real because it is real." Amy took her hand. "Come with me. Let's sit by the fire. I'll explain."

They walked through the blackened forest and onward through the dunes. A six wheeled electric jeep was parked at the edge of a gravel road. A fire burned in a pit close by. Tents were erected on the far side of road. Everything was just how Mira remembered it.

"I'm not the real Amy," the girl said. "I am a construct built from your memories."

Mira stopped.

"So, this is not real?"

Amy moved close and kissed her. Mira tried to compose herself; her mind was a battlefield of conflicting emotions.

"Did that feel real?" Amy asked. Mira didn't, *couldn't,* answer.

"I am a living entity. I am your memories given form. I am capable of independent thought and action within the parameters of the source material. I am built from every detail you remember, both consciously and unconsciously. I am as real as I can be. Just as this place is. Come on, there is a lot to say and time is short."

Mira sat next to the crackling fire. The heat warmed her skin, banishing the chill of the night air. Sweet smoke stung her eyes and made them water. She raised her hand to her face to wipe away the tears. The skin of her cheek was soft and smooth, devoid of scars.

Mira put her hand to the fire, withdrawing it as the flames burned her fingers.

"Careful," Amy laughed. "This world obeys the same rules as the one your body inhabits. If it hurts you there, it will hurt you here."

Mira had played on VR sims that created artificial worlds. Those worlds were simplistic simulacra of real life. This place was intensely detailed and realistic; so much so her lips still tingled from the kiss; her eyes still stung from the smoke.

She struggled to make sense of it. A few minutes ago she was pushing an ancient artefact across a bridge in a chamber beneath the surface of an alien world. Now she was sitting in the Namib desert talking to a girl who had been dead for two years. It was insane. Her senses reeled as nausea gripped her.

Amy was smiling from the other side of the fire.

"It's okay Mira. I am here to help you; they created me because they knew you would trust me."

"The Pharn?"

Amy gave Mira a bottle of water. She took a long drink. It was cold and refreshing; her sickness subsided.

"Yes, that is how you know them. They have many names."

Amy produced a joint from her pocket. She lit it with a battered zippo lighter and offered it to Mira.

"No, I gave that shit up a long time ago," Mira said.

Amy took a long pull. She offered it back. Mira declined again.

"They spoke from the Ark. Why not now?"

"The Ark could only draw a small amount of power from your ship to communicate. They were unable directly commune with you so they manipulated your mind. It's why communication took the form of dreams and voices in your head. In this place they draw energy from the planet's core. They are powerful and our minds are not strong enough to withstand them. For us to commune with the Pharn would be like... I dunno... a sparrow flying into a tornado." Amy seemed pleased with the analogy.

"Is that why I died? They were too strong?"

"It was one of your old injuries, just as you always thought would happen. You suffered a massive cerebral haemorrhage. It was starting when you boarded the Kobo. The Pharn stabilised it so you could complete the task they set you. Without them you would have died days ago."

The headaches and memory issues made a lot more sense. As did the shadow Monica detected.

"Think of it like breathing onto a coal that's all but burnt out. The fire will continue to burn, but only as long as you blow on it."

Mira had always loved the way Amy spoke in hippie metaphors, most were awkward and borderline crass but sometimes she'd pull out something profound.

"When the Pharn left the Ark, they could not sustain you, so your body died."

If you save them, you will die. I did not understand the message. It was never about saving the crew; it was about saving the Ark.

"I guess it could be worse. I can't see any men with pitchforks."

Amy gave a stoned giggle.

"We humans have a peculiar view of life and death. For us death is final, the end, thank you and goodnight," Amy said. "Sure you don't want a toke? It's good."

Mira relented and took the joint.

"It's not like it's going to kill me is it?" she said.

Amy was right, it was good. She buzzed. Perhaps the whole afterlife experience wasn't so bad.

From stoned to eternity. She coughed and giggled.

"The concept here Mira, is what makes *you;* What makes Mira Thorn who she is? Is it the bag of mostly water you shuffle around in or is it the consciousness that moves the blood and gristle from place to place?"

It was an existential argument. Mira understood the point the Amy Construct was making. *I think, therefore I am.*

"The Ark opened a portal to the machine. The Pharn used it to cross over. They took you, or more accurately your consciousness, with them. Congratulations you are the first post physical human!"

Mira gazed around her at the dunes and the stars above. This post physical world was real and detailed, yet somehow sterile. She could not pinpoint what was wrong but something was bothering her.

Amy stared ahead, her expression blank. She moved her lips almost imperceptibly. It was clear to Mira that information was being exchanged between her and whoever was beyond the sky.

"It was always their intention to fix you. They are grateful for what you did for them, in as much as they understand the concept of gratitude. They have a plan for you," Amy said.

"A plan? Amy, who are they? Are they... harmful?"

Amy blew a perfect smoke ring and looked into the flames. "They don't mean us harm, but they don't necessarily want to be our benefactors. It's complicated. Their purpose is to prepare us for a war that will come."

"I saw what happened in the last war. If they couldn't win, what makes them think we can?"

"They see something in humanity they had lost in themselves. You need to understand who the Pharn were and what happened to them."

Amy told her how the First Ones had originated in the Cygnus Vale a hundred thousand years ago. They had been successful spacefarers who spread out through the galaxy. As they encountered sentient life they incorporated it into their society to become a vast and diverse collective known as Pharn.

"Diversity was their strength. They all contributed their differences to a unified whole."

"The Pharn, they were *The Ones Who Came First*?" Mira asked.

"Yes, as we understand it; just as humans will be to whoever comes after us. I think the Verani came up with that idea."

Mira thought of the cycle Jon had described. Life rises, life ends, repeat.

Amy continued to fill in the gaps in the story. Mira watched her as she spoke. Amy was as she remembered her, how she saw her in her mind's eye. She would be. She was born from Mira's memories.

Watching the construct was like watching someone play the part of a person she had known so intimately. Emotional conflict boiled inside her.

"Mira?" Amy said.

"Sorry, it's... hard, seeing you like this. I am listening."

"The galaxy was peaceful for millennia, until the Pharn encountered The Blackened."

Mira laughed.

"Fuck me. Where did they find them? Mordor?"

"You still cuss as well as ever."

"Fuck yeah. Come on get to the point, Flynt."

"The Blackened is the best term; their true name had no equivalence in any Earth language."

Amy continued with the tale, pausing every so often to draw down a lungful of weed. She did not seem to become any more stoned.

The Blackened were an ancient species. They were the antithesis of the Pharn's values and ethics.

"They were hostile, xenophobic bastards. Their technology was advanced and equivalent to the Pharn," Amy said.

Mira thought of the destruction of the city.

"The Blackened eradicated Pharn worlds. The collective was all but extinguished; they built this machine and others like it to preserve their kind. They found a way to abandon their physical form and to live as one consciousness inside vaults like these."

You can destroy cities; you can scrub planets but how do you destroy ideas or thought?

"Surely places like this would be vulnerable?" Mira asked.

"They were and many were lost. Those inside mirrored to a

new vault. The machines were a stepping stone. There came a time when they were able break free and exist between the stars as a single energetic entity."

"And what happened to the Blackened?"

"The Pharn knew they had to defeat them, not just for themselves but for all who came after. They are accomplished bio engineers and they constructed bodies optimised for combat, expendable bodies for which death would not be final. They were unstoppable and they prevailed. The Blackened were wiped out and the Pharn left this galaxy forever."

"Genocide," Mira whispered.

"Survival," Amy countered.

They fell into silence.

A thought occurred to Mira. "So what is the Ark? You said the Pharn could mirror from vault to vault. What was its purpose?"

"When the war was thought to be lost, Pharn society split. Some of the collective chose not to fight. They sealed themselves into Arks, to wait out the war and prepare the way for whoever was left or came after. Arks were scattered throughout the Vale. There is no way of knowing how many survived. Yours might be the only one."

Amy moved around the fire and sat next to Mira. She put an arm around her and pulled her close. Mira could smell the characteristic scent of the Vanilla; the fragrance Amy was so fond of.

The illusion fractured, shattering into the uncountable fragments of an exposed lie.

This is too perfect, too convenient...fake.

Of course it is fake. It's my memories; memories I created because the truth was too painful.

Somehow as Mira followed her own self-destructive path,

the reality of the relationship with Amy Flynt had been lost. Now it came back. The brutal reality surfaced from a dark, shuttered off part of her mind.

The person holding her was Amy the myth, a stylised replica of the best of her; this was the image of Amy she had clung onto for the past two years.

Where was Amy the junkie? Where was the girl who had sold Mira's medals to fund a fix? Where was the girl who beat her? Where was the girl who broke her collar bone, her ribs and eventually her heart?

Amy's descent from a carefree party girl into a violent controlling abuser had been gradual. She became ever more domineering and violent as her substance abuse increased. Endless binges of alcohol and drugs altered her personality. Even when she was clean she was moody and bitter.

Mira had played her part, her thrill seeking personality was all too ready to embrace the excesses of Amy Flynt's world. They were the same kind of crazy, each feeding off the other's profligacy until something had to give. When Mira realised how far she was sinking, she hit the brakes, sobered up and tried to rebuild a normal life. Amy had continued on a downward spiral and blamed Mira for it.

Mira should have left her, wanted to leave her, yet could not. She resigned her commission, knowing Amy could not be trusted to keep herself alive in her absence. It was a decision Mira had made out of love and one she never regretted. Amy reacted badly. Not because she cared about Mira's career; it meant she had to confront her dark side.

Amy had been clean for six weeks. Mira told her of her decision one Sunday afternoon as they sat on the shore of Elliot Bay.

That night Amy erupted into one of her rages. She had been

in Mira's face screaming, yelling and shoving her. Mira stood ground. She snapped and hit Amy, knocking her to the floor.

Mira had stood, looking down on the frail figure sobbing and shaking on the floor of their apartment. She had been filled with rage and guilt as she looked at the poor little rich kid intent on killing herself to live.

Amy Flynt, a girl who had never seen her friends blown to bits. A girl who had never felt the cold caress of death. A girl who never considered that this day, might be her last day. A girl who placed no value on her life.

Mira ran from the apartment into the misty rain of the Seattle night. She spent the small hours of that morning walking alone through deserted streets under harsh Xenon lights. She tried to make sense of her life and eventually did.

Mira returned hours later, soaked to the skin and cold to the bone. She expected to find Amy jacked up with junk, sitting in her own puke and piss. Instead she sat at the ancient oak dining table, her sunken eyes were red and damp. A mug of cold coffee was clasped in her skeletal hands.

Mira gave her a choice; give up the drugs and she would stay, otherwise she would walk out and never return. Amy had not wavered. She had stood, asked Mira to hold her and swore that she was done with the junk, the booze and the pills.

Amy had already spoken to her mother and together made arrangements to go to a clinic in Vancouver. Mira had taken her to bed and held her while she slept.

True to her word Amy had left for the rehab facility the following day. The day *Earth First* bombed the Seattle Metro.

She pushed closer to Amy in an effort to banish the emptiness.

"I'm sorry I hit you."

"You never gave up on me Mira and I treated you so badly.

You stood up to me and you saved me."

"Would you have stayed clean? Did we have a future?"

The Amy construct traced a circle in the sand.

Eventually she answered.

"No, I don't think so. I was never as strong as you. You knew your limits. You knew when to stop. I hated you for it and I hated myself for that."

They sat in silence.

Mira could not be sure if the admission was from her own subconscious or if the construct had somehow modelled the response. Deep down she knew Amy, the real Amy, would have relapsed, just as she knew she would never have left her. In the end one or both of them would have ended up dead.

We have... she thought, smiling at the irony.

She still had questions even if she had all of eternity to ask them.

"So what a happened to the people in the Ark?" Mira asked. "Are they here with us?"

"Yes, this is their realm, their plane of existence."

Above her a shooting star crossed the sky. It glowed an intense blue and faded to nothing.

"They call themselves Sentinels. We are the product of their exile. They have taken the first steps in preparing the way for us. Now they are assimilating the events that took place after they became separated from the collective. I expect they will leave soon, to seek the rest of their kind."

"And what about us? Are we stuck here forever? The same lost souls we always were?"

"I will cease to exist when my purpose is complete. Don't worry I'm good with it. The Pharn used your DNA to construct a new body, you are going back, Mira Thorn."

"How? A clone?"

"Look past the word, this is not cloning as humans understand it. Unlike us, they can produce a mature clone. You'll be the same age; you'll look the same. You will be the same person you always were; the same as you were when you stepped onto the surface of this planet. All your memories and experiences will be present."

It took a moment to sink in.

"A duplicate?"

"No! A continuation. You will be you; think of it as a new bag of blood and gristle to move around in. They could produce multiple copies of you, but only the one in which *you* reside will be Mira Thorn. They cannot duplicate consciousness, only flesh."

"Fuck."

"Is that a good fuck or a bad fuck?"

"An undecided one."

Mira gazed around her at the dunes rising into the starry sky. It would not be the body she had been born with, the body that spent a mystical night here so many years before. Nor would it be the body that had her first kiss, her first heartbreak or the body that had been smashed on the surface of Mars.

"Mira time is short. When the Pharn leave this machine will cease to operate. That is not your concern. Other humans are here and they are lowering a bomb deep into the vault. They want to destroy this world."

"Why?"

"They are agents of the Blackened. They want to destroy the last vestiges of the ones who came first, so their knowledge cannot benefit the ones who came after."

"Can they be stopped? This place must have defences?"

Amy closed her eyes, listening.

"Regardless of the bomb, this planet will end. Humans are

not ready for this world and the technology it holds."

Amy tossed the joint into the fire.

She stood and offered a hand. Mira let her pull her to her feet.

"Buried deep within this machine is a data-core containing knowledge humanity can use against the Blackened. You will need to retrieve it before Arethon is no more."

"Why not just tell us what we need to know," Mira asked.

Amy's face was anxious. It was the way she looked before she went into a rage. She remained calm. "It is their way. Humanity has to earn knowledge, value it and understand it. The power it contains must be wielded with responsibility. Can you imagine what would have happened if someone had given Hitler or Stalin a plasma cannon or an FTL drive?"

Mira understood, excessive power without conditions would be as much danger to an immature humanity as any alien civilisation.

"Mira, know this, the Blackened have returned. They will infiltrate and attempt to destroy humanity from within. When they have divided us and we cannot stand against them, they will destroy us."

"Why?"

"Because we are not them; because that is their purpose."

"So what do we do? What can we do?"

"You are a leader, Mira. You bring people together and you care. You already have allies."

Mira was just a pilot. The best she had ever hoped for was to be a squadron commander and when she could no longer fly, maybe an executive officer on a Steelside.

"That isn't me," was all she could say.

"Mira you overcome everything life throws at you. You survived a crash that should have killed you. You survived me and you survived the destruction of your ship. You don't give up. You fight until you have nothing left and somehow you keep going."

"Maybe I have nothing left to give, Amy. I'm a washout."

"You are here aren't you?"

Mira made no reply.

"Mira, the Pharn know *you*. They looked into you and knew you from…" Amy stopped dead, as if she were about to speak out of turn. She changed tack.

"You have no secrets from them. They chose you. They could have let you die in space and chosen another. They believe you in. Believe in yourself."

Mira stood in silence under a sky lit with first signs of dawn. The stars faded into blue and fog tumbled over distant dunes.

Aspects of life had been brutal. She had fought and she had survived, but there had been plenty of times when she wished herself dead. She thought of Tish growing up at the arse end of the galaxy. Others had suffered far greater hardships than she could imagine.

If Tish could survive what life had dealt her, then maybe there is hope for me… But I am not special; I am not strong. Give me a chance and I'll probably fuck it up.

She snapped her attention back to Amy.

"Mira our present is shaped by the past, both distant and recent. We make choices based on previous choices. Trust me, I ended up dead because of a decision I made. You ended up here because of choices you made."

"So everything is inevitable?"

"We always have freewill, how much depends on the surrounding galaxy. Your galaxy is changing and events will change you."

Conflicted feelings clouded Mira's mind. Before her stood

the Amy she loved, not the Amy who had hurt her so badly and left her alone.

"You know what you did to me?"

A tear ran traced a silver trail on Amy's cheek. "I'm sorry."

It was all Mira needed to hear. Mira held her, feeling her breathe, not caring she was artificial.

Time passed.

Amy stepped back and fixed her gaze on Mira, who was drawn into her deep brown eyes.

"Mira you were my world, my everything. I fucked up my life and you saved me. Now save the galaxy, you dysfunctional hero."

A rapid blur of images and voices flashed through Mira's mind. It was a fleeting dizzying sensation. Before she could say anything more the Deadvlei dissolved into blackness.

Mira Thorn was born for the second time in a rush of colour, sound and sensation. She was immersed in warm viscous fluid yet somehow she could breathe. She floated inside a capsule. It was small and she could barely move. Mira wriggled against the sides of the container and smashed her hands against the inside of the tube. Dull thuds reverberated through the fluid. Outside she could make out light and dark but no detail. A large dark shadow was moving in the gloom beyond the glass. It receded and was absorbed by the darkness.

A tearing, burning pain ripped through her abdomen. The fluid clouded with blood. A flaccid, pink umbilicus withdrew from her navel and retreated to the bottom of the capsule.

The fluid drained in an instant. The front of the cylinder slid up and Mira fell onto her hands and knees. She coughed up lungfuls of the green liquid. Once she expelled it from her respiratory system, she gulped down freezing air. Her ribs painfully expanded with each breath. She shivered, rolled onto her side and sobbed.

Mira did not know how long she lay on the cold metal floor, but eventually she sat up and wiped the remaining fluid from her face. She blinked. She put a hand over one eye, then the other.

I have two eyes! her mind screamed, yet she could not bring herself to believe it.

Mira traced her fingers down her cheek. The scars were gone; the skin was soft and smooth. For the first time in a long time she was unhindered by pain or stiffness. Her back felt supple. She rolled her shoulders in a way she had not in many years.

Reality and constructed reality collided in her thoughts and feelings. Mira could still smell the fire and feel the tingle in her hand where it had burnt her fingers; the taste of the joint lingered in her mouth.

"Dysfunctional hero, thanks for that Flynt," she said. "I'm not sure about the hero bit."

Mira continued to inspect her body. The skin was soft. Her hands were bereft of cuts or callouses. Her hair was longer than she was used to; it reached down to the middle of her back. It was thick and unruly. The same was true of her body hair.

"With all your technology you don't know how to produce a razor? I'm a mouse, not a fucking ape," she said.

Mira pulled her knees to her chest and sat waiting for the shivers to subside while she took stock of her surroundings.

The chamber was small and had dark copper coloured walls. It was rectangular and lit by a low powered hidden light source. A single shelf extended from the far wall, illuminated from above. Different sized pods, similar to the one she had emerged from, lined three walls of the room. She clambered to her feet;

her legs were unsteady and shook like a newborn foal. Once she had her balance, she made a few tentative steps toward the shelf. She stumbled and grabbed the edge to stay upright. She tried to walk again. This time it was easier. Her muscles gained strength as her confidence in controlling them grew.

She found a synthetic coverall on the shelf, a pair of boots and a beaker of what appeared to be water. The coverall was modelled on the base layer of her armour although it was a lighter and thinner. The boots were manufactured from the same material as the coverall, albeit a tougher, more rigid variant.

Her throat was dry and sore. She sniffed the contents of the cup and found it to be odourless. A sip confirmed it was water. She drank it and doubled up with cramp.

Take it easy, everything is new.

The cramps subsided, replaced instead by intense hunger.

Mira dressed. The clothes were a perfect fit for the new body and the boots were sculpted to fit her feet.

Her eyes were now accustomed to the low light. She caught sight of her reflection in the lid of a pod. She walked toward it. Mira Thorn stared back at her with two green eyes.

I look so young. The pain is gone, but I don't feel any different to how I felt this morning. It's just like Amy said... a continuation.

I need to find something... before the planet comes apart. A data-core!

Mira knew what she needed to do where she needed to go. She did not know where the knowledge came from.

The room had a single exit. She found herself in a featureless corridor. It sloped and curved downward, spiralling around what she assumed was the central shaft.

Mira ran. The floor was smooth. There was no sign of the

rock and dust that littered the upper levels. She relished the blood pumping through her veins. A faint sheen of sweat formed on her body. She was alive... So alive.

She rounded a bend and ran into the lanky engineer, knocking him off his feet.

"You! What the hell?" he said.

Mira stared at him, she relished the easy recall of his name. "Zack?" she said.

"What happened? You were..."

"Dead? Yeah I know, it's complicated. We need to get to the weapon."

"I already have. I delayed the explosion time."

"Good. Where is it?"

"Well, that's the thing. Your friend Eden stunned me and took it. I have been wandering around trying to find a way out. I assumed this tunnel must lead to the surface."

Mira wondered what Eden wanted with the Mass Sink. Selling it would be impossible. The Federal Crime Agency would be all over her unless... The Blue Knights.

"You should get to the surface," Mira said. "Go that way, it leads out." It was more a feeling than absolute knowledge.

"What about you?" Zack said.

"I have to get to the bottom. There is something I need down there."

"I'll take my chances with you."

"Let's go then." She broke into a run. "One more thing, this planet will come apart; we do not have long."

"Things just keep getting better and better. How do you plan on getting off world?" he asked.

Mira had not thought about that.

"I'll call my ship or you have an Aurora at your camp. We'll use it if we need to."

There was also the complication of Eden and the Mass Sink; she kept that information to herself.

The corridor continued to spiral downward; each circuit was shorter than the preceding one.

Zack was panting as he struggled with the pace. Mira slowed.

"Do you want to stop?" she asked.

He shook his head, breathing too hard to reply.

"I don't think it's far," she said. She was barely out of breath.

The alloy floor lost its shine and showed signs of dust ingress.

Mira slowed and stopped as the tunnel opened out onto a narrow ridge. They were in a circular shaft. Its featureless grey sides were lined with lights which did little to banish the oppressive twilight. A constant flow of air came from above. It whipped Mira's hair in front of her face. The ground trembled, and a rumble rose from the depths.

"Where now?" Zack asked.

"Down," Mira replied, staring into the darkness below.

CHAPTER TWENTY-SIX

ETHAN'S ankle throbbed, but he refused slow his pace. As the analgesia wore off the pain was becoming intense. Every few steps a ligament would shift and fire a bolt of pain up his leg.

The slope was gradual and the corridor cut from the bedrock; it appeared no different to the one through which they had descended. Barnes kept a steady speed and Ethan fell back, little by little.

"Let me help you," Chloe said. "I'm stronger than I look." She slipped an arm around his waist and her shoulder under his arm. "You are making better progress than Mr Kramer."

Ethan glanced behind him. Kramer was red faced and breathing hard.

"I guess he's not used to this," Ethan replied. He had to admit Barnes was moving them at a ferocious pace. Given the stakes no one objected. Ethan was impressed with Kramer's ability to keep up given his age and build.

"I'm not planning on carrying him," Chloe whispered. Her smile and gentle humour brought relief from the sadness that had fallen over him since Mira's death.

"Do you think we are close to the surface yet? This tunnel seems to go on forever." He guessed they had been moving for four or five hours.

"We passed the point where we inserted about a six kilometres ago, the tunnel incline has not increased. We had to drill to intercept the tunnel so I think we must be over halfway to the surface," Chloe replied between breaths.

They pressed on in silence.

"I'm sorry your friend had to die for this," she said. She sounded awkward. Ethan wanted to say something but could not think of the words so he put his head down and carried on.

"Come on, don't be afraid to lean on me. Like I said I am stronger than I look. I lived on a high gravity world," Chloe said.

The tunnel twisted left, then right, before straightening again. It ran on for about a kilometre. Warm light flickered ahead.

"Daylight!" Luke called back.

Ethan dropped his head and drove onward. The pain in his ankle faded and he was almost dragging Chloe behind him. After a lung-burning, muscle-draining sprint they were confronted by a fine mesh grill. Behind it a fan rotated slowly in a circular opening. Weak sunlight streamed through the holes in the mesh.

"I have a signal!" Luke said.

"Call up Alex! Ask him to triangulate in on this position," Barnes said, inspecting the grill.

Barnes put his hand on the mesh and sharply withdrew it.

"Damn!" he said, he shook his hand. "There is a charge running through it."

"Probably... Charged... To..." Kramer panted behind them "To... repel dust... from the system."

Barnes stepped back and put his hands on his hips.

"Aside from the charge it's not exotic. Private Tate hook up the explosives. Everyone else get back into cover. Be careful, the explosives don't respond well to electrical interference."

Ethan limped forward and wired a chain of blasting wire around the edge of the mesh. The surface was alive with ionised air. Once complete he limped to a safe distance and triggered an explosion. The grill vaporised. Moving forward again and placed a small explosive pack on the centre hub of the fan; he set a 20 second countdown.

"Stay down!" he yelled, lurching into the tunnel as fast as his injured foot would allow. "This will be messy!"

The charge fired and pushed the fan off its axis. Metal screeched as the blades tore free and launched into the corridor and the cave beyond. The explosion rumbled on as the fan tore itself to pieces. As the dust settled Ethan stood. A stabbing pain ran through his ankle as he put weight on it.

He helped Chloe to her feet.

"Are you okay?" he asked.

She nodded. "Just a little deaf." She held his gaze before looking toward the shattered fan.

"Thank you," Ethan said. "For your help back there... and what you said about the commander. She was a good friend."

Chloe squeezed his arm and walked toward the opening beyond the wrecked fan. Ethan limped after her.

The cave opened into a wide, deep canyon.

"Our orbital scans would not have detected the openings if they are all concealed like this," Kramer said, heaving in lung-fuls of air.

Ethan wondered if he was saying it for his own benefit.

Barnes keyed his com-link

"Alex where are you?"

The Naja dropped into the aperture from above. The bow ramp lowered. Ethan jumped back with a startled cry followed by a rush of adrenaline. He pushed Chloe forward into the ship before following. He waited on the bow ramp to assist Kramer. Barnes was the last to board.

"Is everyone in?" Alex asked.

"Everyone who is coming," Barnes said as he sat.

Ethan fixed Chloe's straps and fastened his own.

"Thank you," she said.

Ethan's weight increased as the ship accelerated away from the cave. He closed his eyes and tried to bury his grief in the drone of the drop ship's engines.

Monica Garret sat on a stool in medbay watching a bank of monitors. Each holo-screen displayed a team member's vital signs. The traces had been flat-lining ever since the team dropped below ground and out of radio contact; now the displays lit with the vibrant signs of life.

All but two.

She keyed her link.

"Hey Rich, good to see you all fit and well. Can you ask Mira and Eden to check their links; I'm not picking up a signal from either of them."

"She's gone, Monica. We lost Mira." He broke down.

"How?" she asked.

"I wasn't there, I let her down. Eden said she had some kind of haemorrhage."

Monica closed the link. Once she had regained control, she reopened the channel.

"And Eden?"

"She went below with one of the Lightfoot people to defuse the weapon. She's still subsurface."

Monica sat in silence. "Rich, what do you want me to tell Tish? She was sweet on Mira."

Barnes paused. "Don't tell her anything. Alex and Luke will

fly the ship. We will take care of her when we come on board."

Monica closed her eyes and rubbed her temples.

"Rich are you bringing her back?"

"Negative, the situation is fluid. We don't know if the weapon is disabled."

His breathing slowed, but his voice remained unsteady. "We'll know if Eden and Zack were successful in two hours. We can collect the commander's body when we extract them. Lightfoot has lost one of his people too."

"Understood," Monica said through silent tears.

Eden emerged on a rocky hillside as the drop ship roared into the sky. She watched until it became a dark speck in the grey sky and finally disappeared. She removed her com-link and dropped into the ravine below.

She had chanced on a corridor heading upward, which had in turn led to a lifting platform. It brought her to a cave on the surface.

Eden used the Planetary Positioning System to pinpoint her location. She was on the far side of the mountain relative to base camp. She knew there was a rover there and that would be the fastest way to get to the Blue Knights.

The PPS handset plotted her a course over the terrain. It picked a fast route and advised the journey would take just under two hours. The route was classified as extreme. Eden declined the device's suggestion to plot an alternative route.

With the weapon in her backpack she dropped onto a narrow ridge and shimmied her way along.

Victor Rybov sat in the back of the Rhino listening to Manson brag about how he planned to take control of the organisation.

He made promises of wealth and position to the younger men. Foxhound lapped it up while KK remained silent and concentrated on navigating the vehicle through the difficult terrain.

Saskia Hart sat at the back, next to Rybov. She had barely uttered a word since they left the chamber.

Manson called up Lyle.

"We are on our way back. Get the *Wolf* fired up. I want off this rock as soon as we get on board."

Manson's face darkened.

"What?" he yelled. He punched the headrest of the seat, bending the steel subframe.

"Get it fucking fixed then," he screamed into the link.

"Problem, Boss?" Rybov asked.

"Sand has got into the injectors. Lyle is trying to clear it. When we get back, I want everyone on it. Arseholes and elbows. The weapon is keyed to go off and we have three hours to get it done."

"Three hours?" Rybov fixed Manson with a cold gaze.

"I short timed it."

The atmosphere in the cabin darkened as they all fell into silence.

Once the Naja was in the hangar Alex and Luke made for the exit ramp. Luke tossed his helmet to Spence who deftly caught it.

They ran through the ship and arrived on the flight deck. Monica was holding Tish.

Tish broke away from the Doctor.

"We can't leave, Alex. We can't leave her," she said.

Luke stepped forward.

"Tish we still have people down there, and they will bring her back. We need to prepare the ship."

"No! You don't get it she isn't dead. I know she isn't dead."

"Tish I was there. I'm sorry I saw it happen," Luke replied. His words were harsh but softened by the gentle timbre of his voice.

"She's alive! I don't know how I know it, but I do. We can't leave. We just can't." Tish was agitated.

Monica intervened. "Tish, let these boys get the ship prepped. If she is down there, we'll find her."

Tish's lips quivered. She held it together. She stared at Alex with a fierce intensity.

"She's alive. I know she's alive. I can *feel* her."

Monica whispered to her. She nodded.

"She'll be okay," Monica said to Luke as she led the girl from the flight deck.

"Ready?" Alex asked

"Yeah... I guess... you know..." Luke's voice trailed off as he climbed into the copilot's seat. "Tish has feelings about things, random and impossible things she could not possibly know. They always ended up being true. There was this time when I took her to the casino back on Double T. On the roulette wheel she was on fire. We cleaned up that night."

"I hope this is one of those times. Right now let's get the ship ready, just in case."

Alex began his stage of the pre departure procedure.

Mira scanned the sides of the shaft looking for a way down. She spotted movement in the darkness; something was coming toward them.

These eyes are good!

"Zack, our ride is here."

A circular platform rose out of the gloom and hovered level with the ridge. Mira stepped onto it. It did not move under her weight.

"Come on, it's fine," she said, not knowing where her confidence came from.

Zack followed her and stood in the centre. He looked ahead to avoid looking down. The pad descended. The walls slipped past at a faster and faster rate until they found themselves surrounded by dark towers, ominous black slabs of unknown material. Energy discharges sparked between the obelisks accompanied by rumbles of thunder.

"This place gives me a bad feeling," Zack said.

Mira understood. The darkness was oppressive, the air heavy and charged. The Pharn may have directed her here, but this was a place no human was ever intended to venture.

The pad came to rest in an open area between the towers. Ordered gaps led away in all directions.

"Welcome to Manhattan," Zack said without humour. "Where now?"

Mira looked around. She waited for the same intuition that had led her this far to guide her; it did not come.

"I don't know," she said. The chamber shook. The tremor passed as quickly as it had come.

"That's not good," Mira murmured.

A light was moving between the towers, coming toward them. It hovered in front of them, pulsing with energy. The air surrounding the orb crackled.

"Mira, I am your guide."

"Amy?"

"No."

"Who?"

"We are Pharn. We are not individual units we are one and we are all. We will guide you."

"Amy said you were too strong to talk to us."

"We are. We have adapted. This unit is a subset of the collective. Extended exposure is not advised."

"Can't you give me what I need?"

"Something given has no value." The orb moved toward one of the streets.

Zack wore a puzzled expression.

"I guess we follow that Pharn," Mira said.

The pace was brisk. The orb increased speed, forcing them to run. A second tremor shook the ground, knocking Mira off balance.

"The bomb?" Mira asked.

"No, that was seismic. This place is becoming unstable," Zack replied.

"They told me it was not for us, only the part they want us to have."

Zack spat on the ground. "Your friends are real assholes."

He had a point.

They ran on the past the corpses of two dead aliens, similar to the one they had seen in the corridor.

"Who... what are these creatures?" she asked.

"They are not relevant," the orb replied.

"Are they Blackened?"

"No."

She grew frustrated. "Come on, start telling me something. Stop acting like dicks."

"These units are drones. They were once occupied by the collective. They protected and maintained this facility. They ceased to operate when the threat had passed. Some persist. A unit such as this prepared your birth pod and fabricated the clothes you wear."

The shadow outside the pod.

Zack laughed behind her.

"We have encountered a species more advanced than humanity can imagine and you called them dicks. If it all goes wrong, at least I'll die with a smile on my face."

"You called them assholes first." Mira tried to mimic Zack's accent.

After several minutes they penetrated deep into the interior of the city-like structure. The air was alive with static electricity, the light a murky artificial twilight. Energy discharges occasionally lit the sides of the towers with brutal flashes of blue-white light. The air smelt of ozone. The coverall clung to Mira's body and her unruly hair stuck to her sweat-drenched face.

The orb stopped and rose into the air. It hovered in front of a tower, 100 metres above them.

Mira studied the surface of the obelisk. It was rough and formed from interwoven black cords. She was certain she could climb it.

"Let me set up a safety rope," Zack said.

"No time." The ground shook to underline her point.

She climbed. Progress was easier than she expected. The surface was rough and there were plenty of hand holds.

The tower was coarse under her hands. Her palms were soon sore and blistered yet she hastened her pace. The atmosphere in the city was deteriorating. Aside from the ozone, chlorine and ammonia burned her nose and throat. She approached the point at which the orb hovered. It moved back. The surface of the tower shimmered; it looked like a liquid hanging in the air. Mira pushed her hand inside and her fingers alighted on a square cube. It tingled in her grasp as she pulled it free.

She held it in her hand.

"Is that it?" she asked the orb. "All that effort for this? My Gran had better stuff in her trinkets cupboard." She tucked the cube into her coveralls. The corner dug into her side.

The orb pulsed. Mira sensed a familiarity. A bond between human and Pharn.

"It's you? The girl from the city? You're not a subset. You're an individual."

The orb pulsed and shimmered. The colours changed. Its intensity dulled. "I was the conduit through whom you saw. The memories were not mine, they were ours as a whole. We share a connection, Mira. I volunteered to be your guide in the knowledge I could not rejoin."

The voice different. It was singular rather than the chorus of voices that led her here.

"I wish I could have known you," Mira said. She was filled with sadness as she stared at this ball of light that had once been a living, breathing being.

"You did. As I know you. My name was Zenia; I left my body 12,921 human years ago. During our communication I experienced your feelings, your pain. I dreamt your dreams. I lived as you for one heartbeat. It was fulfilling to feel the physical world again. Thank you, Mira."

Mira remembered the sense of wonder when she joined with the Ark. The joy of floating free of her body lingered in her memory. She had not realised the process had been a two way experience, that her broken body had given another life the chance to experience the world she took for granted.

The orb pulsed. It morphed into a humanoid face. Mira gazed into the eyes of another sentient being. The similarities to a human face were remarkable. The jaw was angular, cheekbones pronounced. The eyes were circular and black; they blinked with iris like movement.

"Remember me," Zenia said as she faded to nothing.

Mira clung to the side of the tower. Now she understood

what Amy meant when she told her the Pharn knew her.

"Clear skies, Zenia."

The descent was harder than the climb. Mira struggled to find handholds and wished she had taken Zack up on his offer of a safety rope.

The tower shook. She lost her footing. She held on with one hand before she regained it. A further tremor hit and Mira slipped and fell. She was twelve metres from the ground. She landed hard and something popped in her knee. She screamed as she fell in a crumpled heap.

"This place is coming apart. Can you walk?" Zack screamed at her. Mira tried to stand but could not. Zack helped her to her feet and half dragged, half carried her through the narrow streets to the platform.

The towers were falling around them. The world became noise and flame.

Zack dumped her onto the transport and she lay staring into the darkness above. The platform rose at an impossible rate. Mira struggled to breathe as the platform sped upward. The sound of the machine destroying itself overwhelmed her senses. Mira closed her eyes. When she opened them, the platform had stopped. They were back in the chamber where it had started. Zack was already searching through the discarded equipment.

"You passed out," he said.

Mira sat up. The rumble of an explosion rose from the shaft. Her leg was sore but not as sore as it should have been. She flexed it before gingerly standing and testing her weight. Everything was fine.

She jumped off the platform.

She looked around. "Where am I?"

Zack gave her a puzzled look.

"Over there, by the pods, next to Jarman." He pointed to a

pair of bodies.

Mira nervously approached herself.

That is not me. It was such an odd thought. The body had her face, yet somehow belonged to a stranger.

Mira stripped and dressed in her combat gear. She flicked on the combat computer and it recognised her. It came as a relief. The device was keyed to the owner's DNA. She fumbled in a pocket and retrieved the picture of Amy Flynt. She placed the crumpled photograph on the body's chest.

"Goodbye, Amy," she whispered.

Mira used her combat knife to tear a strip of material from the discarded coverall and tied her hair back.

She keyed the com-link.

"Barnes?"

Nothing.

"Eden? Luke? Anybody?"

Static was all that came back.

"The depth and energy discharges are blocking my signal. We need to get out of here. We might need your ship."

Mira surmised Eden was probably heading the same way. She would try to talk her down.

Airflow through the three remaining tunnels increased and the roar of machinery grew louder.

The chamber shook as countless blue orbs flew out of the shaft. Mira was knocked off her feet and staggered to regain her balance.

Each orb coalesced into a ball of light high above them. It was flecked with darker bands encircling its surface. Energetic discharges illuminated the walls. Mira squinted as the giant orb's brightness continued to grow. Then without a sound it vanished, plunging the chamber into yellow half light.

"They've gone?" Zack whispered.

Mira nodded.

"Come on let's follow their lead," she said, heading for the nearest tunnel.

"No, wait," Zack said. "I have an idea."

He climbed over the pile of rubble blocking the tunnel they had descended through.

"We have time, explosives and someone who knows what to do with them," he said, pulling at some smaller rocks. "I can clear us a passage through here. It will take us to the drill head. We have a rover and a relay link there."

Mira weighed up the options. She was tired, hungry and the thought of the rover was more appealing than she cared to let Zack know.

"Okay let's do it. What do you need me to do?"

Zack stood on a rock. He spread his arms dramatically. "Stand as far back as possible and watch an artist at work."

Mira sat on one of the merc's discarded transit cases. Zack unpacked his equipment. He sized up the rubble and placed charges. Once he was satisfied, he produced a remote detonator from his pocket and sauntered back to Mira.

He handed her the detonator. She pressed the button. A dull thud produced an unspectacular cloud of dust. When it cleared there was a hole big enough for a human to crawl through.

Eden scrambled down a scree slope. She lost her footing and tumbled for twenty metres before coming to a sudden halt that knocked the breath from her. She drew lungfuls of gritty air. The wind was building as another dust storm blew in. The ground shook. It was the fifth tremor. Each one was stronger than the last. She scrambled upright and checked her position. The Lightfoot excavation was three kilometres south-west of her. Summoning her remaining strength, she ran toward it.

The dust storm intensified as she arrived at the dig site. She would need to get into shelter or the windblown grit would tear her to shreds. A Land Rover Universe was parked on a rocky bluff overlooking the site.

She ran to the vehicle and climbed in. The powerful hydro carbon V12 motor roared into life behind her and she cycled through the vehicle's navigation system and set it to backtrack the last course. The route was projected onto the windscreen as a green directional trace. Eden put the vehicle into drive and swung it around to follow the required heading.

Two figures ran from the tunnel. One was Zack McArdle, the other was short, in full battle armour. *It couldn't be? Could it?*

"Great," she muttered. Her foot hovered over the throttle pedal. She pressed down and accelerated away. She lifted off, bringing the vehicle to a stop. She sat for a few seconds, watching the figures approach.

"I'm sorry," she whispered.

Eden pressed the throttle to the floor and drove away. She did not look back.

Mira stumbled to a halt and rested her hands on her knees. Zack stopped next to her. Her arms and legs were heavy; her head pounded. She was hungrier than she had ever been. She watched as the Land Rover disappeared in a cloud of dust.

"What's she doing?" Zack yelled above the wind.

"She has business with the Knights."

Mira keyed her com-link. It failed to pickup a carrier signal. "We need to get into cover and somehow get a message to the ship."

If Eden was planning what Mira suspected she was, there was going to be one hell of a big bang.

"This way." Zack led her to a prefabricated hut. "This was Kramer's control centre," he said. "He has a hyperspatial relay terminal; it links to the main dish back at base. I should be able to tune it to the local band."

Mira rummaged around the shack. She had a more pressing need. She found a small crate, filled with ready to eat meals. She pulled out a silver sachet and tore it open, using the spoon attached to the package she ate the contents.

"Oh man, that is so good," she said. The tuna and rice had the flavour she was familiar with but it seemed so much more intense. She reminded herself that this body had never tasted food, and it had never had its senses dulled by age or misuse.

Zack glanced at her. "Weirdo," he said. He bowed his head and continued to work on the communications system.

Mira found bottles of water and drank a full litre. She gave Zack a bottle. He drank at a more subdued pace.

"How is it going?"

Zack did not turn around.

"Not good, it uses a multi-layer encryption. Lightfoot is a paranoid bastard. Give me time I'll crack it."

Time is something we haven't got, she thought.

Mira stared out onto the surface of Arethon. She could no longer make out the tunnel entrance. A bulky shape occasionally revealed itself through the murky air.

"What about the merc's rover?"

The vehicle looked intact, but she knew the damage a Viper mine could cause the underside of a truck.

"I can take a look at it if we need to," Zack replied.

Mira pulled her gaze from the window and rested against the wall. Zack was working with a small diagnostic probe and a screwdriver that was too big for the job.

There was a crackling sound; a spark leapt across the terminal's main board. The smell of burnt electronics hung in the air.

"Fuck my old boots." Zack threw the screwdriver at the terminal. It bounced off and landed in the corner of the shack. "The terminal is shot. The main circuit burned out when I tried to bypass the security system. Guess we are looking at that rover."

Zack hunted around the shack and located a pair of goggles and a mouth filter. Mira realised how much she had taken her armour for granted. Zack had covered the space between the tunnel and the control room with no environmental protection save his baseball cap and a hand over his mouth and nose.

They stepped out into the storm, making for the stranded Rhino ATV and their only hope of getting off the doomed planet.

Eden brought the Land Rover to a halt half a kilometre from the base camp. She could see the outline of the prefabricated buildings and the giant bulk of the Nightwolf through the murky air.

She reached for a pair of field glasses she found in one of the gear compartments. The storm was limiting visibility but, in the gloom, figures moved frantically around the starship.

"Have you boys got problems?" she muttered.

Eden picked up her M-871 Spectre assault rifle and the bag containing the Mass Sink. She climbed out of the vehicle. Her visor dropped into place and she trudged toward the camp.

In spite of the weather and the rough terrain, she made good progress. Once she crossed the perimeter of the base she hid behind one of the prefab structures. The mercs were working on their ship. Two clambered around on the top of the vessel while Manson stood below barking orders. She could not see Rybov or Saskia.

Between her and the *Nightwolf* an Aurora freighter rested on a temporary pad. The protective engine cowls had been removed and lay close by. Eden heard indistinct voices carried on the wind.

Saskia and Rybov exited the building she was hiding beside. She crouched and froze. Rybov came into view carrying a stack of transit cases.

"Once you have the contents of this unit loaded meet me in the operations office. I want to download the data core," Saskia said.

Rybov grunted.

Saskia strode toward the operations building. Once she was out of sight Eden followed Rybov up the ramp of the Aurora.

The old merc placed the crates in the ship's small hold. He smiled when he saw her.

"Eden!" he said. "I guess you were serious then."

She kept her weapon slung and made no reply.

"So what now? You going to kill me?"

"No... if I don't have to... what goes around comes around."

It was the unwritten law of the Frontier. If you owed someone, you paid them back.

"I have the weapon, Vic. I am going to use it against your buddies," she said. "You gave me a chance; I'm giving you the same one. You have a ship. Use it and get out of here."

"And if I don't?"

"Then you'll die with the rest of them."

Rybov sat on the edge of a crate. He seemed to age before her eyes.

"Manson is a liability. The other two, well Foxy is an idiot but KK isn't so bad. Hell, I don't owe any of them shit. You have a deal, Eden."

"I need you to do something," she said.

"I thought we were supposed to be square."

"We are, I'm not asking for me. There were two people back at the dig site. When you are airborne pick them up, get them back to their ship or to an outpost. Just save them."

Rybov nodded his agreement and rolled a cigarette. It had a pungent earthy smell. Eden had never seen anyone roll a smoke before; most people used Vapersoles or pre-rolled SynBacco as their personal stimulants.

"What about Snow White's mother?" he asked.

"Take her with you. I expect Lightfoot will pay a good price to get his hands on her."

Rybov blew smoke in a long stream into the air.

"Bring her over. I'll fire up the ship."

Eden walked down the ramp. She used the cover of the buildings to reach the operations centre. Saskia was inside, hunched over a console, copying data to a portable core.

"You took your time, Rybov. This is the last segment. Take the others back…"

Eden hit her over the head with the butt of her rifle. She put the mobile core into her bag and dragged Saskia's limp body to the Aurora.

Rybov met her at the foot of the ramp.

"I'll take it from here," he said.

Eden gave him the data core.

"This might have value."

He took it.

Eden moved toward the *Nightwolf*.

"Eden!" he called after her.

She stopped and turned.

"Good luck."

"You too, Vic."

Nightwolf's vertical lifters coughed into life. Eden ran toward the vessel as the cargo ramp retracted.

KK stood in the bay, trying to raise Rybov on the com-link. Eden ran into him, knocking him off his feet. She landed on him and held her gun to his throat.

"Tell Manson he's on board!"

KK complied. Eden clubbed him with her weapon and ran into the depths of the ship.

She crept through the dark corridors, heading ever forward toward the flight deck. She paused at the crew room, checking it was empty. She removed the Mass Sink from her pack and connected a hand trigger. Steps led toward the flight deck and raised voices reached her ears. She crept to the door. Manson was berating the pilot while Foxhound worked on a console.

"Looks like the Ice Queen has just left, thank fuck," Foxhound said. That was the last piece of information she needed.

Manson was about to reply when Eden stepped into the doorway. He froze, his mouth fell open.

"I told you I would kill you. It's your time Karl."

Manson's eyes flicked from her face to the Mass Sink.

"What the fuck? How did you get that?"

His face flushed red, veins pulsed in his neck.

"We disabled the fail safe and the countdown."

"So what? You thought you'd bring it here and show me? Does Eden want to show big bad Karl how clever she is?" He laughed. "It can't be triggered manually. Foxy kill her; I can't be bothered."

Foxhound moved to draw his weapon.

Eden swung round and shot Foxhound in the stomach.

"Sorry," she said. "I was aiming for your dick. Guess it's too small a target."

Foxhound writhed on the deck screaming in pain.

Eden dropped the Mass Sink. It made a hollow clang as it

landed on the steel floor. In her hand she held a terminal.

"I made some mods Karl. This is a remote trigger. It has a dead man's switch. I squeeze a little harder and you die. I loosen my grip and you die. Either way you and this piece of shit." She kicked Foxhound. "Are taking a one way elevator to hell."

Manson stood and glared at her. He keyed his link.

"KK, Vic get up here."

"KK is out cold on your cargo deck and dear old Vic just blasted out of here on the Aurora. I owed him and I always pay my debts."

Her smile widened as Manson's body went taut and shook with rage.

"So what are you waiting for?" he screamed.

"To see the look on your face when you realise you've lost." Eden took a breath and closed her eyes.

The fabric of the universe flexed as a flash of light lit the horizon. Mira was thrown to the ground as a tide of gravitational waves passed over and through her. They were followed by the deafening roar of a huge explosion. She blacked out.

When she came round the sky was boiling as high-altitude winds whipped the clouds into localised vortices.

She dragged herself to her feet. The Rhino lay on its roof. She looked for Zack. He staggered upright. His face was bloody from a cut above his eye. Somehow his cap remained jammed to his head. He stumbled toward her.

"The bomb!" he said. "She must have triggered the bomb! She's crazy!"

The excavation site was dark. Thickening cloud had brought an early twilight.

The Mass Sink would be forming a singularity, not as big as

the one it was capable of but it was only a matter of time before it grew large enough to consume the ground beneath them. Mira was out of options.

Once again she keyed her link.

"*Nemesis*, this is Thorn. Do you read me?"

The device whined; she unhooked it and threw it into the darkness.

She sat on a rock.

So much for saving the galaxy. So much for surviving the Berlin. So much for escaping the attack on Tarantella. So much for being reborn.

A pair of powerful spotlights ripped through the darkness accompanied by the throb of starship engines. The Lightfoot Aurora hovered above them.

"Eden!" she screamed above the noise.

The ship descended and touched down. As soon as the ramp lowered she and Zack ran aboard. They headed straight for the flight deck.

She stopped when she was confronted by the old merc.

"What the fuck?" she said.

The PlastiSkin of Rybov's face rippled. "It's okay. Eden sent me. I'll take you to your ship."

"What happened back there?"

"Eden did what she had to do," Rybov said, turning his attention to the controls.

"And what's your story?"

Rybov grunted. "I guess, sometimes, we get second chances."

Mira would not argue with that.

CHAPTER TWENTY-SEVEN

ALEX trimmed the ship and commenced preparation for the jump to light speed. He rubbed his temples and rested his head on the back of the pilot's seat. The Navy would have considered the mission a success. The Ark had completed its function, and the Lightfoot team had been extracted with minimal casualties.

None of it mattered. He had lost a friend, perhaps his only friend.

Alex had spent the past ten years his life in pursuit of one goal: the command of a starship. During those years he had pushed away friends and even family. If he were being honest with himself, he would have trampled on anyone if it furthered his career.

Floating in space with Mira Thorn, he had understood that rank was nothing without integrity. As their oxygen dwindled, he realised the person who had been there for him at the end was the same person whose life he had made hell for two years.

The universe had not been kind to Thorn yet somehow she kept fighting. He thought of the defiant single eyed stare. She had a fire burning within her he did not, a dogged determination to succeed. For Mira success was not measured in rank bars and medals, it was just surviving another day. He unsure when he noticed it, but she took her pain and used it to drive

393

her forward. Back on the ship she had used it get through each duty rotation; on the Kobo it had been to rescue her crew mates and bring them to safety. Now she had saved whatever dwelt within the Ark and given her life in exchange. It was not fair; it was not just, but it was honourable.

An alarm pinged.

"I'm detecting an energy discharge on the surface!" Luke said, breaking through Alex's morose thoughts.

The ship shook. Every panel, every screw seemed to come alive. Alex gripped the sides of his seat.

"The bomb!" he yelled.

"Yes... but the detonation is on the surface; that's why we are feeling the effects of the singularity."

The vibration stopped then restarted. The pattern continued for half a minute.

"Gravity waves!" Alex said. The first wave had passed without incident and although the subsequent ones were less intense, he still worried about the effects extended exposure could have on the hull.

"Readings are off the scale. The weather is going crazy. The explosion is centred on the Lightfoot base camp."

"I'm getting us out of here," Alex said. He put a hand on the master throttle and increased power.

"We need to ride it out, Alex. We can't sustain an envelope with gravitational distortions of this magnitude."

They sat reading the instruments and monitoring the ship's systems while gravitational distortions passed through the hull. After fifteen minutes they subsided.

The short range scanner beeped an alert.

"I'm detecting a vessel in low orbit. It's coming up toward us. IFF squawk is Corporate: Lightfoot!" Luke said.

Alex hit the comm-system, broadcasting on all frequencies.

"Unidentified vessel, please state your identification and intentions."

There was a moment of silence.

"My name is Rybov. I have two of your crew on board, a man and a woman. I also have Saskia Hart secured in my hold. Please send me rendezvous coordinates and we can all think about moving on with our lives."

"Rybov?" Luke replied. "Why should we trust you?"

"I've decided on a career change; Eden suggested it. Now are you going to send me coordinates or am I going to be stuck with this pair?"

"Transmitting a vector now. We'll open our bay. Follow the beacon and fly straight in."

"I'm going aft. I'll talk to the Lightfoot guys and give them the news," Alex said.

He gazed at he curve of Arethon as it filled the lower half of the viewport. The system's yellow star emerged from beyond the horizon, dazzling Alex and casting a warm light on the boiling clouds below.

There was a primal beauty to the scene, Alex stared into the sunrise and said goodbye to his friend.

The hangar atmosphere stabilised., and Alex opened the blast door with a stab of the release button.

The grey Aurora dwarfed the Naja and filled every available centimetre the hangar offered. Rybov had piloted the ship to a position perfect landing.

Alex was joined by Chloe Song, Monica Garret and Tish. Monica held Tish's hand; she was unable to stand still, when she did her fingers drummed against her thighs. Alex wondered if this was the best thing for her. She had to accept the loss. It might be brutal but it might help her move on.

The Aurora's hatch slid up and into the hull. The ramp lowered and Zack McArdle walked toward them. His face was black with grime and dried blood. His overalls were torn in places.

"You made it then," Alex said. Zack shook Alex's hand. Chloe hugged the engineer.

"Defused the weapon too, for all the good it did," Zack said. "I'm glad they paid me up front for this job."

A second figure appeared at the top of the ramp.

Mira Thorn smiled and met his gaze with a pair of vivid green eyes.

Tish sprinted past him, nearly knocking him off his feet. She continued up the ramp and embraced Mira. They stood for several minutes. Mira held Tish and whispered to her. Alex coughed. Monica nudged him.

Tish led Mira down the ramp. Monica embraced her.

"Mira I don't think I have been so pleased to see you since you found me on the *Berlin*." Monica could not contain the emotion.

Alex held himself in check, just.

"I told you she was alive. I told you!" Tish said.

"You look like shit, Thorny," he said. "But I can't help but wonder…"

"Later Alex, just later," Mira said. "I need to get this shit off me. It's been a tough day." Her voice was hoarse.

"You need to get to Medbay is what you need to do, Commander Thorn," Monica said, her composure falling back in place, her voice still heavy with emotion.

"Can I come?" Tish asked.

"Of course."

Tish let go of Mira. She jumped up and down on the spot and gave Alex a hug which he returned, awkwardly.

Rybov walked down the ramp.

He approached Alex.

The old man snorted and looked around the bay.

"I need to take a piss," he said.

Mira sat on the bunk in the side room; Kramer was still occupying the main area and Monica had suggested her story was not for his ears, at least not yet.

She told Monica everything. Tish sat next to her wide eyed. Monica took blood samples and ran tests.

"Monica, I don't know what I am," she said. "I kind of look the same, I feel the same but they could have done anything to this body."

Monica swivelled a monitor toward her. "On the left is your current DNA, on the right is you old DNA," she said. "They are an exact match. Your body is mature but unusual as you have no wear and tear. From a genetic standpoint you are the same Mira Thorn who saved me from the wreck of the *Berlin*."

Monica tapped the monitor.

"You know your DNA is interesting," she said. "A mixture of Scandinavian and Asian markers amongst others. There are some copyrighted nodes; I suspect someone went in for some alterations in the past and the code has been passed on."

"I have an ancestor on my mother's side who had work done in the 21st century. It's where my eye colour comes from. At least that's what I'm told."

Mira cast her gaze around the room, still enjoying the novelty of her reacquired binocular vision. She fought the urge to play peek-a-boo.

"You will need to unlearn the adaptive techniques you've grown used to using," Monica said. "You also had a slight astigmatism in your right eye, that's gone. You now have perfect 20/20 vision. It's incredible."

She unhooked the electrodes from Mira's body.

"Here." Tish handed her the battered leather jacket she had scrounged from the Kobo.

"I fixed the hole in the arm. I hope you don't mind. I had nothing to do while you were down there," Tish said.

Mira pulled it over her shoulders. It felt like an old friend.

"You need to rest, Mira," Monica said. "Alex and Luke can fly the ship."

Mira agreed, every part of her new body screamed with fatigue.

"Can she go now, Doctor Monica?" Tish asked.

"Yes but no funny business. You both need to sleep."

Tish blushed and changed the subject.

"You have not seen the stateroom?" she asked.

Mira shook her head.

"Come on, I'll show you," Tish said, taking her hand.

They walked through the ship. Mira wondered what would happen to Rybov and Hart. She pushed it from her mind. Right now she didn't care about anything other than a solid twelve hours of oblivion.

Tish led her to the upper deck and opened the door to the stateroom with a key card. The room was lit with low key lighting. The cabin contained a small kitchen and study, beyond which was a soft seating area, numerous lockers and a bed. A door was open to one side and Mira could see a bathroom with a proper shower.

A holo-screen occupied a whole wall. It cycled through images of nebulae, planets and star systems. A noise cancellation system dulled the throb of the stardrive to distant hum.

"Come on. The decor is Xander's taste, not that he ever uses the stateroom," Tish said, leading her in.

Mira paused in the hatchway. She thought of the empty blackness before her awakening. It could not have been more than a few seconds, but she had never felt as cold and alone as she did in seconds before her birth. She shivered.

"I don't want to be on my own, Tish."

Tish's blue eyes fixed Mira with the same stare as they had when they first met on Tarantella.

"I'll stay," she whispered. Her eyes broke away. A shy, insecure look crossed her face. "I have a gift for you," she said.

Tish unzipped Mira's flight suit. A tingle of anticipation ran through Mira's body as the cool air touched her skin. Her face flushed as the first feelings of arousal made her nerve endings dance.

"Tish..." she whispered. Goosebumps rose as Tish's fingers brushed against her skin.

Tish hushed her and produced a black velvet bag from her pocket. She opened it and emptied a silver sword pendant into her palm. Tish placed it around Mira's neck and clipped it closed.

"I know you are a naval officer, Mira Thorn," she whispered. "But now you are one of us."

She leant forward and kissed Mira. Mira kissed back with an urgency unfelt in a lifetime and an intensity she had never experienced. She gasped and stared into Tish's deep blue eyes.

Mira let her jacket and flight suit fall to the deck and climbed under the covers. Tish undressed and slipped in beside her.

Tish's warm, soft skin pressed against her own as the girl's arms and legs encircled her. "Sleep now Mira. We have all the time in the universe."

Mira rolled over to face her, brushing a wayward strand of

red hair from the girl's face.
    Tish was right.

CHAPTER TWENTY-EIGHT

DAVID Conway snapped awake, sensing movement in his bedroom. He ordered the lights on, tossed the silk sheet to one side and sat up.

A figure stood in the doorway, dressed in a dark suit that emphasised his sickly complexion. The man's skin appeared semi-translucent in the artificial light of the apartment, a mesh of blue veins visible where it stretched over his cheekbones. He rested his weight on a black wooden cane with a polished silver cap.

"Mr Legion," Conway said, brushing away the last vestiges of sleep.

"I'm sorry to disturb you at this late hour, David, but I felt it wise to share my counsel," Legion said. His accent carried an unusual inflection as if standard English were not his first language.

"I know you would not disturb me, were it not important."

"Indeed, not. I will allow you time to dress before we turn to business." Legion left the bedroom.

Conway found a pair of lounge pants and a cotton shirt. He checked the time; it was 3:15am. Events had moved quickly since his trip to Mars. The previous evening his only opponent in the race for the Vice Presidency had dropped out of the contest and tomorrow he would be sworn into office. Legion's timing was unfortunate, but when you had powerful backers sacrifices were necessary.

The old man stood in front of a picture window filled with the curve of the Earth. He held a glass in one hand, a bottle in the other.

"You don't mind me helping myself?" he asked.

Conway gave a dismissive wave. Legion continued.

"Your homeworld looks so small and fragile. We have weapons that could boil it away in the merest fragment of time."

"So do we. It's a miracle we have not done so already. Humanity needs a firm hand."

"Your hand, David?"

Conway did not answer. Legion liked to play games and Conway did not like to be played.

"The reason I ask is that there are those who are doubting your abilities. Not me, I assure you, but I feel it is only fair to bring matters to your attention. We are good friends are after all."

"We are. I appreciate your candour."

"Your mission to Arethon has failed. The First Ones are free. Their numbers are small but they change the dynamics of our enterprise."

Conway had not heard from Manson, now he knew why.

"The mission parameters changed. We did not expect the crew of a Navy cruiser to become involved, nor Xander Rhodes for that matter. Perhaps if you had allowed me to use primary assets rather than mercenaries, the outcome would have been different."

"As you used your primary assets against Rhodes on Tarantella?" Legion asked, his tone mocking.

"The operation was a success we ousted Rhodes, and he is now..."

"On Mizarma with Damien Lightfoot and Senator Meyer. We can only guess what they are discussing. Whatever it may be, I am certain it will not be in our interests."

Conway gritted his teeth. "Perhaps if you would avail me of some of your resources, I might achieve more. I am fighting secret battles on every front. I have a Senate hearing tomorrow to endorse my position as Vice President..."

"Quiet! Rhodes has had direct contact with one of our operations on your Outer Frontier. I suspect he has gathered enough data to realise he is not dealing with an internal threat." Legion turned his back on Conway and continued to gaze at the blue globe orbiting beneath them.

Conway stared at Legion's reflection in the thick plate of sapphire glass.

"And how is that my fault?"

Legion's expression softened.

"True, it is a chance happening. We are operating in a situation that is evolving and changing. Chaotic systems create opportunity and misfortune. We understand this. It excites us. When a system is in flux individuals can affect the outcomes of the best plans. Rhodes is one such individual. We are playing this game at too high a level. We need to get our hands dirty. A decision has been made to recruit our own free operator. Someone unconstrained by public office or rule of law. Someone who can advance both our goals."

Conway poured a large scotch, offering to refill Legion's glass. The offer was declined.

"Who do you have in mind?" Conway asked. He swilled the whisky in his mouth, enjoying the subtle flavours and bracing for the burn that would come when he swallowed.

"David, it is best you do not know, at least not yet. I have yet to speak to the individual concerned. I will in due course."

"So what now?"

"It is not my place to give you instructions, but if I were you and I learned that Rhodes, Lightfoot and Meyer were all on Mizarma I would think it prudent to strike quickly and strike hard."

"What about rules of engagement? May I use Frontier assets?"

"A counter insurgency strike, a fitting first action for the new Vice President, don't you think?"

Conway had to agree.

"One more thing David. Your trip to Mars, did all go to plan?"

"Everything is in place."

Legion returned his attention to the window. "Such a pretty blue world," he said to himself.

Conway drained his glass and placed it back on the oak credenza. When he turned, Legion was gone.

Xander settled back in the copilot chair of the shuttle. He put his hands behind his head. Asha Malik prepped the craft for the descent into the atmosphere.

A fast moving spot of light tracking across the star field drew his attention.

"There goes the Gibson Family," he said. "They're heading to a spaceport on the outskirts of Delain to finish repairs."

"Do you think they'll be okay?" Asha asked.

"Yeah, I think so. I gave them some gold."

"Xander, you can't help everyone. We have repairs of our own to make."

He put his feet on the console. "They're a nice family, besides fleet was paying. It was some of the stash from Mira's Kobo."

"Family means a lot to you, doesn't it?"

"Yeah, Tish, Luke, Martinez, even you..."

The shuttle lurched and Asha laughed as Xander was forced to grab the edges of his seat.

"Sorry, I slipped on the helm," she said as she started the entry sequence.

A three orbit descent brought the ship into a fast approach over Mizarma's western ocean. White capped waves danced and swirled beneath them as the yellow main sequence star painted the blue water with flickering highlights.

The shuttle flew low over Channing's Bay. Asha slowed the approach speed and punched in a course for Lightfoot's headquarters.

"It's quite a view Xander," she said. "Sometimes I regret living on stations and ships the whole time."

He prised his eyes from his datapad. The city skyline was impressive. The Lightfoot tower was a distinctive blue-green structure standing twice as high as the surrounding down town buildings. Early evening sunlight glinted off its many angles, making the building look like an exotic gem instead of a phallic expression of corporate might. In spite of himself Xander found himself agreeing.

Say what you like about MegaCorps, they could produce some pretty planets.

Lightfoot Developments was the exception when it came to the giant interstellar conglomerates. Federal law granted Mega-Corps a fifty year window to develop infrastructure on newly established worlds. In exchange the companies were permitted to claim 90% of the gross planetary output. It was supposed provide a fast track route to developed colonies, however the corporations often turned over incomplete words with facilities incapable of supporting their populations.

"One day, we'll setup somewhere like this," he said. "Assuming we can"

"Xander, snap out of it. You know you need to be on top of your game if you're going to get anywhere with Lightfoot."

Xander snorted. She was right, Asha was always right. He needed more people like her in his inner circle. She was smart, straight talking and there were the other benefits. He laughed.

"What's so funny?"

"Just thinking I need a few more people like you around."

"Martinez is working out pretty well."

"Yeah but you have better legs." He continued to laugh as she focused her attention back to flying the approach.

"What about Thorn?"

"I've not seen her legs..."

Asha flashed him a look that stopped him cold.

"She would fit in... I think she has issues she has to deal with first. You know about Jono's daughter?"

"Yes. So sad."

"Jon told me she was recovering well after the crash. Then Amy... let's say Mira has been left fragile. I don't think our chaotic way of doing things would hold any attraction for her."

"And Tish?" Asha asked.

"What about her?"

"Martinez told me there's a certain chemistry there."

Xander couldn't say he'd noticed. Tish had a thing for the lost and the broken. He had assumed her interest in Mira was just her caring nature.

"We'll see," he replied.

The tower approached. Asha swung the shuttle in onto one of the rooftop pads, alongside a DipCorps Mercury Transport.

A pair of security guards approached and stood at foot of the ramp.

"Let's go do business!" Xander stood and walked aft; once Asha joined him he activated the hatch control and strode out of the ship.

"Hi fellas," he said, raising his hands. "We come in peace. We have come to see your boss. Tell me, does he prefer red or white?"

The guards looked impassively at him.

"You know, wine? I've not brought any, but it's the thought that counts."

The security detachment kept their weapons slung. One man beckoned them to the bottom of the ramp. He first motioned for Xander face away from him and carried out a personal weapons search. They conducted a similar check on Asha.

"Cheeky," she said to the guard as he moved his hand beneath her waist. The man's professionalism broke. He flushed red and hurriedly completed the search.

"This way," the guard said, directing them to a service entrance.

They walked through a featureless access corridor and into an elevator. The guard inserted a key card into the control panel and the elevator descended. It halted and the door opened onto a richly decorated corridor. Xander stepped onto a polished stone floor.

"Want me to take my boots off?" he asked the guard, who made no reply and ushered him along toward a door at the far end go the hallway.

They entered the waiting area of Lightfoot's office. A prim woman in her fifties stood and greeted them.

"Mr Rhodes, Damien is waiting. Please go through."

Xander thanked her.

"Will you be okay out here?" he asked Asha.

She nodded.

"Would you be kind enough to look after my friend?" Xander asked.

"Of course, Mr Rhodes." The woman smiled at Asha. "Make yourself comfortable, my dear. I can order some food if you are hungry."

Asha thanked her, but declined.

"Believe nothing she says about me. She lies all the time," Xander said, walking toward Lightfoot's office. He heard the woman introduce herself as Jane as the door slid closed.

Damien Lightfoot sat behind a giant white desk hewn from synthetic marble. Behind him a wall of glass overlooked the city, now ablaze with lights. The bay shimmered in the distance.

Vanessa Meyer was standing by the picture window gazing toward the deep, dark ocean beyond the bay.

"Mr Rhodes," Lightfoot said standing.

"Xander," he replied.

"Damien."

Rhodes nodded and shook Lightfoot's hand. Despite the man's frailty his grip was firm. He glanced toward Meyer.

"Senator Meyer," he said. "It's been a while, thank you for the information you sent me."

Meyer smiled. It was a politician's smile, yet it carried an unexpected warmth.

"Xander, you are welcome, you are looking well," she replied.

"As are you. It has been too long."

Lightfoot gave a gentle cough.

"So Xander, it would appear we have been pursuing interests in similar areas," Lightfoot said, motioning for him to sit.

"My interest in your artefact was to support my Verani contacts. I am beating my path off the back of helping them. That's what brought me here."

Xander told the story of how Mira had arrived on his station with the Ark and the events that followed.

"They're out there now? Have you heard from your people?" Lightfoot asked.

"No, they have a good ship and lots of weapons. If Senator Meyer's information concerning the Blue Knights is correct, they will be able handle it."

"Thank you, we were warned the expedition may be compromised but had no idea to what extent. I am grateful for your support."

"So... you know my involvement, what is your interest in the Vale? There are countless easier places to prospect."

"Look at me, Xander, I'm wasting away. My doctors give me three maybe four years. I have no heirs and no one to continue this after me." A dismayed frown flickered on his face. "When I'm gone Regina or Quantum will swoop in and buy up my assets and all I have worked for will be no more."

"My quest for technology has nothing to do with any great aims. I am looking for a way to cure this damn disease or at least extend my life a little longer. A lot of the things I've learned along the way have made an enormous amount of money, but LDC-132 offered the best opportunity yet." Lightfoot paused, gathering his thoughts.

"We have harvested data from other worlds that suggests the inhabitants of the Vale were Bio-Engineers with capabilities far in advance of our own. It's the type of technology that can save me... and millions of others."

Meyer stepped forward. She had been watching the two men talk. Xander had almost forgotten she was there.

"Before you arrived, I had an interesting discussion with Damien. Between the three of us we have considerable resources and unexpected common ground."

She sat opposite him.

"Things are changing in the Federation. In the next few hours I expect David Conway to be announced as Vice President, a position from which he will promote his own interests, the interests of the Frontier Company and whoever is backing them."

It was news to Xander. He knew little of Conway, but the little he knew he did not like.

"Conway has made no secret of his desire to give the corporations complete control over the Frontier. FRONCO is big enough to allow him to do it. I can't fight them; they have too many ships and resources," he said.

"If you think Tarantella had a refugee problem, that's a fraction of what to expect once Conway authorises the clearing of non corporation worlds," Lightfoot added. "Vanessa tells me you intend to ask me for a world to house them?"

"I was using Tarantella as a staging post to get displaced people back to the Core Systems. I had a grand idea of an underground railroad running from Tarantella to Earth. I could do with a planet to act as a semi permanent settlement."

"You have one. The southern continent of Mizarma is undeveloped. I have asked President Anderson if we may open it for colonisation. She has agreed."

"I guess you want something in return?"

It was Meyer who answered. "Damien has maintained good relations with all the worlds he has built, which numbers..."

"Seventy two independent, thirty three still in development," Lightfoot replied.

Xander had to admit it was an impressive tally for an independent corporation.

"Thank you," Meyer said. "He has a small fleet of ex-naval vessels providing security for his cargo ships and systems. He will extend that protection to all those wishing to join us."

"Join you?"

Lightfoot replied with a smile that warmed his grey complexion. "We are proposing an alliance comprising independent worlds, my portfolio and commonwealth. It will be an alliance based on trust and cooperation. It will also offer its citizens the protection of a military force independent of corporate control."

"You're mad. The Federation will never let it stand, even if they did EarthGov will override them. Look at what happened on Mars," Xander said. "You'll bring down the might of the Frontier Company on Mizarma and everyone who joins."

"Which is where you come in," Meyer replied.

"I don't see how."

"Your connections with the Verani," Lightfoot said. "We know you have access to their technology and you have contacts within their political caste."

"Whoah," Xander held up his hands. "One simply does not make demands on the Verani, especially when they are going through some kind of political upheaval. Guys we need sanity in the room. Vanessa you might think Earth politics are complicated but you're all rank amateurs compared to the Verani."

"If we secure their support, we can make the Alliance of Free Worlds work," Meyer replied. "Our Navy will be supported by their military superiority. FRONCO may not be constrained by Federal law, but they would not be bold enough to take on the Dominion."

Xander sat back in his chair and thought it over.

Alliance of Free Worlds? They've even come up with a name. I'm like the last guy to arrive at the party who has all the best booze.

"Okay, I'll do it. I can't promise they'll agree to anything, they probably won't. I'll try."

"Thank you Xander, we appreciate it," Meyer said.

He studied her with a cool gaze.

"I guess they'll make you President."

Lightfoot and Meyer exchanged a look.

"Actually Xander, we rather thought you would be a good choice for the job," Meyer said. There was no hint of humour in her voice.

"That would piss a few people off," he said with a wry smile.

The silence that followed was charged and awkward.

Xander glanced first at Meyer, then Lightfoot.

"You are not joking are you?" Xander shook his head. "Seriously you could find no one who is a worse fit for the job."

"Exactly! Xander you are an outsider and you understand people. That makes you better than either of us," Lightfoot replied. A fire burned in his eyes.

Xander was not convinced, but he let it pass. Once he had delivered Verani support, he could head off back to nowhere and leave Meyer and Lightfoot to their power games.

"When my ship returns from the Vale, we'll get it prepped for a trip to Verani space."

He pulled a data core out of his pocket.

"One more thing. When we were en route, we came across a colony that had been completely destroyed."

"I've been hearing rumours," Meyer said.

"Viola Prime, the planet was stripped clean. We were attacked by vessels of a type I have never seen. I have data that needs to be analysed by proper scientists."

He gave the data core to Lightfoot.

Xander stood and stretched his taut muscles. "I'll head back to the *Angel*. I'll make preparations and get some sleep."

"Nonsense," Lightfoot said. He buzzed Jane and asked her to prepare a guest suite.

"We have accommodation on the 165th floor. We'll talk more tomorrow."

Xander stood and shook Lightfoot's hand.

"This is a little odd," he said.

"I won't argue with you on that, Xander."

Xander looked to Meyer.

"Will you be staying on? There is someone I would like you to meet," he asked.

"No, I am leaving first thing in the morning. I want to get back to the Core Systems. I have to keep Conway honest."

He stepped forward kissed her on the cheek. "Take care, Mom."

She smiled. "We'll catch up soon Xander. I promise. I have a grandson and granddaughter I am keen to meet," she said, pulling him close.

Xander took delight in the stunned look on Lightfoot's face. He figured his mother could explain it. She made her living explaining difficult things. He was just a pirate.

He left Lightfoot's office and emerged into the waiting room. Asha was curled into a ball, asleep on a couch.

"Come on girlie, wake up."

She stirred and stretched. "Xander?" Her voice was sleepy, her eyes heavy. Xander realised how stressful the last few days must have been on his crew. He brandished a key card.

"Lightfoot has offered us his guest quarters. We should sleep and by sleep I mean sleep. The kind you get when you close your eyes and when you open them it's later. That kind of sleep."

Asha stood and leant against him. She regarded him with tired brown eyes. He smiled and took her hand.

Strong sunlight streamed into the room, dazzling Xander as he shook himself awake. Asha stood by the picture window, wrapped in a sheet looking out on the down town streets. Xander stood and stretched.

"It's late," he said.

"I let you sleep. You needed it. You internalise your stress too much; it will mess you up in the long run."

He stood and walked to the window. Resting his hands on her hips, he nuzzled her neck, pushing her hair to one side.

Xander slipped a hand under the sheet and onto her breast. The other slid down between her legs. She groaned and leant back against him as he moved his fingers in an insistent circle.

She tensed and pushed his hand away. She wriggled to face him.

"Not now, you dirty old pirate," she said. "Your new best friend wants us to join him for lunch. Besides you stink."

Xander made a show of sniffing his armpits. She was kind of right.

"I've been worse and I'm not a pirate. I'm going up in the world," he said, turning and looking for the bathroom. Asha pointed to the door on the left.

He walked in and slipped off his underwear. The shower was motion sensitive. He waved his hand to start the flow. He set the temperature to hot and let the water wash over him. As he massaged his face under his beard, a thought occurred to him.

"We should get married," he shouted to Asha.

"You're such a romantic," she called back.

He laughed.

"You could be First Lady."

Her silhouette appeared in the doorway. Despite the distortion of the shower door and the steam, a shiver ran through his body.

"They suggested I be president of their little alliance." He paused. "Now how about you join me before I have to pass a law or something."

Asha opened the door. She let the sheet fall to the floor and stepped in with him. Xander slipped his arms around her waist and onto her butt as she kissed him.

With the shower complete he combed his hair and dressed.

"I was serious," Xander said. "None of us know what's around the corner. Why the hell not?"

"There are a million reasons why the hell not, Xander," she said, slipping a simple black dress over her head and smoothing it to her curves.

"Such as?"

"Xander! We are not getting married, okay?"

"Okay," he conceded. "I'm not done with this though. We'll discuss again soon. Once I've worked my moves and laid down my charms, you will be powerless to resist."

"Whatever, come on. I've booked a ride."

Asha suggested taking the stairs. Xander agreed. She said the exercise would do them good as they had been ship and station bound for too long. Halfway to the ground he stopped to gather his breath. Asha was right. He vowed to hit the *Angel's* gym more often.

Arriving at street level, a yellow air car was waiting for them. "Where are we going?" Xander asked as the car rose from the ground.

"To a restaurant on the bay. It was Damien's suggestion."

"Damien's suggestion," he mocked.

"You are such a child. Don't be nasty; he seems like a nice man."

"Nice man? Yeah, *Nice Men* run Mega Corporations." He couldn't believe Asha could be so naïve.

"Xander, stop being an arse and look out the window," she said. "This world is 35 years old. Lightfoot could have continued to exploit it for another fifteen, he didn't. Lightfoot Developments is no Regina or Quantum."

Lightfoot was a venture investor yet he appeared to have a conscience that was lacking in other corporations.

The air car flew over the bay. It descended and skimmed over the waves as it approached a wide strip of white sand, bordered by the turquoise water of Channing's Bay and a line of native Mizarman palm trees.

The trees formed a natural barrier to the tropical forest beyond. Asha mentioned it was a conservation area for indigenous species. He wondered how she had so much local knowledge. He suspected she had been awake before him and learnt what she could about their host from the local UniNet node. It was a typical Asha thing to do.

Structures made from natural materials jutted out of the tree line. People sat talking, eating and drinking at tables along the beach.

The car touched down on the shore and a staff member directed them to a secluded table on a raised wooden deck. Damien Lightfoot sat watching the comings and goings of the day. He wore a linen suit. A straw fedora protected him from the sunlight. Jane sat next to him, sipping a glass of water. She wore a creme business suit.

Xander and Asha approached the table. Lightfoot stood and greeted him with a handshake, Asha with a kiss on the cheek. Jane excused herself.

"No please stay," Xander said. "I'm sure your boss isn't *that* much of a slave driver."

"He is not, Mr Rhodes, but I have things to do."

"Nonsense Jane, sit," Lightfoot said.

Xander was impressed at how much authority his voice carried, it was fairing better than his body. Jane sat.

"How long have you worked with Damien?" Asha asked Jane.

"Forty years, next month," she replied.

"Do you think you'll still be working for me in forty years?" Xander asked Asha.

"You'll be working for me by then." They laughed.

"Senator Meyer has left?" Xander asked.

"This morning. As expected Conway is the new VP. She sends her best wishes."

Xander had hoped she would stay on longer. He wanted to introduce her to Asha, Luke and Tish. It was so typical of their relationship. He had to fight for her attention with the several billion people she represented.

The laughter and small talk continued over lunch. Lightfoot took a sip of white wine and dabbed his mouth with a silk napkin.

"So Xander," Lightfoot said. "My people have compiled a preliminary report on the data you provided. We will provide you with a full copy in due course."

"What have you found out? What were those things? Why couldn't we target them?"

"The ships you encountered are very similar to a derelict vessel we recovered from LDC-97. Your Verani friends will know it as *Zemitha*."

Xander was familiar with the world, a barren mining colony on the Inner Frontier. It was a hellish place, lashed with high velocity winds and near constant dust storms. The colonists lived hard lives below the surface and grew rich off the plentiful titanium deposits.

"Our pathfinders discovered it during our initial survey. We have it in a secure facility." Lightfoot did not allude to where.

"To describe it as a ship is incorrect," Lightfoot said. "It does not have crew space nor does it require a pilot."

"Some kind of drone?" Xander speculated.

"Not in the sense we would understand; it's an autonomous life form."

"What? An animal? It can't be natural. It has hyperspatial capabilities."

"It appears to be an advanced clone; enhanced with bio-electrical interfaces. Its hyperdrive is just that, an electro-mechanical device. Humans have been interfacing with electronic implants since the 21st century. This technology is not new."

"How can something like that survive in a vacuum?" Asha asked.

"It has a hull constructed from a calcium carbonate material, not unlike the substructure of a coral or an oyster shell. It's hard and non magnetic. That's one reason you cannot lock onto it."

"One?" Xander replied. He was grateful that Lightfoot was being so generous with the information.

"The other is their shields. They use a phasing mechanism to oscillate them in a random pattern. It renders them invisible to anything trying to track them."

Xander understood. The Verani stealth system on the *Nemesis* used phase shifting technology. The similarity with Verani tech was more than a little disturbing.

After a brief pause Asha spoke up.

"If we knew the frequency they operate on we could calibrate our sensors and weapons to adapt, track and inflict real damage."

Xander followed Asha's thought.

"If we match an energy weapon to their shield oscillation, it will cut straight through, as if the shields were down!" He slapped a hand on the table. "That's fucking awesome!"

Asha glared at him, her stare laden with disapproval.

"Sorry." He smirked. "Guess you can take the boy out of Tarantella and all that."

Lightfoot waved his hand. "I agree with your initial assessment, Xander. It is useful."

"Asha, we need to get that information to the *Angel* and the *Nemesis* as soon as we can."

She agreed to transmit Lightfoot's data once they returned to the office.

"I have a question, Damien; Xander should have asked it but he is dumb," she said. "Who or what are they?"

"Precursors, those who came first, maybe those who were left. We have few clues. Even from the ten worlds we have documented. LDC-132 offered us a real chance. I hoped our people could salvage something or at least prevent it falling into the wrong hands."

Xander wondered who the wrong hands were. He guessed the mercs were working for a rival corporation.

"This attack on Viola, it seemed random. That system is remote and unremarkable. It's the same with all the systems they have attacked. What are they doing?" Asha asked.

"I have an idea," Xander said. "They're spreading panic."

Lightfoot agreed.

"That would be my assessment. Look at the tension refugees

caused on Tarantella. It gave the Trade Guild their excuse to oust you," Lightfoot said. "Large movements of people create instability and mistrust. There are plenty of human factions who will use mass migration to push their agendas forward."

Xander only had a rough idea of the number of people who had passed through Tarantella. It was over a million. The more worlds these strange alien craft attacked, the more people would retreat to the Core Systems.

"Why is the Federation ignoring what is going on?" Asha asked.

"Because it suits them, Ash," Xander said. "A few thousand lives on the Frontier have little value. GNN would rather report on a holo-celeb's arse than on anything that matters. If they did the MegaCorps would all be brought to their knees, EarthGov with them."

"I agree with you Xander, despite my own vested interest," Lightfoot said. "Are you a student of history?"

"More than you would think."

"In the mid-20th century, the world ignored a man called Hitler for the best part of 20 years; it was easier to ignore him than to deal with him. That man killed 11 million people and attempted the genocide of an entire race."

A gloomy silence fell over the table.

"We won't ignore what is happening out there, Damien. We can't," Xander said with determination.

Mira woke. She propped herself up on her elbows and watched Tish as she dressed.

Tish caught her gaze and clambered onto the bed. She straddled her.

"I'm glad you're awake." She kissed her.

"Thank you for staying..."

Tish giggled and kissed her ear, gently nipping the lobe as she nuzzled her neck.

Mira shivered and rested her forehead against Tish's. "Tish, does this mean we're a... thing?"

"Do you want to be a thing?" Tish asked.

Mira responded with a nod and a blush.

"Then we're a thing." Tish jumped up and pulled her boots on. "I'm late! I have to relieve Mr Alex. He's just pulled a 12-hour shift on top of all the shuttle work and the doctor wants you in medbay, *right now.*" Tish did her best to mimic Monica's stern voice. She did a good job.

Mira clambered out of bed and walked to the bathroom. She had not woken this fresh in years.

"Are you any good at cutting hair?" she called back. "I have to do something about this." She stared into the mirror. Her hair was a tangled mass of black locks.

You can call me Crazy Meg, her reflection said.

"There's a style bot in my cabin. I'll bring it up later."

Mira heard the door shut. She hit the shower and let the hot water flow over her. She took an hour with the razor and felt human again. Her fleet programming guilt tripped her about the water use. *It's not everyday you come back from the dead,* she told herself.

The air car lifted off the beach and headed toward the city. The atmosphere onboard was subdued.

Xander glanced at Asha. She was staring ahead, enjoying her own company. The sunlight shone through her hair, turning it coppery brown.

His com-link beeped. "Rhodes," he said, lazily.

"Xander! Martinez. We have trouble heading our way."

Rhodes straightened in his seat. "Details, Martinez!"

"A Frontier battle group has entered the system. A carrier and two heavy cruisers; the same vessels that attacked Tarantella. Mizarma's Planetary defence forces have engaged but they are ineffectual."

"Martinez pull the *Angel* out of orbit. I have options for getting off world if I need to. Don't risk the ship. We know how capable that battle group is. What about the *Nemesis?* Any news on their arrival?"

"We received a burst message dated yesterday. They were successful. ETA is about eight hours."

Xander closed the link. "Damien!" he yelled. Lightfoot broke off his conversation with Jane.

"The Frontier Company is launching an attack. We need to get off world."

"I can't... Frontier? What?"

"Don't argue..." He was cut off by an explosion. The air car was buffeted by the over-pressure. Six fighters swept out of the sky and headed for the down town area.

"They're going after you... us!" Xander yelled at Lightfoot. "Do you have an alternate spaceport?"

"Yes, south-west of here, a corporate freight facility. We keep two transports fuelled and ready to go." A second explosion drowned his words. The air car's automatic systems lost control and sent it careening to the ground. The vehicle skidded across a concrete plaza, coming to rest against the wall of a building.

Xander's ears rang. He shook his head to clear his vision. The air car lay on its side. Shattered glass littered the ground. Asha stirred beside him.

"Xander?" she murmured.

"Are you okay?" he asked, shaking glass out of his hair. His hand came away bloody from a cut in his scalp. Another explosion rocked the city.

At least they're not nukes...

Asha shifted in her seat. "Yeah, my head hurts, otherwise okay."

A groan from the front of the car caused Xander to twist in his seat. Lightfoot clambered into view. His face was paler than usual. His eyes widened at the sight of Jane. Her head was twisted at an unnatural angle. He felt for a pulse with a shaking hand. Xander knew the old man would not find one.

"Damien, we have to go," he said.

Lightfoot's face was ashen. Blood oozed from a small cut on his forehead. He dabbed at it with a silk handkerchief.

"But Jane... we can't leave her."

"We can't help her," Asha said. Her tone urgent yet not bereft of sympathy.

Lightfoot composed himself. "Follow me," he said, climbing out of the air car.

Xander twisted and kicked the window out.

He helped Asha out of the wreck and scanned the city. Palls of black smoke rose from numerous locations. The whole skyline was swathed in dust and the Lightfoot tower was no longer visible.

"Come on Damien. We need to get under cover," Xander yelled as a squadron of planetary defence fighters screamed overhead.

The air car had crashed in an industrial area on the edge of the city. Xander spotted an underpass where the road flowed under a row of glass fronted buildings. He grabbed Asha's arm and dragged her towards it, checking to ensure that Lightfoot was following.

"Is your com-link working?" he asked Lightfoot.

The older man checked and shook his head. Xander tried his own; static popped and crackled. He dialled in the ship to surface channel.

"*Scarlet Angel!* This is Rhodes, do you read?" The link fizzed. It cleared and Martinez broke through.

"Martinez, we are on the ground; our options are limited. What's going on up there?" The link crackled.

"Multiple inbounds..." Static. "We estimate over 50 fighters..." Static. "Not sure but..." Static. "Bigger ships, around 30 in the second wave. They could be drop ships. It's not just Delain, they are hitting command-and-control centres all..." The link went dead.

They reached the underpass and ducked under cover. More explosions echoed around the city. The ground shook with each blast. "Comms are down, every frequency is jammed," Xander said after checking his link.

He rested his hands on his knees and breathed. He straightened.

"Martinez told me Mira was successful on LDC-132. They are inbound. They will render assistance. We have to get to off the planet and back to the *Angel*."

Asha was breathless, her eyes wide. She sat on the sidewalk and rubbed her temples.

"Xander," she said. "This attack, the timing is wrong. Frontier could not have responded to any communication between the *Angel* and the *Nemesis* this fast."

Asha was right. The battle group had arrived too quickly.

"They must be working off other intelligence. They are targeting us, or Meyer."

"Or all of us," Lightfoot added.

"Martinez said he identified assault ships. They're sending in ground troops. Damien this is not good. How robust are your defences?"

"We have a standard planetary defence compliment. It complies with the Mumbai Accords."

"Not much then," Xander replied. He put a hand on Lightfoot's shoulder. "Damien I need you to get a grip on things. Can we get to the spaceport on foot?"

Lightfoot nodded. "Yes. Our facility is used for confidential movements. It doesn't appear on any official maps."

"So unless they have orbital scans, it's unlikely that they would hit it in the first wave," Xander replied.

In the distance he could hear the sound of sirens and screams. He noticed Asha had lost her shoes. He focused his thoughts.

"Damien, how fast can you move?"

"Fast enough," he replied.

They cut through the underpass and into a busy street. A horde of people ran toward them, looking for cover. An old woman fell and the wave of people swept over her. A young man lifted her back to her feet and helped her to the side of the road.

The crowd thinned after a kilometre. The bombing subsided.

A fighter flew low overhead. The scream of its ion drive echoed between the towers. It banked hard to the right, then left. Two more vessels screamed past. These were different, defence force ships. They launched missiles at the Frontier ship. The missiles arced after the fleeing fighter craft, like white tailed dogs chasing down a rabbit. The fighter jinked left and right, deploying chaff and flares. The first missile hit the ship with a flash of orange. The second finished the job and the FRONCO fighter exploded. Micro debris fell like grim confetti to the streets below. People cheered around him. It was a small victory, insignificant in itself, but hope was hope and small victories could turn the tide of battle.

"Over there," Lightfoot pointed to a large elevated road. "That's the M22. We should be able to find an on ramp..." He was cut off by an explosion close by. A large section of road collapsed.

"I guess we follow the road from below!" Xander said.

The highway they were following veered sharply to the left. They passed bodies, both complete and incomplete. Asha knelt next to the body of a child, a girl no more than ten. She took off her jacket and covered the tiny form. As she stood, she wiped her eyes.

"Asha..." he said.

She pushed him away and walked in silence a few metres ahead of them. A news network holo-cam drone zoomed low over his head. He instinctively ducked.

"Give her space," Lightfoot said. "The attack has slowed."

The explosions were less frequent and fewer ships were crossing above them.

"It's a pause, Damien. They will assess if they have hit their assigned targets. Once that's done they'll send in a second wave of fighters or their assault force."

Lightfoot dabbed his eyes, his shoulders slumped. He appeared broken.

"Why are they doing this? What reason can they have?" he murmured.

"I'm here. My mother was here, and you have been poking around out in the Vale. All are good reasons. Take all three of us out of the mix in one easy strike. They'll spin it as anti-insurgency."

Lightfoot made no reply. He continued to walk. After several minutes Xander stopped him.

"What we spoke of last night."

Lightfoot stopped and regarded him with tired eyes.

"The Alliance? Just a pipe dream now."

"It doesn't have to be. I'll do what you want. I'll bring the Verani to the table, even if I have to drag them there. As for the other matter, I'll be your acting President, subject to you running an open election within a year of me assuming the position."

Lightfoot agreed.

"And if someone better than me runs and wins, you will respect the outcome?"

"Of course."

Xander stared at him. A fire flared in the older man's eyes. There was still fight in the old dog.

"Xander!" Asha called. She was at the crest of a hill. She used her hand to shield her eyes from the sunlight.

"You had better get up there," Lightfoot said. "You don't want to keep the First Lady waiting." He managed a half smile.

Xander clapped him on the shoulder and jogged up the hill.

Several hundred metres ahead of where Asha stood, figures dressed in blue body armour manned a hastily constructed aid station.

"First time I've ever been pleased to see the police!" Xander said. There was no humour in his voice, only relief.

Xander ran toward the checkpoint, raising his hands as the four officers pointed their weapons at him.

"It's okay guys," he said. "I have Damien Lightfoot here. I need to get him off world."

The officers kept their weapons trained on Xander as Asha helped Lightfoot find his way across the rubble strewn roadway.

"Mr Lightfoot," the lead officer said. He lowered his weapon. "Sergeant Jacob Morelli, Sir. My people are at your service."

"We need to get out of the city, Sergeant," Lightfoot said.

"The road to the South is no longer passable. They have knocked out the bridges. You won't make it on foot," the officer replied.

"What about air support? Can you fly him out of the city?" Xander asked.

The officer spoke into a handheld S-UHF radio. Several seconds passed.

"I have a transport inbound," the officer replied. "Where are you heading?"

"The service port, south of the city," Lightfoot replied.

"We were using it as a casualty receiving centre. We lost contact with our people ten minutes ago."

"Fuck it," Xander cursed. A thought occurred to him.

"What about Bryce Field? It's a small cargo dock and repair facility. I have a friend with a ship there."

The officer consulted a colleague.

"Last we heard it had not been hit. It's a long way out of the city though. It's little more than a field with some hangars so these boys probably won't consider it a target, at least not in the initial attack."

He made another call.

"Sir, I can confirm Bryce Field is a viable destination," Morelli said. "Is your friend likely to be there? Traffic movements have been chaotic."

"No idea but in the absence of other options, it's a risk we'll take."

Sergeant Morelli agreed. "You'll struggle to find better odds today,"

"Thank you," Lightfoot said.

"Xander..." Asha murmured from behind him. "I don't

feel..." he voice trailed off and became incoherent.

Xander spun. Asha's face was ashen. She swayed on her feet. He moved towards her and she collapsed, landing hard on the sidewalk.

Xander knelt, feeling for a pulse with trembling hands.

"Asha!" he said. He rolled her toward him. The police officer was at his side.

"Medic!" Morelli yelled.

A police medic barged Xander out of the way as she rushed to Asha. She checked Asha's pupils.

"What happened?" she asked.

"We were in a crash. She said she had a headache. She seemed fine."

"Lucid? Making sense?"

Xander nodded.

"Could be a concussion. Even if I could get her to one of our hospitals I suspect they are overwhelmed. If you can get her to a starship, then do it. I can give her some meds to help."

"I have a doctor on my ship," he said.

"Okay," the medic replied. "The transport is about a minute out. Make sure you keep her airway open. If you don't get her specialist help, she could be in a lot of trouble. I'm sorry I don't have the skills or equipment to help."

Xander rolled Asha onto her side. Her dress rode up. He pulled it down to preserve her dignity.

"Don't leave me, Ash," he whispered. Three distant explosions shook the ground.

"Frontier will answer for this," Lightfoot said.

Rhodes stood and followed his gaze. A thick cloud of smoke and dust hung over the commercial district, a dirty smudge on a sapphire sky. Fires burned in several towers. A building collapsed; the sound reached them a few seconds later.

"I can't believe EarthGov or the Federal authorities will let this stand," Xander said. *Whatever they do, it will be too late and Frontier will have achieved their objective.*

Xander's thoughts were drowned by the roar of engines. A strong down-draft whipped his hair as a civil defence transport set down in the street behind them. Sergeant Morelli motioned them in and spoke to the pilot.

Lightfoot scurried up the ramp. Xander lifted Asha's limp body and carried her to the craft. It lifted off and headed south.

Xander watched out of the window as the smashed city passed beneath them. They flew over blazing neighbourhoods, a deserted sports ground and onward to the Freeman River. All the bridges had been destroyed with heavy ordinance.

The city thinned out. Industrial zones gave way to suburbs; suburbs gave way to fields. Soon the only signs of human habitation came from rural roads linking isolated farms and the occasional village.

The aircraft banked hard and descended. It touched down on a concrete apron. The ramp lowered. Several ships were preparing for departure, one of which was Pete Gibson's cargo vessel.

"You fucking beauties!" Xander yelled. He lifted Asha and followed Lightfoot down the ramp.

He turned to the load-master.

"Thank you and good luck. We'll do what we can to help when we reach orbit."

The crewman nodded and slapped his shoulder. "Look after Mr Lightfoot, Sir. I hope your friend comes through this," he said. "Good luck."

With that the ramp lifted, and the aircraft took off. The transport circled the field. It was turning onto a course back to the city when it exploded in a ball of orange flame. Debris fell into a cornfield beyond the tiny spaceport's perimeter fence. A lone FRONCO fighter screamed over Xander's head. It turned to commence a second attack run, flying in low and lining up with he main runway.

Xander tried to swallow but could not. He stood rooted to the spot watching as a column of black smoke rose skyward.

"Come on Xander," Lightfoot yelled. He snapped his eyes away and ran toward the Gibson family's hauler.

"Pete!" Xander yelled. The big man stopped at the foot of his ramp and waited for them to approach.

"Have you got room for three small ones?"

"Get aboard. You were lucky. Sandy and Mark are prepping for launch. Is she okay?" Pete Gibson pointed at Asha.

"No, she needs help. I need you to get me to the *Angel*."

"I don't know if we have the power or speed to outrun a warship. This is just a..."

"Pete, I know a smugglers vessel when I see one. I've flown enough in my time."

Pete Gibson grinned. "Okay, sorry force of habit. You know how it is," he said.

Xander did. A golden rule amongst smugglers was to assume that no one is who they say they are.

"Strap in. We're out of here in 30 seconds."

Xander and Lightfoot found a bunk and secured Asha before strapping themselves into the passenger compression seats. The little girl, Cathi, came and sat between them. She strapped herself in with the expertise of a seasoned traveller.

Xander's weight increased as the engines roared and the cargo ship blasted clear of the spaceport.

Mira walked with Monica through the now familiar ship. The doctor had drawn blood and topped up Mira's immunity with a series of jabs. Unlike a regular thirty-year-old human, her new body had no natural or acquired immunity. Monica warned her she would be vulnerable to a wide range of common illnesses until her immune system caught up.

"I want to see Vic before he leaves. He could have left us behind but he didn't," Mira said. "I owe him."

Monica stopped.

"Can I ask you something before we get to the hangar? It's a little personal..." Monica said.

"Sure."

"What was it like... dying? Sorry, it's wrong of me to ask. You've been through something the medical profession has never understood."

"There is not much to tell." Mira gathered her thoughts. "When I crashed on Mars, I remember the wing digging in and the ship flipping over. I heard the seat tear free and then nothing. I came round when they transferred me to the medical barge. I couldn't see and all I knew was the pain. I wanted to sleep, to make it all go away. I knew if I gave in and closed my eyes I would never wake up. So I focused on the pain to stay awake."

She blinked. Her voice broke. "One medic whispered in my ear. She said *'it's okay, we have you now'*. Then I knew I could let go and someone would catch me. The next thing I remember was waking up the medical facility on Luna.

"What I went through on Arethon was different. I slipped into nothing. I had no control over it, no clue what was happening. I saw Amy before I went, but I think it was the machine's doing."

"And afterwards?" Monica asked in a whisper.

"Nothing, not until the machine woke me up on the Vlei."

Monica gave Mira's shoulder a squeeze. "I guess the remaining religious groups would be disappointed. This ability the Pharn have to capture consciousness and sustain it is astonishing. That kind of technology could be worth billions to a Mega-Corp."

"I guess that's why they destroyed the machine. They know we would misuse it," Mira said.

When they arrived in the hangar Spence was unclipping the final umbilical lines and stowing them in recesses in the deck. There was a slight jolt as the *Nemesis* dropped out of FTL.

Rybov stood at the foot of the Aurora's ramp, his blue armour now painted matte black.

"You're all set, Vic?" Mira asked.

"Not sure where I'm going, but I have cash stashed away and a few favours to call in. I might go bounty hunting or pick up some private security work. I'm done with the Knights. They're stuck in the past. I'm a forward looking kind of guy."

Mira offered her hand; Rybov took it and shook it.

"Thank you for coming of us."

Rybov responded with a smile that had genuine warmth.

"I did it for Eden. She didn't deserve what life dealt her. The kid was just trying to make a living."

"I'm grateful whatever the reason. If we ever run into each other in some Frontier bar, we'll have a drink to her."

"Count on it, Space Cadet," he said, walking up the ramp. He paused at the top and gave Mira a respectful nod as the hatch closed.

"Clear the deck!" Spence shouted.

They left and the blast door slammed closed.

Mira watched Spence walk toward the engineering section, his equipment swinging from the loops on his overalls.

"Monica, I'm not going back. It's been on my mind since we met up with Xander, now I'm sure."

"Rich told me and that makes two of us," she said. "Before the *Berlin* left Proxima, I received notice I was being discharged from service."

"What? That's ridiculous!"

"Thirty-odd years before the mast. A lot of us don't get that far before someone at Fleet Ops decides we are economically unviable." She laughed. "I planned to take up a teaching position on Luna but I want to see what the Outer Frontier offers. You saw those poor souls on Tarantella? Perhaps my skills can do some good out here."

"I'll miss you," Mira said. Monica took her hand and squeezed it.

"What about you? Do you have any firm plans?" Monica asked.

"I want to go home for a while. I have a bunch of savings, pension rights and my place in Windhoek. I was thinking about cashing it in and buying a ship; maybe see if Tish will freelance with me."

"Are you serious about her?"

"Maybe... yes, it is early days. It isn't complicated... not like with..." She was interrupted by her com-link beeping.

"Mira, I'm getting a burst transmission from the *Angel*. You need to hear it," Alex said.

"Patch it through to my link."

After a pause Martinez's voice crackled through.

"*Nemesis*, the Mizarma system is under attack from FRONCO ships. X is stranded on the planet looking for extraction. We have pulled the *Angel* back. We need you here now! Martinez out."

"Monica, come with me. You need to know what's going on."

They ran for the flight deck.

Alex and Luke were flying the ship. Tish was sitting at the

astrogation station.

"You guys know what's happening?"

They nodded.

"How far out are we?" Mira asked.

"Just under four hours if we show her some whip," Luke replied.

"We need to fight the ship," Mira said. "We can do this. We have the tools and the talent," she added. "Luke, I want you on the main battery with Barnes. Alex, you and I will fly the ship. Tish, I want you to handle the sensor suite and target management."

"We'll be outnumbered," Alex observed.

Mira agreed. "But we have surprise and a fast, stealthy ship."

Alex thumped the bulkhead.

"What the hell are they playing at? Where's the Navy?"

"Keep calm, Alex. They are questions for later. Let's concentrate on getting Rhodes out of there and seeing off the Honourable Company.

"We'll need Ethan and Spence to handle damage control. Alex, I need you to brief them. Talk to Zack too. He's competent and seems willing. We'll need all the hands we can get."

Alex leapt out of the copilot's seat and headed aft.

"Could I request that Chloe Song assists in medbay?" Monica asked. "She isn't medically trained, but she has a science background and knows how to follow instructions."

"Agreed," Mira said. "This could be messy, so I want everyone suited up."

Luke and Mira changed places. She slipped into the pilot's chair and strapped herself in.

She gripped the yoke and steadied her breathing.

"We can do this... I can do this," she murmured.

For the first time in a long time Mira Thorn did not doubt her words.

CHAPTER TWENTY-NINE

DUST motes danced in the sunlight as it streamed through the grimy window. The mid-morning light dazzled Karl Manson as he blinked himself awake. Manson shielded his eyes and pushed his muscular form off the bed in one smooth motion. His right arm was organic, the cybernetic augmentation replaced by flesh and blood. He glanced at his chest. His scars and skin inks were gone.

Manson was home: the farm where he grew up. He had not been here in 30 years. The last time he slept in this room was the night before he left for basic training at Fort Burns. He stared out of the window. Beyond the trees lay the endless cornfields of the American Midwest.

At the foot of the bed he found a familiar denim shirt and well-worn work trousers. He dressed. After lacing his boots he went downstairs to the kitchen. Each step echoed off the bare boards.

A man sat at the worn table. He was old yet spry. He wore a black suit, its style long outmoded. His white hair was swept back from a liver-spotted forehead. Beside him was a cane with an ornate silver cap.

"Mr Manson, so good of you to join me. I trust you slept well?"

"What is happening? How did I get here?"

The last thing he could remember was the smile on Eden's face. He was a dead man.

So what in the name of fuck was this?

"My name is Legion. You and I stand on the verge of a very productive partnership."

"Is this heaven or hell?" He laughed at the idea. Although absurd, he believed the latter was more likely. Even so it looked like home.

Karl Manson had left this farm the day the bank had foreclosed on the mortgage. Falling wheat prices had left his father thinking, no *believing,* he was being robbed. On the day the bailiffs were due to seize the property Karl Manson Senior had shot Nicole Manson with an ancient 12-gauge shotgun before turning the weapon on himself. All this transpired before dawn while their teenage son slept off a hangover in his room. The bailiffs had left empty handed that day, only to return a week later. They seized the farm and family assets, leaving the young Karl to bury his parents and an uncertain future in the local military.

"It has been several days since you died. We retrieved you from the pattern matrix before it broke down. We have..." Legion paused in thought. "Had you on ice, so to speak. There was debate if we could make use of your skills. Men like you are, how do you say it? Dime a dozen? Ten-a-penny? There were those amongst us who considered your friend Eden to be a more balanced choice." Legion gestured for Manson to sit. "Unlike you she has a moral compass which we felt was inappropriate for the role we have in mind."

Manson pulled back a chair. The wood was smooth and worn beneath his hands. He poured a mug of coffee.

Legion's appearance was inhuman yet somehow relatable.

The old man's voice carried a peculiar accent. It combined different inflections and dialectic traits; it was almost an amalgamation of multiple voices.

"My name is Legion, for we are many," Manson whispered.

"Very biblical, Karl, and not far from the truth. We are not here to discuss me. We need to decide if you have a future."

Manson rubbed his hand over his head. "Thanks to Eden I think a future is something I don't have. Mind you, I have to hand it to her. I never saw it coming."

"Indeed," Legion said. "Karl, my associates are powerful people. We have been working with Vice President Conway for some considerable time and through him have been working with you."

"Vice President? He works fast."

"Conway is a useful asset. For all the advantages his position offers it also constrains his actions. Conway is all about the long game. You however are more of a blunt instrument."

"When you want to bang in a nail, you need a hammer. I am a hammer, Mr Legion."

"Quite, you are just that, Karl. A hammer of the gods so to speak. Before I go on, what is it you want?"

The question caught Manson off guard. Legion did not seem a man who would be concerned with what Karl Manson desired.

"What do you mean?"

"It's a simple enough question. What is it you want? What is your desire? What makes you do what you do?"

"Money I guess... no power; wealth is useless if you can't do anything with it." He paused. His eyes were drawn to the wall above Legion's head. He remembered it splattered with blood and cerebral matter, his father's body slumped in the chair in which Legion now sat.

"Revenge," he murmured. "I want to tear the whole fucking system apart. I want to watch it burn. I want to be the last man standing while the whole galaxy goes to shit."

Legion gave a satisfied chuckle. "We can give it to you Karl, all of it."

"What do you want from me in return?"

"We have work for you, well funded work. Mostly you'll be a free agent. Every so often we will call on your skills. When we do, you drop what you are doing and do as we say. Even if you have your hands on the sweetest piece of arse in the Core Systems. When we come calling you are ours."

Manson extended his hand. Legion smiled and shook it, his grip firm.

The old man stood. "Thank you, Karl. I look forward to working with you." He walked to the door.

"Wait." Manson said.

Legion stopped mid stride. Anger flared in his eyes. Manson stared back, unabashed.

"Who are you?" he asked.

Legion's cool gaze lingered on him for a moment. Manson shivered.

"Karl, there are things in this universe that are not for you to understand. If it will help you, we are *Those who Came First,* and we have returned to reclaim what is ours. You are a going to be part of that."

It meant nothing to Manson.

"So what next?" he asked, a slight tremor in his voice.

Legion cast his gaze around the kitchen. "Stay for a day. Enjoy your old life. When you wake tomorrow, you will be in a new body. You will have none of your augmentations, nor will it be able to tolerate any. You will look as do now. Do not make the mistake of thinking you are human. You will be better in every way."

"Where will I be? I mean we both know this is not a real place."

"Oh this place is real, make no mistake about that. Where you awake next will be wherever I choose, Mr Manson. Wherever the wrong man in the right place can make the most difference."

With that he opened the door and stepped out into the bright Nebraska sunlight.

Three steps creaked on the porch and then silence. Manson followed Legion onto the bleached decking. He blinked and shielded his eyes from the sun. Manson was alone aside from the birdsong and the gentle rustle of corn.

CHAPTER THIRTY

THE tension on the flight deck rose as Alex collapsed the envelope. Mira gripped the control yoke and waited.

She and Alex had spent the last hour working thorough the ship's more intricate systems. It kept her mind occupied, but now all she could concentrate on was the battle to come.

The plan followed standard Navy doctrine. They would target the command ship first. It was commonly referred to as cutting the head off the snake. It was an inaccurate description. A battle group was more like the Hydra of myth; if you cut one head off another would take its place. The key to success was to capitalise on the confusion that would reign in the intervening time. If this was the same group who attacked Double T, Mira knew they would be up against a carrier and she hoped the *Nemesis* had the armament to immobilise such a large vessel.

The envelope folded and the energetic clouds dissipated. Mira engaged the stealth system. The only sign it was operating was a small green light on her console. A hand-written label below it read *Invisible!* Tish had told her that the enemy vessels would detect their exit but would fail to detect the ship. It would all change the moment they opened fire.

Let's hope no one looks out of a window before then, she thought.

"Tish, what's out there."

"I have a carrier and two cruiser sized ships. It's the same group that hit Double T!" Her voice was thick with nerves and excitement. "There are sixteen fighters on combat patrol and many more inbound to Mizarma. I am tracking and classifying threats."

"The *Angel*?" Mira asked.

"She's outbound from the star. The lead cruiser is moving to engage. There is a smaller ship out there. I think the *Angel* is attempting to rendezvous with it."

"What about non combatants?"

"Numerous contacts, the closest is half a million kilometres away."

Mira cycled through the data Tish was uploading to her personal display. She stared at it for a minute before turning to Alex.

"The carrier will be their command-and-control ship; do you think we can take her out?"

Alex rubbed his chin

"It'll be a minimum of four nukes and that will leave us under-armed to take on the cruisers. We could knock out her drive system and maybe target comms. She'll still be operational."

Mira considered and agreed with Alex's assessment. Taking out the carrier would slow down the planetary attack, which would give the defence force respite to regroup.

She called up Luke.

"What else have we got up our sleeves, Mr Rhodes? We have six Shipwrecks. Alex thinks it is not enough. Tish is sending you the scan data."

There was a pause.

"We have a pair of Verani Torpedoes. They'll do the job, but they are messy. The yield is all over the place and the blast radius is bigger than a nuke."

"How much bigger?"

"Two thousand clicks."

"You're kidding me! That's five times the requirement of a Shipwreck." Mira wondered what the hell the torpedoes contained.

It also tells me all I need to know about their yield, she thought.

"There is something else, Mira," Luke said. "We have never fired one before; like most of this ship they have been adapted to work with human tech, but we have not tested them. The ship has not been without her teething problems. Xander suggested we avoid using them."

Mira ran through the possibilities: a minimum of four nukes or one Verani torpedo, it was a simple decision.

"Luke, load up the Verani torpedoes, both of them."

She advanced the throttles, and the ship accelerated. Dropping into position astern of the carrier, they closed the distance.

"Tish, line up a spread of energy weapons and as soon as we punch a hole in their shields we'll hit them with Luke's bad boys."

Ever the Navy officer another thought occurred to her.

"Alex, no one has been up close to a FRONCO carrier before. Can you archive the sensor data?"

"Already recording, Thorny."

The carrier grew ever larger in the viewport. A tiny speck of light creeping across the star field grew into grey mass of titanium and steel. As they approached to within ten kilometres, the gargantuan vessel filled the viewport. The glow from her sixteen ion engines bathed the flight deck in cool blue light. Mira held her breath. She could barely imagine they had the capability to disable, let alone destroy a ship of such size. Mira tightened her grip on the yoke as they committed to the attack.

"We are in an optimal position. I have loaded a firing pattern." Tish reported.

Mira keyed the intercom.

"Let's wake them up, Mr Rhodes."

The carrier's shields flashed and sparked under the bombardment from their main battery. The carrier began a slow turn to engage. Mira tried to imagine the scene in the Ops Room as the *Nemesis* appeared from nowhere.

"That got their attention!" Alex said.

"Both cruisers are turning to engage us. They are a long way out and not currently a threat," Tish reported.

Mira smiled. A window had opened for Rhodes to rendezvous with the *Angel*. Things were going better than she hoped.

The *Nemesis* shook under a barrage of incoming fire. Mira's eyes danced over her data display and HUD.

"It's just suppression fire, Mira," Tish said. "It's bouncing off our shields. We're maybe two or three percent down."

Ahead of her the carrier's shields were flickering under the relentless barrage. The vessel manoeuvred at an astonishing rate for a ship of such size. The Nemesis remained tight in behind her stern, blasting her shields.

"This ship is amazing, Tish! It flies like a fighter!" Mira whooped as the adrenaline coursed through her and the yoke danced in her hands.

"His aft shields are down!" Tish reported.

"Luke, fire!"

The *Nemesis* shuddered as the weapons fired. Twin points of light streaked toward the Frontier vessel. She banked the *Nemesis* to starboard and walled the throttles, holding her breath until she saw the vessel pass the edge of the projected blast radius.

She studied the displays, waiting for confirmation of a hit. Once the torpedoes were running the situation was out of their hands. If the carrier could rebuild its shields or the weapons were intercepted, she would have lost the advantage of surprise and be short on ordinance.

A ball of energy bloomed at the edge of her vision. She blinked the after image away.

Mira called up scan information to her console. The carrier had lost steerage, and explosions continued to rip through her stern section. The giant vessel remained intact.

She paged Luke.

"Luke load up a nuke. Tish work up a solution. I want to kill that ship." Her voice was flat, devoid of all emotion.

"Mira!" Alex said. "The carrier is out of the game. What about the crew?"

Part of her wanted to agree, but her resolve remained solid. She would give no quarter.

"Alex, all the time that ship can operate, in whatever capacity, it is a threat. Even if it can only act as a command centre or a staging post for fighters, it can hurt us. That's how we train and we fight how we train. I will take full responsibility."

He nodded his agreement.

Mira aligned the ship onto an attack heading. The carrier was firing back. Blasts of laser energy ricocheted off their shields. Fires blazed in the giant ship's hull. Doubts crossed her mind as she remembered the *Berlin*.

She counted down the kilometres.

"Luke, fire at will."

A single shipwreck torpedo arced toward the Frontier vessel, hitting amidships. The blast tore deep into the carrier's hull with a silent, catastrophic explosion.

"Carrier is down!" Luke screamed over the com-link, his voice sounded as relieved as it did triumphant.

"We have an incoming message, Mira," Alex said. "It's Martinez."

Mira flicked the channel open.

"*Nemesis* is that you?"

"Affirmative *Angel*. I know you had everything in hand, but we figured why should we let you guys have all the fun?"

"You have taken the heat off us for now. I speak for all of us here when I say thanks very much. Be aware you have hostiles inbound."

"Read you, Martinez, we will handle them. Once you've made your pickup we will need your help," she replied. The *Nemesis* shook under a massive blast from an energy weapon.

"Where did that come from?" Mira asked, scanning her screens. The lead cruiser had used the gravity of Mizarma's largest moon to accelerate toward them and into weapons range. Mira was impressed. It was a clever and ballsy manoeuvre.

"Shields are down to twenty percent. He hit us with his main battery," Tish reported.

Another hit like that and they would take hull damage.

Mira changed course and increased the distance between the Nemesis and the cruiser. Tish informed her that there were 30 fighters inbound.

Mira opened a channel to the *Scarlet Angel*.

"Martinez can you engage those fighters?"

"Already on it, *Nemesis*."

"Target the cruiser," Mira said, turning the *Nemesis* to face the incoming vessel. She increased the ship's velocity and closed the distance. The cruiser opened fire with its forward array. The *Nemesis'* shields took a battering, but held.

"Fire!" Mira said.

Luke acknowledged and the main battery fired red bolts of energy at the enemy vessel.

"His shields are holding," Alex reported. They had been lucky with the carrier, his shields were directed forward, leaving the after section under-protected. The *Nemesis* shook under another barrage. The lights went out. Sparks rained down from the overhead panels. The artificial gravity went off and Mira floated in her restraints, only for her weight to return several seconds later.

"Taking hull damage," Ethan reported.

"We're breached, lower deck!" Zack McArdle came over the comm system. "I have it under control. We'll be sealed in a few minutes."

"Casualties, Zack?" Alex asked.

"None."

She changed channel.

"*Scarlet Angel!* We need your help... now," she said.

Silence.

"MARTINEZ!" she yelled.

She pushed the throttles forward and aimed the *Nemesis* at the cruiser.

"Mira?" Alex whispered. Mira glanced at him. His eyes were fixed forward.

Seconds stretched toward a minute as the vessel grew in the viewport. More explosions rocked the *Nemesis*

"Luke, ready up a nuke; we are going to toss it through his window," she said.

They were bearing down on the ship. A collision alarm sounded.

"Mira..." Alex said, panic rising in his voice.

"Trust me, Alex. I saw this in a holo-vid once."

"A freaking movie?" Alex screamed.

The ship shook as they punched through the cruiser's shields, losing relative velocity as the energy field tried to repel the *Nemesis*. Further vibration coursed through the hull as the cruiser opened fire with her close quarters defence system.

"Launch the weapon!" Mira yelled.

"Weapon is away and running," Luke reported.

Mira pulled the ship hard to starboard, tail to the blast. She walled the throttles and their relative velocity increased. The *Nemesis* was fast, but not fast enough. Mira realised she had miscalculated the effect passing through the cruiser's shields. The ship did not have enough velocity to escape the blast radius.

The weapon detonated inside the cruiser's shields. The energy barrier concentrated the blast inward. The hull vaporised as the ship exploded in a violent release of energy.

The *Nemesis* was caught in the expanding blast wave. Mira jolted in her seat, smashing her forehead on the overhead console. Alarms rang out throughout the ship. The engines stopped and went offline, leaving the *Nemesis* helpless without power or steerage. Mira blacked out. The last thing she saw through a fog of blood droplets was the remaining Frontier cruiser moving into range.

Captain Virginia Cochrane stood in the Operations Centre of the cruiser *Ardent*. She studied the situational map. The tide of battle had gone against them in the blink of an eye, proving that nothing could be taken for granted in combat, not even a certain victory.

The last order *Ardent* received from Admiral Parker on the *Ariane* was to engage the ship hidden close to the star. Cochrane had relished the opportunity to take on the ship known as the *Scarlet Angel* and right a wrong that had stained the company's history for too long. It would be fitting that the ship forced to limp out of battle at Tarantella would be the one to kill Xander Rhodes.

She had ordered the ship to a position of advantage when the carrier *Fortitude* had come under attack. She watched in horror as the vessel had been torn apart.

Uncertain of how to proceed Cochrane had continued with her orders to engage her assigned target; only to see the *Ariane* reduced to a cloud of cosmic dust.

Losing *Ariane* and Admiral Parker gave Cochrane overall command of the battle. Her actions in the next few minutes would decide the course of the engagement. Her decisions would have far-reaching effects for the company and her career.

She focused on the situational map, gripped by the paralysis of indecision and the weight of responsibility.

"Ma'am," the XO said. "It appears the unidentified vessel was caught in the blast and has been disabled. It no longer poses a threat."

Cochrane nodded. The *Ardent* was almost in range with the unidentified ship and much further from the *Scarlet Angel*.

She made her decision.

"Helm bring us about. Target that vessel; send them to hell."

The Executive Officer stared at her, disbelief etched into his face.

"Ma'am? The *Scarlet Angel* poses a significant threat..."

"You are dismissed, Mr Franklin," she hissed. "Weapons, destroy that ship!"

The power built. The deck shook as the ship pulled onto an intercept vector.

Mira floated in her seat, constrained by the straps. She blinked and tried to clear her vision, muffled noises coalesced into the sound of alarm sirens and panic.

Alex shook her hard.

"THORNY!" he screamed.

Everything came back into focus.

Alex was trying to bring the engines back online, she called up Luke.

"What's our status?"

"Weapons are off line, shields are rebuilding, currently at 12%."

"Fuck," she whispered. She thought of Tish, Monica, Rich and Ethan...she had killed them all.

"How long before that cruiser is in range?" she asked.

"Thirty-three seconds." Alex replied.

They did not have time to abandon ship.

"I'm sorry Alex." It was all she could say.

"We are not done yet, Mira. Keep the faith." He continued running software bypasses to start the engines.

She cycled through her own instruments, trying to bring the ship to life.

Tish gave her an update.

"They've locked on. Their main battery is charging," her voice was steady, devoid of emotion.

"Tish I... want you to know I... think I..." Mira was interrupted when the console lit up.

Mira stared in disbelief as every board flicked green.

"Flight deck what are you waiting for?" Spence yelled over the public channel.

Mira rammed the throttles to the wall and pointed the ship onto an escape vector, the g-force pushed her back in the seat and forced the air from her lungs.

Virginia Cochrane stared in disbelief as the target vessel moved out of range at a velocity unmatchable by any vessel she had ever encountered.

"Open fire, everything we have!" she screamed.

"The vessel is out of range, Ma'am, no shots on target," The weapons officer reported.

Cochrane balled her fists. The situational map told her everything she needed to know. The *Scarlet Angel* was closing and adopting a firing potion. The other vessel was turning toward them with its shields recharging and no doubt working on a firing solution.

Cochrane's mind raced. She drummed her fingers on the console. Looking up, she swept her gaze around the Ops Room. Twenty expectant faces were looking at her, waiting for orders.

"Jump us clear," she whispered.

Mira brought the *Nemesis* onto an attack vector and rapidly closed the distance to the FRONCO vessel.

"Weapons online!" Luke reported.

The cruiser came into view; Mira could see a moving point of light further aft of the target. The *Scarlet Angel* was coming into play.

She was about to give the order to fire when she stopped.

"Open a channel to them, Alex."

"What? Why?"

"They're beaten and they know it. We should give them the chance to stand down."

"Like they would give us?" Alex flushed red. Mira was surprised given Alex's unease about destroying the carrier.

Mira was about to answer when the cruiser went FTL.

"*Nemesis* stand down. We did it. We bloody did it."

Mira was shaking and could not decide if she were crying or

laughing. She called up engineering. "Spence, when we get somewhere civilised I am buying you the biggest bottle of whatever you want."

"I could do with a decent plasma torch and a new pair of goggles," he replied from engineering.

"Done!" Mira said.

"That was intense," Alex said. "As you are buying, put me down for some clean underwear."

Mira wiped the drying blood from her cheek. She winced as her fingers brushed against a deep cut on her temple.

She called up Martinez. "*Scarlet Angel,* do you read?"

"Five by five, *Nemesis.* That was quite a show. Can I ask you a favour?"

"Go ahead."

"We're carrying a lot of inertia. Can you head back and dock with Rhodes? He's screaming down the line. He has a casualty on board."

"Alex, you heard the man, make it happen."

She stood. Tiredness set in as the adrenaline wore off.

"Mira, I am detecting six envelopes! We have vessels inbound all warship sized," Tish said.

Mira looked to the viewport. She saw three flashes of collapsing envelopes. Her heart pounded. They were low on munitions and carrying damage. She didn't think she could fight one ship, let alone many.

"They have Lightfoot Transponders!" Alex said. "It's his fleet."

Tish confirmed it. "Three Europa and three Africa class vessels."

"Tell them we're friendly. I don't want to die as the result of a misunderstanding."

"*Valhalla* has also entered the system," Alex added.

Mira squeezed Alex's shoulder as she left the flight deck.

Tish stood and embraced her holding her tight.

"We did it!" she said. Her tone became concerned. "What's wrong Mira?" she asked.

"I gambled, it nearly didn't pay off. I could have got us all killed."

"Is that all?" Tish laughed and pulled Mira close. "I've lost count of the number of times Xander has *nearly* got us killed. Being scared of dying is a good excuse to enjoy living, don't you think?"

Mira let Tish's words sink in. The girl had a certain logic.

"I'm going to find Monica. We are bringing Xander aboard and he has someone needing medical attention," Mira said.

Tish enquired who.

"I don't know," Mira said. "But Martinez says he's going batshit."

"I'll come with you," Tish said, taking Mira's hand and leading her through the ship.

"One thing, Mira Thorn," Tish said. "You didn't finish your sentence, back there, before the power came back."

Mira shuffled. Tish gave a half smile. Mira didn't know if she was serious or just playing with her. Some words were hard to say.

"I was just going to tell you, just that... can we talk about it later? Let's get Xander."

Tish squeezed her hand and giggled.

Xander watched as the *Nemesis* drew alongside. Her brilliant white paint was scorched in places, her hull plating buckled in others. Despite himself he marvelled at how well the vessel had performed. He glanced down at Asha, strapped to a body board and breathing through a tube. Xander had been amazed when

Lightfoot had intubated her. He had rolled up his sleeves and slid the tube down her throat with a practised, gentle movement. Xander did not understand someone he had once viewed as little more than a corporate suit had acquired such a skill, but he was grateful.

The ship to ship docking tube connected with the slightest of vibrations.

The airlock hatch opened. Monica Garret, Mira Thorn and a girl wearing a Lightfoot sweat top entered the ship. Monica knelt over Asha and conducted an examination.

"Get her to medbay," she said. "How long has she been unconscious?"

Xander thought for a moment. He had lost all grasp of time.

"Five, no six hours," he replied.

Xander lifted one end of the stretcher, Mira the other. They made their way through the *Nemesis*.

Monica fired questions at him as they carried the unconscious woman. He answered as best he could. He glanced at Mira and realised she was different.

"Your eye! Your face! What happened?" he asked.

"I'll explain everything Xander. Let's get Asha sorted first."

Monica rolled Asha onto a surgical litter. "Chloe, I need you to assist. Are up to that?"

Chloe Song agreed.

"You two, find somewhere to sit down. This will take time. Xander, don't worry, this is what I do," Monica said.

Mira took his arm.

He was numb. His mind was clouded. Mira led him up to the ship's communal lounge. Tish was waiting with Luke, they both hugged him. The happiness at seeing his family made his world feel right again.

Four hours dragged into five. Mira told Xander her story. She left nothing out, even the encounter with Amy Flynt. She felt uncomfortable going into some details in front of Tish, but the girl just watched her talk.

"No wonder Damien is so keen on acquiring their technology." He frowned. "Poor Eden. If I had any idea what she was planning I would never have allowed her onboard."

Mira held his hand. "I don't think she had a plan. An opportunity presented itself and she took it," she said.

They lapsed into silence and Mira dozed off. She stirred an hour later when Monica arrived, still in her blood stained scrubs.

Xander stood. Mira dragged herself to her feet, all too aware that her eyes were heavy and her hair stuck to the congealed blood on her face.

"Xander," Monica said. "Sit down please."

Monica's face was tired and drawn. Mira feared the worse. A whimper escaped from Tish. Mira took her hand.

"Asha came through surgery well. I stopped the bleed and repaired the vessel."

"And the but?" Rhodes asked.

"The next few hours will be critical. I have lowered the temperature of her brain and suppressed all neural activity with drugs. I'll monitor her and gradually bring her back to us by reducing her dosage. There may be lasting damage. We won't know until she comes round. I am confident all will fine but head injuries are unpredictable."

"What about the outcome?"

"She has every chance of making a full recovery. It was a serious bleed. We got to it in time and fixed it. There are no certainties, but I think she'll be fine."

"Can I see her?"

"Of course."

Damien Lightfoot waited in the corridor outside. Xander introduced him to Mira.

"I have made arrangements for Asha to be transferred to a military hospital in Delain," he told Xander.

"How bad is it down there?" Mira asked.

"It isn't good. They took out power and water infrastructure in Delain, Derry and Belmont," he said. "Casualties are in the thousands already. The security forces are mopping up remaining Frontier Company troops and my ships are taking care of their fighters. I have promised the President all the help she needs. We will rebuild. We will make something even more beautiful."

Mira studied Lightfoot. His sunken eyes burned with a combination of passion, anger and resolve. She realised he and Xander were so similar yet still opposites. Lightfoot was a force for order and stability while Xander was a master of chaos and anarchy. They both wanted the best for the peoples of the galaxy, only their methods differed.

Xander excused himself, then stopped. He caught sight of the silver blade hanging around Mira's neck and lifted it.

He smiled.

"You and Tish?"

Mira nodded.

"You always have a berth with us, Mira. I could do with someone like you to keep Martinez in hand. Damien wants me to visit the Verani and I could be away for a while."

"Thanks Xander. Let me think it over; besides your son is a capable young man."

"He is. The offer is always open." Xander bowed and excused himself.

"Let me look at that cut, Mira," Monica said, producing her

kit.

Mira sat and let Monica clean away the blood.

"Is it deep? I just got rid of some scars."

Monica stared at Mira, her face puzzled.

"There is nothing there Mira, no cut, no nick. Not so much as a graze."

"Are you sure? It stung like fu... I mean it hurt a lot and there was claret everywhere."

Monica frowned. "Mira Thorn, I'll have you know both my parents were respected neurosurgeons, and I have been treating everything from facial trauma to STDs for the past 35 years. I am certain. You have no wound to dress."

"Nose bleed?"

"Unless you have a nose on the side of your head, no." Monica finished cleaning up and excused herself, leaving Mira with Lightfoot. She put her hand to her forehead. The swelling and cut were gone, maybe it was the heat of battle... she had no idea.

"I see you found my coat." Lightfoot nodded at Mira's stolen jacket.

"Oh," she said. She made to take it off.

Lightfoot smiled.

"It's yours. It suits you far better than it ever did me," he said.

Mira thanked him.

There was an awkward silence.

"You killed two capital ships today," Lightfoot said.

"I have a good crew and an outstanding ship. They made it possible." Mira didn't handle praise well. She preferred to concentrate on her faults and what needed improving.

"You did, but good people are at their best when they have a good leader. It's something I forgot when I sent Hart and Jarman to 132. Even Kramer couldn't sort them out." He gave an indifferent shrug. "But no matter."

Lightfoot pursed his lips and paused. Mira felt he was sizing her up, judging her worth.

"I've been building my fleet to bypass the restrictions the Honourable Frontier Company place on trade. I need good people to run the military side of the operation. We have 16 ships, all decommissioned Navy vessels. It's not as grand as the Federal Navy, but all the ships have all been modernised and automated to current specification."

"Damien, I need time. It's been quite a ride," she said.

Two offers in under an hour... Don't they know about my reputation...

Lightfoot offered his hand. She took it.

"I understand. In the meantime let me know if you need anything."

Mira was about to leave. She stopped. "Now you mention it. Maybe there is..." Mira explained her plan.

"Is that all? It will be my pleasure, Commander Thorn."

Mira met Tish outside medbay. She stepped close to her and took both her hands in hers.

"Tish I have an idea. I'm not asking you to go along with it. It's your choice."

"Okay..." Tish replied.

Mira told of her discussion with Lightfoot. Tish smiled and rushed off to her cabin.

Mira walked into medbay. Monica sat with her feet on the desk, a glass of brandy in her hand. From the look of her, it was far from her first.

"Recreational refreshment," Monica said.

Mira smiled.

"Pour me one?"

"Aye Captain," Monica replied, reaching for the bottle. Mira wondered just how much her friend had drunk. It did not matter, she had earned every drop.

"Monica, can I ask you something?"

Monica put her glass down.

"The medic, on the *Endeavour,* the one who spoke to me. It was you wasn't it?"

Monica nodded.

"I would have told you, but there was never a right time."

"I think I always knew."

Monica gave Mira a glass with a small measure of brandy. They looked at each other and simultaneously threw the drinks back. The booze burned like a comet, the impact just as powerful.

"Fuck!" Mira wheezed as the booze took her breath away.

"You are definitely you," Monica said.

Mira put the glass on the desk. She swayed and giggled.

"Can I see Xander?"

Monica gestured for her to go through.

The room was darkened, lit by only by the lights of the monitors.

Xander was sitting next to the bed, holding Asha's hand. She was conscious, a neck brace and restraints holding her still.

"Hey, Mira," Xander said.

"Hi," Asha said. "Thanks for hauling this pirate's arse out of the fire while I was asleep." Her voice was quiet, her words slurring just a little.

"You're welcome, Asha."

She put her hand on Xander's shoulder "Xander, Tish and I are leaving. Damien has loaned us a ship."

"Leaving?"

Mira nodded. "I promised Tish I would show her Earth."

"Is it permanent? Are you settling?"

"I don't know, maybe. I have my life back. I want to fill it with the right things."

Xander stood. His face was tired. He opened his arms. Mira embraced him.

"You'll look after Tish?"

"Of course. It's more likely she will end up looking after me."

She reached into her pocket and held out the Pharn data cube.

"What's this?" he asked.

"A souvenir from the Vale," she said. "It's a data storage device. They told me it holds information we would need one day."

Xander took the cube and studied it.

"Did it come with instructions?"

"No, you can work out what to do with it. Despite all they've done for me, they still creep me out. Whatever they think I am, I will live by my choices, not theirs."

Xander held out his hand, she took it. "Good luck, Mira."

"Good luck, Xander."

The ship fell into its night cycle in high orbit above Mizarma. Mira stood in the entrance to the mess hall and watched Barnes and Monica having an animated discussion. Zack, Chloe and Ethan were watching a holo-vid.

They had been fine shipmates.

Tish appeared at her shoulder. "It's time, Mira. The ship has just docked. It's a Kobo. I have loaded our luggage," she said.

Mira took a last look, trying her best to commit their faces to memory, before following Tish to the central airlock.

Luke and Xander were waiting. Mira embraced them both.

"I'll leave you guys alone," she said.

She walked through the connecting tube and into the lower deck corridor of the Kobo. It felt like home.

Mira went forward and climbed the circular staircase. The lounge area was not as ornate as the last ship, but still well appointed and fashionably decorated.

She made her way to the flight deck and prepped the ship. She disengaged the autopilot and started the departure procedure.

Tish arrived. She was tearful.

"I'll miss them," was all she said.

They worked in silence.

"I have plotted the course and optimised it. We will require a refuelling stop. Baikonur Station is a better option than Tellerman," Tish said.

It was a long journey; but Mira was sure she could think of plenty of ways to fill their time.

She called up the *Nemesis* flight deck. "Alex, it's me. We are ready."

There was a pause.

"Okay Mira. You're sure this is what you want?"

"It is Alex. Thank you for everything."

"Good luck Thorny. Stay safe." His voice trembled with suppressed emotion.

She closed the link and the docking tube retracted. Mira edged the freighter away from *Nemesis,* letting the larger vessel slide ahead of them. Once she was clear of the ship's wake she powered up the sublights and broke orbit.

"We should give this ship a name," Tish said.

"Okay, any ideas?"

Tish lapsed into silent thought.

"*Second Chance*," she said with a smile.

"I like that."

Mira advanced the throttles and jumped the *Second Chance* to FTL.

Epilogue

Mariner City, Mars

THE roller shutter lifted on servo motors that creaked and popped under the strain. The room was lit by grimy industrial lights; they cast deep shadows that danced around the walls of the rundown warehouse.

Max Von Hagen cast a long, wide shadow over the worn concrete floor. He stepped inside and let the shutter crash closed behind him.

He rested his hand on the concealed weapon under his coat. Satisfied he was alone he relaxed.

In the centre of the warehouse sat a zero-grav pallet, on which rested a pair of transit cases with diplomatic identification tags. He walked toward them, circling like a curious dog.

Von Hagen pulled a scribbled note from his coveralls and typed the six digit code it contained into the first case. The locks popped and he opened it.

The crate contained twelve Earth Security Force uniforms, body armour, communication equipment and authentic Department 37 ID Tags.

One carried a triple A security identifier and Von Hagen's picture. The name beneath it read: Commander Harry Young.

Von Hagen snorted.

He opened the second; it contained standard issue weapons and ammunition.

Taped to the lid of the second crate was a data core. He removed it and took out this personal data terminal, connecting the core with a ribbon cable.

Von Hagen watched as the data was decrypted and uploaded. When the process was complete, he removed the core and tossed it to one side. He drew his weapon and blasted the storage device, reducing it to smoking fragments scattered across the warehouse floor.

He reviewed the uploaded data; he allowed himself a rare smile as he flicked through the security pass-phrases and authorisation codes, all were marked *Ultra Classified*.

So far Conway had been true to his word.

He shut case's lid and headed for the warehouse door. Footsteps clanged on the overhead walkway, echoing around the warehouse. He turned. A figure stood at the top of the steel stairs, a big man standing with his arms folded.

"Who are you?" Von Hagen asked, his hand moved to his weapon.

The figure descended, each footfall heavy and deliberate.

"Hello Max. You know you have friends you never knew you had."

The man's voice was light-hearted but beneath the jocular tone was a hint of aggression. Von Hagen had dealt with characters like this before. They could flip at any moment.

"I don't deal with outsiders. Conway said nothing about sending anyone else."

The man laughed.

"I don't work for Conway, not any more. After a tough couple of weeks at work I've been given a promotion. What with everything that has been going on over on Mizarma I think the Vice President will have his hands full. So consider me your new bestie!"

The man continued to walk down the stairway. He was dressed in a synth leather jacket over a pair of black combat pants; he had the look of a small time Martian thug. The man rocked back on his heels.

"Would you look at me? I've forgotten my manners!"

The big man folded his arms.

"Max, my name is Karl and I'm here to help you get your planet back."

Max Von Hagen studied the newcomer. Despite his misgivings, he could see this man was dangerous and useful in equal measure.

Von Hagen was certain of one thing.

Independence Day was coming.

Afterword

Dear Reader

Thank you for reading Ark of Souls and joining me on this journey. I hope you enjoyed the story.

The fact that you are here, reading the afterword means a lot to me. Authors may write books, but it's the imagination of the reader that brings them to life. I love the idea that everyone has their own Mira, Tish and Xander.

You can keep up to date with news on books, spinoff stories and even the occasional freebie on the links below.

Wishing you clear skies and a fair wind.

Paul
September 2019

Website: www.paulgrover.co.uk
Facebook: www.facebook.com/paulgroverwrites
Twitter: @Paul_Grover_SF

BOOK 2 OF THE VALE SERIES

GHOSTS OF THE VALE

The Terran Federation stands on the brink of collapse.
After decades of exploitation the outland colonies of the Frontier are poised to join the Alliance of Free Worlds.

Fires of revolution re-ignite on Mars and from the ashes a new galactic order is born.

Deep in the Cygnus Vale a lone survey vessel discovers an artefact of incalculable power; an artefact that hides a darker secret.

Ghosts of the past awaken, and Mira Thorn is drawn back to the Vale.
An entity known only as Legion forces Mira into a brutal choice.
She can prevent a war that threatens the existence of humanity, but only if she is prepared to pay a painful price

Printed in Poland
by Amazon Fulfillment
Poland Sp. z o.o., Wrocław

51245481R00282